Sophie Green is an author an
She has written several fictio
under other names. In her spa
music on her blog, *Jolene*. Sh
and will holiday by the ocea.

Her first novel *The Inaugural Meeting of the Fairvale Ladies Book Club*, a Top Ten bestseller in Australia, was shortlisted for the Australian Book Industry Awards for General Fiction Book of the Year 2018, longlisted for the Matt Richell Award for New Writer of the Year and longlisted for the Indie Book Award for Debut Fiction 2018.

ALSO BY SOPHIE GREEN

The Inaugural Meeting of the Fairvale Ladies Book Club
The Shelly Bay Ladies Swimming Circle
Thursdays at Orange Blossom House

THE
BELLBIRD RIVER COUNTRY CHOIR

SOPHIE GREEN

SPHERE

SPHERE

First published in Australia and New Zealand in 2022 by Hachette Australia
This paperback edition published by Sphere in 2023

1 3 5 7 9 10 8 6 4 2

A CIP catalogue record for this book
is available from the British Library.

ISBN 978-0-7515-8520-9

Printed and bound in Great Britain by Clays Ltd, Elcograf S.p.A.

Papers used by Sphere are from well-managed forests
and other responsible sources.

Sphere
An imprint of
Little, Brown Book Group
Carmelite House
50 Victoria Embankment
London EC4Y 0DZ

An Hachette UK Company
www.hachette.co.uk

www.littlebrown.co.uk

FOR

Isabelle Benton, longtime gig buddy and cherished friend

AND

Neralyn Porter –

thank you for the music, sweetie darling sweetie

JANUARY 1998

Bobbird

CHAPTER 1

'It's really brown,' Kim says.

Alex half-turns her head towards her daughter, who's sitting in the back seat, and sees her gazing out the window.

'What is?' she says, quickly turning her head back. She's not used to driving on country roads. Her old colleague Garry warned her that she would need to pay attention or she'd find herself in a paddock – or, worse, crashing into a tree. Long, straight lines, he'd said. So easy to become bored. And that's when they get you.

'Everything,' Kim says with a sigh and Alex hears her turning a page of her book.

'I really don't know how you can read in the car,' Alex says, laughing. 'It always made me sick.'

'*This* is making me sick,' Kim mutters.

'What, bub?'

'*Nothing.*'

Alex emits a sigh of her own. She has been telling Kim for weeks now that they'd be moving away from Sydney. It's the city of both their births but as it's built up to the 2000 Olympics it's become a different place – fast and breathless and crowded. More cosmopolitan and more interesting, yes; harder to live in, also yes. Every day there seem to be more cars on the road and fewer parking spots, more new buildings and not enough space for them. It feels to Alex like the city is swelling, as if it's a blister heading for bursting, and she doesn't want to be there when that happens – which will probably be around the time of the Opening Ceremony.

It might have been easier if she had an extra set of hands to help her – someone to run Kim to her Saturday sport, for example, while Alex did all the housework that accrued during the week. Her mother, Marta, helped a little bit but she didn't drive, nor did she live close by, so Alex knew she had to rely on herself most of the time. And for a gal on her own trying to bring up her kid, Sydney was tough. It took her an hour to get to work each day and often more than that to get home. On the nights when Marta wasn't looking after Kim, Alex would arrive to find her daughter asleep on the neighbour's couch. It was great to have such a friendly neighbour but Alex decided she'd rather see Kim more. So she told the Department of Education that she'd go to a country town, she didn't really care where, and they sent her here. Bellbird River, New South Wales. A pit stop of a place along the road to Tamworth. Not that Alex knows anything about Tamworth other than stopping there once on a school trip.

'I want to spend more time with you,' she explained to her only child. 'If we move to a country town the school will be around the corner. Won't that be better?'

Kim gave her the baleful eyes she'd perfected as a toddler. 'What about Grandma?' she said.

Well, Grandma had told Alex not to leave Sydney.

'Don't take my Kimmy so far away!' she'd said, laying on the guilt the way she likes to. The way she did when Alex, aged eighteen, told her she was pregnant and her mother had asked her why she wanted to ruin both of their lives. As Alex used to joke to her friends: 'Marta by name, martyr by nature.'

'Get rid of it,' Marta had said, as if the foetus was a pot plant that hadn't made it through a stinking-hot summer. Now that foetus is Kimberly, all she wants to do is keep her near.

Alex knows why: Kim is her mother's chance to get things right. She thinks she failed with Alex – pregnant in her last year of high school, never saying who the baby's father was, not finishing her Higher School Certificate, even though she did it two years later *and* got into uni *and* managed to find a good, stable career – and if only Marta can keep Kim in her clutches she'll right that wrong.

Alex appreciates all Marta has done with Kim – Alex could hardly have managed without her in the early years – but she wants to stand on her own two feet now that Kim is older. She chose to have Kim on her own but she's felt like a kid herself for most of the time she's been a mother.

Now she's almost thirty Alex needs to stop reacting to things and take action. Motherhood just happened to her. Teaching just happened to her in a way – it was the career that made the most sense when she had a child to think about. She really wanted to be a lawyer. Lawyers are in charge. Lawyers have comfortable lives. Lawyers can afford to take nice holidays. But she's not a lawyer, so moving to a town where she will be paid the same as in Sydney but won't be paying Sydney rent is a chance for her to save up some money and maybe take Kim to the Gold Coast for a trip. Maybe even put a little away each month so she's not always worried about whether or not she can cover the bills.

She couldn't say any of that to Kim, of course. Money worries aren't something children should have to hear about – which Alex knows because they're all she heard about growing up.

So when Kim asked about her grandma, Alex smiled brightly and said, 'Bellbird River isn't so far. It's just five hours. That's nothing in a country this big!' And certainly not as far away as Moree, which was the department's other offer.

Alex rotates her head just a little so she can keep one eye on the road while observing the landscape. It *is* brown – and also golden in parts, and khaki in others, depending on how the farmers are working it, by the looks. There is land with furrows in its soil and staccato stands of eucalypts. Ahead she can see a dam, and galahs at the water's edge.

Then the speed limit changes to sixty and a few hundred metres on is a small white sign with black writing: *Bellbird River*.

The real estate agent told her the house she's rented is on the main road, so when Alex spies the sign saying *Town Centre* she puts her blinker on and turns left onto Drury Street. Although she doesn't remember the address being Drury Street and she's left the slip of paper in her handbag, which is on the floor below the passenger seat.

Kim keeps sighing as they drive slowly past heavy-brick single-storey shops with wrought-iron lace adornments, a pub whose heyday was clearly several decades ago, some weather-board homes and a couple of solidly constructed two-storey houses that look as if they were built around the time Queen Victoria entered her dotage. There's a stone School of Arts built in 1901 – the first blush of Federation – and a town hall dated 1904, as well as a park with a slippery dip, swings and a ceno-taph. The park has a vibrant stand of roses of various colours, almost in defiance of the sunbaked palette of the natural land-scape around it. There are several bushes with lush pink blooms, a few with vermilion, a stumpy white rose bush and a pale yellow that is taller than the rest. Clearly someone cares enough about this park to go to the trouble of creating an oasis of colour.

'Look at the roses, Kim,' Alex says. 'Aren't they beautiful?'

'S'pose so,' Kim says and Alex can hear the shrug in her voice.

It's only when they pass a sign pointing to the council swimming pool down a side street and the dwellings run out that Alex realises she should stop and check the address of the house. It's on Jumbuck Way, number 98. And Jumbuck Way is . . . the road she turned off, which she knows because her instructions were to take the Kamilaroi Highway from the New England Highway, passing through Quirindi, then the 'tourist route' on Jumbuck Way. If she kept going on it she'd reach Tamworth, if she didn't choose to turn off to Gunnedah. In other words, it's the main road. The main road *into* town, just not the main road *in* town.

'Where are we going?' Kim says as Alex does a U-turn and drives back along Drury Street.

'I must have missed the house,' Alex says, turning left onto Jumbuck Way. She feels unsettled, as if she's made a mistake coming here. 'Look out for number 98.'

She passes the service station, then about three hundred metres along there's one house, and another. A couple on the other side of the road too.

'Ninety-eight!' Kim shouts and Alex pulls the car onto the shoulder outside the house.

'Charming country cottage' was how the real estate agent described the place, which Alex leased without inspection because she didn't have time to drive ten hours to Bellbird River and back just to look at a house. As Alex gets out of the car she sees that the charm of the cottage is debatable. Although maybe it's meant to come from the fact that it's old. About the same age as the two-storey houses she saw on Drury Street but not nearly as well preserved.

Kim hops out of the car, her Trixie Belden book tucked under her arm.

'What do you think?' Alex says, squinting into the afternoon sun.

'Um . . .' Kim also squints as she looks up at the dilapidated roof. 'Is this really it?'

Alex looks down the road to her right, where the next house is a good fifty metres away, and to her left, where there's a vacant lot sporting some old tyres.

'I don't think there's much room for error, bub.' She raises her voice as a passing semitrailer rumbles over her words. 'This is number ninety-eight.'

Kim glares at the back of the truck. 'I hope there aren't many of those.'

'There might be,' Alex says. 'For fifty dollars a week we probably can't expect much. And this is a highway.'

'Great,' Kim says, rolling her eyes.

Alex wants to laugh – at eleven, Kim is still cute enough to be funny when she's mad – but that would just make Kim cross at her. It's so easy for a mother and daughter to get on each other's nerves when there's no buffer between them. Instead, Alex makes a face at her child and pulls the house key out of her jeans pocket. She picked it up from the real estate agent on the way through Quirindi, along with the instruction: 'Don't lose it, love, it's the only one.'

The lock turns easily, and they walk into a short corridor and turn left into a light-filled room.

'It's nice!' Kim says, sounding as surprised as Alex feels as they go back into the hallway and on to the sitting room.

Alex leased the place furnished – the real estate agent said the owner's late mother used to live here and he's never been inclined to sell her furniture – so Alex was expecting lace doilies on

8

everything and embroidered cushions with quaint designs. Instead there's a couch that's definitely out of style but in very good nick, highly decorated lamps that look sturdy, and armchairs that appear not to have been sat in for many years.

'Let's find your bedroom,' Alex says, nudging her daughter, who skips back to the hallway.

Alex takes the room at the front of the house, Kim the cubby-like room next to the kitchen, which isn't as old-fashioned as Alex feared.

'The beds are coming tomorrow,' she says, because second-hand beds were where she'd drawn the line, and the agent had agreed. 'So we may need to sleep in the sitting room tonight.'

'That's fine!' Kim skips again, this time out the back door and its flyscreen into a small garden that has two lemon trees, a cumquat in a large pot, and native plants that Alex knows she should be able to identify but can't.

'Can we call Grandma?' Kim says breathlessly as she inspects the garden.

They've never had a garden of their own – their apartment block in Meadowbank just had a concrete courtyard – and Alex can see curiosity on Kim's face.

'Not yet, bub,' she says and smiles cheerfully. She wants to feel settled before she has to listen to Marta's guilt trip. Plus she has to get the phone turned on.

'I'll bring in the suitcases,' Alex says, turning back into the house.

'I'll help!' Kim says, but she has her nose buried in a gardenia. Which is where it should be. Her daughter shouldn't be carrying her mother's baggage.

'It's fine. You explore.'

Alex walks down the hall, taking in the vague lavender scent of the house, and heads out the front door to the car.

She's congratulating herself on having found such a great place to live when she sees a woman across the road, a hand on her hip and a glare on her face.

'Hi!' Alex calls and waves, only to see the woman turn swiftly and walk up her front steps.

So maybe the congratulations were premature. Maybe that's one friend she's not going to make in this town. She'll have to worry about that later, though. For now she has bags to unpack, a child to feed, and no bed to crawl into as she contemplates the changes she has wrought on both their lives.

CHAPTER 2

The house has never seemed so empty. Perhaps because it has never been this empty. Victoria has lived in it all her life; her father grew up here, and so did his father. Or, rather, no – Grandpapa built the house. Right in the centre of town. Or was it Great-Grandpapa who did that? Someone at the library will know. They keep all the records there. All the local stories. Plans. Maps. Et cetera. Victoria has never needed to know because this house is an extension of her, and she of it, and there is a timeless quality to that.

At least, there was. Before she found herself alone in it. Her children have their own homes now. And Victoria has no brothers or sisters to make a claim on her ownership of the house. Until this morning her husband was here, but he won't live here again. Not if she has anything to do with it. No doubt his mistress doesn't want him living here any more either.

Victoria would love to have a story of hapless discovery and righteous confrontation to tell the women at the badminton club when she sees them on Thursday. She's fairly sure they all know that Arthur has been having an affair. Hard not to, as his mistress is the wife of the mayor. Except Victoria didn't know. Had no clue. Didn't even go looking for clues. Hence she didn't make any kind of discovery about his misdeeds and had no opportunity to confront him.

Arthur simply appeared before her this morning and told her he was leaving her for this – this – this *Celeste* because they were in love.

'In love?' Victoria shrieked. Shrieking seemed apt in the moment. '*In love?*'

'I don't expect you to appreciate my emotions,' he said condescendingly in the same tone he used to refuse milk in his tea when they were visiting friends. *I don't expect you to remember that I don't drink cow's milk.*

'That's because you don't *have any*!'

She was outraged, of course. They're in their sixties. Affairs are meant to happen when you're still of an age to have the energy to carry them off. When they had two children under the age of three Victoria might have been relieved if Arthur had had an affair and saved her the bother of looking after his needs as well as the children's. But, no, he had to wait until now, when the children are grown and it's been just him and her trying to fill the many rooms of this grand old house in this formerly grand town. Now, when they'd settled into a companionable groove. Or so she'd thought. Perhaps she should have taken his willingness to tend the back garden as something other than an interest in helping to beautify their home. Perhaps one should never trust a husband who starts discussing the merits of American Beauty roses after a lifetime of indifference to flowers of any kind. Perhaps one should take it as an indication that he has developed an interest in a woman who is known for carefully tending to the roses in the mayoral garden.

'That's unfair,' Arthur said after her outburst, and she thought she saw a pout. 'Celeste says I'm very sensitive.'

'To yourself, perhaps,' Victoria said, looking around for a missile to throw at his head. She might never have the chance again, and forty-two years of marriage really deserved a big send-off.

'You have to understand, Vicky—'

'Don't call me that,' she snapped. 'You're no longer entitled to it.'

'Celeste makes me feel like a man,' he went on.

'What have you been prior to this point?' she said, spying the large leather-bound Bible her father had left on the sideboard and which had stayed in its place since he died, Victoria not being a fan of the good book after she once asked a teacher why Jezebel supposedly deserved to be put to death for wearing eye make-up and never received a satisfactory answer. Because, as she knows now, there wasn't one. She picked up the tome. Time to avenge Jezebel. Or just make herself feel better.

'What are you doing?' Arthur said.

'I plan to hit you.' She felt the heft of the old book – it would be the perfect weapon to use against an adulterer.

'Victoria, you're being ridiculous!'

She turned, Bible in hand. 'Am I?'

'Celeste said you wouldn't understand,' he said disdainfully.

'She's clearly a very perceptive woman.'

She stepped closer and Arthur held up a finger.

'I don't know what you think you're proving,' he said, 'but you're making yourself look pathetic.'

She stared at him, at his drooping eyelids and his sloping shoulders and his slack waist. All the things that a wife forgives – overlooks, even – because if she doesn't she may start to question her choices in life.

'*I'm* pathetic?' she said sternly. 'You're sixty-six. She's forty. Get a grip.'

With that, the urge to strike him left her. What would be the point? He'd go crying to Celeste, and possibly to the police, and she really didn't want to end up spending the night in the cell at the local station, no matter how agreeable the constable is.

She put the Bible back on the sideboard and remained facing it until he left the house.

Since then she's been wondering not about how he could have cheated on her – that's a turn of events so commonplace it's almost banal – but about how many people in the town knew before she did. How many of her friends kept this from her? Because there is just no way, in a place as small as Bellbird River, that the wife of the mayor can have an affair undetected. Let alone Arthur, with his prime position at the Rotary Club and his prize-winning fruit cake at the local show.

Shame. That's what she's really thinking about. That's what she's been insulated against most of her life. She was captain of the primary school and of the hockey team. She was head prefect of her Sydney boarding school. She married the first young man who even breathed in her vicinity.

She supposes she should feel sad. She and Arthur have known each other for a long time. He was the head prefect at their brother school, a height of responsibility he never reached again. He was given money by his father to invest in various businesses that did moderately well but did not reap the fortune Arthur felt he deserved. Then he started asking Victoria's father for money to invest and still the fortune failed to manifest. But he did well enough for them to maintain their respectability. It was important to Victoria that they be respectable. If a person doesn't have her dignity she doesn't have much at all. Accordingly, not once in her life has she done anything to bring shame on herself. Yet here it is, visited upon her.

Failure. That's also what she's thinking about. Despite her efforts, she has failed to keep that shame away and in doing so she has let down her parents. They're long dead, but there are still people alive in this town who knew them. How awful to know that they'll soon know – if they don't already – that Victoria has failed to protect her family's good name.

She jumps as the phone jangles.

'Yes,' she says. She doesn't have the energy to be anything other than curt.

'Vicky?'

'Who is this?'

'It's Gabrielle!'

Her cousin. Who did not sound like that the last time they spoke.

'What's wrong with your voice? I didn't recognise you.'

'I, ah . . . It's a long story. I'll tell you when I get there.'

'Where?'

'Bellbird River.'

'Why are you coming here?' Victoria is not in the mood for a house guest, no matter how fond she is of her cousin, and a house guest is what Gabrielle will expect to be.

'I'm moving home.'

Victoria's mouth opens but nothing emerges. Gabrielle moved away when she was a teenager and their contact with each other has been mainly in the form of postcards and letters, and the occasional expensive phone call, as Gabrielle sang with one opera company or another around the world. Victoria is proud of her. There have been write-ups in the newspaper and even the occasional album documenting her magnificent voice. But there are no opera companies in Bellbird River, so Victoria has no idea why she'd want to live here again.

'Don't worry,' Gabrielle says, laughing nervously, 'I won't ask to live with you.'

'I'm not worrying,' Victoria says quickly.

'Yes, you are.' Gabrielle pauses. 'Vicky, I just need to come home.'

Her voice contains longing and a certain weariness that Victoria understands, mainly because she's a decade older than Gabrielle and weariness comes with the territory.

'Then come,' she says more gently. She glances around the vast sitting room and down the empty hallway beyond it, thinks of all the bedrooms and no other occupants, and feels her resolution thawing. 'And you can stay if you like.'

There's a little noise of satisfaction on the other end of the line.

'Oh good,' says Gabrielle. 'I arrive in four days time.'

'Come to the house,' Victoria says. 'I can't imagine I'll be anywhere else.'

'Lovely.'

There's a pause.

'I've missed you,' Gabrielle goes on.

'No, you haven't.'

Gabrielle emits a husky laugh. 'I'm glad you haven't changed,' she says, 'but I really have missed you. We haven't seen each other since . . .' There's a sigh. 'Milan, 1995.'

Victoria smiles into the handset. 'That's the blink of an eye ago.' She's missed her cousin too, but she's not going to tell her that yet. Gabrielle can work for it – that's what she gets for being away for so long.

'See you soon, then. Bye, Vicky.'

'Ta-ta.'

Victoria hangs up but doesn't replace the handset. Instead she leaves the phone off the hook – something she has never once dared to do in her whole life – puts her feet up on the couch and closes her eyes for a nap that turns into a ten-hour sleep.

CHAPTER 3

'Did the boys behave themselves at breakfast?'

Debbie turns at the sound of her employer's voice and quickly works out that Bea means the workers, not her own sons. Mainly because her sons are standing on either side of her, holding their sports bags. Ready for Debbie to drive them to tennis lessons in town because their mother will be too busy to do it and, besides, driving is part of Debbie's job description.

> Housekeeper wanted
> Wattle Tree, near Bellbird River, NSW
> Must be able to efficiently clean and manage large
> house and outbuildings
> Experience in cooking for large numbers valuable
> Sewing and dressmaking a plus
> Must have driver's licence

That was the original ad. 'Wattle Tree, near Bellbird River' turned out to be a thousand or so hectares of a mixed-use farm that has a modern house for the owners – after the original was torn down, Debbie was told – as well as cattle yards, three cottages for the workers, various sheds and a semi-successful attempt at a large vegetable garden. The workers are the large numbers needing cooked food. And 'Must have driver's licence' turned out to mean 'must be willing to chauffeur school-age children to school on weekdays and sports on weekends, because their parents are too overwhelmed to do it'.

Debbie hadn't had a lot of other employment options at the time. In fact, she'd had none. Bea hadn't asked questions beyond whether or not Debbie had the skills she was looking for, but Debbie wanted to tell her everything – didn't want there to be secrets. Wanted Bea to know that her driver's licence was the first thing she attended to when her sentence was up, because she wanted to be free.

Debbie didn't care that she had to take the test again, as if she was a teenager on L plates. The licence was her ticket away from her past and towards the future she hoped to salvage. Towards her children, who were living in Tamworth with their father, who'd divorced Debbie after she was jailed. He had custody of the children, so it was simple for him to take them wherever he wanted to, away from her and the prison visiting hours that would keep the kids in touch with their mum. Debbie had had no recourse. Both parties didn't have to agree to a divorce provided they'd been separated for a year, and Greg didn't find that hard to prove after Debbie'd been in prison for that long. She was hardly in a position to go to the Family Court to say she didn't want the divorce or demand that Greg brought the kids for a visit here and there.

Besides, prisons are no places for children. Even Debbie understood that, no matter how often she felt that by taking them away Greg had punched a hole in her chest that will never fill up. The only thing that can fill it is spending time with her children to make up for what's been lost. And the issue with that is she's the cause of that lost time. She, and she alone, stole money and was found out. So she is the cause of her own devastation, and suspects she'll never forgive herself for that.

It has occurred to Debbie, usually when she's driving Bea's sons around to visit their friends or play sport, that it's strange Bea trusts her with these children but Greg can't trust her with her own. That's what he said when she told him she wanted to make arrangements to see Emily and Shaun on a regular basis. It was after that phone call that she realised she'd need to move closer to them to try to make it more inevitable for him to say yes. Also because he told her he'd remarried and she can hardly believe that another woman spends more time with her children than she does.

'Deb?' Bea prompts her.

'Sorry – away with the pixies.' Debbie smiles as brightly as she can.

She always wants to be the no-trouble employee. Needs to keep this job. Doesn't know if anyone else would be as prepared to ignore her past as Bea has been. When Debbie confessed it Bea had nodded slowly and said, 'We all make mistakes.' Then looked at her meaningfully, as if there was more she could say but she was choosing not to.

'Did the dogs wake you up?' Bea shakes her head, looking annoyed. 'I swear to god, I told Phil to move them further away from the house but he seems to think they're guard dogs. I keep saying they are working dogs. We don't need guard dogs out here. What are they guarding us from – snakes?' She snorts. 'They're more likely to get bitten than we are.'

'Mu-um, we'll be la-aate,' says Ryan, the youngest of Bea's two and the only one who's keen on the tennis lessons they've been attending in the school holidays. This will be their last lesson; school starts soon and they'll have to switch to a weekend sport.

'Sorry, darling, I know.' Bea makes a pleading face at Debbie. 'Sorry, Deb, I'm holding you up. But were the boys all right at breakfast?'

'Oh – yes. Fine.' Debbie thinks of the five burly workers who crowded around the table in the shed, inhaling the food she'd toiled to prepare. 'But they finished those rolls so I'll pick some up in town on the way back.'

Bea nods. 'Just let me know if any of them get, you know . . .' She makes an awkward face. 'Rude. I don't want them driving you away!'

'I can handle it,' Debbie says, thinking of everything she's dealt with over the past three years. It would have been five but she was so well behaved she barely even had to apply for parole, and no one fought her application to report to the police in Bellbird River instead of what used to be her local station in Sydney.

That's her – well behaved. Most of the time. She became an accountant because that was the sensible thing to do. Changed to being a bookkeeper after Emily was born so she could manage the work around the kids. A sedate occupation. She's not a drinker, nor a smoker. Doesn't take drugs. Doesn't eat junk food. Just likes to gamble and doesn't know when to stop. That's why she needed that money. No, that's wrong – it's why she took that money. From her clients. Slowly, and over time, she fiddled the figures enough to squirrel away money to fund her habit. Or her hobby, as she thought of it. What a pity she became worse at that hobby over time.

'Mu-ummm.'

'All right, Ry,' Bea says sharply. She regularly seems to be mildly irritated by her children and it makes Debbie want to grab her and tell her that, yes, children can be irritating but you should never take for granted how much you'd want them to irritate you if you didn't have them around any more. But she doesn't say that. Because, as she's figured out, if a parent hasn't experienced what she has, they just don't understand.

'Come on, kids,' Debbie says chirpily. 'And don't worry, Ryan – I'll put the pedal down until we hit the main road.'

She grins at Bea, picks up the car key from the hook by the back door and leads the boys out to the carport.

'Stop it, Steven!' Ryan says as his older brother shoves him. They always jostle for position before getting in the car. Maybe Debbie's own children do it; there's no way for her to find out.

'Boys – in,' she commands.

They fuss and squawk but eventually settle themselves into their seats and click in their belts.

In the rear-view mirror Debbie sees Bea giving them a wave but she doesn't tell the boys because the wave is over in an instant. Instead, she keeps her promise and puts her foot down on the dirt road and they almost fly to the gate, the boys giggling in the back as stones and sticks hit the side of the four-wheel drive. Debbie thinks it's the sweetest sound she's ever heard.

CHAPTER 4

'Is that all, Mrs Singh?'

Janine pushes the half-dozen brown bread rolls over the counter and blows air up towards her fringe despite knowing it won't do any good. With the shop door open and letting the heat in, no ceiling fan and the ovens hardly cool behind her, there is no way even one hair is moving off her forehead. Just like there's no way her cotton dress is going to unstick itself from her armpits.

'Um . . .' Mrs Singh squints and bends down to look at the cakes. The same way she does every time. She comes into the shop and says she's 'only here for bread, you know', and while Janine's getting it she doesn't even glance at the cakes. Just before she hands over her dollar twenty for the bread she decides she wants a finger bun, but she'll never say that. She'll look at all the cakes while any other customers who might be in the shop smile patiently at Janine, because they know Mrs Singh and her routine. She did it to Janine's parents for years, and now she does it to Janine.

A few months ago Janine memorialised the experience in an oil painting she called *Pink Finger Bun*. It's in the shed out the back of her parents' house, along with all her other paintings.

Not that many people see her paintings. She doesn't show them to her parents often because when Janine did art for the Higher School Certificate her mother told her she was wasting her time and she'd never get a good mark. They were right about her not getting a good mark overall, but she came eighth in the state in art. Her parents didn't say congratulations and she knew it was because they thought it would just encourage her. They wanted her to go to uni and become someone. When it was clear that wasn't going to happen, they let her work in the bakery. Janine supposes she should thank them, but she's never been good at letting go of petty resentments.

Another reason is that her mother said Janine's paintings looked 'messy'. Janine tried to explain that oils can be imprecise but her mother just said she should try to be more like Renoir. Bloody chocolate-boxy Renoir. Janine prefers Van Gogh, with his brilliant colours and brilliant mind that turned in on itself. His heart, his distress, his passion all there on the canvas. She wishes she could be so brave in her art.

Of course, Janine is lucky to have the shed at all. It's attached to her parents' house and she's been living there for far too many years; she's lucky they don't kick her out. Probably because they feel sorry for her. Thirty-six and still working out what she wants to be. Who she wants to be. Everyone else seems to know where they slot into this life and perform their roles cheerfully. Janine just hasn't worked out how to do that yet.

'I'll have a finger bun with pink icing,' Mrs Singh says triumphantly as she stands up again.

'One dollar seventy altogether, Mrs Singh.' Janine slides the finger bun into a white paper bag then puts it in a plastic carry bag along with the bread rolls. She smiles and nods as Mrs Singh leaves.

'Still with the finger bun, eh?' says Davo, shoving his fist into his shorts pocket and extracting the correct amount of change for his daily sausage roll.

Janine nods and turns towards the cabinet that holds the sausage rolls and pies.

'Why don't you just get it for her before she asks?' he says, as if he's come up with a genius idea.

'I tried that once,' Janine says, putting the sausage roll in a bag and picking up the coins on the counter. 'She got upset and didn't come back for two weeks.'

'People, eh?' Davo picks up his breakfast. 'Thanks, luv.'

'See you tomorrow, Davo.'

Janine waves a limp farewell then wipes her forearm across her forehead to stop sweat trickling into her eyes. She knows from years-long experience that the breakfast rush is now over and she might have a few minutes to tidy things up before the morning tea crowd arrives.

Within a few seconds she's humming one of the songs they're practising in choir at the moment. The choir she joined because her mother said she needed to make some friends. Which is true – she's failed to keep her high school friends, for one reason or another. One teacher described her personality as 'anti-social', so Janine guesses that's why she's had trouble finding any new friends. A small town offers a limited pool of acquaintances and she's paddled in both deep and shallow ends and still found no one.

Her mother thinks the choir will mean Janine is more interested in going to the annual Tamworth Country Music Festival, held up the road. Her parents love it and, her mother says, there are 'nice country boys' there. Emphasis on boys. As Janine told her mother, boys aren't looking at women her age. Nor is she looking at them.

She's not a singer. Not a good one, that is. The choirmaster, Warwick, says that absolutely everyone can be taught to sing and Janine's the living proof. The choir is an outlet, though, as well as an outing. Singing feels freeing – she's literally getting something off her chest. She doesn't have a natural ear for harmonies but she learns them all right, with some practice. It was her homework to sort out the mezzo harmony for this song and she's not sure if she's cracked it. So she gives it a try while she retrieves more sausage rolls from the back and lines them up in the cabinet.

'Is that ABBA?'

Janine jumps, although she knows full well that people can walk into the shop at any time. She just forgot that someone could catch her singing.

The speaker is a short woman with grey-streaked brown hair that is, oddly, in plaits. She looks like she's at least forty and plaits are for schoolgirls, Janine thinks. Her forehead is lined and so are the corners of her eyes. But while the rest of her face looks hard, her brown eyes are bright, like she's trying to take in as much as she can, even though her smile is nervous. Janine is very sure she's never seen her before – she's seen everyone who lives in this town. That's what comes of not only growing up here but being the second generation to do so.

'Um, yes,' Janine says bashfully.

'It's "My Love, My Life", isn't it?' The woman smiles tentatively.

'Yeah, it is.' Janine isn't sure how much to tell her. Perhaps she's an ABBA nut? Janine is not an ABBA nut. She prefers rock music to pop. Pop's a bit too sweet for her. So she doesn't want to enter into a conversation about whether or not *Arrival* is better than *ABBA: The Album*. She found herself in just such a conversation at choir practice last week and couldn't extricate herself fast enough.

'I'm in a choir,' she adds, hoping that will distance her from the song choice.

'Really?' There's another tentative smile and the woman's eyes flicker away.

'Yeah. Can I help you with something?'

Janine knows she should be friendlier to a new customer but she can see Mr Fordham crossing the road, which means he'll be in here within thirty seconds wanting his two pies with sauce drizzled on top.

'Oh. Sorry.' The woman shakes her head. 'I'd like two dozen white bread rolls, please.'

'Feeding an army?' Janine says cheerfully as she picks up enough bags for the rolls.

'I work out at Wattle Tree,' the woman says, naming a property that all the locals know because the previous owners went bankrupt after the place had been in their family for over a century, and they sold it for a song to some lawyer from Sydney who thought he knew more about beef cattle and sheep than they did. He moved his wife and kids in, and everyone's been waiting for them to fail. No sign of it yet.

'The rolls are for the staff,' the woman explains. 'I, ah, usually do the shopping in Tamworth.'

'Thought I hadn't seen you before,' Janine says. 'Four dollars eighty.'

The woman hands over a five-dollar note and Janine gives her twenty cents.

'Thanks.' The woman drops her eyes and picks up the rolls.

'Thank *you*,' Janine says. 'See you next time.'

There's always a next time. This is the only bakery in town. Even the people who go to Tamworth shop local on occasion.

The woman nods almost imperceptibly and steps back as Mr Fordham barrels his way into the shop.

'Morning, Mr Fordham,' Janine says, moving quickly to get his pies.

'Janine,' he booms, putting his hands on the counter as if he's surveying his kingdom.

As Janine squirts the sauce on the pies she glances up and sees the woman standing outside the shop, looking in at her with something like regret. But once their eyes meet, she walks away. *Weirdo* is the first word that comes to mind, even though Janine knows that's unkind. You get all sorts here – everywhere, no doubt. It's just that they're more noticeable in a place where the streets are mostly unshaded and there aren't many nooks and crannies between houses. Nowhere to hide. Nowhere to stash your secrets.

Which means Janine will find out exactly who the woman is before too long, whether she wants to or not.

'Thanks, Mr Fordham,' she says as she takes his money. And as he walks out the door she starts singing her harmony again, this time imagining she's Frida singing along with Agnetha instead of Janine just trying to get her notes right, and it helps.

CHAPTER 5

After spending her youth determined to flee Bellbird River and never return, Gabrielle has to admit that she is disappointed in herself for coming back, especially without a good reason. Having nowhere else to go is not a reason so much as an imperative. She is an opera singer who can no longer sing opera, thanks to a surgeon who thought that repairing her vocal cords meant accidentally removing the three top notes from her range. An opera singer without opera is a singer without work, as Gabrielle has discovered. Her voice is not as well suited to rock or pop or jazz. Nor to folk or, heaven forbid, country music.

She has steadfastly resisted country music and the people who like it, because she decided long ago that it's the music appreciated by people who are too unsophisticated to appreciate opera. Yet here she is, back in the Slim Dusty heartland. Her father used to send CDs of Slim's music to wherever Gabrielle was in the world, 'to remind you of where you come from' he'd say in his notes. She never listened to them. She was trying to escape where she came from, and besides, as far as she was concerned Slim was no singer.

'Turn right here, driver,' she says as the taxi approaches Drury Street.

The taxi is an extravagance, but she didn't want to ask Victoria to pick her up. How positively twee, being met at the airport by your cousin. Neither one of them would endorse that kind of showy sentimentality, so instead Gabrielle told the taxi driver she'd make it worth his while to take her from Tamworth to Bellbird River. Not that she should be spending money on taxis given she's unlikely to work anytime soon. Still. *Still.* One must maintain standards, and driving up in some little rental car is not a standard, it's a compromise.

As they pass the Bellbird River Hotel she sees the chalkboard out the front that advertises upcoming musical acts. Apparently a 'jug band' is to play there tonight. Wonderful. The pub is only thirty metres from Victoria's house so they'll both be able to enjoy this band of jugs.

'Just here,' she commands. 'The big house.'

The taxi pulls up in front of two grand sandstone storeys and a wrought-iron first-floor balcony beneath a roof that is so high it's almost disproportionate.

As a child Gabrielle was in that house several times a week, wandering in after school to see her older cousin Victoria, whom she so wanted to emulate and impress. Victoria could be terrifying – she was tall and had very good posture – but she never treated Gabrielle like an annoying child. Not even when those passing visits turned into nights staying over because Gabrielle's parents were fighting again, sometimes physically.

Gabrielle waits for the driver to open her door, which he doesn't. This should not be a surprise as he didn't see her into the car either, so she reluctantly shoves open the door and swings her feet onto the footpath. He can earn his tip by taking her bags out of the boot.

'Jeez, you've got a lot of stuff,' he says, dropping her Louis Vuitton trunk almost on her foot.

'Be *careful*,' she admonishes, but she's talking about the luggage, not her foot. The foot can be fixed. The Vuitton trunk would have to go back to Paris to be mended and the northern hemisphere suddenly feels like a whole planet away.

'Keep yer shirt on,' the driver mutters as he drops another, smaller bag onto the footpath.

Gabrielle resists telling him that she would prefer him to not only keep *his* shirt on but to tuck it in, pays him the fee, and a tip.

She turns to see a woman around her own age wearing a tired-looking apron and an even more weary expression on her face, standing inside the gate of the house next door, one hand on her hip, the other holding secateurs which she must be about to use on the droopy hydrangea next to her.

'Yes, *hello*,' Gabrielle says smarmily. 'Just visiting my cousin. Victoria. I'm sure you know Victoria. Everyone does.' She waves her hand at the wrist, as if she's Princess Margaret on the Buckingham Palace balcony, then walks up to the door, not waiting to see if the woman is still watching. No doubt she'll see her again. Every day. Probably more than once every day. Ad infinitum.

Oh *god*, what has she done coming back here? Europe is full of cities so busy that no one has time to mind their own business let alone anyone else's, and now she's returned to a place so small she'll soon know the number of chin hairs on every elderly woman in town.

The original knocker is still on Victoria's door and Gabrielle knocks in the same code she always used: two taps, a pause, then three, another pause, then one.

A minute or so passes but Gabrielle knows it's because Victoria will be walking from somewhere in the bowels of the house. Finally the door swings open and there stands her cousin, still imperious with her customary French roll, which is greyer now than it was when they last saw each other.

'Gab-ri-elle,' Victoria trills and follows it with a small smile, as if they only saw each other yesterday instead of a few years ago.

'Vicky.' Gabrielle glances to one side and sees another curious neighbour. 'Hello!' she calls, waving vigorously. 'Yes, I'm visiting Victoria!'

'Who are you waving at?' Victoria cranes her head out the door. 'Oh, he is preposterous. Get inside.'

Victoria yanks her arm and Gabrielle almost trips up the step.

'What's wrong?' she says after Victoria has firmly closed the door on the luggage sitting on the footpath. Not that Gabrielle is worried about it – nobody would dare steal from Victoria's cousin.

Victoria moves past her down the hall. 'Everyone's being nosy now that Arthur's left me.'

'What?' Gabrielle stops. So this is why Victoria sounded so odd on the phone.

'He's run off.' Victoria flaps a hand. 'Well, not off. A few streets away. He's shacked up with the mayor's wife.'

Gabrielle pauses to consider this information. Arthur has never been known for his sex appeal so she is finding it hard to imagine how he managed to ensnare not only her vivacious cousin but another woman too.

'Is she still living with the mayor?' she asks.

Victoria glares at her and Gabrielle starts laughing. 'Because that would be awkward,' she continues.

'Gabrielle, are you making fun of me?' Victoria says, but she doesn't sound too cross.

'Absolutely not. I'm making fun of him. Come on, Vicky, you were always too good for him.'

'Was I?' Victoria frowns. 'I see you're dyeing your hair.'

'What makes you think I'm not still naturally brunette?' Gabrielle puts a hand to her crown even though she knows it makes her look unsure. Which she is – just not about the colour. No, it's her old insecurity about Victoria always looking soignée with her thick mane, while she, little cousin Gabby, struggles to keep her wisps under control and, despite attempts to wrestle her hair into submission with the aid of combs and bobby pins, always manages to end up with a bird's nest after an hour.

'Brunettes are *definitely* grey by your age,' Victoria states.

Gabrielle sniffs. 'Well, I can't have people thinking I'm old. Not in my line of work. We can't all look as dignified as you do with your grey hair.'

'I'm fairly sure that's not a compliment.'

'It is.'

'Hm.'

'Which room have you given me?' Gabrielle says brightly.

'Mine. I hardly need the main bedroom any more. I've moved into a guest bedroom.'

'Does that mean I'm sleeping in your marital bed?'

'I burnt it,' Victoria says, leading Gabrielle up the stairs to the bedrooms. 'It's a single bed from one of the guest rooms.'

'Fair enough.'

They arrive at what Gabrielle remembers as the main bedroom. She and Victoria used to sit on the bed – back when the room belonged to Victoria's parents – and talk about composers and painters. Gabrielle always felt so grown-up finding out about the things Victoria loved, things her high-school education hadn't yet introduced her to. If it wasn't for Victoria she wouldn't have discovered opera, would never have dreamt she could become a singer. So if it wasn't for Victoria she likely would never have left Bellbird River; nor would she have had cause to return. She needed to come home, yes, but that was only possible because Victoria is here.

'I have missed you,' she says, and now that they're standing still she can see how age has changed her cousin and how it has not. Victoria still has her big forehead and her strong nose and chin, it's just that now her skin folds around them in different ways.

'I'm sure you have,' Victoria replies, 'even if you are a haphazard correspondent and haven't come to visit in three decades. I'm not sure I've forgiven you for performing in Sydney that time and not bothering to drive up here to say hello.'

'I took you for granted,' Gabrielle admits.

They stare at each other for a few seconds, then Victoria sighs. 'I think all humans take other humans for granted. Including ourselves.'

She picks up Gabrielle's hand and pats it; an intimate gesture for a woman who doesn't hug or kiss easily. 'I'm glad you're here. And you can stay as long as you wish.'

'Thank you,' Gabrielle says, and suddenly feels tired. In-her-marrow tired. She yawns. 'I think I need a nap after that drive.'

Victoria gestures into the room. 'All yours. Now, I'll retrieve your luggage from the street. The nosy neighbour should have gone back inside.'

'Thanks, Vicky,' Gabrielle murmurs.

Now it's a pat on her cheek. Times certainly are changing. 'You're welcome.'

Flopping on the bed, Gabrielle vaguely hears the front door open just before she falls into sleep.

CHAPTER 6

Alex feels like a nervous first-day-of-school student as she stands at the gates of Bellbird River High School. She's already sent Kim ahead into the primary school next door so she can wander around the grounds and see where everything is, then Alex will pop over and introduce herself to the headmistress.

This will be the first time Kim has ever been a student anywhere near the location where her mother is a teacher and Alex has no idea how that will go.

'If you see me over the fence, you have to call me Miss Markovich,' she said earlier that day. 'You can't call me Mum.'

'I knooow, Mum.'

'Practise.'

'What?'

'Practise. Call me Miss Markovich.'

'I knooow, Miss Markovich,' Kim said and wrinkled her nose. 'They're all going to ask why we have the same last name if you're a miss and not a missus.'

'Just say it's none of their business,' Alex said, although she felt an anticipatory pang of fear for her child. She hated putting Kim in this position – it was bad enough she was the new teacher's daughter, she'd also be the kid who had no father – but

Alex had to hold on to the hope that this move would be good for both of them.

'Yeah, like that works,' Kim said, and her face dropped.

By the time Kim had left their local primary school in Sydney, Alex knew she'd heard every possible variation of 'You have no dad' or 'You're so ugly your father didn't want you'. When Alex had given birth to her perfect little girl it had never crossed her mind that she was signing her up for years of taunting by other children, or over a decade of disrespect from other adults directed towards both of them. Alex still has no idea why people have to be so cruel when she and Kim have done nothing to provoke it.

'Bub, it'll be hard at first but you'll be fine,' she said as reassuringly as she could.

'Don't call me bub!' Kim snapped.

'Sorry. I forgot.'

Kim had decided yesterday that certain terms of endearment were no longer acceptable. So when Alex said goodbye to her at the primary school gate she just called her by her name, and watched her walk away, her shoulders drooping a little but her feet treading firmly.

Alex puts her own shoulders back as she tries to find the high school principal's office. She's learnt many things over her teaching career, even if it hasn't been that long, and one of them is that posture is important. It signifies so much to everyone around you.

Teenage girls usually start slumping as soon as their breasts begin to develop. Alex did it too, so she understands, but the rounded shoulders make them look like cowed puppies, and other students target them. The girls who have the easiest time of it are usually the sporty ones, partly, Alex is sure, because they walk around with their shoulders back and their spines long, ready to throw a netball at any moment.

'Mr Sheridan?' Alex says as she knocks on the principal's door.

Vince Sheridan looks up and she watches his face change from neutrality to something resembling glee. She sighs, because she's seen this before and knows what it means: she's younger, and more attractive, than he was expecting. Male principals always think female maths teachers are going to have warts on their double chins and claws instead of hands.

'Miss Markovich!' He springs from his chair. 'How delightful that you're here! And please call me Vince!'

Alex smiles politely. 'Thank you.'

She's not going to say he can call her Alex. She doesn't want him to call her Alex. It will undermine her credibility in front of the students. It's hard enough that she's young. But she has no trouble calling him Vince, if that's what he wants.

He shuffles loose papers together on his desk then steps out from behind it. 'Let me give you the tour,' he says.

She moves aside to let him go first out the door and he looks confused.

'After you,' he says, gesturing.

'Oh. Thank you.'

'If you turn left that will take us towards your classroom.'

Alex glances from left to right as they walk along the short corridor. The school doesn't look much bigger than a large house so she doesn't think she'll have trouble finding everything.

'We're not a significantly sized school,' Vince says, pausing outside a classroom. 'Only thirty students in each year, or there-abouts.' He beams at her. 'I was really thrilled that you wanted to move to this little town. We haven't had a proper maths teacher here for a couple of years. The students are going to benefit greatly from your presence.'

'Let's hope so!' Alex lets him have a bigger smile this time.

He reaches around her and opens the door. 'In here will be your room. We have the students move around rather than the teachers. It gives them a chance to stretch their legs.'

'I see.' Her last school was so big she almost had to sprint between classrooms to be on time.

'And we give them fifteen minutes every second class to go for a run around the paddock.' He nods to the large open space adjacent to the school.

'A run?'

'It helps settle them down. Most of them live on properties. They're used to being active. If we don't wear them out somewhat they get restless.'

He shrugs as if to say, *What else are we meant to do?* But Alex can see the logic.

'Can the teachers go for a run too?' she says.

Vince looks surprised. 'Sure! Most of them don't want to, though. They'd rather have a smoke or a coffee.'

'That won't be me.'

She looks around the room. Smaller than she's used to, but there are shelves occupied by textbooks and other volumes. It looks lived in. Comfortable.

'Thanks, Vince. I'll get settled before the first class.'

He nods vigorously. 'Right, then. Good luck! I'm just down the hall if you need me.'

Alex matches his nods and watches as he pauses at the door, gives her a vague little smile and leaves.

Taking the measure of the room with its high ceiling, like those she's seen in houses built many decades ago, she wonders if this actually was someone's home. She notes the two ceiling fans turning slowly, barely moving the warm air around the room. No air-conditioning unit. Typical. There weren't any in her school in Sydney either, but the temperatures didn't get as high as they can here. Another sweaty summer. She'll have to buy some sleeveless tops at the one dress shop she's seen in town. And some running gear.

As Alex checks her watch she sees she has only twenty minutes to pop next door, say hello to Kim's new headmistress, and get back for her first class.

There's a knock on the door. It's Vince again.

'Hi,' he says, 'just wondered if you'd like a cup of coffee? I'm about to make one.'

'Thank you, Vince, that's really nice of you but I have to run to the primary school.'

He looks confused, then his face relaxes – he must have remembered that she told him she has a daughter who will be attending the primary.

'Say hello to Mrs O'Reilly for me,' he says, and Alex presumes that's the name of the headmistress. 'Coffee at recess, perhaps?'

'Sure,' she says, although she has no idea if she'll have time for that. But she doesn't want to be rude on her first day.

'All right, I'll let you get on with things.' He nods once and waves as he retreats.

Now Alex has only seventeen minutes to get next door and back. She slings her handbag over her shoulder and breaks into a trot as she heads for the corridor.

CHAPTER 7

Victoria keeps her head down as she enters the super-market. Not that there's much 'super' about it. It's more the size of a decent shop. Which means it's all too easy to bump into other people while she's there, and she knows they'll either snigger or sigh and bite their bottom lip and look at her as if she's grown a large goitre. Because those are the two reactions she's been getting so far.

The other day one of the local councillors, a pinched-looking woman named Prue, even went so far as to attempt to hug her, saying, 'Such a *shame*, Victoria, such a *shame*.' Victoria side-stepped the hug and fell into the gutter.

She would rather avoid all such encounters for at least the next few months; however, she can't avoid the shopping, because although Gabrielle isn't singing opera professionally at the moment she likes to keep her zaftig opera figure and is rather fond of baked goods as a means to that end. So Victoria – glad to have the distraction of putting dormant baking skills to use – has been choofing off to the supermarket to stock up on flour, butter and eggs. She's going through more of them than she did when her son was a teenager playing sport four days a week, even though she's quite sure Gabrielle has also opened up a line of supply at the bakery.

As Victoria is extracting two dozen eggs from the pile near the fridges she senses a large male presence.

'How are you, Victoria?'

She looks up to see Jimbo French and his mane of white hair.

He's a former mayor, so it's not his wife with whom Arthur has been enjoying himself; in fact, Jimbo's wife has long since departed this world. Jimbo is better known as a long-time captain of the Bellbird River First XI – undefeated against their rivals, the Quirindi First XI – as well as the unbeaten over-sixties men's singles champion at the local tennis club, and current hardware store owner, ever since his wife died and he sold their property because he didn't want to live out there on his own.

Victoria has known Jimbo socially for years but they have never been what she would call friends. Although, as she's been discovering, her friends aren't who she thought they were – several women she's considered friends for years seem to be incapable of talking to her now that she's the subject of town scandal. So perhaps she isn't who *they* thought she was, either. And Jimbo is the first person, outside of her family, to ask her how she is.

'I've been dumped, Jimbo,' she says, and her eyes flicker towards the checkout, where the middle-aged woman at the till widens her eyes.

'I know,' he says. 'That's why I came over to say hello.'

It's on the tip of her tongue to say something sharp about people wanting to rub salt in her wound, but she stops herself. She doesn't know Jimbo well enough to judge that.

'He's a bastard,' Jimbo says, his weatherworn chestnut-coloured hands on his hips. 'I'd clock him one if I came across him.'

'Would you?' Victoria says, surprise making her voice several notes higher than usual.

Jimbo waves his hand like he's swatting a fly. 'Idiot. He always thought he had a ticket to ride being married to you and now he's ridden all the way into a ditch. Some blokes . . .' He shakes his head. 'They just don't know how good they've got it.'

Victoria isn't sure what to feel. Flattered, perhaps, that this man she barely knows but who is familiar in the way everyone in a small town is clearly thinks highly of her? Or should she be disconcerted that he's formed an opinion of her when she has none of him?

'I think Arthur feels he has a much better ticket now,' she says and offers Jimbo a tight smile.

'He's wrong,' Jimbo says forcefully and she's surprised once again.

'Look,' he goes on, 'it's none of my business but, ah, I found myself on my own when May went and I could have bloody moped at home, y'know?' He folds his arms across his chest and Victoria realises that he still has the physique of the sturdy farmer he used to be. 'But it's the worst thing to do.'

'I'm not moping,' Victoria says with a hard edge. Because she *is* moping, and she's channelling it into baking for her cousin.

'Even if you're not, it's good to have an . . . activity, y'know what I mean?'

He looks so serious that Victoria feels like laughing at the improbability of receiving advice from Jimbo.

'I suppose so,' she says.

'I'm in the choir,' Jimbo announces with what sounds like a hint of pride. 'I reckon you should join.'

'The town choir?' She's seen them perform from time to time. Christmas carols. ANZAC Day. The usual roll call of civic musical appearances.

'That's the one.' He beams. 'We're practising for the town Easter concert. Good lot of songs. Something for everyone.'

'I don't sing,' she says quickly.

He laughs. 'Of course you do. Everyone sings.'

'My cousin is the singer.'

'I heard she's back.'

'She is.'

'Bring her with you.' He looks pleased with himself, like he's checkmated her.

'I don't sing,' she repeats.

'Victoria,' he draws out, '*everyone* can sing. It's just that not everyone knows it yet.'

'Did you come in here specifically to recruit me?' she says, wondering how on earth he'd even concocted such a scheme.

'No.' He looks slightly hurt. 'It just occurred to me while we were talking.'

She presses her lips together. 'I'll tell Gabrielle that you're looking for members. Although I'm not sure it will be her cup of tea. Opera is . . . not choir music.'

'We have some good singers.' Now he's the one with a hard edge.

'I'm sure you do.'

'And Gabrielle would be fine,' Jimbo says, 'but, ah, I really hope that *you* come along too.' He looks at her with meaning but she doesn't know how to decipher it.

'I'll think about it,' she says to end the conversation. She's aware that at least two other people have just walked into the supermarket and she'd like to complete her shopping before she's forced to talk to – or ignore – anyone else.

He nods. 'Righto. We rehearse on Tuesday evenings at the town hall. Seven o'clock.' He pauses, an expectant look on his face.

Victoria offers what she hopes is a warm smile, although she's out of practice on that score. 'Thank you, Jimbo. Nice to see you.'

Turning away, she feels his hand on her arm. 'I really do hope you'll be all right, Victoria,' he says, and his large blue eyes look sincere.

'Oh, I'll be fine,' she says, although his unexpected kindness is making her feel strangely emotional. She must get out of here. 'See you.' And clutching the eggs to her chest, she walks swiftly towards the flour aisle.

CHAPTER 8

This painting isn't too bad. Better than the one she was working on last week. Janine peers closer at the canvas to better see the beak of the magpie depicted there, the one who visits her every day at the shop. She knows it's the same bird because she took a mental picture of its markings after she saw it at about the same time each morning on the footpath, looking around as if it was expecting a welcome. Or food.

She wipes her hands on the apron she wears to make sure her clothes have no paint marks on them, because it's not as if she has a big budget for clothes and she doesn't want to ruin the ones she has.

'Neenie?'

Her mother's voice outside the shed makes her jump. That woman has a habit of sneaking up, and Janine knows it's because she wants to see inside the shed.

Whenever she asks Janine about her paintings she always looks guilty, probably because she remembers what she said about Janine's art all those years ago. But Janine built this shed – that is, she bought it prefabricated – for *her* stuff. Her father has a workroom at the back of the house and Janine has the shed, which she secures with a padlock.

'Yeah, Mum?'

'How are you going?'

Janine once more considers the canvas in front of her and the shade of grass underneath the magpie that's not the green she wanted but also not a green she doesn't want – which happens sometimes when she's trying to find a colour – and wonders how she should respond.

'Getting there,' she says.

Her mother is silent and Janine knows it's because she's working out if there's a way she can ask to see Janine's paintings that's different to all the ways she's asked before. And been rebuffed.

But even if her mother were more enthusiastic about her work, Janine still wouldn't show her – or anyone – what she's working on while she's working on it. It could be due to superstition or, as her brother once said, latent perfectionism. Regardless, Janine just doesn't want anyone to see and that's why she keeps the shed locked.

'Dinner's ready,' her mother says meekly after a while. Obviously deciding to accept defeat.

'Be a minute,' Janine calls.

Silence. Her mother will already be up the back steps and inside the kitchen, making sure the sausages are the right temperature.

The kitchen is her mother's domain of perfection. That's where Janine first learnt how to decorate cakes: her mother showing her how to do it. Her mother's cakes made the bakery famous as far as Tamworth; once someone even came from Armidale. Janine is merely keeping up the tradition, even if she thinks she's a better painter than cake decorator.

Hanging up the apron, she steps out into the soft light of evening and looks up. She loves these New England skies on summer nights. The blue is so intense and the sky is so big that she can feel as though she lives inside a blue marble.

Sometimes she and her father sit on the back steps and watch the light changing. They've been doing it since she was a kid and she's never lost interest. Her brother used to join them, but then he got sick. Not in the body. That would have been easier.

No one likes to talk about people who are sick in the head, least of all her parents. What happened to Bradley hadn't happened to anyone else they knew, so they were ashamed of him. Her father once said it would have been easier if Bradley had just stolen a car here or there. Going to jail, yeah, that'd be easier to understand than him losing his mind.

Schizophrenia. That was what the doctor in Tamworth said. Her parents didn't believe it. Couldn't understand it. Getting sick in the head was for other people. No one in their family had ever had that problem. Bradley was so bright. Had so much promise. This schizo business just wasn't possible.

Except Janine knew it was. She knew Bradley was smoking pot, taking Valium, drinking too much. He even tried heroin a couple of times but it made him vomit. He told her not to tell anyone. Told her he needed it all to feel better. She didn't understand why. Then she did. He was sick and he was trying to find a way to feel better.

Then he was gone. The Bradley she'd known her whole life – the brother who was a better painter, a better person, than she'll ever be – started taking his medication like the good son he'd always tried to be and he disappeared. The medication is his personality now, and she's been grieving for the real Bradley for seventeen years, even though when she visits him at his group home in Tamworth she's still looking at the brother she loves. If only she knew how much of his personality was left inside him. How much of her own too. Some days she can barely comprehend what's happened to him, and is tangled up with guilt for not being able to do more for him.

When Bradley was diagnosed Janine felt like the world, the future, everything in and around her, would be forever unsafe. Bradley had always made her feel safe, even more than her father had, and when he was clearly ailing she still thought he'd pull through and be Brad again. Her protector. It was so selfish of her, but it was real. It was how she felt.

In the weeks, the months – even the years, if she's honest with herself – after the diagnosis she tried to make herself feel safe again. Feel in control of her life. Of the world. Her world. She resented her parents for the way they failed to support Bradley, even if it was because they were scared of an illness they didn't understand, and she wasn't sure if she could trust them any more. Everything felt so unsteady.

It was so easy, at the start, to refuse food. Food was how her parents earned a living and how her mother expressed her own creativity and love, so Janine knew that by not eating she was making a statement: *I am rejecting you and everything that is happening in our lives*. A few months passed before anyone noticed that she was thinner than she should be. By then she was high on her low blood sugar and her sense of victory over her circumstances. She was addicted to the euphoria of succeeding in her mission. Or what she thought of as success.

She's still addicted. Sometimes. Although she's trying to find the euphoria in painting more than in not eating.

Janine pushes open the flyscreen door to the kitchen and sees a round mound of mash, some peas and two skinny sausages on her plate – as always, more than she wants to eat – and her father entering from the sitting room.

'Looks great, darl,' he says, sitting down to his own plate with its bigger mound of mash and more sausages, and whipping the serviette onto his lap. 'Thank you.'

He always thanks his wife for food, which makes him more polite than his daughter. She remembers half the time; the other half her head is still in the shed.

'Thanks, Mum,' she says.

'Pleasure, Neenie.'

Janine tries to smile. Her mother only started calling her Neenie after her brother was diagnosed, almost as if she wanted to keep Janine as a child. Her one child. Janine doesn't want to be thought of as a child but she can never ask her mother to stop using it.

Her father takes a too-big mouthful, as he usually does, then grunts in pleasure as he chews. 'Delicious, darl,' he says, then takes a sip of his barley water.

Never been a drinker, her dad. Says he's high on life. When Janine was younger she heard other men giving him stick about it, but he'd always be good-humoured in response. 'You fellas have your beers,' he'd say, 'I like my barley water. It tastes better.' There'd be guffawing from the others, and occasionally someone would try to force him to drink a beer, but her father is tough when he wants to be. He stands his ground. He always says he knows who he is and that man isn't a drinker.

Imagine knowing who you are. Or even who you want to be. These are certainties Janine hasn't had since her last year of school when everything felt like it was in its right place.

'Thought I'd pop in on Friday for a few hours,' her father is saying.

Janine isn't fully tuned in and it takes her a few seconds to register his words. 'Hm?' she says, trying to play it cool. 'Friday?'

No, not Friday, it can't be Friday. Ross visits on Friday. Ross who nobody knows about but her.

'My golf game's been cancelled. One of the boys has a bung

knee and the others don't want to play if we can't get a four together.'

'Do you need good knees to play golf?' Janine asks, knowing she's clutching at a slender straw.

'It's the swing, love. You twist on the swing. The knees have to go with ya.' He leans across the table towards her. 'If you'd just come and have a game with me, I could show ya.'

'I don't want to play golf, Dad. It sounds boring.'

He sits back in his chair and smiles mysteriously. 'You're missing out. It's glorious out there.'

She swears his eyes are about to go misty.

'Green grass, beautiful trees,' he goes on. 'You wouldn't want to be anywhere else.'

'Sounds like you should still play on your own. On Friday,' she says, squeezing that straw.

'Nah.' He waves a hand. 'No fun on your own. All that glory needs to be shared.'

'I'm, um, I'm fine, Dad. On Fridays. I don't need help.' She pops a pea in her mouth. That's how she likes to eat these days: one morsel at a time.

'I know you don't, love! I just want to keep my hand in. You know, serve the odd sausage roll.' He winks.

'Sure.'

Janine swallows. She'll have to call Ross at his workplace and warn him. Even though he comes after closing, her father might stick around. Except calling Ross at work is risky – what if someone else answers and asks who she is? If she says she's an old schoolfriend that sounds suss.

Not my problem. She's already decided that about her situation with Ross. She's not the one who's married. That's his problem to manage. She's a single woman and she can see who she wants, when she wants. Just not where she wants. Not this week.

'That'd be great, Dad,' she says, eating another pea. She smiles at her mother, who looks worried.

'Are the peas all right?' she says.

'Lovely, Mum.' This time Janine uses her fork to spear several of them. 'So good I was just making them last.'

That's an excuse she's been using for years and her parents pretend they don't know why.

For the rest of the meal her father talks at length about some golf player called Tiger Woods who is apparently the best thing since sliced bread, number one in the world and he's only twenty-one or something.

Imagine being Tiger Woods and knowing so completely who you are that you become the best in the world at it. People like that remind Janine that, at thirty-six, she has no excuse. Except she has lots of excuses, which she likes to repeat to herself whenever she remembers that her life isn't turning out the way she wants it to.

After dinner Janine does the washing up, then her father hands her a beer and picks up his barley water, and they go and sit on the back steps in the nicest warm evening temperature you could ever imagine, and watch the light changing until the moths come out, which means it's time to go back inside.

CHAPTER 9

Well, well, well – this town has not changed one single weensy-weensy iota. In thirty-odd years there appear to have been no new licks of paint, no construction, and no one moving in or out. This is the only conclusion Gabrielle can reach as she strolls down Drury Street and peruses the shops and businesses, because they all look very much the same to her.

Or perhaps it's just the way memory works, tricking you into thinking that nothing has changed when everything, in fact, has changed. Gabrielle has changed, and she is confident about that. When she left Bellbird River for the last time in her early twenties she was uncertain whether she would make a career out of the thing she loved most. Now, returning in her fifties, she is so far past confidence that she could be accused of teetering on the border of arrogance with a visa to high-handedness. Even though her voice is not as it was – not as she wants it – she knows who she is and what she has achieved.

As she sang to herself in the bathroom this morning she heard Victoria call out, 'There is really *no need* for you to rub that in.'

'What?' Gabrielle poked her head out the door, wet hair plastered against her skull, moisturiser dabbed on one cheek.

'I know how well you sing. Do you need to remind me?'

Victoria appeared to be teasing her but she might also have been serious. They haven't lived together for many years and Gabrielle no longer feels she can rely on what she knew of the Victoria of old. Each time Victoria visited – not that there had been many occasions – they would be as familiar with each other as ever, but it's not the same when you actually live with someone, when all the niceties that one keeps up even with familiars are stripped away by the sheer drudgery of day-to-day existence.

'I'm not reminding you,' Gabrielle said, withdrawing back into the bathroom. 'I'm amusing myself.'

Singing is as natural a part of her as walking or eating or dressing. She doesn't want to say 'breathing' because it's such a cliché and she has no wish to be hackneyed. But the two often go together: if she is breathing she is singing. It was ever thus.

On the street she stops in front of a familiar sight. Mrs Maddelin's Hair Coiffure – still there, although Mrs Maddelin must be long dead because she had one foot in the crypt when Gabrielle was a teenager. So that older lady Gabrielle can see through the window, the one who closely resembles Mrs Maddelin, must be her daughter. Or granddaughter. Gabrielle has lost track of which generation is where in this town, but she does remember Victoria's mother popping into 'Mrs M' for a wash and set once a week.

Before any of the customers see her gawking she walks on, glancing across the road to the old cinema, now closed, still bearing a poster for *Jaws*. When she was a teenager she would go in and watch newsreels and matinees. The cinema was how she kept up with the world. That and the wireless, and her aunt and uncle's stereo, because they used to order in records.

That's what's changed – the record shop is gone. In its place is a sporting goods store that seems to also sell camping equipment.

Where would people camp around here? It's so . . . dusty. And dirty. Hardly conducive to an enjoyable bucolic experience.

Someone asked Gabrielle to camp once, in Croatia, near a beach. He was a married tenor with mistresses in three countries. She was tempted – he was extremely handsome – but said no. She's never had regrets, about him or her lack of camping experience.

Gabrielle turns the corner down Clarence Street and heads for Connaught Street, where there's the bakery and the service station, and past the old School of Arts on the corner, which is probably closed up now like the cinema. A boy she had a crush on worked at the service station, putting petrol in cars and wiping windscreens. She hasn't thought about him in a very long time. He was one of the people, and things, she had to put out of her mind once she decided that music would be her life. In the pursuit of excellence there is little room for attachments or sentimentality. Little, but not none.

As she nears the bakery with its flat roof, narrow door and large windows, she can see that it hasn't changed its colour scheme since she left – and the striped awnings look like they haven't been raised or lowered in thirty years, either. Although the sign saying *Bellbird River Baked Goods* looks new and has been nicely decorated.

Victoria gave her strict instructions *not* to go to the bakery. She said neither of them needs the calories, but Gabrielle disagrees. Baked goods can provide a great deal of solace when a person is dealing with changed circumstances, as both she and her cousin are. It's temporary solace, of course – but aren't they all?

'Hello,' she says melodiously as she pushes open the door and hears a little tinkle. Oh, how twee – there's a bell on the door.

'Hi,' says the pale woman behind the counter. She appears to be glaring at Gabrielle. Doesn't she want the business? There's no one else here.

'I've come to peruse,' Gabrielle says, peering at the shelves of teacakes and buns and sponges. 'And, most likely, to buy.'

She straightens up and offers a smile, which is not returned.

The woman narrows her eyes. 'Gabrielle Reynold.'

'What?' Gabrielle sometimes likes to perform this charade of pretending she isn't who she is, all the while feeling thrilled that she's been recognised. After all, a person doesn't go on the stage to be ignored.

'You're Victoria Crighton's cousin.'

She should have expected this: Victoria is still the bigger star in this town. Yet it rankles just a little.

'I am,' Gabrielle says, pressing her lips together and squeezing her eyes shut in her favourite impression of a smile that isn't really a smile.

'Mm,' the woman says.

'A friend of Victoria's, are you?' Gabrielle asks.

The woman shrugs. 'Everyone knows Victoria.'

'Very true. But how did you recognise *me*?' Gabrielle knows she shouldn't ask but she really can't help it.

She's rewarded with a faint smile. 'Well . . . you're famous,' the woman says.

How reassuring, Gabrielle thinks, to know that her fame hasn't disappeared during her absence from the stage.

'I suppose I am,' she says chirpily, then returns her attention to the baked goods. 'I'll take that Victoria sponge. It seems fitting.'

The woman nods slowly and slides open the glass door at the back of the cabinet, pulls out the cake and expertly manoeuvres it into a box.

'I haven't asked your name,' Gabrielle says as the purchase is rung up.

'Are you asking me now?' An eyebrow is raised, an attitude adopted.

Gabrielle's nostrils flare. She's not used to cheek, although she quite enjoys it from time to time.

'I am,' she says.

'It's Janine.'

Gabrielle's memory produces an image of a toddler in this very shop, hair in pigtails, greeting customers at the door. How can that be this same person standing in front of her now? How can so many years have passed yet everything about this town feels the same?

'Oh,' Gabrielle says. 'How are your parents?'

'Enjoying retirement.' Janine takes a ten-dollar note from Gabrielle and gives her change.

'They should. They worked hard.' Gabrielle remembers the queues out the door on Saturdays, the early openings and the late closings. Back when Bellbird River was more heavily populated.

'Yeah,' Janine says.

The bakery door opens and Gabrielle stands aside as a young man in a singlet, shorts and workboots enters. In her day a gentleman would never show his shoulders to a lady in a public setting, but times have obviously changed.

'Thank you, we'll enjoy the cake,' she says as she picks up her parcel and moves out the door and onto the street. Now she just needs to keep the paper from touching the cream on top of the sponge as she walks home.

She takes the long way: down almost to the end of Connaught Street, then across to the part of Drury Street that is opposite the park, and back up towards Victoria's house, which stands sentinel in the middle of town and in the centre of Gabrielle's heart.

She opens the front door – unlocked, as always, because everyone here leaves their houses unlocked – places the cake on the kitchen table and makes for the stairs.

'Which room are you in?' she calls as she ascends.

'The little sitting room,' comes the response. 'I haven't moved.'

Gabrielle hears her cousin cough. 'You're doing it again,' she says as she enters the room and sees Victoria in the same spot as she was earlier, still holding the *Australian Women's Weekly*.

'Doing what?'

'Coughing. You cough quite a lot.'

'I do not.'

'You do.'

'When?'

'*Vicky*. Stop fighting me. You know I wouldn't make up something like that.'

When they were younger, even though Victoria was older than her, Gabrielle used to tell her what was what – 'that colour doesn't suit you', 'you shouldn't go to that party' and so on. Each time Victoria would fight first, then concede. Perhaps it's because she's an only child and never had to negotiate with a sibling – until Gabrielle started to take up so much of her life.

'It's probably just a cold,' Victoria says, sniffing as if to make her point.

But it's not a cold, because she hasn't been sneezing.

'Have you just been sitting there since I left?' Gabrielle says, putting her hands on her hips.

'No, I made some calls.'

'To whom?'

'Listen, Gestapo, I don't have to tell you everything!'

56

'I just like to know.' Gabrielle sits on the couch and reaches over to drag the magazine from Victoria's lap. She may as well keep up with what Australian women are doing these days. 'And I thought you weren't talking to anyone? Or they weren't talking to you.'

Gabrielle has listened to Victoria moan about how ostracised she feels, although she wonders if it's exaggerated. Victoria is too much of a fixture in Bellbird River to be an outcast.

Victoria's face twists itself into a strange expression. 'I have my contacts. We just don't talk about . . . gossip.' Her eyes are briefly shuttered. 'Anyway, I wanted to ask some people about something I heard about the other day from someone.'

'What?' Gabrielle starts laughing. 'That sentence said nothing.'

Victoria frowns and looks away. 'I'm not sure how to say it.'

'That would be a first!'

They stare at each other for a few seconds and Gabrielle realises how much she has missed being in the company of someone she can feel connected to even when they say nothing. She and Victoria used to spend hours together and speak rarely, just keeping each other company while they did schoolwork or knitted or baked. They could communicate with a glance. When she left Bellbird River Gabrielle didn't think about what it would be like to lose that, because she took it so much for granted that she wasn't aware it was rare. She hasn't had it since. There is no one on this planet who accepts her the way Vicky does.

'You know there's no wrong way to say anything to me,' Gabrielle urges gently.

Victoria makes a noise of satisfaction. 'There's a choir,' she announces.

'All right.'

'Jimbo mentioned it.'

'Who's Jimbo?'

Victoria flushes. 'Never mind.'

'I think I *do* mind, thank you!'

'Never *mind*. Anyway, he mentioned it and said I should go so I keep myself busy because of, you know . . .'

'Arthur.'

'Yes. But I can't sing—'

'That's not true.'

'I can't. But you can. I wanted more information about it, though, because obviously I do not want you going to some dreadful amateur-hour business.' She takes a breath. 'So I checked with one of the ladies I know from badminton and she said it's actually quite good.'

Gabrielle stares at her again. 'You want me to join a choir?'

'I thought you might enjoy it,' Victoria says brightly.

'I'm a professional singer,' Gabrielle says, her voice flat.

'Yes, but . . . not at the moment.'

Now it's Gabrielle's turn to flush, because what Victoria has left unsaid is that Gabrielle may never be a professional singer again. As if she doesn't know that.

'I thought you could use the practice,' Victoria goes on.

'I *am* practising!'

Victoria raises her eyebrows so they almost disappear into her hairline. 'Singing in the shower isn't practising,' she says almost meekly, like she's scared of Gabrielle's reaction.

Which would be a first. It used to be the case that Gabrielle was the one who desperately wanted Victoria's good opinion, in all things.

'I can't join a choir,' Gabrielle says. 'That would be . . .' She knows what the right word is but also knows how rude it will sound if said out loud.

'Undignified?' Victoria says it for her.

'That's perhaps a little harsh.'

'You know it's what you're thinking.'

Something Gabrielle hasn't missed as much is Victoria presuming she knows what she thinks, even when she's right.

'How do you think I feel walking around town, knowing everyone is aware that my husband has left me and is living with another man's wife just a few streets away?' Victoria says quietly.

Gabrielle is chastened. 'Undignified?'

'Yes.' Victoria presses her lips together. 'Life takes us in twists and turns and most of them are not in our control. What happened to you was something you couldn't prevent. Just as I couldn't prevent Arthur doing what he did.'

'Because your husband is a jerk and so was my doctor,' says Gabrielle.

'That's a perceptive assessment,' Victoria says drily.

Gabrielle looks down to give herself a moment to think. What is she doing all of this for if she doesn't even try to sing again – not just for herself but for others? It's her whole identity, as unhealthy as that might be. Perhaps the antidote is to try to find the fun in song for once.

'I'm prepared to be undignified if you'll do it with me,' she says, sneaking a look at her cousin.

Victoria makes a face. 'I told you, I can't sing.'

'You *can*. I've heard you. You just think you can't because that awful teacher said you couldn't hold a tune. But that's because her daughter wanted to sing the lead in the musical! And that was years ago. *Decades*. You should be past it by now.'

'Oh, should I?'

'Does this choir have a name?' Gabrielle asks, hoping that by acting interested Victoria will see that she's trying.

'It's the Bellbird River Country Choir.'

'How pedestrian. And it's not a . . . *religious* choir, is it?'

Gabrielle's antipathy for hymns is well established. Everything except 'Jerusalem'.

'I don't think so.'

'Or a country music choir?' The horror.

'No. Apparently a city person started it and they thought "country choir" sounded appealing.'

Victoria purses her lips, then lets out a little huffing sound. 'Perhaps I should visit the choir first. Just to make sure it's not . . . churchy. Or country music-y.'

'To make sure? Or to see this Jimbo?'

'Gabrielle, if I want to see this Jimbo I can go and knock on his door. I know where he lives.'

Another huffing sound, then Victoria starts coughing.

'There it is again,' Gabrielle says.

'What?' Victoria says between spasms.

'The cough.'

'It's the damp, I suppose.' Victoria pushes herself off the chair as if to end the conversation.

'We'll have to get it looked at.'

No point in not humouring her even if it can't possibly be the damp. The house is drier than the Sahara.

'Of course,' Victoria says dismissively as she stands up and leaves the room before Gabrielle can call her bluff.

CHAPTER 10

I t's past three o'clock: time for Janine to shut the bakery for the day after nine hours on her feet. Her parents always opened at 6 a.m. because they were on the premises anyway, baking – a job that has been shared by Janine and a couple of local teenagers – and truckies came to know they could always get something early at Bellbird River Town Bakery. Some of those same truckies are still turning up early.

When Janine started working at the bakery at fourteen it was her before-school and weekend job, which meant that after school she was free to hang out with Ross, her boyfriend. They'd go to the pool or listen to music at his house. Her parents were always home in the afternoons, but Ross's were always out. That lasted as long as school did. Then Ross went away to agricultural college.

'Are you still open?'

It's the woman with the plaits from the other day. The ABBA fan. She's standing with two little boys dressed in uniforms from the Catholic school. They look nothing like her, both of them ginger-haired and pale, one of them with lots of freckles, while she is dark-haired and olive-skinned.

'Just.' Janine smiles quickly to signal that she's not unhappy about the woman's custom but doesn't want her to feel comfortable enough to linger. 'There's not much left, though.'

'I promised the boys a treat. With their mum's permission,' the woman says nervously.

As if Janine cares about who gave permission, but it's confirmed that these kids don't belong to Plaits.

'What are you after, kids?' Janine says, picking up the tongs.

'Can we have a donut, Debbie?' says the littlest one, pointing to the limp pink iced pastry sitting in the cabinet.

'Sure.'

'I want a biscuit,' says the other one.

'That's okay. Your mum said you can have whatever you want. Just let the lady know.' Debbie smiles at Janine apologetically.

With the boys' treats in separate paper bags, and cash slid across the counter, Debbie smiles in a more relaxed way. 'How's your choir going?' she says, so quietly that Janine has to lip-read the last part of the question.

'Still going,' Janine answers brusquely, wanting to move them along because she has an appointment. Her regular appointment.

Debbie's gaze dips. 'Are you, um . . .' Her eyes flicker around and Janine remembers this from the first time she came in: the nervous glancing, almost like she's scared of other people.

'Are you, um, looking, um, for new members?' Debbie finally gets out.

Janine assesses whether or not she wants this woman to join the choir. It's not as if other customers aren't in it – the whole town comes to the bakery – but this woman is new to Bellbird River and Janine doesn't know anything about her. Maybe she's a really good singer and she'll show them all up? Maybe she'll insist they sing Cliff Richard's 'Wired for Sound' like the last new recruit did, claiming it was a 'choir staple' and they needed to 'get with the times'. So many possibilities, and not all of them good. But it isn't her place to decide. Warwick can do that.

'You have to audition,' she says, knowing it isn't strictly true – she joined at a time when they were between choirmasters and no one ever made her audition – but figuring it will sort out if Debbie is serious.

'Oh . . . I can do that.' Debbie smiles briefly.

'Tuesday nights at seven. Town hall.'

Debbie's face falls. 'Oh – weeknights?'

'Uh-huh.'

'I'll, um, have to think about it.' She puts her hand on the littlest child's shoulder. 'Come on, boys – we'd better go. Thanks,' she calls over her shoulder just as someone else enters the bakery.

The someone else Janine has been expecting.

'Hi,' Ross says as Janine rushes to close the shop door and turn the *Closed* sign to the front. He's grinning at her in that way he has sometimes, like he's a lion and she's lunch. Sometimes she likes it. Sometimes it makes her wonder if he's interested in her or just in the opportunity to be with a woman other than his wife.

'Hi,' she says, brushing past him to go to the back of the shop.

He goes to kiss her on the lips and she turns so he meets her cheek instead.

'What's up?' he says.

'It's too obvious.' She leans to the side so she can see into the street. 'We shouldn't be doing this. It's daytime.'

'No one saw me,' he says, rubbing a hand over his close-cut hair.

He keeps it short so he can cut it at home. But Janine remembers when it was past his ears and she'd twirl it around her finger. She also remembers when he was skinnier than any other boy in their class; now he's grown sturdy with age.

'The other people at your work must notice that you're gone. And Miranda has to wonder where you get to every Friday.'

After she and Ross bumped into each other at the pub a couple of months ago – not long after he moved back to the area with his wife and children in tow, which Janine knew about because everyone knows everything in this place – he turned up at the bakery one Friday at closing. He said he'd missed her all these years. That he had regrets about the way things turned out.

Janine's been worried about Miranda, his wife, ever since, because he kissed her that Friday and he's been kissing her every Friday since, telling her that his wife doesn't understand him, that she doesn't show him affection any more, and he misses the way Janine used to love him.

It made her feel special at first – she's the one who can give him that affection he's craving. Then she started to wonder if it's just a line. But she doesn't have anyone she can ask about how to interpret it, and there's a part of her that wants to believe she can be special to someone. That she can give them something they need. Maybe because what she really wants is someone to give her the kind of affection that she longs for but thinks she doesn't deserve – because who would want her? She's a nothing person in a nothing town, stuck and staying that way.

'She knows where I get to,' Ross says, leaning against the bench. 'I'm having drinks with the boys. And I will be. After this.'

His hazel eyes stare into hers the way they used to when the two of them were sixteen and lying on his sitting room floor listening to records. Janine thought everything she needed was there, with him, and she believed he thought that about her – right up until he left and she didn't hear from him after a short phone call telling her that they were over because he had a new girlfriend in the city.

When he takes her hand now she feels as skittish as she did when they went on their first dates.

'We really can't keep doing this,' she says, although she doesn't mean it. There's part of her – not a part she likes, but right now it's stronger than any other part – which wants him to say that he just can't resist her. That she's so beautiful and wonderful that he's risking his marriage for her. Isn't all great love meant to involve pain? That's what the movies tell you.

'We're not doing anything much,' he says, squeezing her fingers, then his lips find her neck and he sucks at it like he's a vampire.

'Why are you even spending time with me?' she says.

She says it every Friday. Because she wants to hear his answer. Also because she hopes it will change one day. One day he'll say it's because he's leaving his wife and his life for her. That he was wrong to break it off with Janine. That he's always loved her and they're meant to be together.

Life's supposed to turn out like that, isn't it? The heroine gets her hero and all's well that ends well. She can tell herself there's still time for everything to work out for her.

'Because you're the only person who really understands me,' he says.

There's so much she wants to say, like: *Why did you marry someone else, then? What would happen if you left her and we got together? Would you want to have more children? What would people say about us?*

Instead she feels grateful for the slivers of time he grants her, and finds her mind turning thoughts of him over, like a revving car engine, when they're apart.

If Janine had a friend to tell about this, she imagines that friend would say she's being stupid. That married men never leave their wives for their mistresses. Even Prince Charles wasn't going to leave Diana for Camilla Parker-Bowles. It was Diana who didn't like the arrangement. And look where that got her.

Janine knows she should be her own friend and set herself straight. But she isn't strong enough.

'Tell me about your week,' she says, taking Ross's other hand with hers, staring up into his eyes, wanting to believe that her love story will be the exception.

He talks and she listens for fifteen minutes, maybe twenty, and tells herself that's enough to keep her happy. Then they kiss for a while, and he puts his hand under her T-shirt like he always does, and she says 'no' like she always does, because there are some boundaries she's not prepared to cross. Not yet.

Then he kisses her goodbye and goes to see his friends, and she turns out the lights, locks up and walks home, down quiet streets, past windows without curtains and gardens without fences, because everyone here pretends they're not trying to hide anything.

But we're all trying to hide, she thinks. Hide the past, hide the present, hide the truth of what we really want but can never have.

When Janine reaches her parents' house she goes to the back garden and looks at the sky for a while. Watches the blue of early evening become deep blue, with golden light hovering on the western horizon, until night lands with a thud.

Sometimes she hopes she'll discover something in that sky: the meaning of life, maybe. She hasn't been able to find it here on earth, that's for sure.

The back screen door opens. 'Janine, love?' she hears her father call.

'Yeah, Dad.'

'You've been out here a while.'

'Yeah, Dad.'

'Your mother's kept some tea for you.'

She turns but in the dark she can't see his face. 'Thanks, Dad,' she says, and walks towards the house.

CHAPTER 11

Debbie should never have told Bea about the choir. Bea heard her humming 'My Love, My Life' one day while she was peeling carrots and asked what song it was. Debbie explained how it had been stuck in her head for days, ever since she heard the woman at the bakery practising it for her choir.

'Choir?' Bea had said.

'It's in town,' Debbie said, not wanting to get her hopes up.

'You should join!'

'It's at night,' Debbie mumbled, as if that was the end of the conversation about it.

'Perfect! Which night?'

'But you need me here at night.'

'Debbie.' Bea put her hands on her hips and dropped her head to one side. 'As soon as dinner is on the table, you're off the hook. And given people around these parts all keep similar timetables I'm fairly sure the choir time is designed to fit in. Which night?'

'Tuesdays. Seven o'clock.' Debbie let herself feel hopeful.

Bea grinned. 'Sounds good. Take my car.'

'What if you need to go out one night?' Someone would have to stay with the children.

'We'll work something out. But, really, have you ever known us to go out on a weeknight?' Bea rolled her eyes. 'We're too bloody tired!' She hooted, then half-turned away. 'You have your own key for my car, so just use it. That way at least one of us can get out and have some fun.'

Tonight Debbie's taken Bea up on her offer, but now she's feeling so nervous she's decided the choir is a bad idea. Not as bad an idea as stealing other people's money, but not as good as deciding to learn how to cook when she was fifteen. The latter was a life decision that has turned out to be very useful. The choir is a life decision that is going to involve introducing herself to people and possibly getting to know them better, which then means having to work out which version of her story to tell – the one that's true or the one that conveniently omits the worst parts of her past. And that's if she makes it through the audition.

The man she spoke to on the phone – Warren or Warwick, she can't remember which – said he'd audition her at the start of practice. That means it'll be *in front of other people*. She hasn't sung in front of other people on purpose since Year Ten. Sometimes someone, like Bea, will catch her singing and they always say something nice, but Debbie finds the niceties hard to believe.

Her high-school music teacher told her that she was a mezzo soprano instead of a soprano – 'And sopranos are, as I'm sure you're aware, preferred' – and that they had two mezzos already and didn't need more, and Debbie couldn't sing with the sopranos because she was 'ruining everything', so that was that. She'd left the choir room trying not to cry.

It's why she loves ABBA so much. Frida is a mezzo, which means there are always parts for Debbie to sing along to in an ABBA song, and while that's not important as far as life goes, it's given her some joy. She just hopes there's room in the Bellbird

River Choir for a mezzo, although as she enters the hall she sees there's only a dozen or so people there, one of whom is the woman from the bakery.

The hall looks bigger than she expected from the outside; the building is narrow but longer than she'd thought when she'd parked across the street. From the front it looks like an old building, maybe Federation era; from the side it looks like it was once quite small and has had extensions tacked on in different eras. It doesn't look as grand as some town halls she's seen. The one in Leichhardt, the Sydney suburb she lived in, was imposing and impressive. Bellbird River's town hall looks like it's just trying hard.

At the far end of the hall there's a stage with chartreuse velvet curtains draped at the sides and a piano below it, pressed into a corner. There are chairs of various types arranged down one side of the hall in a slightly semicircular fashion. A photograph of Queen Elizabeth II from what looks like her coronation year adorns the middle of one long wall, and on its opposite side there's a black-and-white photograph of Sir Robert Menzies. Given that Menzies hasn't been prime minister for a while, Debbie wonders if whomever looks after the hall stopped doing so around the same time.

'Deborah?' says a tall man with an aquiline nose, a floppy black fringe and far too many clothes for this heat.

'Debbie,' she corrects. Her mother named her Debbie, for reasons she can no longer remember.

'Not Deborah?' He frowns.

'No.' She smiles, so it doesn't seem as though she's being difficult.

'I'm Warwick.' He clicks his heels together like Captain von Trapp and bows slightly.

'Hello.'

'Are you ready to audition?'

'I suppose so.' Her voice quivers as she speaks and she wishes she could sound more confident. She knows she's not a bad singer. Just bad at meeting new people.

He'd told her that the piece would be George Gershwin's 'Someone to Watch Over Me' as sung by Ella Fitzgerald, which Debbie thought was a bit cruel – *Ella*, for heaven's sake! – but she knows the song, and knows she can manage it, or make a decent attempt.

Warwick also told her that he's both choirmaster and accompanist, so he expects his singers to be able to keep time with the music as he won't be conducting.

'Do *I* have to audition?' says an imperious-looking woman who has appeared to Warwick's right.

Suddenly Warwick is on his feet, looking as if he's about to bow. 'Mrs Crighton!' he says, almost breathless.

'Ms Reynold,' the woman replies with a tight smile.

'I didn't realise that you are, um, divorced,' says Warwick, his face pinched.

'I'm not,' the woman says. 'But I have no wish to use that man's name if I don't have to. My family name is well known in Bellbird River, as you are, of course, aware. How are you, Warwick?'

He looks inordinately pleased. 'You remembered my name!'

'Indeed.' Another tight smile. 'It's quite memorable.'

Her eyes flicker towards Debbie, who immediately has the sensation of being in trouble with the headmistress, because this Ms Reynold is looking at her as if she's done something wrong.

'I don't recognise this person,' Ms Reynold says, glancing sideways at Warwick.

'She's, ah . . . she's new.' Warwick smiles at Debbie, almost like he's hoping she'll give him courage. 'Her name is Debbie.'

'New to the choir *and* new to Bellbird River.' Ms Reynold looks at Debbie expectantly, but as it wasn't a question Debbie isn't sure if she's meant to answer.

'That's right,' Warwick answers for her.

Ms Reynold steps closer and holds out her hand the way Debbie has seen older ladies do, with her fingers curled in.

'I am Victoria,' she announces. 'Lovely to meet you.'

Debbie takes her hand and feels the same impulse to bow that must have come over Warwick. But she doesn't feel afraid because Victoria's face has softened and she's now offering a warm smile.

'And you are joining the choir?' Victoria goes on.

'Yes,' Debbie says, trying on a smile of her own. 'I heard it's good.'

'I've heard the same thing.' Victoria glances towards where a group of men is sitting.

A man with snow-white hair and moustache beams at her and Debbie wonders if they know each other.

'Does that mean you're joining us too?' Warwick says, bouncing on the balls of his feet like a child on Christmas morning.

Victoria turns back to him with another tight smile. 'I'm considering it. Especially if I don't have to audition.'

Warwick looks nervously at Debbie, then back to Victoria. 'Well, I, ah . . . it's somewhat of a rule.'

'Oh, rules.' Victoria waves a hand. 'I'm of an age where I'm no longer interested in them. Now, how about this: I will observe this evening's practice and see if it's the right thing for me. If it is, I shall return and we can discuss an audition then.'

It doesn't sound as if Victoria is asking so much as telling Warwick, so Debbie isn't surprised when he simply nods and gestures to an empty seat.

'Please,' he says. 'It would be an honour.'

'I thought so,' Victoria says, and she glides towards the seat and gracefully sits down.

'Debbie?' Warwick says softly, gesturing to the piano. 'Do you mind if we continue?'

For a second Debbie wonders if she could offer the same deal to Warwick, except she's already agreed to the audition. So she nods and swallows, then closes her eyes as Warwick starts to play.

The key isn't quite what she's practised, but not too far away from it. She connects to the lyric and gives it all the feeling she believes it needs.

After the last note she opens her eyes and the first person she sees is the bakery woman, whose mouth is slightly open.

Then she turns to Warwick, who looks a little stunned.

'*Brava!*' he says, standing quickly and walking towards her. 'Wonderful, Debbie. Wonderful!'

'So . . . am I in?'

She lets herself glance around at the others, who are of all ages and almost equally male and female. The older man with snowy hair is grinning and nodding his head.

'More than in,' Warwick says, offering her his hand and shaking her own with vigour. 'That was stunning. Just . . .' He shakes his head. 'Stunning.'

'Oh.' Debbie allows herself a smile. 'Thank you.'

'You're a mezzo?'

She nods, then feels a pang in her chest. Maybe he's going to change his mind about her.

'That's excellent news. We need one.' He squeezes her arm. '*Badly.*'

He looks around the hall. 'Why don't you go and stand with Janine? She's our other mezzo.' He gestures towards the bakery woman. 'We have Enid, too, but she's in Queensland at the moment.'

'Oh. Sure.'

Debbie scurries as quickly as she can to take her place and feels a sigh leaving her as she arrives.

'Hi,' she says, turning briefly to meet Janine's eyes.

'Hi.' Janine raises her eyebrows. 'You could have mentioned that you're really, really good.'

Debbie shrugs. 'I didn't know.'

'Yeah, right.'

'Honestly. I haven't sung since school. Not like this.' She waves her hand to take in the hall.

'Guess I'll have to work harder, then.' Janine looks like she wants to smile but doesn't quite make it.

'I'm looking forwards to singing with you,' Debbie says truthfully.

'We'll see how long that lasts.'

As Janine shuffles the sheet music on the stand in front of her, Debbie notices some other people arriving in the hall. She tries to count – there are about thirty people here in total.

'We're about to do "Chains" by Tina Arena,' says Janine. 'Know it?'

Debbie nods. She listens to the radio while she's working.

Janine squares her shoulders and Debbie feels almost like she's being shut out, but she catches Warwick's eye and he gives her a wink, and she realises that this choir idea wasn't bad after all. She needs to start realising that some things, sometimes, turn out all right.

CHAPTER 12

Victoria is barely inside the hall when Jimbo appears next to her. Clearly he enjoys being like a limpet, because as she concluded her first choir attendance last week he seemed to want to discuss it at length, asking what she thought of the song selection and of Warwick. She told him she hadn't yet formed an opinion, which was a falsehood, obviously – she has opinions about everything.

'I'm glad you decided to come back,' he says, looking like a proud parent. He shouldn't get too excited: she hasn't decided if she's going to join the choir herself. Tonight, she has a different mission.

'I'm merely accompanying my cousin.' She turns to her right but sees no one. 'Gabrielle?'

Jimbo taps her arm and Victoria yanks it away. She is a believer in the principle that men should not take liberties with women they barely know. Or any women, for that matter.

'Is that her?' he says, nodding towards the door.

Gabrielle is standing there, eyes narrowed, lips pursed, and one hand making a fist.

'It is.' Victoria sweeps away from Jimbo – she has perfected this sweep in the wake of Arthur's perfidy, thinking it gives her back some of the dignity lost.

'What are you doing?' she says when she reaches Gabrielle.

'This is . . .' Gabrielle throws up her hands. 'This is amateur hour!'

'As discussed. So why are you surprised?'

'I'm not.' Gabrielle makes a sound of disgruntlement. 'But now that I'm here it's very . . . real. Not what I'm used to. Plastic chairs! And that piano is *old*. Not in an expensive or historically interesting way.'

Victoria flares her nostrils as she inhales. 'Stop taking yourself so seriously. We're here to try to have *fun*. *If* you can put your self-importance aside for the evening.'

They glare at each other and Gabrielle looks away first. 'Fine,' she says. 'One night. A trial.'

'Ms Reynold!' Warwick approaches Victoria, stooping slightly in the way he has that suggests an imminent bow.

'Ms?' Gabrielle arches an eyebrow.

Victoria is tempted to kick her in the shins because Gabrielle is just trying to make trouble. She knows full well that Victoria is not one of those feminists, but that doesn't mean she can't make use of feminist language. 'Miss' is a title for a much younger person. Or a ghastly old spinster. Which, she supposes, is what Gabrielle has become – except given Arthur's behaviour, spinsterdom doesn't seem like such a bad lot any more.

'I think, as it's my second visit, you should call me Victoria.' She offers Warwick one of the smiles she saves for dogs she likes – mostly golden retrievers. 'Who knows? I may even keep up my attendance.'

'Really?' Now Warwick looks as eager as a puppy, and if his ears start flapping Victoria won't be surprised. 'That would be *wonderful*. We have so much going on this year. There's the Easter concert, and the town anniversary in May. And the

Bellbird River Show, of course – we spend *months* practising for that. It would be such an honour to have you sing with us there.'

'Would it?' Victoria feels quite flattered, also mildly suspicious that Warwick is so desperate for choir members he's saying whatever he thinks will persuade her to join permanently. Then she remembers her real reason for being here.

'I'd like you to meet my cousin, Gabrielle,' she says, pivoting towards the female thundercloud at her side.

'Gabri-Gabrielle Reynold!' Warwick flushes more deeply and brings one hand to his chest. 'I can't believe it. You're a legend!'

'Am I?' Gabrielle's smile is insincere, but Victoria is sure she's enjoying the recognition. People like her always do – they complain about having 'fans' but are always looking around to see if they're being noticed.

Victoria knows this because they once had a crew from *60 Minutes* in the town reporting on the only murder that had taken place here in sixty years, and the 'star', such as he was, spent a lot of time walking up and down outside the pub, glancing inside, then refused to sign an autograph for the only person who asked for one.

'I have several of your albums,' Warwick gushes. 'I knew you were from Bellbird River, of course, but I thought you never came back to visit.'

'She does now,' Victoria interjects before Gabrielle can say anything about the town that may offend.

Warwick moves closer to his target. 'What brings you here tonight?'

'She's joining the choir.' Victoria matches Gabrielle's insincere smile with one of her own, directed at her cousin.

She's rewarded with a look of confusion on Warwick's face.

'But – why?' he says, his head swivelling from Gabrielle to Victoria and back again, just as Jimbo once more materialises, looking expectant.

Gabrielle turns towards Victoria. 'I want to leave,' she hisses at a low volume.

'I don't!'

Victoria pinches her cousin's cheek, having realised there may be entertainment in joining the choir just so she can watch Gabrielle try to deal with it. Except she'd frame it differently, telling Gabrielle that she's sacrificing herself by joining the choir just so Gabrielle can perform. Because she loves performing more than anything, even cake.

'She's taking some time away from opera, Warwick,' Victoria goes on, 'and I thought it would be wise if she keeps up her performance skills. No matter how long one has been an artist, it's never good to let the paintbrush dry, hmm?'

As Warwick appears to cogitate that notion, Victoria slips her arm through Gabrielle's just in case Gabrielle decides to attempt an exit.

'Wonderful additions, both of you,' Jimbo says, again with a note of pride.

If Victoria didn't know better she'd think he is to receive a bonus from bringing in two of them instead of just one.

'I'm not going to make you audition, of course,' says Warwick to Gabrielle. 'But Victoria . . .' He grimaces. 'As I said last week, we do need one from you.'

'If I don't have to audition, I don't think it's reasonable to make my cousin do it,' Gabrielle says, and Victoria is impressed with how sweetly she's made the statement. Almost as if she's trying to charm the man. 'I can assure you that she is a *very* good singer. She sang all the time when we were growing up.'

Warwick looks from one cousin to the other with a moderately stricken expression. 'I just don't want to look like I'm playing favourites,' he whispers. 'It's not very fair.'

'I think you'll agree that *life* isn't fair,' Gabrielle trills, putting a hand on his arm. Victoria wonders if she'd like to try these wiles on the young man who comes to mow the back garden's lawn once a fortnight and always does a half-hearted job. 'Perhaps you could announce that we auditioned privately?'

'What a brilliant idea!' Warwick's face is alight. 'Please, take a seat – sopranos are on the far right. I presume, Madame Reynold, that's where you'd like to be?'

'*Please* call me Gabrielle,' she purrs, and Victoria wonders if Warwick is about to faint.

'Right – Gabrielle, thank you. Thank you.'

'Is he going to bow at last?' Victoria mutters to her cousin and is met with a wink and a smile.

'I hope so,' Gabrielle replies.

Victoria feels another tap on her arm but this time she doesn't move. If Jimbo didn't get the message the first time, there's little point repeating it.

'I'm in the baritones,' he says, nodding to the chairs on the far left.

'Congratulations.'

'Perhaps we can have a cup of tea at the break?' He gestures to a trestle table bearing two packets of biscuits, an urn and an open packet of tea bags.

Victoria has no idea why Jimbo is so keen to socialise with her, but she also reasons that agreeing to one cup of tea now may satisfy his curiosity and she'll never have to do it again.

'Perhaps we can,' she says. 'I shall see you anon.'

She turns to make her way to the back row of the sopranos. As she moves between chairs she spots Janine from the bakery sitting nearby, a startled expression on her face. That girl hasn't looked right for years, and Victoria has no idea why. She used to be such an outgoing little thing.

'Hello, Janine,' she calls and receives only a nod in reply.

'I really think I should leave,' Gabrielle whispers as Victoria sits with a thud. 'This won't be my sort of music.'

'How do you know?'

Gabrielle points to the sheet music on the stand: a song called 'Ironic' by someone called Alanis Morissette.

Victoria sniffs. 'I hope this Alanis has used "ironic" properly. You know how annoyed I become when that word is misapplied.'

'Oh dear,' says Gabrielle, squinting at the lyrics.

'Never mind.' Victoria waves a hand, then sighs and sits back.

Gabrielle may be right: they *should* leave if this is the sort of song they'll be expected to sing. But she'll wait until the evening is over to make a final decision.

CHAPTER 13

'Is that book on your homework list?' Alex asks Kim.

Her daughter is sprawled on her front on the thin rug that covers the splintery floorboards. Alex told the real estate agent about the boards – saying she was worried about Kim getting splinters – and the agent said Kim should wear shoes inside. Alex didn't like that answer so she went to the haberdashery shop in town and asked if someone could make her a rug for the floor. In Sydney she wouldn't have known what a haberdashery was; life in Bellbird River has been an education already.

'*No*,' Kim says, and Alex imagines the face she's making behind the curtain of her thick brown hair.

'Okay, all right, I'm just asking.' Alex tries not to sound defensive, although that is what she is. She can't help being a teacher sometimes, even though Kim doesn't need monitoring. She's always been a conscientious student.

'I finished my homework book for this week,' Kim says, waving her legs from side to side.

'Already?'

Kim turns her head and glares at her mother. 'You don't believe me,' she states.

'I do, sweetheart,' Alex says brightly.

How can she explain to Kim that what she's really trying to do is make conversation, to be cheerful, because she knows that Kim resents her for moving to the country where there is no grandmother, no favourite local park, no next-door dog and, as yet, no friend for her to play with.

'What are you reading?' she continues.

'*Playing Beatie Bow.*'

'Isn't that a little old for you?'

'*No*, Mum.'

Alex searches her memory, wondering how old she was when she read it herself. She might have been Kim's age, because she thinks the book was published when she was ten or eleven. She always read books meant for older children and her parents, whose first language wasn't English, never tried to stop her. She was about Kim's age when she read *The Outsiders*, but she wouldn't want Kim reading that now because she doesn't want her to know such a panorama of how cruel life can be. Which makes her a hypocrite, but that's a prerogative of parenthood.

'Do you have any excursions coming up?' Alex asks as she sits on the chair nearest to Kim, trying to see her daughter's face.

Kim is hiding something from her, she knows – because she knows her daughter better than Kim knows herself. Her memory holds the full catalogue of all the ways Kim has moved her face and hands and feet over her lifetime; the clues she gives away in her tone of voice; what she's like when she's tired or hungry or bored. Kim will never know as much about Alex, and that's the way it should be. It's her job to watch over Kim, even after Kim is old enough to look after herself.

That's one of the reasons Alex moved them here, so she can spend more time watching and cataloguing, and so she can give Kim a chance to discover herself without the noise and bustle of the city.

'Dunno,' Kim says, then makes a noise.

'What did you say?'

She sighs. 'I don't know, Mum.'

'Kim, please put down the book.' Clearly gentle prodding is not going to help Alex detect anything.

'No.'

'Kim.'

Her daughter slams the open book face down on the floor, then sits up suddenly and glares at her mother again.

'What's going on?' Alex says, keeping her voice gentle.

She knows that Kim resents her for prying but it's her job. Her daughter is eleven. She doesn't get to be upset and not tell her mother why.

'You don't care,' Kim says spitefully.

Being a teacher has given Alex practice in not taking children's spite personally, but it requires more effort than usual where her own child is concerned.

'You know that's not true. You know I love you more than anything.'

'You don't!' Kim rolls onto her front again and puts her forehead on the floor, almost as if she's about to beat the boards with her fists and feet, except she hasn't done that since she was three.

'I do.'

Alex reaches down and puts a hand on Kim's back, only to be met by a furious shake-off.

'Kimberly, please tell me why you're upset,' she tries again.

Kim pushes up to a sitting position, her face red, her freckles almost disappearing inside the lines made when she screws up her eyes and mouth.

'Why don't I have a dad?' she says, and Alex feels her guts turn to water.

She hasn't needed to address this for years, but she should have guessed it would come up when they moved to a new place. Should have prepared her daughter for it.

'We've talked about this, sweetie,' she says, although that's not a helpful statement.

'They said you're a bad person,' Kim says, her face still red.

'Who did?'

'The . . . the kids.'

Of course 'the kids' means 'their parents', because they have to be the source of these barbs, as they have been in other places. The worst thing in this world, apparently, is a single mother. Worse than men who rape and pillage and start wars; worse than people who have children and don't look after them properly; worse than someone who rips off the life savings of little old ladies. Because none of those people have committed the sin of having sex while unwed, then dared to brag about it by giving birth to a child without a father visibly attached. The sin of being the parent who stuck around.

'When did they say that?' Alex asks. The school year is barely a fortnight old – the local rumour mill obviously works quickly.

'I want to go home,' Kim says, and now Alex can see what no parent wants to: her child's bottom lip trembling, tears imminent.

'We can't leave, bub.' Alex's throat constricts as she realises she's used the banned term of endearment, but Kim doesn't react.

'I have a job here,' Alex continues. 'We have a home.'

'Everyone knew. At home.' Kim sniffs and starts to cry. 'Everyone knew I don't have a dad. It was okay there.'

Alex slides to the floor and wraps her arms around her only child. 'I know it was. And it will be okay here too.'

She hugs Kim as tightly as she can but her daughter resists. Her skinny arms are rigid. Her spine feels like a rifle.

'Where's my dad?' Kim sniffles into Alex's arm.

'I don't know,' Alex says truthfully. She never saw him again after she told him she was pregnant and intended to carry it through. She's never needed him. *They've* never needed him. The fact of his presence wouldn't make Kim's problems go away, not that she's old enough to understand that. Just because you have a man standing there saying he's your father doesn't mean he *is* that person in your life. Alex has met fathers at parent–teacher nights who are present but completely uninterested. They've ticked the turn-up box and they think that makes them a good parent. She asks them questions about their children and they never know the answers.

The mothers are the ones with the information, although even then not all the time. Some mothers don't care either. Some people just don't want to have to bother with other people, and they really shouldn't have children in that case. But Alex doesn't get to make those decisions.

The only decision she could control in that respect was the one that gave her Kim. And as hard as that decision has been on Kim sometimes, Alex will never regret it. Her life is unimaginable without her daughter in it. Kim may never understand that but Alex will always try to help her do so.

'Why not?' Kim almost whispers.

'I just don't. I'm sorry you're upset.' She rubs Kim's back, a circular action that Alex knows she loves.

Kim sniffs. 'Are you a bad person?'

'I don't think so,' Alex murmurs. 'A bad person couldn't have a daughter as wonderful as you.' She hugs Kim tightly.

'I know it's not easy being here,' she goes on. 'Kids say horrible things. They did to me too, because of my last name. We can't stop them being mean, but we can stop letting it make us sad.'

Kim's shoulders relax a little.

Alex lets go of her and looks into her worried eyes. 'I'm always in the building just next door, okay? If someone is mean to you at school, come and find me.'

She's probably meant to tell Kim to be brave and soldier on. But Alex remembers what it felt like to be taunted each day. She would have given anything to have her mother close by, so she could run to her and try to make the pain go away. Providing that succour for her own child doesn't mean either one of them is weak. Resilience doesn't come from stuffing down the pain but from acknowledging it and dealing with it, which is hard to do if you don't have anyone to comfort you.

Kim nods slowly and Alex kisses her on the forehead.

'I think we'll like this place more if we do some fun things here,' she says. It's a subject she's been giving some thought to, because the teaching staff isn't large in number and if she doesn't branch out from school life she simply won't meet many people.

'Like what?' Kim says, plucking at a loose thread in her T-shirt. Alex tries to remember where she put her sewing kit when they unpacked.

'I heard about a choir when I was in the bakery the other day. The woman who works there said something about it. You know that amazing cake I brought home? She decorated it.'

Kim nods slowly and offers a quick smile.

'So she mentioned she's in this choir on Tuesday nights,' Alex continues.

Kim glances up. 'Do you sing?'

'I used to. I was in a band once. In high school. They sacked me. And they were my *best friends*!' Alex laughs softly. 'But I don't think that was because of my singing.'

'Why, then?' Kim's eyes are wide.

'The drummer said he was in love with me but I, ah . . .' She closes her eyes against the memory of the confession, so awkward, so unwanted. 'I didn't feel the same. And the worst part was he was going out with my other best friend who wasn't in the band. So, yeah . . .' She shrugs.

'That's mean,' Kim says.

'I guess it was.'

Alex thinks back to how much she loved being in that band, and how much she was made to feel like her departure from it was a necessary sacrifice in order to preserve the drummer's dignity. And his relationship.

Kim gives her a purposeful look. 'People were mean to you at school too.'

Alex returns the look. How can she not have realised this before? All Kim has wanted is someone to understand her pain, but Alex was so good at blocking hers out that she didn't ever consider that Kim may actually want to know the details. To know how it felt for her mother, in case it's the same as it feels for her.

'Yeah, they were, bub,' she murmurs. 'And it was awful.'

Kim sighs and lays her head on her mother's arm.

In moments like these – so rare these days – Alex wants her daughter to stay in place for hours. Forever. Just the two of them, connected by years and fate. Her heart has never felt so full, nor so capable of breaking.

'Why don't you tell me about Beatie Bow?' she says, clearing her throat. 'I've forgotten pretty much everything.'

'You read this book?' Kim looks up, her eyes wide.

'Mm-hm. A long time ago. How about I lie down and you read to me? I'd like that.'

Kim nods quickly and Alex can see a little smile.

She closes her eyes as Kim starts to read. If she keeps them closed her daughter won't be able to tell that, despite what she said, Alex is worrying about whether or not she really has done the right thing bringing them both here.

What she can't say to Kim is that her job is harder than she thought it would be. Smaller class sizes mean that individual personalities can be more pronounced and Alex finds some of them tricky to manage. She also wasn't prepared to see so many parents of her students when she goes about her business in town, shopping, getting petrol, trying to find a hairdresser. In Sydney she never once bumped into a student's parents because she didn't live anywhere near where she worked. She was naïve not to consider what might happen when she lives and works in the same place.

None of this, however, is something Alex can solve this afternoon, on this thin rug. So she tries to concentrate on what Kim is reading out to her, even if it only lasts a few seconds before she shifts to worrying about something new.

CHAPTER 14

'Greg, please.'

Debbie never used to be a person who begged but she seems to do a lot of it these days, and all to her ex-husband.

'I don't want to disrupt them,' he says.

She can hear the TV in the background and imagines her children are sitting there, watching it, while their father is on the phone telling their mother she can't see them, all because she made a mistake a few years ago.

As if he's never made mistakes. He lost a lot of money on a bad investment, which is why Debbie ended up working five days a week, and sometimes nights, as well as raising the kids and doing all the housework, to support the family while he paid back his debt slowly. The stress of it . . . Debbie is often tempted to think that's why she gambled, but she's determined to take responsibility for her own behaviour, so that means she can't blame Greg.

Except *he* blames *her*. Says she humiliated him when she was convicted. She never said he'd humiliated her when he lost all their money. Just put her head down and tried to earn it back.

'I'm their mother, Greg,' she says as calmly as she can. 'I have a right to see them.'

'Well, uh, not really,' he says flatly. As if he's talking about whether or not she's allowed to walk on his path.

'If I went to court now they'd say I can see my kids, even if I can't have custody of them.'

Debbie doesn't have the money to hire a lawyer, so the issue is moot, but she wants to make a point.

'You'll never get custody of them,' he says, and again there's that emotionless tone. He's so used to winning now. He doesn't need to become bothered by anything.

'I just want to see them.' She tries to match his tone, thinking that keeping the emotion out of it may be the key. 'It's important that they know I love them. That I haven't abandoned them.'

'They don't really need you, Debbie. They have a mum.'

'Julia is not their mother. I am.'

She hears him sigh. The sigh a parent emits when a child is being annoying.

'Debbie, they never ask about you.'

'Do you ever talk about me?'

'No.'

'So they probably think they're not allowed to ask about me. But they can't have forgotten me, Greg. They weren't babies when I went away.'

'Went inside.'

'How is that different to saying I went away?'

'I think you know.'

'*Greg*. Please. They are my children.'

'Not any more.'

She's never sure if he really believes this or says it to get a rise out of her. Either way, it doesn't change the outcome of their conversations. The conversations they've been having every week since she was released. She doesn't know why he keeps taking her calls; perhaps he likes torturing her. Well, she has a trump card now and she's going to play it.

'I'm living just down the road now,' she says.

'What?' He sounds alert.

'Near Bellbird River.'

Silence.

'What the hell do you think you're doing?' he says, his voice a low rumble.

'Trying to see my children.'

'You have no right—'

'I can live wherever I want to,' she says firmly, because it's the truth.

'No one said you can move near us.'

'No one has to say, Greg.' She keeps her voice light, just like she told herself to when she rehearsed telling him what she's done.

'What about your parole?'

'They're letting me report to the police station here.'

Another silence.

'So, what?' he says after a few seconds. 'You're just planning to turn up?'

'I don't want to do that. But if you won't let me see them I'll talk to the police about my options. They might be able to give me some advice.'

He laughs coldly. 'Like they'd help a crim.'

'I've done my sentence, Greg, and I accept that people are going to find out what happened, although obviously I don't want a lot of people knowing. I made a mistake. I'm sure you know how that feels.'

He starts to bluster then stops. 'You can't see them,' he says. 'You'll upset them.'

She pauses to take a breath. She knew he wouldn't agree easily. Knew it would take some time. But she's not going to give up. These past three years she kept writing letters to the children, although she's sure they never received them. When she sees them, though, she'll tell them that she didn't give up. That she has always loved them. So she has to play the long game, and that means not letting Greg wear her down.

'Debbie?'

She turns to see Bea standing behind her, pointing vigorously at the phone.

'I need to make a call,' Bea whispers exaggeratedly.

There's one phone line in the whole place, along with one mobile phone that's permanently attached to Bea's husband. Debbie knows she's tied up the landline long enough.

'I have to go,' she says to Greg and hangs up. It's not as if she won't have this conversation with him again soon.

'Sorry, Bea,' she says, giving her the handset.

'No worries, chook.' Bea smiles. 'I have to put in a feed order. Wally forgot and now he's panicking.' She makes a face. 'Hopeless.'

Debbie smiles. 'I'll head off to get the boys.'

'Thanks!' Bea calls after her as Debbie reaches for her handbag and keys by the back door.

As she heads out along the gravel drive, she thinks about how long she should leave it until she calls Greg again. Maybe a week. No more than that. Now that school is back Emily and Shaun will be as busy with activities as Ryan and Steven. Debbie doesn't want them to run out of time for her.

She turns on the car stereo. The Kate Ceberano CD she popped in there this morning is up to track four and Debbie sings along.

She missed music so much when she was away. When she was *inside*. There was the radio, but she couldn't play anything she wanted to when she wanted to. That, along with so much else, is something she will never take for granted again.

CHAPTER 15

'Ivan, I have to tell you, this choir is woeful. *Woeful.* Wouldn't know their Mimi from their Mariah Carey! They seem to think Wagner is the name of an actor who was married to Natalie Wood. Terrible!'

Gabrielle is hamming it up for the benefit of her old opera-company friend from Sydney but she does have her reservations about the choir. At her second practice last night there were at least two women singing out of tune in her immediate vicinity; and what nails on a blackboard are to some people, out-of-tune singing is to Gabrielle. She was rigid with indignation bordering on fury for most of the night.

'Dear me,' purrs Ivan comfortingly. Which is the reason she rang him: he's good at being reassuring.

When she was first offered a place in a company in London, many years ago now, she panicked, sure that she wasn't good enough. Ivan had reassured her that she was more than good enough otherwise they wouldn't have wanted her. Two years later he came to one of her performances at Covent Garden and insisted that she was the best singer on stage, even though at that time she wasn't singing solos. He's been a good friend. She's been a slack friend. For every three letters Ivan wrote her, she wrote one. Yet he has persisted, so she tells herself that it's because she's such a wonderful person and he wants to be around her.

Victoria would say Gabrielle's kidding herself and that she should take better care of those who care for her, but Gabrielle's of an age now where she *really* doesn't need to pay attention to what her cousin says about life. They're both crones now – at least, Victoria definitely is one and Gabrielle certainly feels like one. That means they have pretty much equivalent experience and wisdom. Or so she would like to think.

'I know. It's outrageous!' she says to Ivan. 'I left this place because it was full of philistines and now I'm back.' She sighs loudly. 'I suppose I shall just have to *educate* them.'

'Who are you talking to?' Victoria hisses as she walks past.

With profound irritation, Gabrielle waves her away.

'So when are you going back to Europe?' Ivan enquires.

Gabrielle swallows. She hasn't told anyone – apart from Victoria – that she can't sing the way she used to. The surgery took place after her last contract ended and before her next engagement was due to begin; the story she's spun is that she liked having time off so much that she's still doing it. She's only fifty-five years old, so she's not really at retirement age. Her hope is that singing in the choir, even under sufferance, will prepare her voice for a return to the work she prefers. Hope is all it is, though. She doesn't have anyone to ask about it, so all she can do is wait and see.

'Oh, not for a while,' she answers breezily. 'My cousin needs me. Her husband has left her.'

Victoria's face – featuring a glower – appears around the doorframe and Gabrielle blows her a kiss.

'But how are you, darling?' she goes on. 'How's Felix?'

'Carrying on like the old diva he is,' Ivan says with a chuckle. 'You know what he's like – always has to have the best.'

'And you always give it to him,' Gabrielle says with affection.

Ivan and Felix are her favourite couple: completely devoted to each other, each knowing his role in the partnership and playing it to perfection. Gabrielle used to think she could find that for herself, but around the age of forty decided that heterosexual men were, on the whole, a failure at devoted relationships. She hasn't completely given up on the dream – or thought she hadn't. Living in Bellbird River isn't likely to make it come true. Every man around her age is married or widowed, and she doesn't really want to inherit a wife either way.

'He's good to me,' Ivan says. 'And I'm still at Opera Australia, toiling away in the service of the arts.'

'What has that been – twenty years?'

'Twenty-five.'

'They're lucky to have you.'

'So I keep telling them. But sorry, darling, I have to run. We're going to the symphony tonight and the taxi will be here shortly.'

'Of course, go. Go! Have a wonderful time!' She means it truly but also wishes she could be going to the symphony. Instead she's about to sit down to Victoria's lamb chops.

'Kisses,' Ivan says, then the line goes dead.

'Who was that?' Victoria demands from the doorway and Gabrielle jumps.

'Could you *please* stop scaring me like that? It's the third time today.'

Victoria steps into the room. 'If you would pay more attention to your surroundings you'd hear me coming. Honestly – you're so wrapped up in that head of yours.' She huffs. 'You always were.'

'I'm an *artist*, Vicky, what do you expect?'

'Just because you're an *artist*, Gabby, it doesn't mean you get out of being a functioning human being.'

'I think it does.' Gabrielle sniffs. 'I'm a very sensitive person. I have different needs.'

Victoria laughs heartily and Gabrielle blanches. When she's used that line before, her interlocutor has always nodded sympathetically and said they understand.

'Different needs?' Victoria keeps laughing. 'So you don't have to eat and drink and poo like the rest of us?'

'Don't be vulgar. That's not like you.'

'Then don't *you* be so ridiculous. I know you, Gabrielle Reynold. You were a pretty tough little kid.'

Gabrielle purses her lips. 'I had to be.'

'I know. You had to put up with a lot.'

Victoria pulls up a chair opposite to where Gabrielle is sitting on the 'bad couch', as Victoria calls it – the couch that has the most wear and tear.

'But you made it,' Victoria continues. 'You outlasted your parents and you made a success of things. I'd say that's not because you're so *sensitive*.' She arches a neatly groomed eyebrow. 'Anyway, sensitivity goes both ways. If you're as sensitive as you say, you should be sensitive to other people too, and that means being a little more kind about the choir.'

'I was just making a joke!'

'You weren't.'

They stare at each other for a few seconds.

When Gabrielle was younger she believed that she and Victoria could communicate without words, almost as if they were twins. They'd sit at family dinners and Christmas lunches and make tiny facial expressions at each other; gatherings were more bearable that way. It wasn't until Gabrielle was living abroad, constantly meeting new people, and didn't have Victoria any more that she realised how comforting it is to know someone so well that you don't need to explain anything to them.

Now Victoria's visage is inscrutable, something she's no doubt learnt over the years of being a town identity. She's the queen of Bellbird River and, like HM The Queen, can't betray her true feelings to anyone lest she offend. Each time Gabrielle walks down the street with her she finds it exhausting – everyone has to stop and say hello to Queen Victoria, who nods and smiles and waves as if she's in a carriage being driven down Pall Mall – so she can only imagine how it affects her cousin.

'I realise that being here is not your ideal,' Victoria says slowly. 'And that the choir is not of a standard you're used to. But there are decent people in it. People who are impressed by you. Please try to make the best of it. You may be surprised and find yourself enjoying it.'

'But you didn't even want to go! How can you lecture me?'

Gabrielle can hear herself whining and she feels like a teenager again, when Victoria's mother used to tell her to sit up straight and use her cutlery properly.

'I'm not *lecturing*, I'm *suggesting*. And I still don't want to go but I am going for you.' Victoria smiles tightly. 'I make sacrifices for the people I love, and you, my dear cousin, need this choir. You love singing and you love performing. The choir is your only opportunity to do that here.'

Gabrielle picks at the skirt of her flouncy cotton dress. She bought it in Italy the last time she was there, planning a Capri summer that never eventuated because she had her surgery, then her world shifted off its axis.

'I think you're going because you're sweet on Jimbo,' she says, teasing.

'Gabrielle, that's outrageous! I'm still married.'

'That didn't stop your husband from stepping out.'

Gabrielle hiccups with surprise at herself for saying something so risky.

Victoria's nostrils flare and she says drily, 'How true that is. Please remind me to visit the solicitor on Drury Street to begin whatever legal process is needed to formally evict Arthur from my life.'

'You mean . . . he hasn't done anything yet?'

'No. Probably thinks he can come back to me when that Celeste tires of him. *As she will*, because he is tiring. But he will be on his own then.'

They sit in silence for a minute.

'I admire you, Vicky,' Gabrielle says, her hands now resting in her lap. 'You keep your head held high and you forge onwards.'

'It helps to have a distraction. Like the choir.' Victoria smiles. 'And my cousin.' She stands and offers her hand to Gabrielle. 'It's lamb chop time.'

'Again?' Gabrielle groans as Victoria pulls her up.

'Would you rather do the cooking?'

'You know I can't.'

Victoria shrugs. 'Then you're stuck with mine.'

CHAPTER 16

'Kim, you can sit over there,' Alex whispers, pointing to a chair in the corner of the hall. It doesn't look comfortable – it's one of those bare iron-legged jobs with a narrow seat – but it's no worse than anything to be found in a New South Wales school.

'Okay.' Kim sighs dramatically and takes her book and her bad attitude to the corner.

All the way here she was complaining about being out at night, and Alex kept replying, 'But you're always asking me to stay up late.'

'So I can watch TV!' was Kim's rationale. 'I don't want to hear you sing.'

'Thanks very much,' Alex said. 'I've listened to you sing in school concerts.'

'You're my mum. It's your job.'

And so it is. Alex is aware that Kim being here is not in the job description of being a child, but with no babysitter there wasn't another option.

Not that Alex tried to find one. She thought she might have come across a student who'd be a reasonable babysitting prospect, but so far the girls are either rushing home after school to help their parents feed sheep or whatever happens around here – she hasn't really paid attention to which animals they have on their farms – or they're on sports teams, or they're trying to impress the unworthy boys.

Alex knows they're unworthy because she can already tell they're going to be the types to get someone pregnant or drunk or both, or they'll write off their parents' cars, and because they're good-looking and passably sporty they'll be forgiven for all of it. Their lives will peak in high school, after which time they'll drift into middle age lamenting the fact they never reached their 'potential'. These are types she's taught or grown up with, and it never ceases to surprise her that humans can be so predictable in so many ways.

'Hi.'

Alex turns away from watching Kim make a display of not finding the chair comfortable to see the woman from the bakery standing before her in what she thinks is the same T-shirt and pair of jeans she saw her wearing a couple of weeks ago. The T-shirt features Salvador Dali's melting clock, and the jeans look like they have flour on them. Janine, she said her name was. Amidst all the student names she's had to retain these past few weeks, Alex is pleased she can remember this.

'Hi, Janine! Nice to see you.' She points at the T-shirt. 'You like Dali.'

'Oh.' Janine glances down. 'My dad gave it to me. I'm more of a Van Gogh girl.'

Alex smiles. 'That's catchy.'

Janine blushes. 'I didn't mean it to come out like that. Um – Warwick's over here. I'll introduce you.'

Alex does her audition and sees Warwick wince only once, when she goes for a high note she shouldn't have. It's a note she used to be able to reach confidently when she sang in her high-school choir but it's a long time since she's tried it.

'Thank you, Alex, I think we'll put you in the mezzos,' Warwick says. 'So that makes four of you in total, which is more than we've ever had. I'm hoping for some robust harmonies, ladies!'

As Alex takes her place next to Janine, she notices a woman sitting hunched over on Janine's other side. She looks to be in her forties and her forehead is puckered, as if she's thinking hard about something.

'This is Debbie,' Janine says.

'Hi.' Alex gives her a little wave.

As Debbie turns her head her forehead relaxes a little. 'Hi.' She nods once then looks away again.

Okay, one antisocial in the group. It won't stop Alex saying hello to Debbie but she won't try to be too friendly. If someone doesn't want to communicate it's pointless to force the issue.

'Enid is sitting next to Debbie,' Janine says quietly. 'She and I were the only mezzos for a while. She liked it that way.'

Alex sees a woman who's at least sixty years of age with a prominent bosom and jawline to match. 'Noted,' she responds, then turns her attention to the sheet music on Janine's stand. 'Alanis Morissette?'

'Warwick loves her.' Janine snorts. 'He also loves Kylie Minogue. We did "Better the Devil You Know" for an Easter concert once.'

'I'm sure that went down well with some of the religious locals.'

'Yeah,' Janine says, laughing. 'I did wonder why the priest from St Brigid's was glaring at us.'

Alex notices that an older woman with an impressive French roll, her hair thick and grey, is looking at her with curiosity bordering on suspicion, and realises she should shut up and pay attention. If this were her classroom she'd have already decided she's a potentially troublesome student. Which she was when she was still at school. Becoming a teacher has been a form of penance, but also a belated acknowledgement that her own teachers did more for her than she realised at the time.

There's just one thing she needs to say before she forgets. 'Kim loved your cake,' she whispers to Janine and is given a smile in response.

Alex glances towards Kim, who, thankfully, has her head buried in her book. She decided that she's old enough to read *The Hobbit*, which she found when Alex unpacked their boxes. Alex was sure she'd have given up on it by now but she's persevering. Or pretending to. Tomorrow, after school, Alex is going to take her to the local library because clearly the primary school library isn't offering her anything of interest.

'All right,' Warwick booms, looking so much taller now that they're all sitting down and he's standing in front of them. 'We're practising in earnest for the Easter concert.'

'No hymns,' the woman with the French roll says loudly, to tittering from other members of the choir.

'Victoria, it's *Easter*.' Warwick smiles benignly and Alex admires his patience with the somewhat unreasonable request. 'It's a religious holiday so I don't think we can avoid hymns.'

Victoria's nostrils flare.

'I'm happy to take requests for other songs,' Warwick says. 'It doesn't have to be all hymns.'

'"Folsom Prison Blues!"' calls one of the older men. More tittering.

'Um . . .' It's Enid, the other mezzo, who looks startled as all eyes turn to her. 'Oh, I . . .' She smiles bashfully.

'All suggestions are welcome, Enid,' Warwick says encouragingly, 'even if we can't accommodate them.'

Enid nods vigorously, as if he's energised her. 'Righto, well, I like that Celine Dion song.'

'Bloody hell,' mutters one of the baritones.

Warwick holds up a hand. 'Roger, let her speak.'

'You know the one?' Enid smiles brightly and starts humming the chorus of 'My Heart Will Go On'.

'Not the sinking ship!' Frank throws his hands in the air and Alex sees Warwick stifle a smile before speaking kindly to Enid.

'It's a *very* impressive song, Enid. But, ah, unless someone wants to volunteer to do Celine's part, we may have to leave it out.'

He glances around, but no one speaks.

'It's a tricky vocal,' he says, 'so I'm not surprised. But thank you, Enid. Any other songs we should consider? Anyone?'

Alex can see Debbie fidgeting. Her eye catches Alex's and Alex smiles, hoping to encourage her.

'Um . . .' Debbie starts, and Warwick holds up a hand to quieten the others. '"We've Only Just Begun" by The Carpenters?'

Warwick beams. 'Such a lovely song. We can consider it.'

'Oh great,' Janine mutters. 'It's so sappy.'

Alex doesn't answer because she's quite fond of The Carpenters.

'How about Johnny Farnham?' says one of the other men. 'Everyone loves "You're the Voice".'

'Come off it, Frank,' says another. 'Are *you* going to sing that?' He guffaws.

Frank looks offended. 'Dawn says I do an all-right Farnham.'

'She has to say that – she's married to you.'

'Now, hang on—'

'Gentlemen.' Warwick has his hand in the air again and Alex wonders if choir practice is always this rowdy. And also if they are ever actually going to sing, even if tonight she intends to mostly listen. It's been so long since she's sung in company and she won't know enough to get anything right. She's just pleased that she's here. Her first proper outing since she moved to Bellbird River, and it's doing something that will challenge her. She wanted to make a change, and that includes taking part in activities she would never have tried in Sydney.

'You'll remember we have a no-Farnham policy,' Warwick is saying and Alex turns to Janine, eyebrows raised.

'Why?' she mouths.

'The mayor insisted on singing "Burn for You" a couple of years ago, when he was in the choir.' Janine shudders and shakes her head. 'He left the choir after that and the rest of us are still recovering.'

Warwick now has both hands in the air and Alex pays attention.

'I've made some changes to our arrangement of "Ironic" and I'd like to run through them now,' he says. 'And we'll talk about the Easter concert during the break, when we've all calmed down a little.'

Alex glances at Frank, whose feelings still appear to be hurt, then at Debbie, who looks more settled than she did before.

As the music starts Alex follows the sheet music on Janine's stand, and when the chorus comes around she decides to join in. It feels more natural than she remembered, and when they run through the song again she performs it the whole way through.

CHAPTER 17

Sunday afternoon. The one time of the week when Janine is guaranteed to not be at the bakery and not needed anywhere else either. The bakery is closed on Sundays, so the morning is for washing clothes and helping her parents with whatever needs doing around the house and garden.

'Going for a drive?' her father says after she's changed out of her grungy T-shirt and shorts into a clean T-shirt and pair of cotton pants.

He says it every week. He knows she's going for a drive; she thinks it's his way of trying to start a conversation but he's lacking imagination.

'Yep,' she says, nodding, checking her handbag for wallet, sunnies, tissues.

'Where are you off to?' He looks wary.

She's seen this before, too, and she can interpret it.

'Just for a drive, Dad. You know I like to get out on the weekends.'

He nods slowly. She knows what he wants to say, but he can never say it so she usually does it for him.

'I'm not seeing Bradley. In case you're wondering.'

Her father's eyes are bright blue and they're at their brightest now. 'No?' he says.

'He can have visitors,' she says.

They've gone over this so many times: her parents steadfastly resisting seeing their only son; Janine trying to nudge them towards it. Bradley would benefit so much from seeing them, not least because she knows that the shame he feels about his illness comes in large part from the shame their parents feel. But she's Sisyphus in this situation and the rock isn't getting any easier to move.

Her father peers at her. 'Is it . . . safe?'

'Dad, he's not dangerous.'

'He *was*!'

'That was a long time ago,' Janine murmurs.

It's not a memory she visits often: her brother, before he was diagnosed and probably after he'd taken a drug of some kind, punching walls in the house, punching the fridge, punching the car. Punching her. She always maintained – because she believed it to be true – that he hit her because she was in the way, like an object. Like the car. He didn't know he was punching his sister. Or perhaps that's just what she wants to believe, because if she didn't she might not be able to have a relationship with him. It would make her far sadder to not see him, so it's easier to keep telling herself the story that makes seeing him possible.

'I don't want anyone hurting my girl,' her father says gruffly, turning away.

'Righto, Dad.'

Janine picks up her handbag and her keys, kisses him on the cheek and walks to her old sedan. She packed her paints, easel and a board into it last night, the way she always does on Saturday nights, ready to see where Sunday takes her. Once she drove to Manilla, another time to Armidale. Sometimes she doesn't even get out of the car; she just likes to see what she can see beside the road. If there's something to paint, she stops.

Today she turns left on Jumbuck Way and heads north so she can cut across towards Goonoo Goonoo, then maybe she'll go on to Nundle. Or maybe she'll find a spot by a river or a creek and stop.

The sky is almost as blue as her father's eyes, and with the full heat of the sun overhead she winds down the window. There's no air conditioning in this car so even though the air outside is warm there's enough of a breeze to provide some relief.

Cher's 'If I Could Turn Back Time' comes on the radio and Janine smiles. The other day at choir practice one of the older ladies tried belting it out in the hope of impressing Warwick with her vocal abilities. Instead she sang flat, couldn't reach the highest notes in the chorus and stopped, muttering something about pop songs not being what they used to be. Then Gabrielle piped up about how people should just apply themselves, or something like that, and perhaps Warwick could include some songs that were not just by 'pop tarts' – Janine smiles remembering the phrase – perhaps some Rodgers and Hammerstein, Stephen Sondheim, Mr Cole Porter? Warwick didn't like being told what to do, that was clear. Janine thinks the other members of the choir enjoyed the stoush as much as she did. Gabrielle may be a snob but she's entertaining.

At any rate, Janine is partial to a pop tart and she gives the chorus of 'If I Could Turn Back Time' a crack now, with the volume up loud. There's no one to hear her on this road, with mostly pastoral land on either side and only some Friesians observing her as they chew grass near their fence.

Nah, she can't get those notes either. And she doesn't care.

There's an ironbark up ahead, then another. The signs that the turn is near. She doesn't bother with her blinker, just swings to the right and heads down the narrow road that leads east.

This road's so quiet that a flock of galahs has gathered on the roadside, picking their way through the meagre green shoots there. They barely register her passing, only two of them flying away. They'll be back. They always come back.

There are heavier, greener trees up ahead, leaning towards each other from either side of the road, a tangle of leaves in emerald and olive shades.

The names given to colours never express what they feel like to her. One shade of green feels warm, another cool; one may make her gut feel unsettled, another can calm her.

As a child she would sit, sometimes with Bradley and sometimes not, on an escarpment looking over Bellbird River. Their parents would let them go exploring, trusting in their common sense. Sometimes it would go wrong – they both had their share of falls and scrapes – but they learnt how to take care of themselves. Most of all, they had time and opportunity to appreciate the countryside around them. It's how, Janine is sure, she developed her eye. As she surveyed the landscape she felt physically connected to it, like the browns of the soil were seeping into her feet and hands, and the trees were extending their branches inside of her. She doesn't talk about it to anyone, because how could she? It's weird. Instead she expresses it through painting.

Round the bend there's a stand of shorter trees next to a stump, marking a side road that, Janine remembers, goes to the creek. In high school she had a friend who lived near here and they'd spend the occasional summer afternoon lying by this creek, working on their tans. She's paying for that now with her freckles.

She turns down the road and pulls up near what the locals call the beach – actually a stretch of dirt, not sand, that goes for about ten metres. The creek isn't running, and she didn't think it would be – there hasn't been rain for weeks. But it's the creek bed she's after.

She pulls the easel from the car, along with a milk crate to sit on and her paints and the board.

It's cool here, some gums providing cover. Janine sets herself up so she can paint the biggest dip in the creek bed and the trees on either side, with their varying barks of white and tan and a rough brown that she can never quite name but which she sees everywhere.

When she saw Ross on Friday he asked her what she was doing on the weekend – a question she avoids asking him because she knows it will involve his wife and children. She said she might try to paint the hills that form a western border for Bellbird River, with their rich green trees and bulging outcrops.

'Painting?' He'd frowned. 'You can't even draw.'

She'd opened her mouth to correct him: she could draw, she did draw, when they knew each other in high school. She used to draw him. Maybe that's what he was referring to. Maybe he'd lied all those times he told her he loved her drawings of him. So she closed her mouth and kissed him instead, and hated herself a little bit for not sticking up for the past as she remembered it.

Then he'd patted her hip and said, 'You have a bit more fat on than you used to.' He'd smirked, she'd blanched, and he'd patted her again and said, 'Don't worry, babe, I like it.'

If only he knew that the fat took years to put on and represents a victory over her stronger demons, even if she hates it. Because she does. Every time she looks in the mirror she sees a failure. That is her instant reaction, before she talks herself around, reminds herself that it's not good to be as thin as she was. Except Ross clearly disagrees.

He's not here now, though; nobody else is. It's just her and the trees and the sky and the dappled light, and a couple of cockatoos that have noisily decided to shred a nearby tree.

Spreading paints on her palette, she dips in a brush and starts.

Soon, she knows, time will lose its form and she won't realise that the afternoon is fading, and she'll stay here until she can't see anything well enough to paint it.

Then she'll pack up and drift home, content that she's had this time to herself, to be herself, and tonight she'll set the alarm so that tomorrow morning she can get up and start another week of that whole other life that holds her in stasis.

CHAPTER 18

It's her fourth choir practice yet Debbie still feels nervous each time she parks the car near the hall. It's not the singing she's worried about – when she sings she actually forgets about every other concern she has.

When she was a child she and her sister would sing together while their parents sniped at each other down the hall; it was their way of comforting each other and blocking out the noise. They sang nursery rhymes and hymns and songs their grandfather taught them. He said they were special songs he knew as a boy, but once she was older Debbie realised he probably made them up.

He was creative, her grandpa. Liked to do woodwork and sketch flowers and animals, which she knew because she lived with him and her grandmother for a few months while her parents were 'sorting things out', or so they said. Debbie sang with her grandfather, and with her grandmother too for that matter. Sometimes fragments of her grandfather's songs come back to her; she's never stopped wishing she wrote them down.

Her sister, Rosemary, went to their other grandparents. Debbie didn't know why she and Rosemary weren't kept together, but she's never really stopped regretting it. They grew apart and they've never quite grown back together. Rosemary was her best friend; now they're barely acquaintances. She visited Debbie in prison twice and each time the conversation was so stiff it was as if Debbie was being assessed for the position of failed sister of the year. All Debbie wanted to do was ask Rosemary if she still sang, because she thought maybe that could be a point in common, but the moment never felt right.

Their parents reconciled eventually, but Rosemary had left school and home by then, and Debbie wanted to stay with her grandparents. The whole thing was a mess. Her parents were ill suited to each other and to parenthood, but that didn't stop them resenting the fact that Debbie didn't want to live with them again. Her solution was to start her own life, in a new part of Sydney. That was going pretty well until she was arrested.

It was so tempting to blame her failings on her upbringing – her lawyer said she should, because she might get a reduced sentence – but most of her memories of her younger life are of her grandfather and his songs, of the freedom she felt when she sang them, of how music made her feel lost and found at the same time. Lost inside the notes, found within herself. Grandpa understood that. No one else ever has.

So, no, it's not the singing she's nervous about. It's the people. They all know each other and talk to each other, and Debbie feels like the gulf between being one of the people they know and not is too vast for her to cross. It's so hard, trying to talk to strangers, and some of the choir people seem like they'd be more difficult to talk to than others.

One woman, Victoria, completely changes the room when she enters it. Some people start frantically whispering to each other, while others go quiet. Debbie just hopes that Victoria never looks her way, because she wouldn't know what to say to someone so formidable.

Victoria's cousin, Gabrielle, seems more approachable, mainly because she's so loud that it's like she's advertising her presence. Not that anyone can get near her with Warwick fluffing around. '*Madama* Reynold' he called her the other day, which Debbie thought was a bit much.

As Debbie walks into the hall for tonight's practice she sees Warwick standing near the piano talking to the very same Madama and it looks as though he's blushing. He's fanning himself with sheet music.

If she weren't sure he's gay, Debbie would think he has a crush on Gabrielle. And Debbie would probably have a crush on him herself. He's quite handsome, and he's been kind to her, checking on her at least once every practice to see how she's fitting in.

She feels nervous when she sees him tonight, although she isn't sure if it's because she wonders if he's being honest about liking her singing or if she's just excited to see him.

'Those two, honestly,' says a voice near her left ear and Debbie flinches.

'Sorry, sorry!' the voice adds as Debbie turns and sees the young woman she met last week, with brown hair and wearing a pair of well-worn jeans. Alex, that was her name. 'I shouldn't have done that unannounced.'

Debbie smiles quickly. 'That's okay.'

'But, really, look at them. They're like teenage lovebirds.'

Debbie glances towards the piano and the animated pair beside it. 'I, um, don't think he's interested in her like that.'

'Really? I could have sworn he has a thing for her. He blushes when she speaks to him!'

'He likes her in a fan way maybe.' Debbie smiles nervously. She doesn't really want to be gossiping about the choirmaster. She wouldn't want someone to gossip about her, which is probably inevitable anyway because if they don't know her story yet, they will. That sort of information always gets around.

'In-ter-es-ting.' Alex raises an eyebrow. 'So you're a local?' She points to the chairs and they walk towards them.

'No. I moved here a little while ago. I work on a property. You?'

'Same as you without the property bit. Moved here from Sydney. Teaching at the high school.' She stops and waves at a girl sitting in the corner near the stage. 'That's my daughter, Kim,' she explains. 'I don't know any babysitters so she has to come along.'

'You don't have a husband?'

It comes out in a rush and Debbie doesn't know why she said it, because she's hardly in a position to be judgemental about other people's family arrangements.

Alex's eyelids flicker. 'No,' she says. 'Never.'

Never is a bold statement and no doubt Alex knows it. Debbie hasn't met a single parent before – that is, not one who has always been on their own. She doesn't even count herself as one because the children aren't with her.

'Do you?' Alex says, and Debbie knows she should have anticipated the question in return even if she doesn't want to answer it.

'I, um, I used to,' she says, holding her breath as she looks at Alex, who simply nods and stops at a chair.

'Mu-um.'

Debbie jumps and turns, then stops herself as she realises it's not her daughter calling out but Alex's.

Alex gives Kim a quizzical smile. 'What is it, Kim?'

'I need to go to the toilet.' Kim glances at Debbie then drops her head.

'Oh, I . . .' Alex looks around.

'I think it's out that door,' Debbie says, nodding towards the opposite side of the stage. 'I need to go too.' She smiles at Kim. 'I'll wait until you come back. There's only room for one person at a time.'

It isn't the truth – she doesn't need to go – but she can see that Kim is shy about mentioning the loo in front of a stranger.

'Thanks,' Alex says, smiling gratefully. 'Want me to go with you?'

'No!' Kim whips around and starts for the door.

Alex sighs. 'She doesn't like me very much at the moment.'

Debbie is probably meant to ask why, but she's not sure if that's prying. So she opens and closes her mouth, then pulls out the sheet music from her handbag.

'She misses Sydney,' Alex says softly.

'Understandable,' Debbie murmurs. She misses it herself sometimes. Or, rather, she misses the version of it she knew years ago.

'I'm surprised Janine's not here,' Alex says more brightly, sitting down. Then she nudges Debbie and nods towards Victoria. 'How funny is Victoria? I thought she was Lady Muck at first, but then I heard her talking to Gabrielle and she sounds like a character. The two of them together are a *hoot*.'

Debbie glances over at the impressive older woman and feels startled when their eyes meet, almost as if the headmistress has caught her smoking. But Victoria gives her a crinkly smile instead of a detention and Debbie feels oddly proud of herself.

'Anyway,' Alex says in a loud whisper, 'it looks like Warwick and Gabrielle have finished their love-in, so we're probably about to start.'

'Oh . . . right.' Debbie puts her sheet music on the stand in front of her. She's appreciative of Alex chatting to her but the music is still her focus. Will always be.

'We'll start with "We've Only Just Begun",' Warwick announces, and Debbie feels as pleased as she did last week when he told her they'd be singing it for the Show.

Now, as Warwick plays the opening bars, Debbie prepares to lose herself in Karen Carpenter's hope for the future. And as they start singing, she can't stop a smile from forming.

CHAPTER 19

The house is modest: one storey made of blond brick with a terracotta-coloured corrugated-iron roof, discoloured blinds in the front windows and desperate sasanquas in the front garden. It's two blocks from the West Tamworth Leagues Club and three blocks from the last house Bradley lived in, where Janine visited him a couple of weeks ago. He moves around a bit. At least he calls and tells her where he'll be. Calls the bakery, because he knows it will be only her answering the phone. He hasn't spoken to their parents in a long while. Why would he?

Janine tucks limp strands of hair behind her ears. Autumn isn't too far away but summer is hanging on. 'At least it's a dry heat,' a customer said recently. Yeah, Janine wanted to say, there's dry heat in the Simpson Desert but not too many people want to live there.

There's a screen door that shows a long, dark hallway. The knocker is on the door that's pushed back, out of reach behind the screen.

'Hello?' she calls. 'Bradley?'

'Round the back,' grumbles a nearby voice.

Janine scurries down the side of the house to where she saw a low brick fence and a gate. It unlatches easily and she follows the lawn around until she spies her brother. He's slumped in a plastic slatted chair better suited to the beach, arms folded across his chest, his chin dropped and his eyes closed, his legs stretched out, belly hanging over his pants, and his crew cut growing out in tufts.

'Hi,' she breathes but he doesn't move.

She steps closer. 'Hi, Bradley.'

He opens the eye closest to her. 'Hi,' he says, then closes his eye again.

She knows she should be used to seeing him like this. The medication makes him sluggish, if not drowsy. It's why he's put weight on. He doesn't do any exercise. Not like he used to. As a teenager he was captain of the high school cricket team. He rode a bike everywhere. He challenged her to skipping rope competitions that she knew she would never win, but she participated anyway because he was her big brother and she didn't want to let him down. She never wants to let him down.

She never wants to become used to seeing him like this, either. She wants to believe there'll be a cure for him someday, although she's pretty sure no scientist is working on how to make schizophrenics better. There are never articles in the newspaper about that.

After Bradley was diagnosed their mother worried he'd become dangerous. One of her friends is a nurse and said the schizophrenics could be violent. Janine did as much research as she could and told her parents that there was no proof of that but they should really help him stay on his pills because they would temper his extremes.

That time he hit her happened when he wasn't taking his prescribed medication but he seemed to have found something else to take. That's when their parents organised for him to go to a home. That way a professional could keep an eye on him, they said. Their embarrassment about his mental illness had nothing to do with it. So they said.

Janine felt like she'd failed him. But she had to work; she couldn't be the one to monitor him all the time.

He opens his eye again. 'You just gonna stand there?' he mumbles.

'Um . . .' Janine gestures to the empty chair opposite him. 'May I?'

He jerks his chin towards it. 'Course.'

'Keep your eyes open,' she orders as gently as she can. She's had to get used to bossing him around. It feels strange telling your big brother what to do. It's not as though it's some form of revenge, either, because he never gave her orders. He just let her be herself.

'Why?' he says, sighing.

'So I can see them.' She tries smiling but it feels unnatural. He nods slowly.

'How are you feeling?' she asks, and reaches across to take his hand, to show him she cares.

A couple of visits ago she realised that Bradley would never have anyone touching him. She hardly has that herself. Now that she's seeing Ross, there's more than there was, but her parents aren't demonstrative that way. Whose are, though? Her schoolfriends never had parents who hugged and kissed either. That doesn't mean it isn't important. She once saw a documentary in which a ewe gave birth and the lamb lay on the ground, still. It looked dead. This went on for a minute or so, then the farmer picked up the lamb and put it next to the ewe's nose. The ewe nudged her baby, which immediately sprang to life. Janine has never forgotten that. The power of touch. She and Bradley have never said 'I love you' to each other, but maybe she can show him by touching him.

Except he pulls back and scowls.

'What are you doing?' he says.

'Trying to be your sister.' She sits back and crosses her arms.

'By holding my hand?'

'Not exactly,' she huffs. 'I just thought I'd show you I care.'

He pulls a packet of cigarettes out of his tracksuit pants pocket and lights one.

'You're here, aren't ya?' he says, blowing out smoke. 'I know you care.'

'Sorry I haven't been for a couple of weeks.' Usually she's here every Saturday while one of the local teenagers works the afternoon in the bakery.

He shrugs. 'No worries.'

'Really?' She's agitated by his nonchalance, and not for the first time.

'What?'

'You really don't care that I haven't visited?'

He shrugs again. 'I dunno, Neen. Some days I don't care about anything at all.'

She knows this is true, because she's tried to rile him up about various things – cricket scores, election results, even the bloody Golden Guitars one year – and he usually just shrugs when what she wants him to do is *feel*. Even though she knows that, for him, feeling could be dangerous. But she doesn't want to be the only person she knows with feelings. With passions. Ross says he's passionate about his work but she thinks that's different; what he's really passionate about, she suspects, is making money.

Bradley used to talk about music with her. They'd listen to the radio; they'd lie on the floor while records played and talk about which songs were the best. Which bands were their favourites. She had plenty of feelings then, and so did he. She misses that version of him. The boy who never thought she was odd for getting hung up on an album for weeks on end or trying to get creative with her sports uniform.

'I can see you don't care about your hair at the moment,' she says, trying for levity, for her own sake if not his.

'Haven't been able to get to the barber,' he mutters.

She pauses while she formulates a plan.

'Come on,' she says, standing and holding out her hand again. 'I'll take you now. I drove past one that was open.'

He drags on his cigarette and looks as though he's considering her suggestion.

'It's next to a milk bar,' Janine goes on, 'so there might even be a hamburger in it for you.'

She thinks she sees a glimmer of a smile on his face, and it's like the sun has come out after the darkest winter.

With his free hand he takes hers and she pulls him up to standing, feeling the thrill of tiny progress. It disappears once he's on his feet because he lets go, but as he shuffles to the gate behind her she can sense that he's not far away. And at the moment he reaches forwards to open the gate for her, the Bradley she knew is made flesh once again.

Then he's gone, and the Bradley she's come to know keeps smoking his cigarette as he trails her to the car.

CHAPTER 20

Victoria lets the letter fall to her lap. It's so very tempting to screw it up into a ball and throw it out the window, but that wouldn't solve the problem.

She sighs and picks it up again. Reads it again. Feels her blood boil. Makes a noise that sounds like a muffled war cry.

'Victoria!' Gabrielle calls from the piano room down the hall.

'Yes?'

'I can *hear you*.'

'Sorry.'

This time as she reads it she clenches her teeth and makes a fist, then bashes it down on the coffee table. She's rewarded by the sound of heavier-than-needed footsteps.

Gabrielle stops in front of her, puts her hands on her hips and juts her bosom forwards in a fashion she no doubt learnt playing Brunhilde.

'I'm trying to learn a new piece,' she chides. 'Very *hard* when you're making such a racket.'

Victoria raises her eyebrows. 'That's all?'

'What do you mean?'

'I thought you might stomp your feet for effect.' Victoria sniffs and turns the letter towards her cousin. 'Arthur's lawyer has sent me a list of demands.'

'It's a bit early for that,' Gabrielle says. 'You need to be separated for a year to get a divorce.'

'I imagine Arthur thinks there's no harm in making a start.'

'No.' Gabrielle makes a hurrumphing sort of noise. 'He's only interested in the harm that comes from dipping his wick in someone else's wax.'

Victoria is momentarily surprised at her cousin's ribaldry then grateful for the opportunity to laugh.

'I'm sure she does wax actually,' she says. 'Celeste is very well *groomed*, shall we say.'

'Ridiculous amount of bother. Now, show me this letter.'

Gabrielle almost snatches it up then reads it, expressions quickstepping across her face accompanied by gasps and guttural sounds.

'Out-*rageous*,' she says, thrusting it back. 'He can't have this house. It's yours!'

Victoria glances around the sitting room that she has known since childhood; the same one her mother sat in when she was pregnant, therefore it's the room she's known since before childhood. She takes in the paintings on the wall, some of which were commissioned two generations ago, some newer.

'He bought the Streeton,' Victoria says, nodding towards a small painting next to one of the windows.

'Whoop-de-doo,' Gabrielle says, barely glancing at it.

'You didn't even realise that *was* a Streeton, did you?' Victoria says, amused. Her cousin loves the arts – but not all of them.

Gabrielle flaps a hand. 'Irrelevant. He can have the Streeton. *I'll* take it to him. But if that's all he contributed I hardly think he has a claim on the whole house.'

'Oh, he only wants half. The value of half.'

Victoria closes her eyes and wonders if, when she opens them again, the letter might have disappeared. How can anyone possibly assess the true value of this house? How can a person ascertain the worth of over a century of family life here? And why would any lawyer think his client should be entitled to that just because he happened to live here for some of it? Arthur is probably saying that Victoria forced him out because she was unwilling to allow him to 'explore' his relationship with Celeste. And that's true: she has no interest in staying with him while he carries on with another woman. Arthur forced himself out, though, the second he told her he was in love with someone else.

'Vicky – wake up!'

When she opens her eyes she sees Gabrielle's snapping fingers.

'You need to get organised,' Gabrielle says. 'Who is his lawyer?' She peers at the paper. 'Some drongo in Muswellbrook. Right. Listen. *You're* getting someone from Sydney.'

'I wouldn't know where to start finding a lawyer in Sydney,' Victoria says wearily. The mere thought of having to go through the administration that comes with a divorce is enough to make her want to nap for the next week.

'I'll call my friend Ivan. His boyfriend knows *everyone*.' Gabrielle beams as if she's solved all the world's problems.

'I have no wish to travel to Sydney to see a lawyer. The local man will do.'

Gabrielle pinches her arm and Victoria yelps. 'What on earth are you doing?'

'Trying to *wake you up*. You can't afford to be complacent, Vicky. There was a conductor I knew who was shtupping every soprano he could get his hands on and when he left his wife she thought he'd be nice during the divorce because she'd been so understanding about his affairs. *Wrong*. She got *nothing*. Women should be paid danger money just for having to go near men, let alone bear their children and stay with them for years. No. *No!*' This time she really did stomp her foot. 'Arthur is not getting *anything*. You need a lawyer who has experience in such matters and Monsieur I-Do-Mostly-Conveyancing from Bellbird River won't cut it.'

'But I don't want to offend the man. He'll know that I'm not using him.'

Gabrielle crosses her arms and glares down her nose. 'Arthur has no problem using a drongo from Muswellbrook. He is clearly not worrying about the local solicitor's delicate feelings. Why should you?'

Victoria wants to laugh at her cousin's performative outrage, but instead she's touched. Since her parents died she's never had anyone care that much about her. The children appear to care when they call to say hello, but she doesn't believe they think about her at other times.

When she called to tell them about Arthur's affair her son cleared his throat and muttered something about how he was due at the local tennis courts and her daughter said, 'Well, men have needs, Mum', as if that made it all right. Victoria tends to think Helena was brainwashed at university by those women's studies courses she took; she talks a lot about 'equality' and seems to think it goes hand in hand with hopping into bed with random men. But Victoria doesn't believe that pandering to men's sexual urges makes women equal; it just makes them fools. And she was not brought up to be a fool.

So perhaps Gabrielle has a point. One cannot be complacent in the face of a foe who is determined to win at all costs. One must, instead, prepare for war. And the required armaments are thicker on the ground in a city where there are battlefields everywhere and warriors on standby.

Victoria makes a face but it's for show. Gabrielle likes a show. 'All right, all right,' she says with an exaggerated sigh. 'Make the call to your friend.'

Gabrielle looks like a proud mother at a prize-giving.

'Are you sure he won't mind?' Victoria goes on.

'Not at all,' Gabrielle says breezily. 'Besides, he owes me.'

'How so?'

'I introduced him to his boyfriend and they've been together for *years*.' She narrows her eyes. 'You know, I'm quite good at matchmaking. Maybe I should set you up with someone.'

'I'm not even divorced yet!' Victoria has no interest in adjusting her life to suit yet another man. She made too many accommodations for Arthur. Never again.

'It'll give you something to look forwards to.'

'No.'

'We'll see.'

'No.'

Gabrielle smiles mysteriously. 'I may already have someone in mind. But I'll keep that on the simmer for now.'

Victoria doesn't wish to know what her cousin has planned unless it pertains to this currently hypothetical Sydney lawyer.

'I'll leave you to make the call,' she says as she heaves herself off the couch. 'I'll use the piano room to practise piano, the way God intended.'

Victoria leaves the room, feeling lighter with every step.

CHAPTER 21

'Frank, as I've already reminded you, *no Farnham*.' Warwick is shaking his head, looking like he's fed up, and practice hasn't even started yet.

Alex puts her handbag in the corner and watches as Kim takes her usual spot near the stage, her shoulders slumped more than usual. It was another friendless day at school.

'Cold Chisel, then?' Frank looks hopeful.

'Frank, we've talked about this.' Now it's that snowy-haired older gentleman – Jim, from memory – who looks almost as fed up as Warwick. '"Khe Sanh" is never going to happen.'

'What about "Flame Trees"? That's a bloody good song.' Now Frank sounds desperate.

'I agree with you but we did it two or three years ago,' Warwick says, crossing his arms.

'Time to do it again, then,' Frank says triumphantly.

'The show committee has requested more contemporary songs,' Warwick says.

'But they're all by women!' Frank sounds exasperated.

'That's true. I think you'll find that a lot of the more popular songs lately are by female artists. The Spice Girls and so on.' Warwick sounds like he's talking to a toddler.

'But us blokes need something!' Now Frank is pouting like a toddler. 'The choir has blokes in it too!'

Alex takes her seat next to Janine and looks at her, eyebrows raised.

'This happens at least once a month,' Janine mutters. 'Maybe it's a full-moon thing.'

'I'm aware of that, Frank,' Warwick says with a soothing tone. 'But the show committee said they're hoping to appeal to younger people this year and these are the sorts of songs younger people like.'

'Don't worry, mate,' Jim says, patting Frank on the shoulder. 'I'm still campaigning for a Slim Dusty.'

Alex thinks Warwick might have just rolled his eyes but from this angle she can't tell for sure.

'We've had plenty of songs that appeal to men,' Warwick says. 'Just see this as the ladies' turn. They're overdue.'

Frank lifts his eyes heavenward, as if appealing to God, then mutters something Alex can't hear and shuffles off to his seat.

'Wow.' Alex starts to laugh. 'Is it always this dramatic?'

'Frank misses the good old days,' Janine says, pulling herself up from her slumped position. 'You know, when women were seen and not heard.'

'Oh, right. You mean the days that never existed anywhere but in their imaginations?' Alex nods. 'I've worked with some men who think like that. Sadly they're teaching boys to think like that.'

Janine tilts her head and narrows her eyes. 'You're not a big fan of men?'

Alex shrugs. 'I like looking at them. Sometimes I even like being around them. But I'm not a fan of the things they get away with, no.'

She puts her music on the stand. While she likes Janine it's too early in their acquaintance for Alex to talk about how it feels to be dumped by your boyfriend when he finds out you're pregnant, and how people – including other women – blame you, the dumped one, and how it's all symptomatic of how their society is constructed, to nobble women, and it makes her worry about Kim and whether or not life will be different for her. Because she thinks it may not be and that's just too depressing to ponder on a regular basis.

Yeah, far too early for that.

'So what's new with you?' she says instead.

Janine looks at her as if she's a bit odd. 'What's new with me?' She snorts. 'Not much. I don't go anywhere other than the bakery or do anything other than sell baked goods.'

'That's not true – you come here.'

Janine makes a funny face. 'Big whoop. It's a whole ten-minute walk from home.'

Alex can see Warwick fluffing around the piano, which is usually the signal they're about to start.

'Are you going to try out for those solos Warwick talked about last week?' she asks. 'For the Show?'

Another askance look from Janine. 'No. Alex, you've been sitting next to me. Haven't you worked out that I can't sing all that well?'

'You sound fine to me.'

It's the truth – Janine is a good singer. If she were more enthusiastic about it she'd probably be a better-than-good singer, but Alex gets the sense that she's in the choir just for something to do.

Janine nudges her. 'You sure you should be singing? I don't think your hearing's all that accurate.' She smiles impishly.

'Ha ha.'

Now Warwick has moved away from the piano and is talking to Gabrielle. Alex is mildly – no, greatly – intimidated by Gabrielle's presence in the choir, because every time they sing she suspects Gabrielle must be judging them. How could she not be? She's reached a level of professional achievement in music that the rest of them never will. Which is why Alex won't be trying out for the solos either – she does *not* want to sing solo in front of the great Gabrielle Reynold.

'Hi,' comes a soft voice from Alex's left and she turns to see Debbie, looking timid. Although last week Debbie barely spoke to her, so saying hello is probably a big step.

'Hi, Debbie,' Alex says. 'I bet *you're* going to audition for a solo.'

'What? Why?' Debbie frowns.

'Janine and I were just talking about those solos. The ones Warwick mentioned.' She glances at Janine, who raises a hand in greeting to Debbie.

'Oh – those.' Debbie nods quickly. 'I don't think so.'

'You should,' Alex says. 'You have a great voice. I can hear it even when we're all singing.'

Debbie looks surprised, then shrugs. 'Thanks. I'll, um . . . I'll think about it.'

Alex smiles encouragingly, then realises she hasn't checked on Kim since they arrived. She glances over and sees her not reading, as usual, but writing. Probably about how much she hates her mother for bringing her to a place where she's finding it so hard to make friends *and* for telling her they're not going to have ice cream for a month because they've been eating too much of it. Or Alex has been eating too much of it. It's been comfort food while they adjust to life in Bellbird River, and she knows she shouldn't punish Kim for her own overindulgence, but if they have it in the house at all she'll eat it, and at this rate her arteries will be hard by the time she turns forty.

Kim glances up and catches Alex's eye, glowers, then bends her head over her exercise book again.

'We're ready to start.' Warwick's booming voice cuts across the chatter. 'Jimbo's going to hand around your new sheet music. "Spice Up Your Life" by the Spice Girls. Ready-made for a choir, considering there are five-part harmonies.'

There's a loud groan from the tenors and baritones.

Janine chuckles. 'Unreal,' she says softly, and Alex turns to her with an enquiring expression.

Janine shrugs. 'Sometimes I think Warwick does it just to piss off those old blokes. Keeps life interesting.'

Alex glances across at Frank, who looks like his world has just ended.

'Somehow I don't think the old blokes enjoy being pissed off,' she says, and readies herself for the challenge of learning to sing like Scary Spice.

CHAPTER 22

Debbie's heart thumps as she approaches the park. Greg chose a place in South Tamworth that he told Debbie would be easy to find, but she drove over the Peel River and up into the north of the town before she realised she'd gone too far. So she's late, and he'll make a point of saying it, and he's probably told the kids that she doesn't care about them. *See, kids? She went away for years and now she can't even be bothered turning up on time.* Or maybe she's being ungenerous. Maybe he hasn't said anything.

'Couldn't be bothered to turn up on time?' he says, sighing, as she walks up to him. His hands are on his hips and he's shaking his head.

But Debbie doesn't care. She's looking around trying to see her children. To see how much they've grown. If they still look like they used to, or if time and distance have changed them the way they've changed her.

'I got lost,' she says.

'It's a bloody country town, Debbie – how lost can you get?' More shaking of his head.

He never used to say mean things. At least, not to her. Right up until the time she went to prison he wasn't mean. So when he told her he wasn't bringing the kids to see her any more, she was shocked. It was a bigger shock than her sentence, because she kind of expected that, really.

Prison isn't that much of a surprise when you do something illegal. Or maybe it is to people who tell themselves they'll never get caught, but she was always convinced she'd get caught. That belief didn't stop her doing what she was doing. Which made her wonder if maybe she'd wanted to get caught. Maybe she'd wanted someone else, something else – a force outside of herself – to stop her because she couldn't think of a good reason to stop herself. Not even the kids were motivation enough for her to decide that gambling was the wrong path. As Greg has pointed out in just about every conversation they've had since he took their children to a different part of the state: *You didn't even care enough about the kids.*

Except she did. She loved the kids more than anything. More than life. But once she was inside she had time to think and wondered some more about the fact that she didn't stop stealing and gambling, about how the highs of it were so high and that's what she kept chasing, to the detriment of everything else. And she came to the conclusion that she was a fairly worthless human being and maybe the kids deserved a break from her. Not that she could explain that to Greg. All he saw was a wife who dumped all the child-rearing on him.

'Where are the kids?' she says, choosing not to tell him just how lost you can get in a town the size of Tamworth.

'In the car.' He nods towards a Commodore parked a hundred or so metres away.

'Thanks for changing your mind,' she says nervously, as if he could change it back at any moment.

'Thank Julia. She's the one who said you deserve a chance.'

Julia, her children's stepmother. Julia, the woman who has more of a relationship with Shaun and Emily than she does. Julia, who is now getting out of the front passenger side of the car.

Her hair is dyed blonde and scraped back with combs. She's wearing tight jeans and a loose top, and her face crinkles in what looks like a smile in Debbie's direction.

'She's pretty,' Debbie says, and her eyes flicker to Greg.

He smiles smugly. 'Yep.'

Debbie feels nothing. He stopped being hers a long time ago, and jealousy isn't an emotion she used to feel much anyway.

Now Julia is opening the back door of the car and Emily steps out. Her legs look so much longer than they did the last time Debbie saw her two years ago, even though she's only seven.

Shaun slides out after her. He's lanky, like his father, and his sandy-coloured hair is falling in his eyes, like Debbie's father's used to.

All she wants to do is run to them and scoop them up, hug them so close they'll never escape her, but she can't. They're not hers any more either. Not the way they used to be.

They stand next to each other, looking at her. Not smiling.

Despite the fact she has rehearsed this meeting in her imagination, tried out all the different ways she and the children may greet each other, she hasn't prepared herself for a moment like this, when her children are staring at her as if she's a stranger. It feels like a fissure has opened in her chest, so deep that she thinks she might actually split in two.

But she can't. These are her children. She needs to hold herself together. Today is the first step in becoming their mum again. Greg may not want that, but she *needs* it.

'Kids,' Greg calls and jerks his head towards Debbie.

Emily glances up at Shaun, who frowns then starts to walk slowly towards his mother, his sister half a step behind.

'Hello, Shaun,' Debbie says as he draws near and she can see how his face has matured, his cheekbones becoming more angular even as he retains a youthful roundness to his jaw. She wants to call him 'darling', the way she used to, but she knows that's presuming too much.

'Um, hi,' he says, pushing his hair out of his eyes.

'Hi, Emily.' Debbie crouches so she's looking up at her daughter.

'Hi,' Emily says, tugging on the side of her blue sundress.

'How are you?' Debbie risks an arm around Emily's shoulders and finds it met with a recoil. So she takes it away and feels the recoil in her heart.

'Good.' Emily looks at the ground, then up at Greg.

Debbie pushes herself up to standing. 'I've missed you both so much,' she says, aware of how inadequate that phrase is to describe the enormity of what she's felt, even though it's the truth. But what else can she say?

They're not going to say it in return, she knows. That's her punishment. In so many ways a far greater punishment than anything else.

'I'm sorry you had to . . .' Now it's her turn to look at the ground. 'I'm sorry that everything changed,' she says in a rush. 'I never wanted anything bad to happen to you.'

'It didn't,' Greg says tersely. 'They're fine.'

Debbie glances towards the car, where Julia is standing with her forearm on the top edge of the open door. Like she's waiting for the kids to turn around and get back into the car.

'I know, Greg,' Debbie says. 'I can't thank you enough for looking after them.'

'They're my kids,' he says. 'I wasn't looking after them. I was raising them.'

'I know,' Debbie says quickly. 'I know. Sorry. Sorry.'

She closes her eyes and puts one hand over them as she tries to think what she should say. What she *could* say to try to set them all on a new course where she's involved in her children's lives and her ex-husband stops snarling at her. Because she needs to have her children back, if not physically with her then at least part of her life. The thought of them is all that keeps her going.

She looks from one to the other. 'I don't really know what to say, kids. I stuffed up so badly. You probably thought I didn't love you, because I went away, but I love you very, very much. I never stopped.'

Emily's biting her bottom lip just as she used to when she was upset, and tugging harder on her dress. She glances at her father. 'Dad says you were really naughty.'

'I was,' Debbie concedes. 'But I'm not any more.'

'You might be again,' Shaun says matter-of-factly, and his lack of emotion makes that fissure in Debbie's chest widen.

'I won't be,' she says. 'I promise.'

Shaun shrugs. 'Can we go?' he asks his father. 'I have that party.'

'Already?' Debbie's voice comes out strangled, her throat closing around the thought that this is all she's getting: a couple of minutes in a park in the middle of a town she doesn't know, with no certainty about ever seeing her children again.

'Yeah, sorry,' says Greg, although Debbie knows that sorry is the last thing he is. He would have designed it like this. A reminder that the kids have different lives now. Busy lives. Happy lives. That they're just fine without her.

'When can I see them again?' she says, trying to sound calm when she's the furthest thing from it.

'Not sure. C'mon, kids.'

'Wait, Greg, please – just a couple more minutes?'

But Shaun looks at his father and Debbie can see his indifference and she knows, as surely as she can know anything, that there won't be a couple more minutes.

'I'm sorry, Shaun,' she says, trying to keep him there. 'I let you down. I'm sorry.'

He glances back at her, his lips pursed. Punishment. Which she deserves. But not forever.

'I'm still your mum,' she says. 'That didn't change.'

Her eldest child doesn't respond, though, just turns and heads back to the car. It's Emily who lingers, a worried look on her face.

'What is it, darling?' Debbie crouches again, hoping she sounds like the mother Emily remembers.

'You look different,' Emily whispers. 'Are you really my mum?'

Now the fissure hardens with despair and regret and grief, all the ways she's let her children down, all the ways she will have to find to make it up to them.

'Yes,' she says, taking one of Emily's hands. 'I know I look different. But you still look like my favourite girl.'

A little smile crosses Emily's face then, right before Greg takes her other hand.

'We have to go,' he says, and he pulls Emily away.

Debbie stays crouching, one hand in the grass, the other shielding her eyes against the late-morning sun.

She stays there as they all get into the car; it seems fitting that she's bowing before her children and their new life. If she were still the Catholic she was brought up to be she would prostrate herself before them and beg for forgiveness, plead for another chance.

Instead she remains bowed as they drive away, and tells herself that she has to believe she will see them again.

CHAPTER 23

The soft tap on the bakery door tells Janine that Ross has arrived. The lights are off everywhere but there's enough light outside for her to make him out and she feels excitement mixed with guilt. It's a bad cocktail – she shouldn't put herself in a situation to feel guilty about seeing a man – but she hasn't been able to resist it yet.

'Hi,' she says as she opens the door.

'Hi,' he breathes and steps in without looking behind him.

Janine looks out, wondering if anyone can see him, at the same time knowing she shouldn't be wondering that. What they're doing isn't good. She stops short of telling herself it isn't right, because she's convinced herself that they're both adults who can make choices about their lives, so it's justifiable. She's single; she doesn't owe anyone any loyalty. If Ross wants to cheat on his wife that's his business. Janine isn't making him do that.

Besides, this is the best she can get in this town, and she deserves affection. Sometimes she'll have a second's self-reflection about the fact that there are better types of affection than this, than sneaking around to be with someone. But she doesn't have access to them. She's lucky anyone finds her attractive, really. Or attractive enough to see once a week in her parents' bakery.

Ross kisses her and she feels the prickles of his nascent beard. He's always been hairy – he shaves each morning and has growth by the afternoon. He says it's because he's from good Irish stock and the Irish needed the hair to keep warm; those who moved to warmer countries haven't evolved.

His greeny-blue eyes are staring into hers and she runs a hand through his thick chestnut hair.

'I've missed you,' she says, which is a phrase that applies to the week just past and to all the years since they broke up.

He kisses her again, with force, his hands grabbing at her bra strap.

Sometimes she likes that he pushes, because she thinks it means he wants her so much he's overcome by it. Sometimes it frightens her. Sometimes she likes that it frightens her and she wonders what that means.

'I bet you did,' he whispers into her ear, then he nips her earlobe and she winces.

She told him she doesn't like pain but ever since then he seems to make sure he does something painful to her. When she's protested he's said he just can't help himself. Janine's read books and seen movies that tell her that's how desire goes: men can't help themselves when they really desire someone. Sometimes she feels like that can't be right, that if someone cares about you they should, well, *care* about you. But it's not as if she's had enough real-life experience to prove that. And she doesn't have any right, really, to ask Ross to care for her. She just hopes he does.

'Let's go out the back,' she says, as she does every week. Out the back no one from the street will be able to see them.

She leads him by the hand to the storeroom and switches on the naked bulb. He perches on some sacks of flour and takes off his jacket, draping it over the nearby stepladder.

'I don't know how you can wear that thing in summer,' Janine says. Small talk. That's what they do: talk small. Kiss small.

As teenagers they were under each other's skin and every little thing seemed epic. Now they keep things superficial and pretend that his skin isn't also being touched by his wife.

Janine is fed up with that. She needs more from him. She wants more. She wants to be the one he cares about. It's her turn. Isn't it? She's had no relationship since Ross left town; no one to make her feel desired, to feel like their only one. Other women have that, even if Janine knows she'd never choose the husbands they chose for themselves.

'Real estate agents need jackets,' Ross says, grabbing her around the waist. 'No one respects us if we don't wear them.'

His accent has changed since he moved to the city. His vowels are rounder and he now has 'g's on the ends of words.

'Where did you tell your wife you are?'

She always says 'your wife' like she's trying to remind him of what he's doing, but in reality it's because she doesn't want to say the woman's name. If she has a name she has feelings. If she has a name that means Janine is doing a real thing to a real person, not just acting on her own needs.

Not that she's entirely clear about what those needs are. It's not as if she set out to do this; she doesn't know what the outcome is meant to be. Which hasn't stopped her from having the occasional daydream about what would happen if Ross left his wife for her. She'd be a stepmother. Maybe she'd even become a mother. She'd be wanted and needed. Someone would care for her.

Ross smiles, showing his uneven teeth. Orthodontists aren't that easy to find in small country towns.

'Drinks with the boys,' he says. 'Same as every week.'

'I thought you might come up with another story.' Janine kisses the tip of his nose.

He shrugs. 'She buys it. No need to change it. And I did go to the pub for one before I came here.'

'Yes,' she says, 'I can smell it.'

'Can you?'

He pulls her right into him, so his mouth is near her nose, which she wrinkles.

'Tooheys Old,' she says. Her uncle drinks it; she's been smelling it since she was a baby. 'Lovely.'

He wiggles his eyebrows. 'You can taste some of it too, if you like.'

She wants to laugh because he's so corny, but then he might think she's laughing at him. She doesn't want to upset him. His temper has always been on a hair trigger. When they were young she thought it was because he was so passionate. That's the story she's still telling herself.

'All right,' she says and puts her lips to his.

His kisses are more urgent now that they're older. When they were teenagers they had time. They *took* time. They enjoyed kissing, or she did at least. He seemed to as well. Now it's like he's trying to take something from her and she's trying to take something from him too. Or maybe she's trying to take back what he's taking. It's a negotiation and it never feels like either side gets what they want, just a portion of it.

She breaks off the kiss because she feels like making a demand. 'Is this all we're ever going to do?'

He frowns. 'What do you mean? I said we can't go to my place. And you live with your parents. Why?' There are the wiggling eyebrows again. 'Do you want to do it here?'

He nods at the flour sacks and nudges a knee between her thighs.

Do it. Like it's a bodily function, not something she's daydreamed about.

They used to 'do it' before, but it was never just about that. They had fun. They said they loved each other. Maybe they did love each other. Who knows when you're that age?

'Not really,' she says softly.

He sighs and scratches the side of his head. 'I know this isn't much but it's better than nothing, isn't it? We get to see each other.'

'I guess.' She looks down for a few seconds, to work out what to say next. 'I mean, it's nice that you want to see me, but what do you think is going to happen?'

He frowns again. 'What else is meant to happen? We're hanging out. We're making up for lost time. And we'll, uh . . .' He runs a hand up her thigh. 'Figure something out. There's a house coming up for sale. Gonna be empty for a while after the owners move out.'

His knee pushes her legs apart and his lips latch onto her neck and she gets the message. She sighs, and he stops what he's doing.

'What?' he says, irritated, his eyes boring into hers.

They're not the eyes she remembers from teenage Ross. They're harder. They remind her that they're both grown-ups now and they need to talk about grown-up things.

She clears her throat. 'What happens, Ross? What happens from here?'

He seems startled. Probably because she's never been one to make demands.

Maybe she should have been. Maybe he'd respect her more now if she had. Maybe she'd respect herself.

'Janine, I thought we were just having a good time. I'm, uh . . .' Another head scratch. 'I'm married. Right? I'm not going to leave her.'

This is the point, Janine knows, at which she should tell him he's a terrible person and that he's been leading her on. Except she's been leading herself on; and if he's a terrible person so is she, because she's made this whole situation possible.

Instead, she stares at him for a few seconds. 'Yeah, we are having a good time,' she says. It's the only good time she's having, even if he seems to enjoy it more than she does sometimes. 'I guess I . . .' She makes a face. 'I don't really know what you expect from me.'

His face relaxes. 'Oh,' he says, grinning, tugging at the waistband of her jeans, 'I just expect you to be your gorgeous self.'

If the compliment is designed to charm her, it works, and she hates herself a little for being won over so easily.

'You know all the right things to say,' she tells him.

He keeps grinning. 'You should see me when I'm selling a house.'

And he kisses her before she can think too hard about the meaning of what he's said, and how it might relate to her.

They only have an hour together. After he's gone, she turns out the light and sits on the bags of flour for a while, fantasising about what she might have the gumption to say to him next week. Knowing she likely won't say anything at all.

CHAPTER 24

Gabrielle clears her throat, presses the key on the piano and tries again. At a softer volume this time. Rodgers and Hart's 'I Didn't Know What Time it Was' is one of her favourite songs. She has sung it, oh, at least a *thousand* times. Now it's a problem. She has to slide up towards the top of her range and even though they're notes she can still reach, the journey isn't as smooth as it used to be.

It's a side effect of her perhaps not taking as much time to rest her voice after the surgery as she was instructed. The surgeon could hardly blame her for being keen to find out how her voice sounded, though, could he?

And the notes that she's having real trouble with – well, they're not her fault. It's just the uncertainty around these other notes she needs to take responsibility for. And now she needs to take responsibility for making them right.

Instead, she bashes the keys as if that's going to help. It never has, but that doesn't stop her trying.

This time she begins with the first line of the chorus, hoping that if she keeps going over it, she'll unlock something. Opera is what she has to get back to, because otherwise she'll never work again.

Unless she can develop the other modes of singing she used to do passably well. Jazz. Torch songs. Rock songs. She's been known to belt out a Pat Benatar track when no one's around – Pat was trained in opera too, so Gabrielle feels she's a kindred spirit – but even that seems to be beyond her now.

The surgeon who did this to her wasn't even sorry. When she told him she'd lost some notes he just nodded, as if he'd expected it.

'It can happen,' he'd said when she'd booked an appointment two months after the surgery, after she realised that her voice had changed, perhaps irrevocably.

'But you didn't *tell me* it might!' she'd retorted, as if pointing this out would somehow alter the facts.

'Didn't I?' He looked confused. 'I'm sure we discussed it.'

They certainly hadn't, because Gabrielle would have remembered if she'd been warned that she might lose her livelihood.

'You said I might have some *temporary* loss of function,' she told him. 'You said nothing about it being permanent.'

He'd frowned and nodded again, as if this was a very serious matter and he was taking her concerns to heart. 'Mm, I see.'

'I don't think you do.'

'But your voice would have been further damaged if you'd continued the way you were,' he'd said.

'How would that have been worse?' Gabrielle heard her pitch rising.

'Madame Reynold, you were going to lose some notes altogether. Those nodules would not have stopped growing.'

'So now I have all the notes but I just can't sing them?' Her pitch was so high that she knew her words sounded strangled.

The surgeon had blinked, looking a little like a child who was ready for a nap.

'There are exercises you can do,' he'd said.

And she's been doing them, ever since. But while she has some improvement in quality, there are notes she just can't reach without making a horrible squeaking noise.

There's no point trying to explain any of this to Vicky. Only someone else who is musical would understand.

Actually, that's not true. An instrumentalist wouldn't really understand, because their instrument is always external to them. Gabrielle's instrument is within her. It's not just part of her – it *is* her. When it fails, so does she. So each time she tries to sing those notes and all she hears is a voice that doesn't sound like it belongs to her, she feels like she will never come back to herself again.

She has cultivated her voice, as any professional singer must. When she was a teenager and had a music teacher at school who was both envious of her prowess and encouraging of her ambitions, there was a point at which she had to decide whether to pursue opera or to explore the other options for her voice. Opera was her main hope of singing professionally, and that was definitely what she wanted to do. There wasn't much prospect of making a living out of other kinds of singing; everything else promised a tenuous lifestyle at best, booking shows ad hoc and trying to win people over all the time. With opera they were already won over – who doesn't love the tubercular Mimi, after all?

Mimi was one of Gabrielle's mainstays. Every opera company in the world puts on *La Bohème*. It's a moneymaker for everyone involved – but not for Gabrielle any more.

She strikes the note in the song again. One more shot before Victoria returns from her bridge game.

When Vicky left that morning Gabrielle had asked how she came to have so many activities with other people.

'I've lived here all my life,' Victoria said, looking bemused. 'I've never left.'

Gabrielle didn't think it was meant as a dig at her own peripatetic lifestyle. Rather she realised the truth in it: moving frequently had left her with mostly superficial friendships.

'Is anyone giving you trouble about Arthur?' she asked.

'Not any more!' Victoria seemed to be . . . chuckling. 'They think I'm well rid of him. Turns out he has a reputation for being a bit free with his hands, if you know what I mean. I was mortified, of course, and I wish I'd been told sooner, but it means that many of the women I know understand completely why I threw him out.'

'When are we going to Sydney to see that lawyer?' Gabrielle pressed, as she's been doing regularly.

'Soon,' came Victoria's usual reply.

Gabrielle thinks it's not because Victoria is reluctant to go to Sydney but more that her life in Bellbird River doesn't provide many opportunities to get away. Whereas Gabrielle would positively love to escape to the city, perhaps even take in a concert or something. Except she doesn't have a car and her New South Wales driver's licence expired long ago, so she's stuck.

Now, that note. She hums it. Holds the tune in her mind. Starts the verse again. Goes for the chorus.

She feels the vibrations of sound within her, enters the place where she's almost unconsciously singing the song because she knows it so well, begins to take flight – and stops.

The note isn't there. Not the way she wants it to be. She can't feel it the way she used to.

Her voice, she has long believed, comes from a place beyond her. From the ether. Or from a higher plane. It's not for her to pin that down; she's just learnt to trust it and accept it.

So if these notes aren't there any more, where have they gone? Are they on that plane? Can she visit them? Can she coax them into coming back with her?

No one has any answers for that. And Gabrielle doesn't want to ask anyone she knows, because that would reveal what has become of her.

Instead she puts her forearms on the keys, crushing them discordantly, rests her head on her hands and allows herself a few moments to weep.

AUTUMN 1998

CHAPTER 25

'We'll go back to the library tomorrow,' Alex says as she pulls the car into a spot near the hall, then turns and looks over her shoulder at Kim in the back seat. Kim makes a show of sighing. 'You said that *yesterday*.'

'I know.' Alex tries to smile as brightly as pretence allows, because she's growing tired of being reminded of all the ways Kim thinks she's a bad mother.

Alex loves her daughter unconditionally and absolutely, but she doesn't always like her. A mother's not supposed to say that though, is she? Children are wonderful; children are a gift from God; where would we be without our children . . . Yes, children are all of those things, and they can also be annoying pains. The real test of a mother's love is not, Alex thinks, how often you tell other people that your offspring are the best thing that ever happened to you but, rather, how much irritation you can tolerate without cracking. Love is far less present in the easy bits than in the hard, because it isn't needed as much when things are cruising along.

Her own mother, for example, is probably experiencing those hard bits right now, because Alex has taken Kim away and Marta is finding that very difficult, as she reminds Alex during her regular phone calls.

'When are you bringing back my Kimmy?' is usually what she says right after – sometimes instead of – 'Hello'.

'Gee, Mum,' Alex said during their phone call last night. 'It's so nice to know that you miss me too.'

'Of course I miss you,' her mother had snapped. 'But you don't let me tell you.'

Alex hadn't had a chance to ask her mother to explain that statement before Kim had pretty much snatched the phone out of her hand and the two best friends started their usual marathon chat.

So perhaps Kim's behaviour is a form of cosmic revenge on Alex because she's disrupted all their lives.

Not that Alex believes in that stuff: karma, fate, planets doing this and moons doing that. Life is luck and no luck and all the things you can make with that.

Take falling pregnant. A lot of people would think that lucky, especially if they've been trying for a while. When Alex fell pregnant in her last year of high school she felt like she was being punished for stupidity in having sex with someone she barely knew and having to display the consequences in front of her classmates, all because, thanks to her irregular periods, she didn't realise she was pregnant until it was too late to do anything about it. Bad luck cascading onto bad luck.

Except it wasn't. It was, actually, the best stroke of luck ever, because Kim – for all the times she makes Alex grit her teeth and dig her nails into her palms – is a gift. Her gift. Alex really doesn't know where she would be without Kim and she has no desire to imagine it. And it's at the times when Kim really tests her that she notices it the most. Like now. Kim is frowning as she unbuckles her seatbelt and flings open the car door, and all Alex wants to do is make things better for her. Her heart almost physically aches at times like these. That is love reminding her that it hasn't gone away.

'You still have some of your book left to finish tonight, don't you?' she says as she joins Kim on the footpath.

'No,' Kim says grumpily.

'Oh.'

Damn it, damn it, *damn it*, she should have checked before they left home. It's bad enough for Kim that she has to put up with listening to choir practice – now she doesn't even have a book. They could have brought some blank paper and pencils so she could draw. Or a doll or something. Not that Kim is interested in dolls any more.

'Come on,' Alex says as they walk towards the entrance. 'We'll find something.'

She can hear a low buzz in the hall that grows louder as she pushes open the door and sees Gabrielle in full conversational flight with Jimbo, whose gaze is actually on Victoria, who is looking across at two women who are wagging fingers in each other's faces in a disagreement, from what Alex can make out, about the next best time of year to fertilise roses.

Quiet little Debbie with the big voice is chatting to Warwick, who is laughing with his head thrown back. At something Debbie said? Alex wouldn't have thought she had it in her.

Now Debbie is tilting her head to the side and looking up at Warwick as if he's the best thing since sliced bread. Interesting. Warwick isn't Alex's type and she's pretty sure women in general aren't his type, but maybe Debbie is seeing something she can't.

Alex sees Janine walk in and waves, before putting a hand on Kim's shoulder to guide her towards the corner. She's rewarded with a flounce. Then Kim glances back and smiles shyly. Alex turns to see Debbie waving at Kim, before Kim's face is set to glower mode again.

'Hi, Warwick,' Alex says as she and Kim pass him.

'Hello,' Warwick says, standing up from the piano stool and regarding Kim with curiosity. 'Someone's not happy to be here, I see.'

'She's out of books.' Alex smiles apologetically. 'I meant to take her to the library today but I had to stay back at work.'

'Hmm.' Warwick leans against the piano. 'Kim, would you like to help me tonight?'

Kim's eyes dart from her mother to Warwick and back again. 'Why?'

'Well, we're rehearsing songs for the Bellbird River Show in July. It's one of our *big* concerts. There's a *lot* of new material and, frankly, I'll be flat out trying to tell the choir what to do let alone playing piano at the same time.'

He smiles ruefully, as if he's oh-so-hopeless, but Alex is absolutely sure Warwick has managed such rehearsals just fine in the past.

'So, Kim, I really need someone to turn the pages while I'm playing,' he says seriously, for which Alex could hug him. So few adults take children seriously. 'It would make things smoother for all of us. I'm sure our singers would appreciate it, because I can pay proper attention to the music.'

'Um . . .' Kim looks up at her mother.

'She doesn't read music,' Alex says. 'Sorry.' Kim learning an instrument has never been within Alex's budget.

'Completely fine.' Warwick waves off her concern. 'I would just be so grateful to have the help. How about this, Kim – you stand next to me and I'll nod once when I need you to turn. And if you miss it, that's quite all right.' He looks at her inquisitively. 'What do you think?'

'Um . . . okay.' Kim gives a tiny shrug, but Alex can tell she's quietly pleased.

'Great!' Warwick sounds as excited as if his beloved Kylie Minogue were making a guest appearance.

'Thank you,' Alex says to him. 'Are you sure, Kim?'

'*Yes*, Mum!' Kim's nostrils flare.

'All right, all right!' Alex's laugh is strained. Nothing like your child letting everyone know that you're annoying her. 'I'll go to my seat.'

'Thanks, Alex,' Warwick says, then he turns to Kim and pulls the sheet music off the piano to show it to her.

'What's going on there?' asks Janine when Alex reaches her chair.

'My daughter has nothing to read,' Alex says, pushing her handbag under her chair. 'She needs more books from the local library, but I just haven't been able to get there. So now I'm relying on other people to help me entertain her.' She grimaces. 'Bad parent.'

'Single parent,' Janine says softly. 'It's hard on your own.'

'Honestly, I don't know if it would be easier with a husband. I know women whose husbands turn out to be an extra child, they're so useless. Can you imagine how annoying that would be? And how *unsexy*?' Alex shudders. 'I certainly wouldn't want to sleep with a grown-up baby.'

She smiles in case she's inadvertently offended Janine, because once the words are out of her mouth she realises Janine may have a grown-up man baby of her own that Alex hasn't yet heard about. The smile is there to suggest that she might be joking if Janine wants her to be. It's exhausting, all the things a person has to do to manage other people's feelings.

'I wouldn't either,' Janine says, although her nose twitches once and she looks away.

Great, so Alex probably has offended her. The one woman she's even close to making a friend of in this place.

'I haven't had much time to practise,' she adds.

'Me either,' Janine says, and this time she looks Alex in the eye and half-smiles. 'Mainly because I forgot.'

'Oh yeah?' Alex sets up the sheet music on her stand. 'Have you been having hot dates?' She grins.

'Um, no. Not really.'

Janine fumbles with her own music and now Alex is sure she's put her foot in something. Time to shift subject again.

'It's great, though, all this singing,' she says. 'I haven't sung this much in years. I'm really enjoying it. It's fun.'

'Sort of. Yeah.' Janine glances towards Warwick. 'Kim looks like she's having fun too.'

Alex looks over and there's her sullen daughter smiling – actually smiling – at Warwick, who is miming hitting the piano keys with force.

'God love him,' she says. 'That's more of a smile than I've had out of her lately.'

'He used to teach at the primary school,' Janine murmurs. 'Probably good with kids.'

'Really? I hadn't heard that.'

Janine's lips press together. 'Some of the parents didn't like him being there.' She wags her head from side to side. 'You know.'

'No.' Alex frowns. 'What?'

'They thought . . .' Another wag.

'Janine, I'm having trouble decoding this.'

'They didn't want a gay teacher there,' she almost hisses and Alex sees Debbie's head swivel in their direction.

'How ridiculous,' Alex says. 'What does it matter? Are people really like that here?' Not that she can be too sanctimonious, because she's sure it happens in Sydney too.

'Only a couple. But they were noisy about it.'

'How's Kim?' Debbie cuts in, and Alex turns to see the other woman looking at her, eyes bright.

'She's . . . good, thanks.' Alex smiles quickly. First Debbie's waving at Kim and now she's asking about her. Alex wonders if she should be concerned.

'Which year is she in?'

'Five.' Alex frowns. 'Why?'

'Oh, nothing. She's around, um . . .' Debbie presses her lips together. 'Around the age of the boys I look after where I work.'

Ah, so that's it. Debbie's probably wondering if they're at school together.

Just then Warwick stands up and turns to face the assembled singers. 'Right,' he says, 'I have a very special helper tonight. Everyone, please welcome Kim.'

As the choristers applaud Kim looks at her feet then over at Alex, who is thrilled to see a hint of a smile on her daughter's face.

As Warwick begins to play she sees Kim's usual frown of concentration appear, then Alex can feel her own developing on her forehead as the choir launches into the first verse of 'Spice Up Your Life'.

Kim's smile grows and Alex feels herself relax for the first time all day. Yes, this is fun, and even more fun when she doesn't have to worry about Kim. They'll go to the library tomorrow and borrow enough books for a month. And then she'll call her mother so Kim can have a chat.

It's not that Alex doesn't realise that Marta is always the one calling; it's just that Marta calls before Alex can remember to do it first. So that makes her not only a bad parent but a bad daughter.

She can be better. Do better. Wasn't that one of the reasons she wanted to move here – so she could have more time for the things that matter?

That includes spending time on the people who love her, and whom she loves, no matter how hard they make her life sometimes.

CHAPTER 26

The laundry is never-ending – and that's just for Bea and Phil and the boys. Debbie does the house laundry to free up Bea to do the workers' laundry, which seems a little out of whack except Debbie doesn't particularly want to do the workers' laundry either – it's all sheets and towels, and seems to go on constantly.

Yanking the towels out of the dryer, Debbie is rewarded with bits of lint floating into the air. She groans as she pulls the last two towels out and puts them on top of the washing machine.

'You're groaning a lot these days,' says Bea behind her.

Debbie used to jump when people approached her; that was a long time ago. Years of having women behind her, in front of her, to the side of her, women who might not wish her well, have trained her to not react. To react to someone passing close by is to show fear, and controlling her fear was essential to making it through that time, if only to keep her sanity intact. If she felt like she was even a little bit in charge of her mind and her life, she was better able to manage her circumstances. The same goes for this job. She didn't know if she'd be able to do the work, didn't know if her past would be used against her, but she controlled the fear that she wouldn't be good enough and things seem to be turning out okay.

'Sorry,' Debbie says and she turns around with a guilty smile to see Bea with a stack of folded sheets under one arm.

'No need to apologise,' Bea says. Her smile is kind, which is fitting: Bea is a kind person. Debbie suspected it early on and it's turned out to be true. 'I'm just wondering what you're groaning about.'

Debbie picks up another towel to fold. 'Oh, you know,' she says, shrugging a couple of times. 'This and that.'

Bea nods slowly, peering at her. 'How's the choir going? What are you working on?'

'Warwick's decided that "Great Southern Land" by Icehouse should be part of our repertoire for the Show.' Debbie remembers the mystified looks from the older choir members when he announced it.

'I haven't heard that for a while,' says Bea. 'Probably because Phil keeps listening to the ABC. Is there even a music station around here?'

'There's 2TM – it's a Tamworth station.' Debbie puts it on in her room sometimes. Mostly it's country music but she doesn't mind.

'I'll try to find it.' Bea shifts the sheets to her other hip. 'So you're enjoying it?'

'Yeah,' Debbie says, and she feels her cheeks stretching. A smile. She tends to forget what they feel like. 'Warwick's great. Really passionate about the music. Good at dealing with all the personalities.'

'Oh really?' Bea says teasingly. 'What else is this Warwick like?'

Now Debbie's cheeks are hot. 'It's not like that! He's not a, um, he's not a romantic prospect. I don't even know if he likes women.'

She doesn't know why she said that. Actually, yes, she does: she's now quite sure she has a crush on Warwick because, as much as she's been trying to talk herself out of it, her body seems to have some kind of subconscious response to him. She's a woman in her forties. She doesn't *want* to behave like a teenager; she just doesn't appear able to stop it.

'Ah.' Bea smiles knowingly. 'But you seem to like him, so that's nice. Someone with a common interest.'

'Yes, it's good,' Debbie says quickly, hoping her cheeks are no longer red.

'And I've heard you practising – honestly, Debbie, your voice is spectacular. I hope he gives you a starring role in that choir.'

Debbie blinks. She only ever practises when she thinks Bea is out at the workers' accommodation or in the paddocks. Bea must be coming and going from the house more than she realises.

'Oh, sorry – you weren't meant to hear me,' she says.

'Stop apologising for things!' Bea says, laughing. 'I'm *happy* to hear you singing. You brighten up the day. Please keep it up.'

'Thanks,' Debbie says, looking away.

She's never been good at accepting compliments. It seems arrogant somehow. When she was in the school choir and singing her little heart out, one of the other girls used to say, 'You love yourself, don't you?' over and over again. After a couple of choir practices the others started saying it too. Eventually Debbie pretended she couldn't sing well at all, until the music teacher asked to see her parents to find out what was going wrong. But teachers and parents didn't do anything about bullies – that was up to kids to figure out – so Debbie kept herself quiet and small and unremarkable, and the other kids stopped being mean. About her singing, at least. They found other things. By the time she left primary school she was an average student and her parents were so confused. She'd been the top of her class in Year Three. In high school she kept her head down and didn't outshine anyone. It was safer that way, even if she never really felt like herself.

Not that she's really being herself in this choir, either. She saw the looks on the faces of some of the others when she auditioned. They looked like that girl in the school choir. Part of what's so mystifying about being an adult is that you can go through so much and work so hard on becoming a better person, only to discover that there are adults around you who are still as jealous and mean as when they were kids. It's enough to make a person give up.

'I'm just going to put these sheets away, then maybe we can have some lunch?' Bea says.

'Sure.' Debbie smiles briefly. 'That would be great.'

'You can catch me up on your kids. You didn't say anything after you saw them.'

Debbie swallows. She purposely didn't tell Bea how that visit – or non-visit, really – went and she thought Bea would be too polite to ask. Except Debbie set herself up for this by telling Bea about the visit in advance.

'There's not much to say.' Debbie gives what she hopes is an I'm-okay-don't-worry-about-me smile.

Bea stares at her. 'I'm sure there is.'

'Honestly, there's not. I only saw them for a minute. And I mean a minute.' Debbie laughs, as if it's the funniest thing in the world instead of the saddest. 'They had to go somewhere else.'

'Yeah. Right.' Bea raises her eyebrows. 'I'm sure they didn't.' She chews on her bottom lip. 'You have to try again.'

'I don't think so.'

'Debbie, they're your kids.' Bea is frowning at her.

'Not any more,' Debbie says quietly, and she angles her body slightly away from Bea, hoping that will signal the end of the conversation.

'Yes, they bloody well are,' Bea says. 'And you shouldn't have to suffer forever because you made one mistake.'

'It was a fairly big mistake.'

'Sure.' Bea smiles weakly. 'Sure. My brother made a mistake once. He was a kid but, you know, not in the legal sense. According to the law he was old enough to be held responsible as an adult. He went to prison. Lost all his friends. Our parents had a hard time with it. But I said the same thing to him: he shouldn't have to suffer because of that one mistake. No one died. It was just a stupid thing.' Her face clouds. 'He's lost, though. He's let it ruin his life. I just don't want what you did to ruin yours. It was *one mistake*, Debbie. You shouldn't lose your children forever because of it.' She smiles faintly. 'But if you don't want to talk about it, I won't push.'

Now Debbie turns her head away so Bea won't see her crying. Crying has been her regular night-time activity since she saw the children. Something else she can't help, like her crush on Warwick. She spent all those years learning to control her mind and now her body is betraying her all over the place.

'I – I appreciate you asking,' she says, her voice catching. 'But I just don't think there's any point trying.'

She feels Bea's hand on her arm. 'If they matter to you there's always a point. I can help you, if you want. Like I said, though, I'm not going to push.' Bea squeezes her arm then lets go.

'Thank you,' Debbie says, her eyes wet as she turns to smile at Bea. 'I'll think about it.'

Bea looks dubious but says, 'Okay. And let's still have lunch. I'll just stick to talking about the weather.' She grins, then she's gone.

Debbie wipes her eyes with the back of her hand and avoids wetting the towels as she moves them aside. Then she tosses a load of clothes into the washing machine and presses the start button.

Familiar routines, daily rhythms. These are the things that lull her back to life.

CHAPTER 27

Victoria can't remember the last time she drove to Sydney. It's so easy to become ensconced in one place and not explore outside it, and that tendency has become especially pronounced since her children left Bellbird River and she hasn't been tearing around the countryside driving them to sport and parties and friends' houses. They've been gone for a while, though, so as she drives down the New England Highway she realises that she really has let her world shrink.

Moreover, it was always Arthur doing the driving if they went anywhere. She's been a passenger for years – in more ways than one. She let him drive their life together off the road because she was too busy looking out the window. Now that Victoria actually has her hands on the wheel, it's Gabrielle in the passenger seat.

They pass through the lush greenness of Murrurundi, caused by the precipitation that comes with being on the fringe of the Great Dividing Range. That countryside gives way to dramatic rolling hills then browner fields in the horse country around Scone, with its busy main street, then the grittier outskirts of Muswellbrook and its mines, through the Upper Hunter towards Maitland, and Sydney.

'You haven't practised your singing,' Victoria says as they cross the Hawkesbury River. She holds the steering wheel tightly as a semitrailer thunders past.

'Why would I?' says Gabrielle, winding down the window. 'We're in the car, not a rehearsal studio.'

'I just thought you'd make use of the time.'

Victoria glances at her cousin and sees that her head is turned firmly away. She hasn't heard Gabrielle sing much at all, come to think of it. Playing piano and humming along, yes; from time to time there's the occasional run of notes as if she's working out a tune. But nothing full-bodied. Nothing that would indicate that Gabrielle's voice is approaching its old strength. Victoria feels stupid for not noticing this before but, in her own defence, she *has* been very busy thinking up revenge plots involving Arthur and Celeste.

'I don't need to practise as much as you mere mortals,' Gabrielle says, but her head is still turned away and Victoria is sure her voice just wobbled.

'Perhaps not.' Victoria has to raise her own voice as the sound of cars on the road bounces off the rocks beside the freeway, creating a dull roar. 'Could you close that window, please? I don't want to shout.'

Gabrielle huffs, or something that sounds like it, and winds up the window.

'Still, I'd like to hear you sing something,' Victoria persists. 'The last time I had a private concert was just before you left us.'

'I'm not going to sing in a *car*. That's for amateurs and truck drivers.'

'Oh, fine, then.' Victoria makes a face. 'I'm an amateur, so I can sing.'

She opens her mouth, then feels her cousin's hand across it.

'Please don't,' Gabrielle says. 'I've heard you sing and there's not enough space in here to let me escape it.'

Victoria swats her hand away. 'How rude. And there you were pretending to Warwick that I'm a good singer. But I understand. Which means you really do have to sing instead – I can't listen to any more Classic FM. It sounds like they're doing Medieval Music Hour and you know I detest recorders.'

'Who doesn't?' Gabrielle says, laughing.

'Gabby,' Victoria says sternly, 'you're a professional singer. Why haven't I heard you sing?'

'My voice is still recovering,' Gabrielle says meekly.

'By my calculations it's been almost a year since your operation. You should be fine by now.'

'Well, I'm not!' Gabrielle snaps. 'All right? I'm not. My top notes are not coming back and I don't . . . I don't . . .' Her voice catches and she puts a hand to her chest.

Victoria reaches over and takes her wrist. It's not the same as a hug but it's all she can manage in the circumstances.

'I don't know what to do,' Gabrielle whispers. 'If I can't sing the way I used to, I can't work.'

Victoria sniffs. 'No, you can't.'

She puts both hands on the steering wheel again and concentrates as the freeway exit looms. Country driving is so straightforward that she can become confused in the city. Once she went back and forth over the Sydney Harbour Bridge three times because she couldn't work out how to exit at North Sydney. That was a rather distressing day, and it wasn't helped by Arthur laughing at her when she told him the story. He really was a very disappointing husband. Why didn't she notice earlier?

'Look,' she says, 'we're in Sydney to talk to this lawyer chap and part of what I'm going to ask him is not just how I can stop Arthur getting half the house but also how *he* can pay *me*. *He* was the one having the affair. I'm sure there's a penalty there. So if all goes according to plan I'll have some money to live on, and you can live on it with me, and we'll be *fine*, darling, just *fine*.'

She beams, so Gabrielle knows she means it. Because she does. Or she wants to. She wants to believe it, more than anything.

'And what if it isn't?' Gabrielle murmurs. 'What if there's no money and I can't work?'

Victoria thinks about her father coming home one day and telling her mother they had to sell the last of the properties that had been in the family for three generations. The loans were too big to repay, the weather too hard to predict. The land was a liability even as it was all they knew. Selling up was the only option, before the whole enterprise took them under.

The house in town had been the family headquarters from which her forebears ran their small empire. All that was left after the properties were sold was the soft drink factory in town, and that was enough to keep them going financially until her father died. Then Victoria had to sell it just so she had something to live on.

Arthur did whatever it was he did – speculating on shares and businesses. Sometimes he ended up in the black but there were plenty of times in the red. All the while they kept up the veneer of success because Victoria knew her father and grandfather and great-grandfather would have expected nothing less from her. Once Gabrielle had loaned her money so Arthur could pay off his debts without them needing to take out a mortgage on the house. She'd tried to pay Gabrielle interest but her cousin wouldn't hear of it. It was a mortifying experience and Victoria should never have put Gabrielle in that position, but she couldn't see another way out of it. Her marriage survived that, but it's clear now that nothing in Victoria's life has been as solid as she thought it to be. Even her house could now be taken from her.

Yet that means she's more adaptable to change and challenge than she realised. She's been in this place before, with sands shifting, and she has managed to keep herself strong. In turn, that has helped keep the people around her from crumbling. It's important work, this business of being a family buttress. It's unpaid and usually unacknowledged, but Victoria knows her worth – to herself and to Gabrielle.

'Then we shall sit down and make a plan,' she says to her cousin as she navigates the traffic lights down the Pacific Highway, through the north shore of Sydney.

Traffic lights! What a concept. The only time Victoria has to deal with them is when she comes to a city. She'll have to keep reminding herself that amber does not mean 'see if you can make it through in time'.

'You could teach singing, for example,' she continues. 'I could clean houses or do ironing. Or cook. I can cook!' She beams again. 'There are plenty of people who don't want to cook for themselves. There's always something we can do to earn money. Luckily it's cheap to live in Bellbird River. Not like here.' She gestures to the houses beside the road.

'But we're old, Vicky,' Gabrielle says mournfully. 'We shouldn't have to do that.'

'Our grandmother was smoking half a pack a day and drinking whiskey neat when she was ninety-two,' Victoria says. '*And* she made all the cakes for the family. We have some of those genes in us somewhere. We're not *old*, Gabrielle, we're *old-er*. There's a difference. We need to remember it. And we need to not let anyone tell us how we should be, at any age.'

A sign comes up for roads heading west to Homebush and east to the beaches.

'Where on earth am I going here?' she mutters.

'Straight ahead,' says Gabrielle. 'Ivan's in Waverton.'

'It was very sweet of him to organise this appointment,' Victoria says.

'It was. I haven't seen him for years.'

'Are you looking forwards to it?'

'I think so.' Gabrielle gazes out the window again. 'I'll look different. So will he, I guess.' She taps Victoria on the leg. It's something she used to do when they were young and she wanted to get someone's attention. 'I don't want him to know about my voice.'

'I certainly won't be saying anything,' Victoria murmurs.

She marvels at how built up this part of Sydney has become in the years since she last visited. It must be those Olympics – everyone's moving in to Australia's largest city. Or perhaps it's just that cities continue to expand. Or that Sydney specifically does. People come to visit, fall in love with its beauty and decide to move here.

'Thank you,' Gabrielle says softly. 'I just want to be me for a while longer. To Ivan, I mean.'

'You're still you without your top notes, Gabby.' Victoria jumps on the brakes as the car in front of her stops inexplicably. 'Bloody city drivers.'

'I'm going to stop talking,' Gabrielle says. 'You need to focus. How about some recorder music?' She turns up the radio.

'Fabulous,' says Victoria drily. 'How helpful.'

This time Gabrielle pats her leg instead of tapping it. 'I'll let you know when we're near his place.'

Victoria nods and smiles, and keeps both hands firmly on the wheel as she steers them down the highway.

CHAPTER 28

The cigarette smoke is thick in the public bar and Alex would very much like to leave. She hasn't smoked since she found out she was pregnant and she loathes the smell the way only someone can who desperately doesn't want to remember she was addicted to it once. But she can't leave until Vince has said whatever it is he's gathered all the teachers here to say. He organised these drinks a fortnight ago; even arranged for Kim to go to the science teacher's house because his children are teenagers and they can tolerate a younger child for a couple of hours.

Alex sighs and sips her lemonade. She can't even have a proper drink because she's driving. One of her colleagues told her that the Bellbird River cops don't even know how to give anyone a random breath test – moreover, they're just as likely to drive after a few as anyone else – but her Sydney habits die hard. At home RBT might pop up anywhere and it wasn't worth taking the chance. Everyone knows someone who's lost their licence for drink driving.

When she told that to the same colleague he guffawed, slapped her on the back and said, 'Drink drivin'? Round here we just call that drivin'!'

Alex felt the expression of shock on her face but changed it quickly. Something she's learnt here: not to appear to judge other people's behaviour. The place is too small and information travels too fast. Use the wrong adjective about a person and that person's grandparents, second-best friend and the local hairdresser will know about it within the hour.

She sighs again and glances towards the door just as it opens and Janine walks through. Janine, whom Alex has never seen outside of the bakery and choir practice. It could be interpreted as divine intervention to get her away from her colleagues. Putting her lemonade on the bar, Alex almost flies in Janine's direction.

'Hi!' she says as she steps in front of Janine, who looks startled and says 'Hi' back, with a small smile.

'I'm here with people from work.' Alex gestures at the group by the bar. 'Saw you walk in.'

'Oh, yeah. Right.' Janine's eyes flit from side to side.

'Looks like you're on your way to meet someone,' Alex says, wanting to delay Janine for selfish reasons but not wanting to be rude.

'Um, no. Not really.' Janine tucks her hair behind one ear and looks at the floor. 'Just, uh, going to the bottle shop. My uncle's coming over and he likes a particular type of beer.'

She looks hesitant, almost as if she's not sure if they should be talking.

'It's weird, isn't it?' says Alex, taking a guess as to what might be the issue. 'Seeing someone out of context. Sometimes I don't recognise students if I see them outside of school.' She makes a face. 'How bad's that?'

'Oh, I recognised you.' Janine glances around again. 'It's just been a while since I've been in here of a night. It's busier than I thought it would be.'

A tall man with a slight paunch, not much chin and a haphazard haircut appears beside Janine and touches her back briefly.

'Hello,' he says, smiling in a way Alex identifies as sleazy.

Janine turns and her face colours, then her mouth opens and her eyes meet Alex's briefly. 'Oh, hi, Ross. Um, Alex – this is Ross. We were in high school together.'

'Hi, Ross.' Alex holds out her hand and is unimpressed with the handshake Ross offers. Her father used to say you could measure a man's character by his handshake; if that's the case, Ross is weak and useless. 'I'm in the choir with Janine.'

Ross looks puzzled. 'Choir?'

Janine's head shakes imperceptibly and Alex is confused: if she and Ross were at school together, surely they've known each other for years. Why would the choir be a secret anyone would keep from a schoolfriend? It's not like Janine can be trying to play some game with Ross, or impress him. He's wearing a wedding ring, and Alex knows that Janine is single and there seems to be nary a flicker of a boyfriend on the horizon. Not one that she's mentioned.

'It's just a thing. Nothing big,' Janine says dismissively and looks up at Ross.

That *look*. Alex knows it. She's seen it. She's done it. It's the look of a woman who's trying to impress a man who's not all that impressive but the best she can get at that point in time, and she's trying to impress him because that's what she thinks she needs to do, because she should be coupled up – what is a woman without a man, after all? – and he's the nearest prospect. That look is desperation and vulnerability and eagerness to please all in one.

So this Ross is married but Janine is keen on him. How tricky.

Then Ross smiles at Janine. The sort of indulgent smile you give someone who knows you so well that they won't think you're being condescending. The smile of intimates.

Alex breathes in sharply. She really doesn't want to be a party to whatever is going on here. Janine is friendly to her but they're not friends; this is not information Alex wants to have about her or Ross. Especially since Alex may bump into Ross one day, possibly with his wife in tow. And she will definitely bump into Janine again.

'I'm here with a mate from work,' Ross says, his pelvis angling towards Janine, making Alex even surer that she doesn't want to witness this.

'But I'd better get back,' he adds. 'Just didn't want to not say hello.'

He smiles at Janine again, then glances at Alex, who purposely keeps her face in neutral.

'All right,' Janine says. 'Bye.'

Ross winks at her then turns to Alex. 'Nice to meet you,' he says, but Alex can't bring herself to say the same.

As he turns to go she sees his hand trail along Janine's hip. When she looks up Janine is staring at her.

'Haven't seen him in ages,' Janine says, biting her lip.

Alex considers her response. She doesn't want to upset Janine but it would be really disingenuous to accept what she's said. It would also make it hard for Alex to become any friendlier with her, because she'd always be conscious that Janine lied to her and she said nothing about it. Life is hard enough to navigate when people tell the truth; trying to circumnavigate lies makes it almost impossible.

'I don't think that's true,' Alex says as gently as she can.

'What?' Janine approximates a glare.

'You're very familiar with each other. Like very old, close friends.'

'We used to go out together,' Janine says quickly, but what Alex saw wasn't faded familiarity. There was an energy to it that indicates it's very much a present-day concern.

'And perhaps you still are?' she nudges.

'He's married!'

'I'm aware.' *And that wasn't a no*, she wants to add, but she thinks Janine knows it's hanging there anyway.

'He just moved back,' Janine goes on, tucking her hair behind her ear again. 'We've had a chat here or there, that's all.'

She looks defiant and Alex realises that this conversation can't go any further without making the next choir practice very uncomfortable. There is nothing to be achieved by persisting, apart from unpleasantness. She's made her point: she knows what's going on, even if Janine wants to deny it.

What Alex really wants to say is that she's not asking questions because she's concerned about the morality of it – that's Janine's business, and Ross's. She just thinks Janine deserves better than hanging around with someone else's husband. Every woman deserves better than that, even if they tell themselves it's the best they can get. She's had friends in that situation, who rationalised what they were doing by saying it was so hard to meet decent men that they couldn't be choosy. Except the men they were involved with were nowhere near decent. They were cheating on their wives and stringing along their mistresses.

Alex had quoted Oscar Wilde to one of her friends – *When a man marries his mistress he creates a job vacancy* – but instead of seeing it as a warning that such men never change, the friend asked, 'So do you really think he'll leave his wife and marry me?'

It's too early to tell if Janine would have the same reaction. So there's nothing else for it: Alex has to move on.

'I see,' she says, and smiles to show Janine that she's not trying to be antagonistic. 'I'd better get back to the others. See you on Tuesday?'

Janine regards her warily. 'Yep,' she says.

Alex's smile is bigger this time. 'You'd better get that beer.'

Janine nods and turns in the direction of the bottle shop.

'See you,' Alex says, then heads back to her rowdy colleagues, just in time to see the PE teacher pouring a beer over the science teacher's head and Vince crying out, 'Not again!'

CHAPTER 29

Autumn is lovely in some places. The leaves of deciduous trees turn brown then fall, revealing skeletons of branches that create stark, beautiful shapes. The air has a nice cool edge to it, heralding the change in season. In Bellbird River all that happens is sometimes rain falls, which makes the grass greener than in summer, and sometimes it doesn't, which makes everything more brown. There are very few deciduous trees, as it's one of the only towns in the eastern third of Australia that hasn't tried to turn itself into a little England. Instead the streets have ironbark and stringybark trees, and the few council park areas box gums and pines. Bellbird River, which runs past the edge of the town centre and after which the town was named, has native flora on its banks.

Gabrielle loathes it all. All these greys and khakis and unappealing browns. And dirt. Actual under-the-fingernails dirt. Each day, as she takes her constitutional around town – or her *passeggiata*, as she prefers to call it, no point giving up on European culture altogether – she ends up with dirt on her person, just as she will today.

'Hello,' she says as she takes the path through the main town park and passes Mrs Daley, who is pulling her worn-out shopping trolley – more like an appendage.

Mrs Daley gives her that narrow-eyed smile common to women who know they have to be polite but in reality cannot stand you.

Gabrielle has become inured to it. While she was at school none of the mothers liked the fact that she could sing better than their children, and some of them are still holding on to that all these decades later. Including Mrs Daley.

'Lovely day!' Gabrielle calls after her, because the best way to annoy your enemies is to be pleasant to them.

As she passes a pile of eucalyptus bark she feels, in her body, how much she misses the Jardin du Luxembourg and the forests of Germany; she longs for a nice Welsh meadow, even a rocky Spanish outcrop. She left Australia to get away from these native colours, these surroundings, that were never as vivid as she believed the world to be. She'd met Australians overseas who told her that she'd get homesick, that she'd miss those big blue skies and all those wide open spaces. But she didn't.

What she missed was her supportive cousin, and even then only when she realised she needed a soft landing after the hardest ordeal of her professional life. Victoria wasn't on her mind for much of the time she was away; now she's on her mind a lot.

The other night Victoria was up late, sitting at the kitchen table, going through papers. Which Gabrielle discovered because she'd wafted in looking for a snack.

'What are you doing?' Victoria muttered without looking up.

'Eating,' Gabrielle said.

'It won't bring your voice back.'

'What?' Gabrielle snapped.

'You keep eating because you're sad. It's not a good policy.' Victoria pushed her reading glasses further up the bridge of her nose.

'And why do you eat?' Gabrielle could fight that fire with one of her own. 'I don't see you dropping kilos out of despair over that husband of yours.'

Victoria deigned to glance at her. 'You're younger than me. You should be thinking of your health.'

Gabrielle sniffed. 'Just because you're older doesn't mean you shouldn't be thinking of yours.'

'I'm not buying – or baking – any more cakes,' Victoria said, as matter-of-factly as if she'd said she was no longer having the paper delivered.

'You've been eating them too!' Gabrielle thought of the sponge that came home yesterday, and the chocolate cake made last week. Victoria was right: she *was* eating because she was sad, but it was bloody enjoyable.

'We can both do without them.' Victoria had coughed then, wheezing with it, and put her hand to her chest.

'Are you all right?' Gabrielle asked, all thoughts of her snack forgotten.

'Asthma,' Victoria replied, still coughing.

'Since when were you an asthmatic?' Gabrielle had her own theory about the cause of her cousin's recent coughing bouts.

Victoria waved her off as if she was an annoying child.

'I don't care if you're smoking again,' Gabrielle said as she turned to leave.

'I am not smoking! I haven't done that since my second pregnancy.'

'Fine.'

They didn't speak about the coughing, or the eating, again, but Gabrielle has been worried all the same. Victoria has been sleeping in later than normal. Which could just mean she's depressed.

Gabrielle has heard about depression, although she's not sure she believes in it. For that matter, she's quite sure Victoria wouldn't either. Victoria's mother, the redoubtable Augusta, believed in ire and revenge, which were probably healthier options when it came to dealing with life's disappointments. Perhaps Victoria should consider a tactic more strident than sleep when it comes to dealing with Arthur.

Certainly that's what the Sydney lawyer suggested. 'You should set the terms of the settlement before your husband has a chance,' he'd said.

'But it's only been three months since he left!' Victoria said. 'Surely we should wait?'

'The decree nisi will go through at twelve months,' the lawyer said. 'To ensure it's taken care of smoothly I advise you to have the settlement done. That is, unless you're hoping to reconcile?'

The look of outrage on Victoria's face had told the lawyer all he needed to know.

On the way home from his office Victoria announced that she was going to start thinking about how to protect 'her assets'.

Gabrielle isn't sure Victoria has many assets but she assumes it's the sort of thing a person has to say in the circumstances.

She arrives at the end of the park, where one has to make a decision: go right onto the street, or left to take the narrow path to the river. If she goes by the river it will be a longer route home, which means she burns off more calories and can use that as a justification for buying more cakes. Left it is.

The path cuts through some thick bush, then there's a clearing where locals have been known to take picnics.

Locals such as Arthur and his lady friend, who are sitting on a blanket and doing what Gabrielle can only describe as canoodling. *Not* that she has ever, in her life, wanted to think of Victoria's husband doing any such thing.

'Arthur,' she says bluntly, and is pleased to see him look startled. Serves him right, flaunting his affair in a public place.

'Gabrielle?'

He gets to his feet – creakily, Gabrielle notes, because the old fool *is* old, although he's no doubt convinced himself that he has the vigour of a spring chicken.

'And this must be your sweetheart,' Gabrielle says, offering a narrow-eyed smile.

Arthur holds out his hand to his companion, who takes it and hoists herself up. 'Yes, this is Celeste.'

'Ah, Celeste,' Gabrielle says, clasping her hands in front of her and keeping up her smile. 'Rhymes with "Wicked Witch of the West", doesn't it?'

Celeste gawps and Gabrielle feels pleased. Which is bitchy of her, but she can't help it. Or, rather, she does not wish to help it.

Arthur is a walking cliché, with this younger woman in her stonewash jeans, chambray shirt, fob-watch chain necklace and Alice headband. He could have ordered her out of the Country Girl Catalogue. What does he think he's doing? What does *Celeste*? What could she possibly see in this rickety senior citizen when she can't be more than forty herself?

'Gabri-Gabrielle is Victoria's cousin,' Arthur stumbles and Celeste responds with colour in her cheeks.

'I'm glad to see you're embarrassed,' says Gabrielle. 'And you should be too, Arthur. You're the Bill Clinton of Bellbird River, fiddling with a younger woman who clearly needs to think more highly of herself if she believes *you* are a good deal. I'm only glad Victoria didn't take the Hillary route and stand by her man. A ridiculous policy if ever there was one.'

She raises her eyebrows and leans slightly away from him, to make herself seem more grand. It's something she has practised in many a dressing-room mirror, and she's pleased to see that Arthur now looks a little afraid.

He swallows. 'What are you doing in Bellbird River?'

'None of your business, Arthur. What are *you* doing in Celeste?'

Arthur looks like a guppy stranded in five centimetres of water, his mouth opening and closing, his eyes blinking.

'How dare you!' squeaks Celeste. 'We're in love!'

Gabrielle chortles. 'Love? I see. That makes it all right, does it?' She turns her gaze on Arthur. 'You've been in business, Arthur. If you had an employee who wanted to embezzle money from you because they were in love with an expensive car and just had to buy it, would that be all right too?'

'It's hardly the same thing,' Arthur says, indignation written across his otherwise unremarkable features.

'I believe it is.' She turns to Celeste. 'Not to worry, dear. I'm sure you can trade him in for a newer model when you're finished with him. Or he'll trade you in. Depends on who gets bored more easily, I suppose.'

With the dastardly duo glaring at her, Gabrielle realises that her walk is now ruined, so she may as well turn back the way she came. She'll just lie to Victoria about how many calories she burnt.

'I'll leave you to your picnic,' she says, 'or whatever it is you're doing. As ever, Arthur, it was a great displeasure to see you.'

She is tempted to stomp away but it would be more fun trying to glide, the way she likes to glide offstage. Regal exits and all that. So she daintily puts one foot in front of the other and moves as smoothly as she can down the path, resisting the temptation to turn around and see what Arthur and Celeste are doing.

As she walks back through the park, towards the main street then the house, she has only one regret: she really should have pushed Arthur into the river.

CHAPTER 30

Janine would like very much to not see Alex at rehearsal tonight. The other night, at the pub, it was quite clear from the look on Alex's face that she didn't approve of whatever she thought Janine and Ross were up to – and that was only from observing them together for a minute or so. It also seemed as though Alex didn't believe Janine was really at the pub to buy beer, which Janine wanted to be mad about but couldn't, because she might have been hoping to bump into Ross and that's why she volunteered to go for beer after her father offered to do it.

Ross had said he might be meeting two of his mates from school for drinks that night and Janine thought she'd surprise them. Those two mates are men she sees around town. *Isn't this funny*, she was planning to say, *Ross being back in Bellbird River?* Then they'd all hang out together as if it was so innocent, except it would be her and Ross in the same place, in plain sight. Getting away with whatever it is they're doing.

Maybe Alex saved her from a potentially treacherous situation. She stopped her going too far with Ross in public and the risk they could get caught. News of that would have made it back to Janine's parents probably before she even arrived home with the beer. She'd have embarrassed them. Embarrassed herself, although that's a secondary consideration.

Or maybe it's not, considering how lousy she felt about Alex seeing her and Ross together. There was judgement in Alex's eyes. Janine was sure of it.

So she doesn't want to see Alex tonight because Alex might ask her questions, which she'll try to avoid answering, but the avoidance will be its own kind of answer. Not turning up to choir would be its own kind of answer too.

'Hello.' Here is the very same Alex, smiling awkwardly.

Janine attempts a smile of her own. 'Hi.'

'May I sit?' Alex gestures to the empty chair in the spot she always sits in.

'Yeah. Of course.' Janine makes a show of shuffling over on her chair even though Alex doesn't need extra room.

She glances around to see if anyone is noticing that she and Alex aren't chatting the way they usually do. Because people notice things like that in this town. They notice if you're using a new lipliner and if you're taking in your newspaper and if you're fifteen minutes late on your daily walk.

Although they didn't notice that Victoria's husband was having an affair. Janine couldn't believe it when she heard that. Arthur must have been crafty. There wasn't even the whisper of a rumour about it. Janine felt so sorry for Victoria when she heard, but didn't for a second compare Ross to Arthur because it didn't suit her to. That makes her a terrible person, doesn't it?

No one is looking at her and Alex, though. They're all looking at Gabrielle, who appears to be telling a story to some others. Warwick has that expression on his face he gets when they're late starting and he can't control it. He likes things to run on time.

Alex puts her sheet music on the stand and taps it into a neat stack. 'I think I put my foot in it the other night,' she says quietly, not looking at Janine, who isn't sure what to say next.

'Oh,' is what she comes up with.

'What you do at the pub – anywhere – is none of my business,' Alex says. 'Sorry. Sometimes I can't help being a schoolteacher, thinking I have to regulate everyone the way I do my students.'

She makes a can't-help-it face. Janine isn't sure it's genuine but she can hardly call her on it.

'It's fine,' she says lightly, sensing an opportunity to get out of this without having to explain anything.

Warwick is walking over to Gabrielle, probably to attempt to get her to wind down her story so he can start practice. Janine sometimes wonders if Gabrielle has always been like this – showing off every chance she gets – or if she learnt it. It must be nice to be so outgoing, but kind of tiring too.

'Um . . .' Alex clears her throat. 'I saw in the paper that there's a good band playing at the Imperial in Tamworth on Saturday night.'

'The Impy,' says Janine.

'Hm?'

'The Impy. Locals call it the Impy.' She smiles in a conciliatory way.

'Oh, right. Thanks. The Impy.' Alex returns the smile. 'Anyway, I think the band is good. I don't really know.' Her laugh sounds a little forced.

Warwick is walking to the piano and Gabrielle has sat down. They're about to start and Janine can see that Alex has noticed.

'One of the teachers offered to babysit Kim any time I want to go out,' Alex says in a rush. 'So I thought I might go. Would you . . .' She raises her eyebrows. 'Would you like to come along?'

Janine is so surprised that anyone – let alone Alex, who she was sure would judge her for eternity – would ask her to do anything social that she thinks her mouth may have dropped open.

'Sure,' she says before Alex can change her mind.

Alex looks relieved. 'Do you know if they do food there?'

'Yeah, they do, but it's not that decent. The Tamworth Hotel is better.' She glances to the piano and back to Alex. 'We can eat there beforehand.'

'Great.' Alex grins.

'All right,' announces Warwick. 'We're a little late starting, my apologies. Now, we're making good progress with the songs for the Show but we need to stay sharp so it continues. And let's not forget I'll be assigning the solos soon. So I'm paying attention to your every note.' He glances around with intent. 'Let's begin with some warm-ups. Scales.'

Janine groans along with half of the choir.

'Come, come,' says Warwick. 'We have to do the boring work in order to get to the fun.'

'But the fun never comes!' says Jimbo. 'You promised we'd do "Lights on the Hill".'

'Shut up about Slim Dusty, Jimbo,' calls one of the basses.

'I haven't forgotten that song,' says Warwick tolerantly. 'We just have to get through the Show first. Then I'll think about adding it to the program for the Christmas concert.'

'Christmas?' Jimbo groans. 'That's a way off.'

'Think of it as my present to you,' Warwick says with a tight smile as he takes his seat at the piano.

'Pick you up at six?' Alex whispers in Janine's ear.

Janine nods. 'I'll give you my address later.'

And just like that, for the first time in more years than she can remember, Janine has a social activity to go to.

Her parents probably won't believe her when she tells them, but Bradley will. He remembers when she had friends. He remembers when he had friends too. They pretty much both lost them around the same time. The time Bradley lost himself. Now, maybe, one of them can start to come back to life.

CHAPTER 31

Going to choir practice is one thing. Being in a noisy pub where people are talking and laughing, slapping each other on the arm, nudging, winking, where music is playing, where drink orders are shouted over the bar . . . this is quite a different experience. Debbie feels like she has gone from a situation where her senses know what to expect to one where they're getting mugged on each street corner. She closes her eyes and is tempted to put her hands over her ears, just so she can slow this down.

Once she was released she went into accommodation that was suburban and quiet. She didn't go out at night. She didn't even go out for coffee during the day. Then she moved to Wattle Tree to work, and her world has been Bea and Phil and the kids, and the other workers. It's been years since she's been to a pub. So many years she can't remember the last time. Because she didn't know, whenever it was, that she wouldn't be back in a pub for this long. If she'd known she'd have paid closer attention, to that and to so many other things. You never know, though, when your life is about to change dramatically. No one gets warnings for that. And the warnings probably wouldn't be believed if they came, because you can't assess loss – the suddenness of her type of loss – until you're in it.

Debbie feels her arm being prodded. 'Why are your eyes closed?'

She opens them and smiles weakly at Jacko, one of the farm workers.

Bea encouraged Debbie to have a night out 'just for fun', and asked Jacko and George to take her. The three of them squeezed into the front seat of the ute together and Debbie didn't know whether to be offended or relieved that neither of them took it as an opportunity to grope her leg or some other body part.

'Guess I'm just tired,' she fibs.

'Not for long!' Jacko says. 'Gonna be a good night. You'll perk right up. Beer?'

Debbie shakes her head. 'Just a Coke, please.'

Jacko gives her a thumbs-up just as George finishes greeting every second person in the place.

'You must come here often,' Debbie says. She's trying to be sociable. It's a skill she had once that she practises on Bea from time to time, but chatting to anyone less familiar still requires concentration.

'Huh?' George's thick sand-coloured eyebrows pucker.

'You know everyone!' She gestures to the full public bar.

'Oh yeah. Right.' He grins. George has very even teeth. Debbie has often wondered if he's had them filed. 'Yeah, done a bit of drinkin' here. And at the Courtyard.' He nods towards a window. 'Down the hill. So who's on tonight?' He scrunches up his face as he looks at the blackboard next to the stage a few metres away. 'Nuh. Can't make it out.'

'Do you need glasses?'

'Yeah. Probably. Definitely!' George laughs.

He's one of the most happy-go-lucky people Debbie has ever met and she wishes she could have a life that allowed her to be the same.

'It says "Tex Trick and the Rough Riders",' Debbie says, quite pleased that her eyesight is impeccable. Not bad for an ageing chook.

'Texy!' George looks like he's won the Lotto. 'Haven't seen him play in ages.'

Jacko returns with two beers and a Coke and hands them around.

'Texy's playing,' George tells Jacko, swallowing half of his beer in one gulp.

'Bewdy! Texy!' Jacko is more circumspect with his beverage, barely sipping.

'So you like him?' Debbie says, hoping this means she'll at least have some good music to listen to.

'He's unreal,' says Jacko. 'Plays all the good songs. Johnny. Waylon. Willie. Old Slim.'

Debbie doesn't know what he's talking about but doesn't want to say so. Not sure what to say next, she glances around and flinches as she sees Alex and Janine from the choir sitting at a table near the stage, looking at her.

Now Alex is waving. Is she meant to go over there? She doesn't chat to them much at practice. Why should she chat to them here?

Because this is what being sociable is, she reminds herself. And Bea will want a report about how her night has gone. Debbie would like to have something interesting to tell her.

'I, ah . . .' She smiles at the boys. 'There are two people I know over there. I'll just go and say hello.'

'Righto,' says Jacko, offering another thumbs-up.

Debbie pushes through the clusters of men. They are all taller than she is and she feels like she's trying to find a path through a forest.

'Hi,' she says as she reaches the table, smiling. Or she thinks she's smiling. She lost the habit a while ago and her face isn't quite used to doing it again.

'Hi!' Alex smiles and points to the empty chair next to her. 'Want to join us?'

'Oh. Well.' Debbie glances back at the boys. George's glass is empty and Jacko is trying to balance a twenty-cent piece on his nose. 'I'm here with some people.'

'I know that bloke with the coin trick,' says Janine, squinting. 'Jack Henderson, right?'

'I, um, I – I don't know his last name.' Debbie doesn't know any of the last names of the workers. First names or nicknames only.

Janine looks at her oddly. 'But you're out for the night with him.'

'We work together,' Debbie says quickly. 'With George, the other one.'

Alex nods. 'Right, right. Janine and I were wondering if the other one was your boyfriend. He's cute!'

'My – what?' Debbie is agape. 'He's at least twenty years younger than me!'

'So?' Alex smiles mischievously. 'Nothing wrong with that.' She pulls the chair out. 'Sit for a while. Go on.'

Debbie glances at Janine and can't tell if she's pleased about this development or not. She's always found Janine to be quite stand-offish. Alex is friendlier but Debbie only knows that by observing. Still, it would be rude not to sit down, so she does.

'You have a great voice,' Alex says, leaning in to talk as the noise level around them spikes. 'I was saying to Janine the other night that I wish I could sing like you.'

The unexpected compliment makes Debbie jerk back. 'That's really nice of you,' she says. 'Thanks. Yours is lovely too.'

Alex laughs and shrugs. 'I have more fun than skill. But that's okay. So you're new in town too? There aren't many of us.'

There's no point in wondering how Alex knows, because Debbie is well aware that news gets around town quickly. Which is why she never wants anyone besides Bea to know about her past.

'Yes. I work out at Wattle Tree – it's a property.' Debbie glances at Janine, who looks as if she couldn't care less.

'Are you from the country?' Alex again.

'No, I . . .' Debbie considers how to say this. 'I just felt like a change.' She clears her throat. To avoid answering any more questions from Alex she'll have to ask some of her own. 'So where are you from?'

'Sydney.' Alex shrugs. 'It was getting a bit too full-on for me. It feels like everyone's moving there because of the Olympics. There's so much construction going on and all the workers . . . And so much traffic it seems like it takes twice as long to get anywhere. I got sick of it. My mum's still there, but I thought I'd move away while Kim's still in primary school.'

Debbie thinks of Alex's serious daughter bent over a book in the corner of the hall, sometimes curling up and falling asleep amidst all their noise. One night Warwick carried her out to the car after Alex said she was too heavy to be lifted. He looked so strong and gallant that Debbie's heart skipped a beat, then a second later she thought it couldn't have because she doesn't like Warwick like *that*.

'How is Kim?' Debbie asks.

Alex shrugs. 'Not happy that I'm out for the night but . . .' She shrugs again. 'Mummy needs to have a life too.'

There's a roar near the bar and Alex glances over while Janine shifts in her seat.

'How's the bakery?' Debbie asks her.

'Fine.' Janine stands up. 'I'm going to get another drink. Would you like one?'

'Oh – no, thanks, I'm okay.'

Janine looks enquiringly at Alex, who shakes her head. 'Nah – thanks. I'll stick with the one. But you go for it – you don't have to worry about driving.'

Debbie gazes after Janine as she walks away, then across to where she can see Jacko gesticulating animatedly while he talks to someone Debbie doesn't recognise.

'She's being a bit abrupt,' says Alex. 'She's not usually like that.'

Debbie glances back at Alex. 'It's okay.'

'She has some stuff on her mind.'

Debbie nods, not sure why Alex is telling her this. Or maybe she's trying to tell herself, because Debbie doesn't know why someone as personable as Alex would want to be friends with Janine.

'Tell me more about you,' Alex says, leaning forwards. 'I always like hearing people's stories.'

'There's nothing too exciting about me.' Debbie smiles so it looks like she's being modest instead of evasive.

'That voice has to come from somewhere. But I don't want to pry. Anyway – look.' Alex gestures to the stage. 'The band's about to start.'

'I'd better get back to the boys,' Debbie says, standing up, although she likes it here, with Alex. She feels calm being around someone who seems to be settled within herself.

'Sure,' Alex says. 'See you Tuesday?'

Debbie nods and walks away.

She passes Janine, whose head is bowed, her lips pressed together. Debbie considers saying something but feels the force field Janine has around her, and recognises it because she has one of her own.

Perhaps she's been too quick to judge. Janine owes her nothing. No one owes her anything. Not their time. Not their interest. Debbie has to earn it, whether it's with new friends or her children. That's the way of her world now.

As she rejoins George and Jacko the band strikes up a two-four beat and they don't much vary it for the rest of the night.

CHAPTER 32

'I don't want to talk about your father,' Victoria says as authoritatively as possible. She buckles in her seatbelt then swivels to give her daughter a meaningful look.

'Mummy, really, that's not reasonable.'

Helena turns the key in the engine and glances in her side mirror, her long, thick hair falling forwards over her shoulder. It's Victoria's mother's hair, which Victoria also inherited. Gabrielle, being from Victoria's father's side of the family, ended up with fluff. But, as Victoria likes to remind her, she has a singing voice that no one else in the clan can claim.

'Put your seatbelt on,' Victoria commands.

'Mummy! I'm not five.' Helena laughs, as if Victoria is amusing and irrelevant.

'No, but you're a licensed driver and you'll lose points if the policeman sees you.'

'The policeman? You mean Craig?' Another laugh.

Children can be so insolent once they reach the age when they decide they know more than their parents.

'Yes, Craig,' Victoria says snippily.

The local policeman most often on daytime duty is the son of one of Victoria's friends from bridge. He grew up with Helena and her brother, Leopold, and is known to be slightly lenient with his mother's bridge friends if they drive over the limit or engage in minor traffic infringements. It's all part of community policing, he told Victoria once – a good cop makes a judgement call about what's really worth enforcing. Victoria isn't entirely sure that's true, but she knows Craig let off Arthur for speeding more than once. Now she wishes he hadn't. Arthur should be made to pay for every transgression.

'You know as well as I do that Craig's not going to ping me for a seatbelt,' Helena says.

She pulls out from the kerb in a hurry and Victoria clutches the side door.

'Don't do that, Mummy, you make me feel like a bad driver!'

Victoria watches the speedometer reach seventy kilometres on the sleepy main drag and widens her eyes. 'Because you *are* a bad driver. And if you're going to keep driving over the speed limit you will need a seatbelt.'

Helena sighs exaggeratedly and takes one hand off the wheel to pull her belt across. 'Happy now?'

'Never,' Victoria mutters. 'Why are you here, exactly?'

'We're going to see your friend.' Helena tears out onto Jumbuck Way without putting on a blinker.

'I know that – which way are you going?'

'I'm taking the Wallabadah road.'

Helena removes a hand from the wheel again and reaches into the car door pocket to extract some chewing gum.

'You could have taken the other road.'

'Why would I go north when I can go south? We're going to Nundle, aren't we?'

'Yes, but . . .' Victoria sighs and looks out the window at the eucalypts and the grass that's greener than it has been in a long time. 'I just like the other road.'

'Then you should have driven.'

Helena chews her gum loudly, and Victoria is convinced she's doing it on purpose.

'So why aren't we talking about Papa?' Helena continues.

'Why *would* we talk about him? He's a wretched individual.'

Victoria sees a dead wombat by the side of the road and shudders, as she always does. They're too precious to lose yet too stupid to know not to cross a high-speed road. When she was on the council she had an idea to put short fences along certain stretches of the road, just above wombat height, to discourage them from crossing, but some greenie complained and said it was a 'curtailment of wombat freedoms', and Victoria was so irritated she abandoned the notion.

'He just wants to be happy, Mummy.' *Chew chew chew.*

'And I don't?' Victoria almost shouts.

'Come on – were you really happy with him?'

Helena winds down her window and her hair starts blowing everywhere. Victoria resists the urge to tell her that she's liable to have an accident with all that hair in her face, because that would be pushing her interference too far and they'll just end up being cross with each other, as they so often do.

It's been months since Helena last visited and that's because Victoria told her she shouldn't be shacked up with her boyfriend because he was getting a live-in maid and Helena was getting precisely nothing except more housework. Helena had told her she was 'anti-feminist' and Victoria had replied that there was nothing feminist about being a live-in maid without even a diamond to show for it, let alone the promise of anything more secure, and they'd barely spoken since. It was only once Helena decided that she was, indeed, sick of being a live-in maid and dumped the boyfriend that she turned up in Bellbird River, with no warning.

'Happiness comes and goes in marriage,' Victoria says. 'And it usually has little to do with the other person unless they act in such a way as to really drive one round the bend.'

Helena snorts. 'And yet you wanted me to get married.'

'*No*, I wanted you to not be living with a man without marrying him. You should value what you have to offer. Men have by far the better deal in marriage and you shouldn't be giving them anything without ensuring you receive something in return.'

'Gee, how romantic.' Helena winds up the window but not in time to prevent her hair looking like a bird's nest.

Victoria laughs drily. 'There's nothing romantic about marriage. No doubt that's why your father has sought romance elsewhere.'

'I thought we weren't talking about him.'

'We're not. Slow down – the turn's coming up.'

Victoria braces herself against the door as Helena does not slow down but takes the corner at speed.

'So who's this friend you're seeing?' Helena asks as she speeds along the road past quiet houses and dogs in front gardens.

'Louise. You remember her.'

Louise was a regular visitor to the house when the children were growing up – not that they would have paid attention. Children are always so delightfully self-centred that way.

'Did she move?'

'Yes. Her husband died and she didn't want to stay on the property. She bought a nice little place in Nundle, in town. You didn't have to drive me, though.'

'I don't mind. Gives me something to do.' *Chew chew chew.*

They reach the highway and Helena stops at the intersection, almost as if she heard Victoria's silent prayer that she do exactly that. There are semitrailers on this road going both directions, and always traffic heading north to Tamworth. If Helena had tried her usual trick of turning without looking they'd probably have ended up flattened in full view of the customers at the one café in this tiny town.

'You wouldn't consider moving back?' Victoria says as they slip in behind a ute which has an unsecured kelpie in its tray, pacing back and forth amongst secured tools. How can a man tie up his tools and not his precious dog? It's one of the great mysteries of bush life, although Victoria has seen it often enough.

'To Bellbird River?' Helena pulls into the overtaking lane so they can pass the kelpie and his owner. She laughs. 'No. There's nothing for me to do there.'

Victoria can't refute this. Helena has a good brain and nowhere to use it in Bellbird River. She didn't want to be a lawyer or an accountant, so there went two staple jobs of country towns other than mechanic. Instead she decided to work in government and there's nary a government office to be found near Bellbird River, unless she wants to work for the Department of Agriculture or whatever it's called now and live in Tamworth.

'I miss you,' Victoria murmurs.

'I know,' Helena says cheerfully.

'Oh, you're terrible.' Victoria smiles to soften it.

'I know.'

The Nundle road is coming up on the right soon, but Victoria resists the urge to tell Helena to slow down once more. Her daughter is an adult – at some point Victoria needs to let her take responsibility for her own decisions.

'It wasn't right, what he did,' Helena says quietly. 'That's what I wanted to say.'

She turns her face briefly towards Victoria, who sees pain on it.

'He may say he just wants to be happy, but Mummy . . .' Helena's inhalation is ragged. 'You did everything for him.'

Victoria smiles sadly. 'Perhaps that was my mistake.'

'I'm sorry.' Helena wipes her nose with the back of one hand and Victoria realises she's crying. 'I really am.'

Seeing her child upset makes Victoria cry too, but she doesn't want Helena to know, so she looks out the window at the khaki and gold and light brown and dark brown of the bush, at the tangle of trees and scrub that provides a home for hapless animals and a reassuringly familiar palette for a heartsick woman who wishes her husband hadn't made their daughter cry.

Victoria clears her throat and blinks back her tears before turning to look at Helena. 'I have no regrets. I have you and Leopold.'

Helena sniffs once, twice, then chews that infernal gum again.

'I wish I could stay longer,' she says.

'So do I, but I have Gabrielle for company so I'm all right.'

Helena laughs. 'She's a hoot. I wish I'd known her while I was growing up.'

'I wish you had too, but she was too busy being Gabrielle.'

Despite her earlier resolve, with the Nundle sign looming Victoria can't help herself. 'Slow down! The turn's coming up,' she barks.

Helena sighs. '*All right*, Mummy.'

She hits the brakes, Victoria gasps, and they make the turn with only minor skid marks left on the road.

CHAPTER 33

As the basses practise their part Gabrielle looks around at the other members of the choir. She doesn't know any of their names – they tell her, but she forgets. It's not that she's forgetful; she's simply had so many years of meeting a multitude of strangers that she's never developed the habit of remembering people's names. All those functions she had to attend to please friends of this opera company and that grand old venue. *Gabrielle, we're so pleased to introduce you to Monsieur So-and-so, our favourite patron. Madame Reynold, it's an honour to introduce you to Herr Whoseywhatsit, our biggest donor.*

If anyone had told Gabrielle when she was a young singer with stars in her eyes that so much of her career would involve and depend on people who knew nothing about opera, or any music, she might have decided that Bellbird River wasn't too small for her.

Actually, no, that would never have been true. Bellbird River was always too small for her. Even her kindergarten teacher said she was too big for her boots, and her Year Four teacher said she was stuck-up because she could pronounce French words correctly. She'd learnt them listening to a recording of Bizet's *Carmen* – what else did the man expect?

And if he'd bothered to find that out he might also have discovered that she listened to operas over and over again because they went for hours and her parents yelled at each other for hours. Opera helped her pretend there was no yelling.

It was Victoria who gave her a turntable and some records; Gabrielle never found out if that's because Victoria knew exactly what was going on in her house. All she said was, 'I've tried to like opera and I can't stand it. Perhaps you'll fare better.'

Victoria preferred other sorts of singers – popular singers like Ella Fitzgerald, Sammy Davis Junior, Frank Sinatra, Dean Martin. It wasn't that Gabrielle thought they were bad, more that she didn't really like their songs: so short, hardly any story. With opera you had guts and glory, high stakes and low dramas. It was the stuff of life and no amount of 'My Funny Valentine' could compare.

'Have you developed a nervous tic?' Victoria hisses in her ear and Gabrielle's attention is back in the here and now.

'What?' she says, refocusing on Warwick and his flapping, conducting hands.

'Your eyes have circled the room about fifty times.' Victoria pulls some sheet music off the stand. 'We're meant to be mentally rehearsing our part but you're being a busybody.'

'I'm not!' Gabrielle is, indeed, a busybody but she doesn't like it when people notice.

'So why are you looking around the room as if a piece of gossip will spontaneously erupt somewhere?'

'I just . . .' Gabrielle tries to think of something plausible then decides to tell the truth. 'I was thinking that I don't know anyone here. Not really.'

Victoria peers over her half-moon glasses. When Gabrielle first saw them she laughed and said she couldn't believe Victoria would choose something so old-fashioned, and was rewarded with her cousin's miffed silence for several hours.

'Do you *want* to know the people here?' Victoria says, her tone clipped. 'Because I know *everyone* here and I can introduce you, if you wish.'

'You don't know everyone! Don't exaggerate.'

'If I don't know them to have a conversation with, I certainly know their names.' Her smile is thin-lipped. 'Years on council. Lifelong resident. I can *assure* you, I know them and they know me.'

The basses have stopped singing and Warwick is back standing in the centre.

'Have you suddenly developed an interest in the residents?' Victoria continues.

'No. I was just passing time.'

Actually, she was trying to distract herself from the fact that she didn't want to get out of bed this morning. When she woke up the first things she thought of were the notes she still can't reach and the career she no longer has. It was enough to make her want to roll over and sleep for the rest of the day, as it is most days, but she heard Victoria on the phone to one of her friends, then a clanging in the kitchen as she dropped something, then there was a knock on the front door because people like to drop in to see Victoria if they're passing by. It all served to remind Gabrielle that her cousin has a full life and she, the previously revered Madame Reynold, doesn't have even a demitasse of one. Cue further desire to roll over and go back to sleep, but Victoria chose that moment to knock on her door and tell her that sleeping-in was for teenagers on holidays and it was time she got up.

'Gabrielle,' Warwick says loudly, and for a second Gabrielle wonders if she's going to be disciplined for not paying attention.

'Ah – yes,' she says meekly, relaxing as she sees Warwick beaming at her.

'This piece has a solo,' he says.

Gabrielle knows this. She has studied the music and seen the solo. But to say so would sound churlish, so she merely nods and smiles and says, 'Oh?'

'I think you'd be perfect for it!' he announces, looking very pleased with himself.

'Oh, really?' She says it flatly, as if he's disappointed her. *How obvious, to ask the opera singer to perform the solo. Tsk, tsk, choirmaster, do better.* She can see on his face that he's understood her.

'You don't agree?' he says.

'Well, Warwick, *darling*, as I'm sure you know, I'm perfect for most things.' A titter; a little who-me? shrug. She's good at playing roles; sometimes she forgets it herself. And the role she's playing tonight is of the diva who is desperately hiding the true state of the voice that made her famous. 'And I'm *so* flattered you asked, really, but I haven't earned my stripes here yet.'

'That's clearly not true! You're a star!' he blusters, but Gabrielle can tell from the stony looks on the faces of some of the sopranos that there's agreement in the room.

'You're so sweet, truly. But I'd like to see . . .' She looks around the room again, but at least this time it's with purpose. Her gaze lands on that quiet woman with plaits. D-D-D-something her name is. Diane? Daisy?

'Debbie do it,' she says, smiling in Debbie's direction and receiving a shocked expression. 'She has a lovely voice, and before you say it, I *know* she's a mezzo, Warwick, but she has range, doesn't she? I'm sure she would be brilliant at it.'

Warwick looks as if he's just been told his car has been stolen, and Gabrielle feels momentarily guilty, but she has to protect herself first and foremost. No point acting to spare someone else's feelings if it puts her in peril.

'Um,' says Debbie.

'You'll be lovely, Debbie, I'm sure of it,' Gabrielle says – because she *is* sure. That quiet little mouse has the voice of a siren.

'Right,' says Warwick. 'I, well . . .' He shuffles his sheet music. 'Debbie, how would you feel about that?'

Gabrielle doesn't hear the response as she's too busy feeling relieved that she's managed such an escape.

'Nicely done,' Victoria murmurs.

'What do you mean?' Gabrielle says out the side of her mouth.

'You get out of doing the solo and make yourself look generous in the process.'

As Gabrielle turns to Victoria she sees raised eyebrows and amusement.

'I have many skills,' she says.

'And fooling me isn't one of them.' Victoria is serious now. 'That voice still isn't right, is it? That's why you only practise when I'm not home.'

Gabrielle puts her shoulders back so her bosom lifts. It's her standard position when she wants to look like the prow of a ship that's cutting through waters of doubt and disagreement. 'This is not the place to discuss that.'

Before Victoria can respond, Warwick and Debbie stop talking and Warwick seats himself at the piano.

'Sopranos,' he says, 'let's hear you.'

Gabrielle plucks the sheet music out of Victoria's hand and places it in front of her. '*You* can look over *my* shoulder for once,' she says, but her guard completely drops when she feels her cousin's hand on her forearm, holding her gently, just the way she used to when Gabrielle was young.

With tears in her eyes, Gabrielle opens her mouth to sing amongst the others.

CHAPTER 34

Janine pauses in front of the photographs of Ross and his dark-haired, brown-skinned wife and their dark-haired, brown-skinned children. Miranda doesn't look anything like Janine, with her pale skin and nondescript hair. Miranda has strong eyebrows and pronounced cheekbones. Janine feels as though her own face lost a distinctive form so long ago that she can't remember what she used to look like. Or maybe that's just the way she sees herself. She is aware – because the one doctor she saw at the nadir of her troubles told her so – that her perception of how she looks doesn't match the reality. Certainly, though, she isn't as striking as this woman with her face worth painting.

What would it be like to have Miranda sit for her? To pretend that she doesn't know her, doesn't know Ross, doesn't know anything about their lives?

'She's beautiful,' Janine murmurs as Ross kisses the back of her neck.

'Mm, yeah, she is,' he says, kissing a different spot.

Janine traces her fingers over the glass of one of the photo frames, then pushes back against Ross and turns around.

'I'm still not sure I should be here,' she says.

Ross had asked her to come to his house, on Sandown Street. Actually, he'd insisted. Miranda had taken the children to visit her family in Wellington. It's a three-hour drive and she'd set off after school had finished. They wouldn't be coming back tonight. Or tomorrow night. They'd have the place to themselves, Ross said, so instead of meeting at the bakery they would meet here.

When he said it Janine knew it was a tipping point. If she said no that would probably be the last time they'd see each other, because Ross wanted more from her and if she didn't give it he'd break things off. But if she said yes that would mean she was letting him know he could get whatever he wanted just by pushing.

She hadn't felt strong enough to say no. She wishes she had. She wishes there wasn't part of her that still thinks she deserves no more than this grasping, furtive interplay with another woman's husband.

She'd walked over here from the bakery, leaving her car parked in its usual spot and the light on out the back of the shop, so if anyone passes by they'll think she's still there. Deception comes so easily to her these days. It both fascinates and appals her. Right now it's making her realise that she's an awful person and she should do something about it before she turns into a terrible one.

'Why not?' Ross looks at her quizzically, then wraps his arms around her waist, pulling her against him. 'I want you here.'

He kisses her, hard, and presses his groin into hers. Just in case she needs a reminder about what he wants. Or, rather, all she's good for.

'And you know you want to be here,' he says into her ear, then nips her earlobe as he pushes her back further.

She breaks off the kiss and folds her arms across her chest to stop him coming closer.

'Now what's the matter?' he says, looking at her like she's a silly child. 'You didn't have a problem with that in the bakery.'

'Because your family doesn't live in the bakery,' she says. She glances around at the worn couch, the bright cushions, the messy stack of magazines. All signs of someone else.

He laughs. 'It's not like you didn't know they exist. What's the problem?'

'It's just . . .' She looks at the photographs again. 'It feels weird. It's your house. There are these.' She gestures at the images of his family. 'I don't need the reminder.'

His eyes narrow briefly then his face relaxes. 'I'm sorry,' he says. 'I know it's not the best place. But we can't exactly go to your house.' He slides one hand under her T-shirt. 'And I'm keen to get out of the bakery.'

With his other hand he grabs her arm, his fingers digging in. Her body pulses out a warning – *this is not the behaviour of someone who cares about you* – but her brain shuts it down: *this is what you get for changing your mind.*

'You're so gorgeous. I just can't resist you,' Ross murmurs, his lips on her neck again, the hand that's under her shirt moving its way to her breast.

You're so gorgeous.

That was the right thing to say. Which he knows. And she knows he knows.

But he's holding her in place and her skin is starting to melt under his lips and there are just enough hormones racing around her body to convince her that maybe this is a good idea after all.

Now he's lifted her T-shirt above her head and his hands are reaching for the clasp on her bra. She has a thought – *just let him do it, then it's done.*

The thought means that she doesn't really want what he's doing. But sometimes it's just easier to relent. She has relented so many times to her own darker urges – to the thoughts that tell her she's worthless, she's ugly, that she should punish herself for even existing – that it's a habit. One she's been trying to break, but oh, how hard it is to stop those thoughts filling her mind, murmuring, chattering, shouting.

Except she has to try. Otherwise why is she here, on this earth, in this town, in this body? What is the point if she doesn't try to make her life today better than it was yesterday?

'Ross, please, stop,' she says.

He makes a noise that's half-grunt, half-sigh, and as he pulls his hand away the hooks on her bra scrape her skin. She flinches but stays silent.

'But you want it,' he says roughly.

In his voice she hears the tone other men have used when they've pushed her too far too fast and she's tried to slow it down. It's anger born of entitlement. And she feels the threat then: real and unspoken. *But you want it.* That's the get-out-of-jail-free card he's given himself, even if it's not true. Her guts turn to water and she can taste fear.

So she does what she's always done when she's been in this situation: she smiles to appease him.

'I never said I didn't,' she says, taking hold of his hands and squeezing them. 'But I'm getting my period.'

That's the tactic that has worked in the past. She hopes it will work now, because his irises are dark and his face hard.

He frowns. 'You could have said that earlier.'

'Sorry,' she says, so meek, so docile. 'I just didn't think you'd want to do . . . that. Since we haven't, um . . .' She pulls an apologetic face. 'I'm really sorry.'

'Just as well you told me,' he says quickly and turns away. 'Periods are disgusting.'

She picks up her T-shirt from the floor and puts it on. 'I'd better go. Mum will be calling the bakery wondering if I've chopped my hand off in the slicer or something.'

It's a lie and he could call her on it, because they were planning to be together for a while tonight.

'Sure,' he says. 'See you next week?'

'Yep,' she says, picking up her handbag from his coffee table, like she's the cleaner heading home.

'I'll be thinking about you in the meantime,' he says, grabbing the waistband of her jeans and kissing her cheek, then her mouth, his teeth nipping her bottom lip. More pain. This time she's sure he meant to cause it.

'I'll be thinking about you too,' she says truthfully, although she doesn't mean it the way it sounds.

As she leaves she checks quickly from side to side and across the street, but there's no one around. She half-jogs the three blocks back to the shop under a crescent moon, the night air cool and only one streetlight to mark her path. Checking twice over her shoulder to see if he's followed her, because for some reason she feels like prey.

CHAPTER 35

'I'm not going.' Kimberly kicks the back of the passenger seat, something she hasn't done since she was seven. Or five. Or eight. Alex can't remember, because all these years of motherhood have at once no form and all form. Each day she colours inside the lines of being Kim's mother and each day she feels like her life is a great big splodgy mess, because no matter how well she follows the rules of parenthood they end up somewhere like here, with Kim refusing to go to school tomorrow, and that's after last night spent refusing to do her homework and nagging Alex about getting a dog. That's her latest thing. She wants a big dog to scare off the mean children.

'You have to go, sweetheart,' Alex says, trying to keep her voice even. Kim doesn't respond to raised volume.

'I do *not*.' Another kick.

'Yes, you do. It's against the law for me to keep you out of school without a good reason, and even if I had a reason I have to go to work.'

Alex looks at her watch. She has papers to mark and dinner to prepare, not to mention the library closes shortly and the whole reason they're sitting in the car outside it is because Kim wanted more books and now she's refusing to go in because she saw some of the kids from school entering a few minutes ago.

'I can't go to school because I'll be sick tomorrow,' Kim says, looking anything but with colour in her cheeks and fire in her eyes.

'Nice try,' Alex says.

'*Mum!*'

Alex turns and sees tears on Kim's cheeks. Her instinctual reaction is to want to reach back and hug her daughter, but she also wonders if she's being manipulated and hates herself for thinking it. Kids can be so good at playing their parents like fiddles, though. Childhood is a full-time job of trying to get what you want by slipping between your parents' strictures and navigating what other children want, all while developing your sense of the world and your personality and your awareness of your place within your family.

What has brought them to this stalemate is that what other children want is for Kim to suffer. The latest campaign – according to Kim, and Alex has no choice but to believe her – is to taunt Kim about her lack of a father by saying she's so ugly that her father ran away when she was born. One enterprising boy threw in the detail that Alex herself must be so ugly that Kim's father didn't want to be seen with her. Alex would like to have a word with that child's parents but Kim won't identify him. Instead, she is refusing to go to school.

'I know it's hard,' Alex says, squeezing Kim's ankle, a compromise gesture.

'You do not!'

'Kim, children are mean. I really understand that.'

Alex thinks of the teenagers who taunt her, and she's meant to be the one in charge. One Year Eleven told her 'your tits are small, miss', then sniggered. There are days when Alex wishes corporal punishment was still available and hates herself for thinking it. Detention does nothing but give the Year Eleven and her friends the opportunity to delay going home, because they always seem to contrive to get detention together.

'But I don't want these mean children to stop you doing things you want to do, like going to the library,' Alex adds.

Kim sighs loudly and dramatically drops her head into her hands. 'I can't go in, Mum. I'm scared.'

This may or may not be true, but it's effective. The last thing Alex wants is for her child to feel scared.

'They're not going to hurt you,' she says as reassuringly as she can. 'I'll come in with you.'

'One of them pulled my hair.' Kim's face is full of accusation, as if it was Alex who did it to her.

'I know, sweetie.'

Now it's Alex's turn to sigh. She spoke to Kim's teacher about that particular incident and was told that 'boys will be boys'. The teacher said it so flatly that Alex was sure she'd seen and heard it all before, and decided she could never change it.

Alex understands that, because it's hard to remain optimistic in the face of children's – and teenagers' – obstinance. The younger generations have less at stake and are prepared to wait you out. Eventually a weary teacher just stops trying to intervene. Or care. Alex never wants to be that teacher but it's oh-so-tempting sometimes.

Except she can see the result of it in her daughter's distress. Kim's teacher is doing nothing to stop these bullies having a go at Kim, and now Alex has a child who not only doesn't want to go to school but won't even enter the library that is nowhere near the school.

'Kim, if I let you not go tomorrow, what's going to happen the day after that?' she says.

'I'm not going then, either! I'm going to call Grandma and she can take me back to Sydney.'

That's been her other refrain. When she's not demanding a dog she's threatening to call Grandma.

Alex checks her watch again. 'The library will close soon. Don't you want some more books?'

Another kick against the passenger seat.

'Stop that, please,' Alex orders.

Kim glares at her, then turns and stares out the window.

Alex has no idea how to change what's happening, but she knows Kim will feel better if she has some new books. She always does.

A knock on her window makes Alex jump.

She turns and sees Debbie peering into the car, with two boys standing next to her. Does Debbie have sons? Alex has never heard them mentioned. Not that they've chatted about many personal things.

She winds down the window. 'Hi,' she says with a tense smile.

'Hi, Alex.' Debbie puts her head closer to the open window. 'Hi, Kim!'

Alex's eyes flicker to the rear-view mirror in time to see a small smile from her daughter. Amazing. She'll smile for Debbie but not for her own mother.

'We're just, ah . . . deciding whether or not to go into the library,' Alex says, raising her eyebrows to make a signal she hopes Debbie can interpret and understand: *my child is being difficult.*

'Oh, we're about to go in too! This is Ryan and Steven. I work with their parents.'

The boys say 'hi' in unison and Alex looks at their uniforms. Not the same as Kim's. So they can't be amongst the cadre of bullies.

'Hi, boys,' she says. 'Which school do you go to?'

'They're at the Catholic school in Quirindi,' Debbie says as Ryan and Steven look with curiosity at Kim.

Alex swivels in her seat to look at her daughter. 'Shall we go in with Debbie and the boys?'

Kim's eyes are wide as she looks at Debbie then Alex then Debbie again.

'Okay,' she says and unbuckles her belt.

'Thank you,' Alex mouths at Debbie.

Before Alex can wind up the window Kim is out of the car and standing on the footpath. With relief Alex watches her skip ahead with the boys while Debbie waits for her to sling her handbag over her shoulder.

'Maybe we can meet you here every week?' Alex says as they walk towards the flat-roofed building. 'I may not be able to get her in there otherwise. Some of the kids are being mean.'

Debbie nods slowly. 'School can be hard.' She stops and turns slightly. 'I'd be happy to take her every time I take the boys. Shall we talk on Tuesday night?'

It is so rare for Alex to have someone else help her with Kim – especially since she moved to Bellbird River – that she almost forgets her manners.

'Thank you, yes, that would be great.'

Debbie gives her the briefest of smiles – almost like she doesn't want to acknowledge what they've just discussed – and stands back to let Alex walk into the library first.

CHAPTER 36

'Hello?' Debbie steps into the hall, surprised by how much noise her footfall makes when there's no one else around to absorb the sound. She's never been the first to arrive at choir practice, let alone been here on her own. But Warwick asked her to come an hour early so they could work on her solo.

'A solo!' Bea had cried when Debbie asked if it would be all right if she left an hour early today and told Bea why. 'That's fantastic!'

Debbie had let herself smile. She doesn't let many things make her smile; working on this solo is the first thing that's made her genuinely happy since she moved to Wattle Tree.

'It's just an ABBA song,' she said, as if ABBA songs are the easiest thing in the world.

She's noticed that Warwick loves giving them ABBA songs – because of all the harmonies, he says. They're perfect for choirs, even if they're technically quite difficult.

'ABBA's the best,' Bea had said dreamily. 'I know it's daggy to like them but *seriously*, they're so good. And I guess *Muriel's Wedding* made them cool again.' She snorted. 'Or I like to think they are.'

She'd given Debbie a quick hug, which was out of character for their relationship but not for Bea herself. Bea hugs everyone. It's just that Debbie likes to emit a 'keep out' signal so Bea rarely tries it on her.

'Of course you can go early,' Bea said. 'And I want a full report later on!' Then she'd put on her hat and walked out the back door, leaving Debbie to continue folding the washing. The washing that never ended and would never end and which Debbie has started to dream about.

She is pleased to have left the piles of towels and the boys' sports clothes behind, pleased to have this time just to be in the hall, singing. It feels like a treat she never thought she'd earn.

'Ah, Debbie.' Warwick emerges from the side of the stage. 'Thank you for coming early.'

'It's fine,' she replies lightly.

He grins and trots down the short stairs to the floor, sheet music tucked under his arm.

Debbie notices that his shirt sleeves are rolled up just so, and she suspects he may have a crease in his jeans but she wouldn't swear to it. Not that she should observe him so closely. He's attractive and talented but not available. And even if he were it's not as if she's looking for that sort of thing. She's lasted for years without going anywhere near a man. She really doesn't need to moon over *this* man, no matter how appealing he is.

Besides, it's the children taking up most of her thoughts. She has to focus on rebuilding her relationship with them, and that means trying to persuade Greg to let her see them more. She's called him twice since that short meeting in Tamworth and each time he's said 'I'll see' when she asks about seeing them again. If that's meant to deter her it's not going to work.

'So, shall we sit at the piano?' Warwick says, pulling out the seat for her. 'That way we can share the music and you can follow along as I play.'

Debbie doesn't know whether to tell him that she can't read music – she just follows the words and memorises the tune from listening to a recording. She's been listening to this song over and over – even went out into one of the paddocks with her portable CD player to practise it, hoping that none of the other workers were within cooee. If they were, no one said anything.

No, she doesn't need to tell him – she's well-rehearsed and she can manage. She smiles compliantly at him.

'It's a big song, "Thank You for the Music". A signature song.' He looks at her meaningfully. 'I know you're up to it. And I had a feeling the lyrics would resonate with you.'

She stares at him. Does he know about her? Is he trying to tell her he knows that, given her recent experiences, she's someone who would think that music can save her from herself, as the song's protagonist suggests? Or maybe he's trying to tell her that he thinks she's not that interesting without music. That her singing is the only thing that makes her interesting. Which means he's actually being a little bit . . .

'I just realised how that sounds!' he says, breaking into her thoughts. 'Gosh – how terrible of me. I don't mean you're boring or anything like that in the song. Not at all!' His laugh is high, false. 'I just meant that you seem to have such a strong connection to music. When you sing you look as if you're being transported to some other place.'

Now he's blushing, and so is Debbie, to think that she's been observed so closely. And here she was thinking she shouldn't observe *him*.

'Oh,' she utters, if only to keep the silence from being any more awkward. 'That's, um – that's a nice thing to say. I guess I . . .'

She tries to think of how to frame her real relationship with music, although perhaps she doesn't have to try too hard. Warwick, of all the people she's met lately, would understand.

'I watch everyone,' he says quickly. 'When they're singing. I didn't mean that to sound odd.'

It's reassuring that she hasn't been singled out – except the look he gives her is so intense that Debbie can't tell what he wants her to think. That she matters, or that she doesn't? That he notices her more than others, or that he doesn't? After years of being a number, of being categorised according to what she did as opposed to who she is, being noticed for her skill may not be so bad.

'It didn't sound odd,' she says, then smiles shyly. 'Or maybe a little. But it's okay. I won't tell anyone.'

Warwick nods slowly. 'But if you want to tell me how you feel about music, I'd love to hear it. Even with all the people in choir, I don't get to talk about music very often.'

'Why not?'

His laugh is lifeless. 'Because this town is full of philistines, haven't you noticed? If you can't talk about a national sporting side, they don't want to know you.'

Debbie thinks about George and Jacko animatedly discussing the band they went to see in Tamworth on the drive back to Wattle Tree, comparing songs and talking about what they loved, and whether or not they'd be able to get back into town soon for more music. They didn't mention sport once. Although they did talk about shooting kangaroos.

'I haven't spent much time in town,' she says, because it's the truth and because she doesn't want to disagree with Warwick when he's giving her such a lovely opportunity.

'You're lucky,' he says with a hint of bitterness.

'Did you grow up here?' Debbie asks, thinking that's the only reason he'd stay in a place he clearly doesn't like.

'No.' He gives her a tight smile and looks like he doesn't want to say any more.

'Right.'

'So where do you live if not in town?' he asks.

His enquiry seems genuine but Debbie's peeved: he wants information from her yet won't give much of his own.

'On a property,' she says. 'Wattle Tree. I work there.'

His face lights up. 'It's beautiful out there.'

'You know it?' She's never seen him there, and when she mentioned his name to Bea she didn't say she knew him.

'I used to have a student who lived there. Previous owner's daughter. I'd give her piano lessons. She wasn't able to get into town so I'd go out there and sometimes stay for dinner.' His eyes close briefly. 'On a summer night it's magic. When the light changes and you can sit and watch those colours in the sky. And the riverbanks are so picturesque in the twilight.' He stops and looks at her as if he's surprised she's there. 'Sorry. I got carried away.'

'Not at all,' she says. 'You noticed more than I have. I'll pay attention from now on.'

He looks thoughtful, then spreads out the sheet music. 'I moved to Bellbird River for a change,' he says. 'And I stayed for the scenery.'

Debbie wants to ask why he needed a change, because it feels like a logical thing to say, yet it also feels like prying. He can tell her if he wants to.

'You know how a piece of music has layers?' he says, gesturing to the music in front of them.

Debbie nods.

'It can look like not much if you extrapolate each part on its own sheet, but when you put all the parts together there is such richness.' He glances at her then back to the music. 'I think the bush is like that. You can look at a patch of grass or a tree in isolation, but it isn't until you put it all together, stand back and let it really show itself to you, that you realise it's a symphony just waiting to be heard.'

Debbie realises her mouth has dropped open but she's never heard anyone talk about the landscape here with such affection. For Bea and Phil it's always about how it's 'bloody dry'; for the workers the land is a source of dust in their clothes and grass stalks in unexpected places. Wattle Tree is too brown or too green at all the wrong times.

'You sound like a romantic,' she says teasingly, because she can't think of a better word to describe his language.

'I probably am,' Warwick says, then frowns. 'Actually, I must be, to stick around.' He looks at his watch. 'We need to start. Time gets away.'

Debbie murmurs her agreement and as he plays the opening bars of the song she hears the first notes of the vocal in her head and hopes that she's ready to deliver them the way that ABBA intended.

CHAPTER 37

'I have no idea why you've asked me here,' Victoria says as she drapes her serviette across her lap and sits up straight in her chair.

'Because I wanted to have tea with you.'

Jimbo smiles at her and Victoria notices that one of the hairs in his left eyebrow has gone rogue. Ah, old age – she has chin hairs that do the same thing but at least she thinks to take the tweezers to them.

'Why did you come if you didn't know why I asked?' Jimbo goes on, leaning towards her.

Victoria sniffs. 'Because it's rude to refuse an invitation without a good reason. And I didn't have a good reason.'

If he analyses that closely he'll discover that her statement alone is rude, but the satisfied little smile on his face tells her that analysis is unlikely.

'I didn't even realise this place is open in the afternoons,' Victoria says as she scans the brief, handwritten menu. Cake, cake, cake, scones, biscuits, Swiss roll. Earl Grey tea. English Breakfast tea. The Twinings quinella.

'The CWA is trying to raise some extra funds. They've been opening each afternoon. Get some more customers.' His eyes are bright as they meet hers.

'You seem to know a lot about them,' Victoria says. 'As you're not a country woman, I'm intrigued that you are *au fait* with their association.'

'They do good work.' He picks up a sachet of sugar and gives it a shake before putting it back in a cup full of them. 'If you've made a choice I'll pop up to the counter and place the order.'

'English Breakfast tea and lemon cake, please,' she says, although she doesn't really feel like eating anything. She's had this odd pain in her stomach for the past couple of days and it's put her off food. But she knows that if she doesn't eat something he'll ask questions, because not eating cake in company in the country is tantamount to renouncing your family and friends.

As she watches him place the order, chatting amiably with the apron-clad woman holding a notepad, Victoria thinks that he's a nice man who's giving her a nice diversion for an hour or so. It's not in her nature to accept social invitations from men she doesn't know well but she's been feeling rattled lately. Gabrielle bumped into Arthur and Celeste by the river, then one of Victoria's friends from bridge said she'd seen them at the Tamworth Hotel having steak with mushroom sauce. Arthur's favourite. Victoria used to cook it for him and took particular pride in that sauce. She hasn't made a sauce since he left, content to use whatever Kraft produces and the local supermarket stocks.

The other day Gabrielle told her 'you're abandoning your identity, Vicky, *honestly*', because she isn't cooking much any more. But is cooking really her identity? Perhaps Gabrielle meant that Victoria is always caring for others and cooking is part of that.

She's a bit sick of caring for others after a lifetime of it. Caring for oneself is by far the nobler pursuit, she's decided, except lately she's felt so exhausted by everything that's happened over the past few months that caring for herself has meant opening tins of soup and doing nothing more strenuous in the kitchen than mashing potatoes. The house is nowhere near as clean as it used to be – and she doesn't care.

Nor does Gabrielle appear to, although Victoria is aware that Gabrielle probably hasn't done any housework since she moved overseas, given that in her letters she'd mention the 'divine girl' who did it for her. Every place she lived in had a 'divine girl'. Victoria began to wonder if it was code for something – was the divine girl actually Gabrielle's divine girl-*friend*? But a cousin shouldn't pry. If Gabrielle wanted to discuss her love life she would. And she never has.

'Shouldn't be long,' Jimbo says as he eases himself back into his chair, wincing as he lands.

'You're in pain,' Victoria states.

'Yep. My coccyx.'

'Your *what*?' Victoria feels it's somewhat early in their association to be so familiar.

'Coccyx,' Jimbo says matter-of-factly. 'Tailbone.'

'Oh.' Victoria blinks. That was close.

'I fell off a horse a few years ago – bam, right on it.' Jimbo shakes his head. 'Never been right since.'

'And the horse?'

Jimbo gives her a look of surprise and starts to laugh. 'Still going. But my son rides him these days. You ride?'

'Not for a long time.'

Victoria remembers her succession of steeds, each less spirited than the last as it became clearer and clearer that she wasn't as strong a horsewoman as her mother. She loved riding, though – the freedom of it. It was the one activity she could do that allowed her to be gone for hours – all day sometimes – and her parents didn't question it. Once she was married and a mother she daydreamed about that long-gone freedom and wished to have it back. Now that she is, in fact, free again she doesn't know what to do with all her spare time.

'I won't try to tempt you back,' Jimbo says. 'It's not much fun for me either.'

'I'm afraid I'd make a pony's knees buckle if I attempted to ride it.'

'What do you mean?'

'Jimbo,' Victoria says with a condescending tone, 'I'm sure you've noticed that I'm not a sylph.'

He stares into her eyes for so many seconds that Victoria looks away.

'I think you look lovely,' he says, sitting back as the apron-clad woman puts their pots of tea on the table. 'You always have.'

'That's very kind,' Victoria says, meaning it. She's gone without compliments for almost as long as she's gone without horses.

'Yeah, so . . .' He spins his teapot round a couple of times. 'I just thought we could get to know each other a bit better.' He looks up. 'We know each other to say hello to each other, but that's just casual stuff. It would be nice to have a conversation.' His eyes twinkle. 'Or two.'

Victoria takes a sip of tea and half-chokes on it.

'Are you all right?' Jimbo says, half out of his seat.

'Too hasty,' she gasps, the pain in her stomach distracting her. How irritating that it now seems to be caused by tea, of all things.

'Might be a bit hot,' Jimbo says, lifting the lid on his pot as if that will prove his theory.

'Might be,' Victoria agrees. Heat or no heat, her oesophagus is telling her to wait a while before she attempts another sip.

'You ever join the CWA?' Jimbo gestures to the crest over the door.

'No. I've never been good at crafts.'

'Really?' Jimbo picks up his fork and starts to hack into his slice of cake. 'You seem quite handy to me.'

'And *you* seem to have a lot of opinions about me,' Victoria says snippily, and regrets it when he looks aghast. Just because she's not feeling well, she shouldn't take it out on other people.

'I'm sorry,' she says. 'That was mean of me.'

'It's all right,' he says kindly.

'It's not.' Victoria fiddles with her teaspoon. 'Living with my diva cousin is affecting my manners.'

She thinks of Gabrielle's high-handedness on the phone when making appointments, or telling someone what she thinks of them when they walk on the wrong side of the footpath. It can rub off on a person if that person isn't vigilant – especially if there's no one around to keep a check on it.

Jimbo chuckles. 'She's a good egg.'

'You think?' Victoria arches an eyebrow. 'I didn't realise anyone else had noticed.'

'All bark and no bite.' He nods knowingly. 'I've seen her type before.'

'I won't tell her that you've worked her out,' Victoria says. 'She likes to think she's an enigma.'

'Don't we all.' Jimbo puts a sugar into his cup and stirs.

'Didn't you run for mayor once?' Victoria says, dredging up a memory, thinking she should do some of the lifting in this conversation.

'I did.'

'Why don't you tell me about it?' Victoria smiles. Not just because she wants to seem friendly to this harmless and well-meaning man who's provided a social opportunity for her, but because she knows that smiling can lighten your mood. And right now, with her body complaining, she hopes it will help her feel better.

Ten minutes later, as Jimbo continues his story of the close-run mayoral race, Victoria takes her second sip of tea and it goes down much more easily this time.

CHAPTER 38

'Are you and Victoria having a party?' Janine asks as she straightens up and slides the cupcakes into a paper bag. 'I beg your pardon?' Gabrielle knows what Janine means but sometimes she just likes to make people explain themselves. It's a quirk of her nature, and may have something to do with playing for time so she can formulate a response that she considers satisfactory.

Janine's nose twitches and she nods at the bag. 'That's a lot of cupcakes.'

Gabrielle presses her lips together. 'And what do you consider a lot?'

Janine looks mildly amused. 'There are six cakes and only two of you.'

'They're mainly for Victoria,' Gabrielle says.

This is an outrageous lie but Victoria isn't here to correct it and, besides, Gabrielle doesn't want anyone thinking *she* is going to eat that many cakes. She likes to tell people that she's on a diet, even if she never is.

'Right.' Janine raises her eyebrows.

Gabrielle hands over the money for the cakes, thanks her and turns to leave just as Debbie from the choir enters, with her hair in a ponytail for once. She looks almost like a different person – younger somehow.

'Hello, Deborah,' Gabrielle says cheerfully.

'It's Debbie.'

'What?'

'On my birth certificate.' She smiles almost apologetically. 'It says Debbie.'

'How unusual.' Gabrielle shrugs. Life is constantly surprising. 'I *am* enjoying your solo at rehearsal, Debbie. Sounding *lovely*. Toodle-oo!'

Gabrielle leaves the shop without waiting for a response, satisfied with having given her benediction. She meant it too: Debbie is a lovely singer. Beautiful tone and plenty of emotion.

The walk home never has a set time because occasionally she will bump into people who want to chat. Victoria's friends mostly, all trying to extract information about Arthur and Celeste that Victoria has clearly not given them and which Gabrielle wouldn't either, if she knew it. Today, however, no one stops her.

Humming to herself, as she so often does, she cradles the cakes as she approaches Victoria's house. And there, standing on the footpath, with his long arms folded across his chest, glaring down at her with his grey eyes in his handsome, if weathered, face, is someone she has moved halfway around the world to avoid.

Inhaling sharply, Gabrielle stops. 'Laurent,' she says, her voice breaking.

'Gabrielle.' He steps towards her.

She wants to say, 'What are you doing here?' but it's such a cliché and she has always been determined to avoid them. They indicate laziness and she has never advocated that – although the last few months of sitting around the house, playing the piano and not much else, suggest otherwise. She's been dealing with her grief, though. Grief about the life she used to have. The life that is now reinserting itself into her current existence in the form of Laurent.

'It has taken me a while to find you,' Laurent says, dropping his arms and standing very close to her.

'How did you?' she says quickly.

'Your friend in Sydney.' He pronounces it *Syd-neigh* in the way the French have.

She knows he means Ivan. Ivan is the only friend she told him about, and Ivan wouldn't know that Gabrielle doesn't want to see Laurent because she didn't mention it. So she can't blame him but she wants to. Because Laurent being here is going to turn into a bloody, sprawling mess, probably very shortly.

Across the road Gabrielle sees a head turning in her direction. Victoria is at bridge but the news will reach her in about twenty minutes that there's a strange man outside her home talking to her cousin. Gabrielle has to take Laurent inside.

She opens the door and nods for him to follow her, leading him into the kitchen where she deposits the cakes. This is as far as he'll get. Whatever he wants from her, he'll have to extract it right here. And she has a good idea of what it is.

When she told him she was going to have the surgery he said she had too much work lined up to take an indefinite break. Which was true: she had contracts all through 1998 and 1999, some into 2000, and as her manager he stood to make a lot of money off her. As her lover, he stood to have quite the glamorous lifestyle traipsing around after her. She sacked him from both roles, but didn't tell him. She just boarded a British Airways flight to London then a Qantas flight to Sydney.

Once she realised that her voice needed more time to recover than she'd allowed for – that's if it *can* recover – she knew Laurent wouldn't care. There were so many times when she hadn't wanted to do operas back to back at the pace he demanded. No, he'd said, she had to make the most of her popularity. Gabrielle said that performing without a proper break between roles could hurt her voice. He didn't care. She turned out to be right, but he never once let her be right about anything and even as she was recuperating he insisted that she had to be ready to perform soon. Instead she wrote a letter of apology to the next opera company that had contracted her and fled.

He'd been good for her for a while. Encouraging. Helpful. He'd made her a lot of money, and himself too of course. She'd spent a lot of it, as had he. They'd both presumed her career would continue and there would be time to save for her eventual retirement. But part of the reason for her leaving him was that she no longer wanted to provide for him.

'I am in debt,' he announces.

Gabrielle waits for him to continue. It's not her fault that he isn't any good at saving.

'Because you have not fulfilled your contracts there is a penalty to pay.'

He doesn't look angry, or even mildly upset, which unnerves her. Is she nothing but a business opportunity to him? They used to have fun. There was laughter. In a restaurant overlooking the caldera in Santorini, eating whitebait. At a nightclub in Monte Carlo. A Christkindlmarkt in Munich. So many times when they had enjoyed each other's company. Or perhaps that was her experience. Perhaps he was just keeping his moneymaker happy. Or it could be that by ditching him she's genuinely upset him and he doesn't want to show it. That would be the generous interpretation.

'You came all the way to Bellbird River to ask me for money? How did you afford the plane ticket to Australia?' Gabrielle keeps her voice steady.

'I have borrowed from friends,' he says evenly. 'As I have to pay these penalties. But they are not mine to pay, Gabrielle.'

His eyes are flinty now, and Gabrielle feels something she hasn't before: fear.

'I'm sorry,' she blurts. 'But you were going to make me sing and I – I – I didn't want to! I need time to recover.'

'Your career is over,' Laurent says with a flip of his hand. 'No one will hire you again after this.'

Gabrielle feels the blood drain out of her face. It has only happened once before, just before she fainted on stage in Milan. Her corset was too tight, which she had told the wardrobe girl *over and over*. But oh no, they wanted a small waist on her, so in they cinched and out she went, like a light.

She doesn't want to faint here, alone with this man she used to trust. Who knows what he might to do her while she's unconscious. So she grips the benchtop and tries to breathe properly while she contemplates what he's said. It simply cannot be the case.

'I don't believe you,' she says.

'Oh?' He sniffs.

'I am Gabrielle Reynold and I *will* return to the opera.' She pushes off the benchtop and gulps down some air, hands on her hips, making her face into a mask of defiance. 'But *you*, Laurent, will have nothing to do with it. *You* are the person who will not be hired.'

'I want my money,' he demands.

'And I want you to fall into a pit of lava, so I guess we are both disappointed!'

She hiccups, surprised at the ferocity of her own words. She can see he is too. Good. Now she has more control than she did before.

Grabbing the notepad that Victoria uses to keep shopping lists, Gabrielle shoves it at him along with a pen. 'Write down the figure then get out.'

She wants to have something to show Victoria, so they can talk about how she can manage this predicament.

For predicament it is: she has no doubt Laurent will take further, possibly legal, action if she doesn't give him what he wants. What he needs, rather. She knew, as she boarded that Qantas flight, that she was probably leaving him with this kind of problem. In the moment, though, she didn't want to think about it. She just wanted to go home. Laurent had always taken care of the business side of things and she thought he'd find a way to take care of this. He hasn't, but that's not his fault. Nor is it hers, really. Well, partially it is – if she'd been honest with those opera companies they may have let her out of the contracts. But she absolutely does not want them to know what's happened to her. Her shame is still real and present.

Laurent finishes writing and Gabrielle decides to look at the figure later. When she has a stiff drink in one hand and Victoria sitting beside her.

'Please leave,' she says.

Laurent frowns. 'That is all you have to say to me?'

Gabrielle makes a face. 'Will *au revoir* do?'

Then she flinches, realising what she's said. *Au revoir* means 'until we see each other again'. She has no intention of seeing him again.

'I think you mean *adieu*,' Laurent says softly.

She turns away, waiting for him to go.

After the door closes she picks up the notepad and shoves it in the pocket of her dress, then stomps upstairs to the piano, deciding that only 'Moonlight Sonata' will calm her down.

CHAPTER 39

It's mildly annoying that Alex has asked Debbie to come with them to this gig, but Janine didn't have a good reason to stop her. When Alex suggested it the other night at choir practice, saying that she thought Debbie was lonely and they should try to be friends, Janine had smiled and said nothing. What she wanted to say is that she thinks Debbie is lonely for a reason – that no one else wants to be her friend, probably because she's weird – but she didn't. She likes Alex; she respects her too. Alex always does what she says she's going to do and shows up when she says she will. If she tells Janine she's going to visit the bakery and buy donuts for Kim, she does.

Janine admires that because she recognises her own flakiness. At a certain point in her late teens she just stopped being reliable, and she's not even sure why. Maybe because she felt like her life had effectively stopped. Or stood still. In her tiny town she wasn't going anywhere, so why try to make anything happen? It's not a healthy way to think but it's there, in her brain. And it's probably why she didn't say no to Ross when he first turned up at the bakery. There was nothing else happening, and besides, he was a relic from the time before her life changed. Before *she* changed. Before Bradley got sick and then so did she.

She hasn't seen Bradley for three weeks. He's stopped calling her for a chat, which he used to do twice a week. It's punishment for her absence, or so she thinks – and she deserves it. It's just so tempting to become mired in her own hopelessness, like she used to. She's embarrassed to tell him that, because he genuinely has problems – serious health problems that he'll never get rid of – so she avoids him instead.

'Thanks for inviting me,' Debbie says as they walk into the pub, and Janine shakes herself out of her self-indulgent spiral.

'It's fine,' she says flatly while Alex turns her head and grins.

'It's great to have you here!' she says, and Debbie smiles bashfully in response.

Her hair isn't in plaits tonight – it's loose, not even in the ponytail she's had the past couple of weeks. Janine is surprised to see that she actually has quite long, thick hair that looks all right when it's brushed out. The sort of hair Janine would kill to have except, like so many other things in life, she never will. Not eating properly for years tends to mean a person's hair isn't in the best condition.

'I hope you like the band,' Alex continues as they push through the hordes of men clustered around the bar, men who are openly appraising them.

Janine can't help wanting their approval. She shouldn't tether her self-worth to the opinions of men she doesn't know, but it's hard not to when she's spent years not being attractive to anyone.

'Have you seen them before?' Debbie asks as they reach an empty table and pull out chairs.

'No, but one of the other teachers said they're good. Meant to have some originals as well as playing covers. All country music.' Alex laughs. 'It'll make a change from our choir roster of pop hits.'

'Warwick does like pop.' Debbie looks around nervously, as if she's worried about being overheard.

'Hey, how's your solo going?' Alex asks. 'Are we going to hear it soon?'

Debbie grimaces. 'I need a bit more practice.'

'I bet you're great.' Alex looks meaningfully at Janine. 'Don't you think, Janine?'

'Oh, yeah. Sure.' Janine nods. She *is* sure Debbie will be an excellent soloist, but right now she just wants the music to start so she can concentrate on something other than her vortex of thoughts.

'Deb!'

A nice-looking young man with sand-coloured hair is standing next to their table, hands on his hips, looking as if they've made his night.

'Oh – hi, George,' Debbie says, standing up as if he's her headmaster or something.

'You didn't say you were comin' into town.'

He's still grinning, so he's obviously not mad at her about it, although his grin is now mainly directed at Alex.

'Sorry, I, um, wasn't sure if you knew about the band,' Debbie says.

'Yeah, Dale's a mate.' He jerks his thumb over his shoulder in the direction of the bar. 'Jacko's here too. So is Mitch. Now – can I buy you ladies a drink?'

He looks as if he'd like nothing better in the whole world.

Alex stands up. 'I'm heading to the bar, so I'll get us drinks.' She looks at Debbie and Janine in turn. 'Chardy?'

'Yep,' says Janine and Debbie nods.

'Well, you can come to the bar with me,' says George, 'but I'm buying the drinks.'

Alex starts to protest but George just offers her the crook of his elbow.

To Janine's surprise, Alex takes it. Alex hasn't struck her as the sort of woman who'd go off with a strange man. But then George clearly isn't a stranger to Debbie.

'So how do you know him?' Janine asks as she watches Alex laughing on her way to the bar.

'We work together. Sort of. We work at the same place. I'm mainly in the house and he's on the land. He was there the other night when I saw you and Alex at the Imperial Hotel.'

Janine stares at her then starts to laugh. She knows it's rude, but she can't help it – although she should stop, because Debbie looks offended.

'Sorry,' Janine says, 'but that's the most you've said to me since you first came into the shop. I guess I'm surprised.'

Debbie presses her lips together and fiddles with the fringing on her leather jacket. 'I didn't think you liked me,' she says quietly. 'You don't talk to me at practice.'

Janine immediately feels guilty. 'I don't talk to anyone,' she says, trying to sound casual about it but aware of how much that makes her sound like the loner she has undoubtedly become.

'You talk to Alex,' Debbie says, almost accusingly.

'Nup. *Alex* talks to *me*.'

It's the truth. And it makes Janine feel tired. Really to-the-bone tired of being who she is. The local woman who knows most people on sight yet who can't be bothered talking to anyone first. She can't remember if she was always like this but she thinks that maybe, years ago – when she and Ross were still a couple, before Bradley got sick – she wasn't.

Being a fully engaged human takes work. And as tired as she is of being herself, she's more tired at the thought of having to do that work. It would have been easier to keep it going than to have lost it and have to build it up again. She knows this from painting: if she does a little bit each day she is more likely to improve than if she stops and starts. Yet she hasn't applied that to life off the canvas and outside her shed. That's because life involves other people, and other people can decide she's unworthy of their company, too boring, too stagnant. Her paints and brushes don't have responses.

'It's nothing personal,' she says to Debbie, because she has to say something. In a corner of her brain there's an awareness that she shouldn't be deliberately hurtful to someone who hasn't hurt her. 'I'm just not very chatty.'

'Hm.' Debbie looks away.

'And you don't talk either!' Janine says, trying to sound jolly, like they're two antisocial freaks having a kumbaya moment.

'I don't know anyone,' Debbie says quietly.

Janine can see Alex and George chatting, three glasses of white wine by Alex's elbow and a schooner of beer next to them. By the look of things, the chardonnay will be warm by the time they drink it.

'Yeah, I figured,' Janine says.

Indeed, she knows that Debbie doesn't know anyone because she also knows – everyone does – that the owners of Wattle Tree advertised for a housekeeper and the person who got the job didn't come from the local area. Janine worked out who Debbie was after she first came into the bakery. Not long after that, some of her more gossipy customers asked if 'the shy lass with the plaits' had been in yet, and had Janine heard that she was out at Wattle Tree with those city people who would probably go bust soon because they didn't know anything about the land?

So, yes, Janine knows a lot about Debbie and has used none of that knowledge to try to get to know her better, even though they have a common interest in the choir. If anything were proof that she's lost the use of her human muscle, this would be it.

'How are you going at Wattle Tree?' she asks, awakening the tendons of that muscle.

Debbie looks surprised. 'It's fine. The people are nice.' She turns her head to glance at George, who now has his hand on Alex's shoulder. 'George is the best of the boys. He's sweet.' She smiles. 'Looks like he and Alex are getting along.'

'Any fellas for you out there?' Janine says, feeling bold.

Debbie's eyes meet hers, and they're darker than they were. Janine can't read them.

'No,' Debbie says. 'I'm not interested.'

Janine isn't sure what to make of that so she says nothing.

'I was married,' Debbie goes on, now fiddling with the chunky silver ring on her right middle finger. 'I think once was enough.'

Janine nods, not sure if Debbie wants her to ask more questions or just listen. *This* is why conversation is so hard. You have to take risks, figure out the stakes for each subject and decide if you push or hold back. It's a lot of work.

Just then Alex returns and puts the glasses of wine on the table. 'Sorry I took so long!' she says, her cheeks pink. She turns to Debbie. 'He's funny, that friend of yours.'

Debbie nods, glances quickly at Janine then away.

'So what have I missed out on?' Alex asks as she sits.

'Nothing much,' says Janine. If Debbie wants to repeat that personal detail to Alex, it's up to her.

'The band's coming on stage,' Debbie says, picking up her glass and taking a long sip.

Alex grins and nudges her elbow into Janine's. 'What a great night!'

Janine nods because that's the thing to do, then nurses her wine until it's warm and she doesn't want it any more.

CHAPTER 40

lex peels the boiled eggs so she can mash them with mayonnaise and salt, then make Kim's favourite sandwiches. The ones she won't take to school any more because some kid started saying she had 'stinky egg sandwiches', then other kids started calling her Stinky Egg.

If Alex weren't so frustrated about it she'd have to admire the creativity of nasty children. They seem to continually come up with new insults, each as hurtful as the last, producing an oeuvre of barbs that would have made Alexander Pope proud, although even he might have thought some of them too extreme.

'Did you really knit that?' she hears her mother say in the living room.

Kim had to knit a scarf for a school project. Alex cast on for her but Kim did the rest. The wool is poo brown and electric blue, a combination only a devoted grandmother could love.

'Yes,' Kim replies, giggling. 'Do you like it?'

It's the first time since they've moved here that Alex can hear happiness in Kim's voice. If only the source of it weren't Marta, because her mother will return to Sydney soon.

Despairing about Kim's glumness, Alex paid for Marta to take the train to Quirindi, where Alex and Kim picked her up.

On the drive there Kim was so excited she kept undoing her seatbelt. Alex wanted to do her bad-cop mothering routine and threaten to take away something that Kim would care about, then realised that the main thing Kim cares about is fairly virtuous: books. So she resorted to threatening the future.

'If you do that again, Kim,' she said in as severe a tone as she could muster, 'there's no chance of us getting a dog.'

It had worked, and the belt stayed clipped in right until they rolled up to the station and Kim was out of it and out the car door before Alex had turned the engine off.

She wanted to yell at her about danger, but out here it's so unlikely another car is going to be driving by at the exact moment she stopped that there's no point. Plus Kim really is a good kid. She usually goes to bed when Alex tells her to. She eats all her vegetables. She brushes her teeth. The only problem Alex has with her is the one she's had a hand in creating: the loneliness Kim has felt since they moved to Bellbird River.

'I love it, my darling,' Marta says. 'May I wear it?'

'Yes!' More giggles from Kim. It is the most delicious sound.

Alex used to wish she'd recorded Kim's baby chortles and toddler laughs, because those were the sounds she'd replayed in her mind when she was trying to get to sleep each night, worrying about money, worrying about time. The remembered sound of her daughter's joy was a balm.

Since arriving in Bellbird River she's wished she'd recorded Kim's slightly older-child giggles too, since they've also disappeared. Not that Alex needs them as she needed the others, because she doesn't have trouble falling asleep any more. The time and money problems have been solved by moving to a small, cheap town on the same salary she was on before. Now she has a Kim problem instead.

'When are you going home, Grandma?' There's a shift in Kim's tone.

'Tomorrow, my darling. You know that.'

Mashing of eggs finished, Alex compiles the sandwiches, tuning her ears more closely to the conversation. Kim may be about to have the same kind of meltdown she had yesterday when Marta mentioned returning to Sydney.

'I don't want you to go,' Kim says, running her words together.

'I know, Kimmy.'

There's a dull sound that Alex guesses is her mother hugging Kim.

'Can I go with you?' Kim asks, with sniffles.

'My darling, I always love to see you, but you belong here with your mother.'

Alex is relieved that Marta is following this line, as they discussed, because yesterday she had suggested to Alex that she take Kim home with her and re-enrol her in her old school so Alex could get on with 'your new life'.

'Kim *is* my life!' she'd shouted, and she shouldn't have, because Kim was in the garden and could have heard her. 'She's the reason I moved here!'

Marta had glowered at her, the lines beside her mouth deepening. With her hair always in a too-tight bun that pulls taut the skin around the hairline, her mother's face is often a combination of ersatz facelift and anger – at least in Alex's presence.

'Don't make excuses,' Marta had said. 'You wanted to move here. You gave her no choice.'

'Because she's a *child*, Mama. She doesn't get to make those sorts of choices yet. Remember? You used to tell me that it didn't matter if I didn't like something you did; I'd have to wait until

I was an adult, then I could make choices of my own. Well, I'm an adult now.'

Marta had pursed her lips tighter, which sharpened her prominent cheekbones, then left the room.

Alex can't blame Marta for taking Kim's side. In fact, she kind of loves her for it, because she wants Kim to have a good relationship with her grandmother. It's comforting to think that – God forbid – if anything were to happen to her, Grandma could step in.

Only once has Marta ever asked if Alex has considered that something might happen to Kim. She only has one child. No second child as an insurance policy. If Kim dies, that's it. Marta had said it so matter-of-factly, and Alex had been so shocked that she'd left the room, although she knew her mother was right. Kim is her everything. That's why she doesn't want to leave Bellbird River – she's seen more of Kim over the past few months than she has in years.

Sandwiches made, she takes them into the living room, where Kim is indeed curled into her grandmother's side.

'Lunch is ready,' Alex says cheerily.

'I don't want it.' Kim burrows further in.

'It's your favourite, darling – egg and mayonnaise sandwiches.'

'I don't want them,' Kim mumbles.

'Come on, my darling, Mummy's made them just for you.' Marta cajoles her like she's six years old. 'And I am so hungry – I can't wait to eat one.'

Alex meets her mother's eyes and sees something surprising there: understanding. No doubt because Alex and her brother also refused food that she'd made them, never for a good reason other than they were in a snit or they had something else they wanted to do.

'I'll eat them if I can move back to Sydney with Grandma,' Kim says, her chin lifting.

Wonderful – Kim has now moved to a more sophisticated level of blackmail, beyond the type that all children practise of the 'I'll brush my teeth if I can have/do/go to . . .' variety. Alex can't wait until she's a teenager and the scheming will really begin.

Now Marta looks away from Alex, and Alex hopes like hell that her mother hasn't been putting ideas in Kim's head. She invited Marta here thinking it would calm the situation, not inflame it.

'Kim, we've talked about this,' Alex says, keeping her voice steady. 'We're staying in Bellbird River. Things will improve, I'm sure. Kids get bored. They move on to other targets.'

She doesn't even know if that's true but she can wish.

Kim's face pinches and her eyes are wide and bright. 'Then I'll run away.'

'Please don't say things like that,' Alex says, exasperated. 'I know you're having a hard time. I am so, so sorry that I can't fix it. But you can't move back to Sydney. Not without me. And I'm not leaving here.'

Maybe she's being selfish. Maybe she's just a bad mother. But given she has all the care *and* all the responsibility for this child, Alex thinks it's reasonable that she protects a way of life that has been beneficial for her. She has time for activities here. For new friends. For going out at night, whoop-de-doo! And she can still keep up her job and her housework and the shopping and the gardening. If they went back to Sydney she would have time only for the non-fun things. And if she can't be content in her own life she can't show Kim how to be content in hers – even if that's a while off.

Kim and Marta look at each other conspiratorially and Alex's heart lurches. They *have* been up to something.

'Then I want to spend school holidays at Grandma's,' Kim says.

Alex's mouth drops open. She supposes it's not an unreasonable request but it feels like one. She's about to say as much when Marta stops her with a subtle shake of her head and a flaring of her nostrils.

Ah, now she gets it. Marta is missing Kim too. Really missing her in a way she's probably never missed Alex.

Perhaps because Marta wasn't on her own when Alex left home. She wasn't a widow yet; her life hadn't changed the way it does when you used to be part of a couple and now you're not, and your friends start shifting the way they socialise with you because they can't figure out what to do with you. Which is pure laziness and lack of imagination on their part, although that doesn't help the pain of it. Alex doesn't know what it's like to be in a couple, but she does know what it's like to have people not know what to do with you because you don't fit into their stereotyped conception of how humans are meant to live.

So Marta needs Kim too, and loves her greatly. They love each other. It's a good thing. A heart-warming thing. It is also, Alex can see, a way that they can possibly all get something they want: Alex can have more time to herself, Kim can spend time with Marta, and Marta's heart can feel full again.

'All right,' she says, and catches the flicker of joy on her daughter's face. Her own heart expands; a parent can go for days on the energy that sort of thing generates.

'Now will you eat my sandwiches, please?' Alex says, smiling to show she's not unhappy about Kim's demand.

'Can I start school holidays early?'

'*Kimberly.*'

Kim looks at Alex guiltily then looks away. But she stands up and walks to the table and picks up a plate. When she takes a big bite of sandwich, Alex feels like they're finally getting back on track.

CHAPTER 41

Debbie's never been sure why people say they feel like they're 'having kittens' when they're nervous. She feels more like she's going to vomit, which is not at all like having kittens and more like having your guts put into a tumble dryer. She even has that acidy taste in her mouth that foretells vomiting. Great. Great. *Great*. She's going to vomit in the gutter and that's what her children will see.

She's still not really sure if they're actually coming, because when Julia called her yesterday nothing seemed to be certain.

The phone rang in the kitchen and Debbie answered it, as she always does when she knows she's the only one in the house. Bea was collecting eggs from the chooks or killing a snake or making damper for a dozen workers or something. There are always a million and one things to do at Wattle Tree.

'Hello?' she said in her cheerful Wattle Tree voice. It's the only place she uses it, because she likes to be professional.

'Hello – is Debbie there, please?'

For a second she wasn't sure if she heard correctly because the only person who's called the house looking for her is Warwick, and the woman on the other end of the phone definitely wasn't him. It was irrational but she immediately thought she was in trouble again. Something she didn't even know about had caught up with her. But she was reporting to the local police when she was meant to, and she hadn't even done so much as speed since she left prison, so she couldn't think what it could be. Which didn't help her galloping, panicking mind.

'Speaking,' she said, her voice quavering.

'Oh. Hi.' A pause. 'It's Julia.'

Julia. Greg's Julia. The panic didn't exactly dissipate.

'Is everything all right?' Debbie said in a rush.

'Sorry. Yes. Yes!' Julia laughed nervously. 'It's fine. The kids are fine.'

The kids are fine. It was so strange to hear another woman say that about her children.

Debbie was silent. She wasn't sure what else she and Julia had to say to each other.

'I actually rang to see how *you* are,' Julia said.

More silence, because this was hard to compute. Julia – the woman who is now her children's stepmother – was making a social call?

'Um . . . I'm fine,' Debbie said.

Silence. One second, two seconds, three . . .

'I don't think you can be, Debbie,' Julia said, as kindly as if she was Debbie's best friend in the whole world, and Debbie almost cried, right there.

There are so few women who have been kind to her. Her own mother doesn't talk to her, too ashamed of what happened. Her sister hasn't called since she got out, although Debbie has left messages with the Wattle Tree number. The closest she's come to kindness is from Alex and Janine, but they're not friends yet. They're not close enough to sound like they care as much as Julia sounds like she does.

But it's not so strange, really, is it? They share children. If Debbie'd had the chance to talk to Julia on her own before this, maybe she'd have been kind too. She knows she's not a bad person, just a mixed-up one. She used to be good to people, back before she stopped being good to herself.

'Um,' was all she could bring herself to say.

She could hear Julia breathing.

'The children miss you,' Julia said. 'I know they do. They just don't . . . want to say it.'

From there Julia made the suggestion that Debbie come to Tamworth to see Emily and Shaun, no Greg, just Julia with them. She would tell Greg, she said, but she thought the children would be more willing to talk to Debbie if he wasn't there.

The thing is, now that Debbie's waiting for them, she feels more nervous than she did when she saw them last time. Last time their reaction to her was unknown. This time she knows how that went: they could barely look at her. She's not sure if she can handle that again.

Except she has to try, because they're her kids and how can she not? With every single cell of her she wants to be part of their lives again. Once upon a time they were part of her body, and that body aches now she's separated from them. Of course she has to try, no matter what she thinks it might cost her.

So she's here at Oxley Lookout, as good a place as any, she guesses. If they have nothing to say to each other at least they can look at the view – 270 degrees, pretty much, to the east, west and south, the town laid out below them. There are blossoms on some wattle bushes near the picnic tables. They're early. Wattle Day isn't until August, Debbie is sure. Or maybe that's changed since she went away. For an autumn day it's not too bad – the sun is warm on her back as she sits at a picnic table, or what she guesses is a picnic table, and watches as a Volvo station wagon pulls up nearby and her children get out of it.

This is the weirdest part of what's happened in her life these past few years: that she feels so wound up about seeing the two people she gave birth to. She never even considered that could happen. She didn't consider much, as it turned out – never thought ahead to the potential consequences of her actions. If she had stopped, just once, and realised that punishment for what she was doing could mean Greg taking her children away, she wouldn't have continued on the same path. Or she likes to think she wouldn't have. Because the truth of it is that she was pretty bloody selfish back then.

'Hi Emily, hi Shaun,' she says as she stands and walks towards them, smiling as brightly as she can.

She sees Julia closing her car door and smiles vaguely. Are they meant to greet each other like friends now? Even if they're not friends? She's not sure what they are. What's the term for this – 'co-mothers'?

'Hi,' the kids chorus. They don't say 'Mum' but nor do they say 'Debbie', which she thinks would break her heart.

'Hello, Debbie,' says Julia, and up close Debbie can see that she is prettier than she looked in the park that day, and also older.

'Hi, Julia. Um – would you like to sit? I brought some cupcakes. There's a bakery in Bellbird River. That's near where I live. I got passionfruit for you, Em, and . . .'

She stops. Is she still allowed to call her daughter Em? One glance tells her that Emily doesn't look perturbed.

'And chocolate for you, Shaun. And, um, Julia, I wasn't sure what you'd like so I brought a mix.'

Debbie gestures to the paper bags as if she's making an offering. Which, in a way, she is. This picnic table is the altar of her future and she hopes to appease the gods.

'Thanks, Debbie, that's thoughtful of you.' Julia smiles encouragingly. 'Greg doesn't like them having sugary things but I think we can have a special treat today, kids, can't we?'

'Yep,' says Shaun as he opens a bag to look inside.

'Thanks, Mum.' Emily opens a different bag, then grins as she sees the contents.

Debbie feels the prick of tears. *Mum.* She's back to being Mum. For this instant at least.

'I thought it might be easier to start with food,' she says, almost apologetically, like she has to explain her parenting methods to Julia.

Julia laughs. 'I get it. If Greg wasn't so strict about the sugar thing I'd probably bribe them with sweets every time they say they don't want to do their homework.'

Debbie sits down on the bench again and is surprised when Julia sits next to her.

'Em, leave it,' Shaun says warningly as Emily puts a fingertip on sprinkles that have fallen on the tabletop.

'But they're yummy!' she whines.

He shakes his head. 'You don't know what's been there.'

'God, he sounds like Greg,' Debbie says.

'He sure does.' Julia nods. 'They're peas in a pod.'

Debbie doesn't know how she's meant to converse with Julia. How do you start a conversation about your own children with someone who knows them better than you do? There's so much to say, and so much that is impossible to say.

'I, ah . . .' Debbie swallows. She wishes she were better with words. Like Alex. Alex could, as Janine said the other night, have a conversation with a brick wall. She's just good at it. Or practised at it. Maybe it's because she's a teacher and she's had to do it with parents and children.

At Wattle Tree Debbie isn't around many people, and Bea is pretty gentle on her as far as conversationalists go. So she decides to just say what's in her heart, rather than what's playing on her mind, because trying to get what's on her mind to her tongue is so often her issue.

'Thank you,' she says, and Julia looks surprised.

Debbie swallows again. 'Thank you for being there for them,' she continues. 'When I wasn't.'

She jerks when Julia pats her hand. 'Sorry. I'm not used to people touching me.'

'Oh, right.' Julia smiles awkwardly. 'I'm a toucher. A hugger, really.' She looks into Debbie's eyes. 'So the kids have had lots of hugs. I just want you to know that.'

Debbie knows she's said it to be a reassurance but instead it makes her feel like collapsing. It's her job to hug her children. More than a job – a vocation. A life. She's had so many years without their hugs.

This time as Julia puts her hand on her back Debbie doesn't flinch. 'I didn't mean to make you upset,' Julia murmurs.

Now Shaun and Emily are looking at them, eyes wide.

'I'm all right,' Debbie says, smiling quickly. 'I'm just so happy to see you both.'

Shaun shrugs and Emily wipes icing off her top lip.

Debbie stands. 'Who wants to come and look at the view? I haven't been up here before.'

'I think we all do,' Julia says, also standing. 'I haven't seen it in ages.'

Clutching their cupcake bags the children race off.

'I think we should make a regular day,' Julia says, 'for you to see them.'

Debbie holds her breath. She wanted this but wasn't going to ask for it. It isn't her place to make demands of Julia.

'Maybe once a month?' Julia suggests. 'Just to start with.'

'Yes.' Debbie nods vigorously. 'Yes, please. I'd love that.'

Julia smiles and shoves her hands in her jeans pockets. 'Maybe we could come to you next time.'

Debbie imagines the children coming to Wattle Tree and wonders what they'll think about her living in a house with other people's children. But she'll worry about that later. For now, she has more than she dared hope for.

'Great,' she says, 'thank you. Thank you, Julia, really.'

'No,' Julia says seriously. 'Thank *you*.'

For a second she looks sad, then she wanders off towards the children, her hands still in her pockets. Debbie follows her two seconds later.

WINTER 1998

Cockatoo

CHAPTER 42

The smell of minestrone – or something very much like it – wafts up the stairs. As Gabrielle descends to the kitchen from the piano room she pulls her thick cardigan tighter and swishes her scarf around her neck. The first floor of the house is warm enough with the fire on in the sitting room, but Victoria doesn't think the ground floor should be heated. Almost as if she doesn't think winter in Bellbird River is as perishing as it actually is. Gabrielle has spent winters in countries that have *snow*, for Verdi's sake, and she has *never* been as cold as she is here. Australians do not understand central heating. Or perhaps they don't believe in it.

She told Victoria she was going to practise her scales, and Victoria of course thought she meant her vocal scales but instead she practised piano scales. It wasn't a lie. Which is what she'll tell Victoria if she's challenged. She simply prefers to work on her voice when Victoria is out of the house, which she will be tomorrow morning because she's going to Willow Tree to see a friend. Or maybe it's Werris Creek. One of them. Both start with W. How can she be expected to keep it straight? She has a lot on her mind. And Victoria knows so many people.

Gabrielle wonders if her cousin was this busy before Arthur left her or if she's filling up her days flitting about. It's almost as if she's running for council. Again. Except Victoria has sworn off local government. All forms of government, although some man from the National Party was here the other day to see if she'd be interested in running for preselection for the state election next year. Victoria informed him that she's about to be unmarried and voters don't like that sort of thing; besides, she's past legal retirement age so she didn't think it a good idea. The man looked somewhat disappointed but was sent on his way with a suggestion for someone else who might do.

'Finished already?' Victoria says as she stirs the contents of the large saucepan. Then she sighs.

She's been doing that a lot lately. Gabrielle would like to ask why, but Victoria is one of those people who thinks it's rude when their most intimate companions ask prying questions. She will offer the information when she's ready. Which may never happen. It's annoying to someone as gossipy as Gabrielle but she's learning to adjust.

'I have.' She peers into the saucepan. 'Is that minestrone?'

'It's whatever was in the vegetable drawer that was about to go off,' says Victoria, adding salt.

'How appetising.' Gabrielle plonks herself at the kitchen table.

'You're welcome to cook for yourself,' Victoria snaps.

'You know I can't,' Gabrielle says with the satisfaction of someone who made a decision long ago to always ensure she could never be responsible for someone else's dinner.

'It's not hard.' Victoria turns and arches an eyebrow. 'Stock. Vegetables. Simmer. Stir.'

'Oh, I'm sure it's more complicated than that.'

Gabrielle is not at all sure because she's never tried it. Although she's pleased to see Victoria cooking, because lately she's seemed too tired to do anything much.

Victoria sniffs, then puts down her wooden spoon. 'I'll leave it for a little while. Glass of red?'

'Why not?'

Victoria moves towards the opposite end of the kitchen, winces and stops, putting a hand to her left side.

'I'll get it.' Gabrielle stands up. 'Is it that pain again?'

'Mmm.' Victoria rubs in the area of her ribcage. 'Like a stitch that won't go away. And given I've hardly been exerting myself, I can't figure it out.'

'Have I not told you to go to the doctor?'

'You have. And I went. As I told you.'

'And?'

'He said I need to eat less. Lose a bit of weight. So . . .' She gestures to the saucepan. 'Soup it is.'

'Well, *I* am not on a diet. Why should I be subjected to soup? What if I want more?' Gabrielle has never been a fan of restricting herself.

'There's bread in the freezer.'

Victoria sits down as Gabrielle takes the cork out of the bottle of shiraz and pours them both a glass.

'So I have something to tell you.' Gabrielle places a glass in front of her cousin.

She should have told Victoria what she's about to tell her the same day Laurent appeared but she didn't, thinking that if she ignored it perhaps the problem would magically disappear. That has, in fact, worked for her in the past but only for minor issues, so it was perhaps naïve to think it could work for this. But there's no harm in dreaming.

'You're pregnant,' Victoria says drolly.

'Hilarious.' Gabrielle takes a swig of shiraz, as if to prove her point. 'No.'

'You're going back to Europe.'

Oh, how Gabrielle wishes it could be that. But, no.

'Not that either.' She sits down opposite her cousin.

'Arthur has left Celeste for you?'

'All right, all right.' Another swig. Her best Pollyanna smile. Victoria now looks weary of guessing. Or of something.

'The other day,' Gabrielle starts, 'I had a visitor.' She pauses, unable to resist a dramatic effect. 'Laurent.'

Victoria's nostrils flare. 'I thought you fired him? Years ago. Didn't you? It was in one of your letters.'

Gabrielle has written Victoria several letters over the years so it's possible she did say this. Because she did fire Laurent briefly. Just before they became lovers. Then he persuaded her to hire him again, which she knew was likely to be a mistake but he was just so talented in so many ways and . . .

No, she needs to stop thinking of those talents. If she'd never gone to bed with him he would have stayed fired and she wouldn't be trying to think of how to get rid of him again. Sometimes, when she wants to absolve herself of responsibility – which is fairly often – she will tell herself that it's hard to meet attractive men in her line of work and she has to take the opportunities that present themselves. *Yes*, it would have been better if she hadn't mixed her business with her pleasure but she doesn't regret all of it. Just the business parts.

'I did fire him but I hired him again,' she says. 'And he was still my manager when I left Europe. More than my manager.' She avoids Victoria's eyes.

Victoria sips her wine. 'So why is he in Australia? Because you broke his heart?'

'I . . .' Gabrielle tilts her head from one side to the other like she's a puppy waiting for a treat. Which she is: she's waiting for Victoria's absolution, because it's so much nicer when someone *else* tells you that you're off the hook.

'I didn't really tell him that I wasn't going to be able to fulfil some contracts,' she says lightly, no big deal.

Victoria lifts her chin and looks down her nose. Gabrielle is familiar with this: her cousin in pre-judgement mode.

'And . . . ?' Victoria prompts.

'And there were clauses about notice periods and penalties for lack of notice,' Gabrielle says in a rush.

Victoria's eyes narrow. 'So you flew to Australia without telling him?'

'Yes.' Sip. Sip. Gulp. Shiraz really is a lovely grape. Of course, Gabrielle had a lot of syrah – its French relation – when she lived overseas and she could be a *terrible* wine snob about it if she chose but—

'How much do you owe him?'

That makes Gabrielle stop. She was expecting Victoria to lecture her before they arrived at the money.

'I, ah . . .' Sip. Sip. Gulp. End of glass. 'Apparently forty thousand US dollars or thereabouts. Different currencies involved, you know, so that's just an estimate using American currency as a common denominator.'

She smiles as if it's all silly-me-I-should-have-known-better. Which she should have. She signed those contracts and she was aware that there were penalty clauses for her failure to fulfil her obligations. But how could she tell anyone that she can't sing the way they expect? It was better to abscond. At least she still has her dignity. As a singer, if not as a person.

Victoria takes a slow sip of her wine and Gabrielle gets up to refill her own glass.

'Oh no,' Victoria says sharply. 'Stay where you are.'

Gabrielle obediently sits as Victoria, perversely, stands and walks to the stove to give the soup a stir, before returning to the table. She does not, unfortunately, refill Gabrielle's glass.

'Well, we have to come up with the money,' Victoria says at last.

'We?' Gabrielle feels excessively relieved and also guilty, because she didn't want to draw Victoria into this. Not really.

'I'm not going to have you bothered by that Frenchman.'

Now Gabrielle feels like a child who is watching someone else being punished for her misdeed: pleased she's getting away with it but aware that she shouldn't be. As she's no longer a child, she probably should say something.

'It's not his fault,' she murmurs with as much contrition as she can muster. 'I shouldn't have done it.'

'As your *manager* it is his job to *manage* these things, not let them get to the point where you owe this much money.' Victoria holds up a hand. 'But it's done now and we have to face the consequences.'

'But I don't have the money. And neither do you.'

Victoria shrugs. 'I have a divorce coming up. My humiliation at Arthur's hands is worth something. I've already talked to my lawyer about it but now I have an incentive to increase the penalty. And I have some money saved. My grandmother – on Mama's side – left me a little. Not enough for this, but it will help.'

She turns her glass on the tabletop, gazing into it. 'If I can offer any advice at this juncture,' she says slowly, 'and it's advice I intend to take myself, it would be that men are to be avoided, romantically speaking.'

She looks into Gabrielle's eyes. 'If he was just your manager he might not have become so aggrieved. But the other involvement raises the stakes. You've hurt his feelings. That's compound interest. You, me, women in general – we can all do without that. Men cost us too much.'

She gets to her feet. 'Now, I have a soup to serve.'

Gabrielle watches as her cousin walks slowly to the stove and pulls the saucepan from the burner.

'Thank you,' she says. 'For helping me.'

'Of course.' Victoria picks up a ladle. 'I love you. Why wouldn't I help you?'

For all her glamorous, exciting years abroad, Gabrielle never once had someone say they love her and mean it. Coming home has cost her in some ways, but it has been worth it in so many others.

She watches Victoria stir the soup for a while longer, as they chat about the parlous state of the neighbour's vegetable garden – seen over the back fence – then have their soup, listen to some music, and sit in companionable silence until the late hour draws them towards slumber.

CHAPTER 43

The sign is turned from *Open* to *Closed*, although the door is unlocked so Ross can get in. Janine has switched off the lights at the front and packed up the small number of surplus goods. They are pretty accurate at estimating how much is going to sell each day, and the locals have been trained to get in early because the bakery can run out of things, so usually there's not much to take home. Today it's three finger buns and a couple of loaves of bread. They'll go into her mother's big chest freezer. Waste not, want not. The bread can become bread-crumbs, or bread-and-butter pudding. The finger buns will be resurrected for morning tea.

In the minutes before Ross arrives Janine always feels like she's pedalling in place, and today she is pedalling harder. She's nervous after what happened the last time she saw him. He wasn't happy that she left. Or, rather, he wasn't happy that he didn't get what he expected to. He hasn't come to the bakery since.

She saw him on the street two evenings ago, as she was walking home from work. She wasn't near his house so she thought he might have done it on purpose. He was on the other side of the road, walking slowly, his hand clutching one of those mobile phones that people seem to like but which Janine can do without. Who needs to phone or be phoned all the time?

His head turned towards her and his mouth opened, as if he was going to say something. Then his mobile phone rang. It wasn't until he answered that Janine realised she felt nervous. Or maybe more than nervous: scared. But she didn't know if she was scared that he would be angry with her for leaving or scared that he might call off the whole thing. Or scared that she wanted it called off but lacked the courage to do it. Because that would involve admitting she's been carrying on with him for no reason. That there was never any reason apart from, maybe, causing herself pain.

He called the bakery yesterday and said he wanted to see her. And she, still not willing to avoid that pain, told him she'd wait for him after work, as she had been.

The phone in the shop rings and Janine walks swiftly to answer it, knowing it can only be one of her parents, hoping that whatever they have to say is quick so they can't hear the door opening when Ross arrives.

'Hello?' she says.

'Janine, it's your father.'

'Hi, Dad.' She waits.

'Your brother has been arrested,' he says.

Your brother. Dad hasn't said his name in years.

'What's happened?' she says, trying to sound calm. Her parents aren't going to deal with whatever this is so she'll have to.

'Drunk and disorderly.' Her father sounds cross, like Bradley is a wild teenager not a sick man.

'Really? He doesn't drink.'

Her father sniffs. 'Seems he does.'

Janine twirls the phone cord. She is sure Bradley wouldn't have been drinking – or is she? When he was diagnosed he told her that he'd never drink again because there was too much else going on in his body, natural and pharmaceutical.

'So he's in a Tamworth cop shop?' she asks.

'Werris Creek.'

'Werris . . . What?' It's over half an hour's drive from Tamworth – she can only wonder what he's doing there.

There's silence on the line.

'I'll go,' she says.

Of course she will. Even if her parents were talking to their son she'd still go, because she wouldn't want them to have to deal with it. It'll be messy, and they've had enough mess – from her, from her brother.

'Thanks, love.'

'I'll go now. Bye.'

She hangs up, then picks up her bag and keys from the store-room, turning off lights as she comes back through the shop, locking as she goes. There's no way to leave a note for Ross – if she puts it on the door some nosy neighbour will see it and ask her parents about it. She can't exactly call him either. He'll just have to turn up and be disappointed.

Maybe she should feel bad about that instead of what she really feels: relieved. Because she's just the tiniest bit afraid of what he's going to want from her tonight, given what he didn't get from her the last time.

She trots home faster than she ever has and yanks open the door of her car, which she leaves on the street so her father can use the driveway. As she hops in she glances towards the house and sees the front curtain shift slightly. Her mother, probably.

Janine wonders if she wants to come out and join her to check on her only son. And if so, why she doesn't just get over whatever hang-up she has about Bradley's illness and do it.

There's no light on Jumbuck Way as Janine turns left and heads north. The moon is new and the stars, though brighter, aren't enough to show her the asphalt. But she knows this road so well she's not worried. She and Bradley would tear along it as teenagers, heading for Tamworth and friends and underage drinking on her part. He'd look after her, make sure she only had one drink – he could hardly stop her having any, he said, when he'd done it too. They all did it. Country life has its charms and its boring bits, and grog alleviates the boring bits as well as that seemingly endless pain of being a teenager.

Bradley would keep track of her wherever they went. Put her in the car, never leave her behind, even when he met a girl he liked. Janine was his main concern, always. So he has to be hers, at least for tonight.

There's a single light on in front of the police station when she pulls up across the road. She hopes the place isn't shut. She hasn't needed to visit anyone here before but she knows they wouldn't stay open all night in a town like this, just like they don't in Bellbird River.

When she gets out of the car she's hit by the cold. It's so much colder on a clear night in winter than when there's cloud cover, which she knows, but she was in such a rush she forgot to grab a jacket from the house. Tucking her hands under her armpits is the best she can do to keep warm as she approaches the old building.

Thankfully the screen door opens and she enters to find a tired-looking officer on the desk, his ginger hair in messy tufts and a half-filled mug at his elbow.

'Yep?' he says, glancing up.

'You have my brother here. Bradley Johnston.'

'Yep.' The officer shifts in his seat and looks at her enquiringly.

'Would it be possible for me to see him?'

She doesn't know if you're meant to ask such things but she knows from other people that cops in these towns tend to be lenient.

'You here to pay the bond?'

'Um . . .' She should have thought of that. She doesn't have much cash on her; not enough, she's sure. She has a credit card that she hardly uses.

'Maybe,' she says. 'Can I see him first?'

The officer stands. He's taller than he looked sitting down. Imposing. She wonders if it helps with keeping people in line.

'Bradley doesn't drink,' she says as she follows him deeper into the station.

'Yeah, right,' he says wearily.

'I mean – he's schizophrenic. He takes medication. It's possible he's off his medication.'

The officer turns to look at her. 'He didn't say anything about that.'

'He wouldn't. If he's off it he probably thinks he's Santa Claus. Or Kieren Perkins. He just seems drunk because he raves.'

The officer nods slowly. 'Righto. Big guy, though. We thought he might hurt someone. Took three of us to get him in here.'

They stop in front of a cell and she sees Bradley sprawled on the bench, one arm over his eyes.

'I'll give you a few minutes,' the officer says, and departs before Janine can thank him.

'Bradley?' she says meekly. She doesn't want to upset him. He may not recognise her. It happened once before, when he was at his then home and off his medication. A staff member called her and asked her to come and calm him down, except she couldn't. All she could do was wait until he exhausted himself, then they asked a doctor to come and sedate him.

Bradley takes his arm away from his face and opens one eye.

'Neenie,' he says flatly.

'Why are you in Werris Creek?'

He slowly moves himself to a sitting position and scratches the side of his head. 'I don't know.'

'Have you been keeping up your medication?' She clutches on to the bars as if they may melt in her hands and she'll be able to magically step through and give him a hug.

He sighs. 'I don't know.'

She puts her forehead against the steel but it's so cold that she moves back straightaway.

'What are we going to do with you, Brad?'

She knows that he knows her question is bigger than what's happening here and now, because it's a conversation they had when he was first diagnosed. What was to become of him now that his brain wasn't working? What kind of life could he have? All his dreams and goals and ambitions were reduced to hoping he could make it through one day living in a straight line.

Janine sometimes thinks all of her dreams and goals and ambitions have stuck to that line too. Someone else – someone grander than her – might have taken that moment as her opportunity to leap headlong into her own future and do all the things her brother couldn't do. But that would have been cruel. She doesn't want to live her life in spite of what's happening to Bradley; she wants to live *because* of him. What better purpose is there?

He opens his mouth as if to speak.

'Let me guess,' she jumps in. 'You don't know.'

He shakes his head, then puts it in his hands; she watches his shoulders heave and hears him sob. Her arms want to enfold him and she wants to put her head on his and hold him until he feels better. Instead she stands there, his witness.

'We'll sort it out,' she says. 'I don't know how, but we will.'

'I'm never getting better,' he says, his voice thick with tears, speaking the truth.

'I know. But that doesn't mean we can't make your life better.'

She closes her eyes and tries to imagine what that looks like. There is no handbook for this. Not even a leaflet. It's up to her to figure it out.

Maybe it starts with her trying to make her own life better. While ever she doesn't help herself she can't help him. If her little troubles are insurmountable, how can she help him with big ones? That's the challenge she has to face.

Something Warwick said the other night comes back to her: *worry about one note at a time*. He meant that if they could all just focus on getting each note right, the piece of music would take care of itself.

Maybe the choir has been useful after all.

She needs to start with the next moment, and continue in each moment after that. Moment by moment is easier to handle than thinking of the bigger, longer, wider arc of both of their lives.

'I'll go and talk to the cop about getting you out,' she says.

Bradley lifts his head and looks at her, his eyes wet, then nods. 'Thank you.'

She walks quickly to the front of the station before she starts crying herself.

CHAPTER 44

'Thank you for having me back here, Victoria.' Arthur smiles obsequiously and Victoria wants to hit him.

'It's good to see you're persistent in your insincerity,' she says, then turns to his lawyer. The drongo from Muswellbrook, as Gabrielle so sweetly called him.

No one between Armidale and Scone would take Arthur on, Victoria heard. At least her family's history in this area still carries some weight and she can rely on others to honour it. The scholarships her father established put plenty of boys through school, and some of those boys are now lawyers and accountants and councillors in this area. Quite an insurance policy, those scholarships. She suspects her father knew they might be; he just couldn't have guessed the circumstances in which the policy would be needed. Or perhaps he did: Arthur was never his favourite person.

'So, Mr Walshe, what do you wish to discuss?' She smiles from her mouth to her cheekbones but no further.

'Oh, Vicky!' Gabrielle singsongs up the stairs and Victoria suppresses a smile.

She told Gabrielle that Arthur and his lawyer were coming to visit and Gabrielle insisted on making sure they know she's in the house, and that Victoria is to pretend it's accidental timing.

'I'm not having you undefended with that weaselly man around,' Gabrielle said. 'That's how you got pregnant – twice!'

Victoria can't help thinking that Gabrielle, lacking the drama of being onstage, is intent on creating some at home.

'I'm busy, Gabrielle,' she says now, pretending to sound annoyed.

'Are you?'

Stomp stomp stomp to the top of the stairs, down the hallway and into the room.

'Arthur!' Gabrielle says, looking surprised. 'Why are you here? You don't live here any more. Victoria, shall I call that nice policeman to come and remove him?'

Victoria tries not to laugh, although she enjoys Gabrielle's show of outrage – both real and *faux*.

'That's quite all right,' she says. 'I knew he was coming. This is his lawyer, Mr Walshe.'

Gabrielle plonks herself onto the settee next to her cousin. 'Oh good – tea.'

She makes a show of pouring a cup for herself, which means that one of the others will have to go without.

'Er – I don't think Miss . . .'

'Reynold. Gabrielle Reynold.' She extends a hand to the lawyer. '*Enchantée*, as I'm sure you are too.'

'Gabrielle is my cousin,' Victoria explains. 'And she can stay.' She takes a breath. She's still feeling so weary, but is hopeful that sorting out things with Arthur will help revivify her. 'Now – what is the matter at hand?'

The lawyer clears his throat. 'We would like to discuss my client's half-ownership of this house.'

'He doesn't have any ownership,' Victoria states firmly. 'This is my family home, it was built by *my* forebears, and has nothing to do with him apart from the fact that he fraudulently lived here for several decades.'

'Fraudulent is a very strong word, Mrs Crighton,' says Mr Walshe.

'*Ms* Reynold.' Victoria draws herself up and narrows her eyes. It's something she has been practising for precisely this moment. 'And he lived here pretending to honour our marriage vows, but the whole town now knows that he was not, in fact, doing that. He was cavorting with another woman. Committing adultery.'

'We're in love,' Arthur protests.

'She's over twenty years younger than you, Arthur,' Gabrielle says forcefully. 'She doesn't love *you*, she loves the idea that you're going to get some money from Victoria. Actually, if you truly believe that woman loves you, Victoria should ask for an annulment, because you're too stupid to have understood your marriage vows in the first place.'

Mr Walshe's mouth hangs open as Arthur gasps.

Victoria turns away so they can't see the look of triumph on her face. Honestly, there are very few times that she's pleased Gabrielle has training in the dramatic arts, but this is one of them. Her cousin puts on a very impressive turn.

Mr Walshe recovers his wits. 'We're not here to discuss the nature of my client's romantic relationship—'

'Aren't we?' says Victoria. 'It's the entire reason we're having this conversation at all.'

'Victoria, come on,' Arthur says, and he starts to move his hand across the coffee table.

Victoria recoils.

'Our marriage wasn't in the best shape before this,' Arthur continues.

'Wasn't it?' Victoria glares at him. 'It was a perfectly good older-people's marriage. Romance is for university students,

Arthur. We had built a life together. We had children together. We didn't hate each other.' She pauses. 'I used to quite like your company.'

She falters as she remembers how lonely she was in the days after he moved out and before Gabrielle moved in. Her cousin's arrival was a godsend in ways she can never let Gabrielle know, lest there be crowing about it.

Arthur makes a face like a disappointed basset hound. 'I'm sorry, Victoria, but the heart has its reasons.'

'Oh, that old Blaise Pascal chestnut.' Victoria wants to stop herself rolling her eyes but gives in to it. 'I believe Edward VIII said that when he abdicated the throne. Life as the Duke of Windsor wasn't nearly so glamorous. So the heart can be a fool.' She sighs loudly. 'However, it's done. But I'm not giving you half the value of this house and that's that.'

Mr Walshe and Arthur exchange glances.

'Actually, Miss Reynold, we would like to propose that *he* buys *your* half.'

'What?' Victoria's cheeks feel hot and she presses her lips together angrily. '*What?*'

She wishes she were limber enough to jump to her feet and loom over the pair of them, but Gabrielle does it for her, putting her hands on her hips and tossing her hair.

'Victoria has already said that Arthur is not entitled to any part of this house.' Gabrielle's bosom is thrust forwards, as if she's the prow of a cruise liner throwing shade on a foreign dock. '*I* would be entitled to it before he would be. Victoria's grandfather was *my* grandfather too.'

Her statement gives Victoria pause. Perhaps Gabrielle has a point. Although Victoria's father inherited this house, and left it to her, she never asked whether his brother had been bought out of his part of it or if her father simply took it.

'I can buy you both out,' Arthur says almost gleefully.

'Where are you getting the money from?' Victoria scans her memories and considers that Arthur might have been hiding funds from her – but how did he make them? He's never been overly industrious.

'Celeste has an inheritance,' he says, smiling smugly.

'Ah.' Gabrielle sits down with a thump. 'So *your* heart's reason is that you love her for *her* money.' She turns to Victoria and widens her eyes. 'This is getting juicier.'

'That's not fair,' Arthur retorts. 'Celeste has a beautiful soul.'

'The subject of this house is closed,' Victoria says with quiet determination as she digests the news that Arthur now has the means to outlast her when it comes to lawyers and settlements.

She has to figure out what to do next, otherwise she could end up in court with no money to pay anyone to defend her, and one can never predict what a judge will decide. Arthur could well get away with his claim.

'Not yet,' says Mr Walshe. 'But I can see we'll make no further progress today.'

Victoria nods once in agreement. 'Please leave,' she says.

She doesn't look up as they go, seen out by an officious Gabrielle; nor when Gabrielle returns to the settee and puts an arm around her.

'What do you want to do, Vicky?' she says softly. 'Shall I hire a hitman?'

Victoria is momentarily shocked, then she starts to laugh. 'You probably know one, don't you?' she says, still laughing and grateful for the comic relief.

'I can find out where one is. Ivan knows *all* sorts of people. Or what about Jimbo? I think he'd like the chance to defend your honour.' Gabrielle squeezes her cousin's shoulder. 'We'll be okay.'

'What – between your debt to Laurent, and my husband with his wealthy mistress wanting the house?'

Gabrielle appears to consider this set of predicaments. 'None of this is ideal. But we'll be *okay*. I'm sure of it.'

'Or you want to be.'

'There's not much difference in the end!' Gabrielle says cheerfully. 'Come on, let's open a bottle of wine and toast ourselves.'

Victoria doesn't actually feel like drinking any wine but she'll keep Gabrielle company. There's nothing else ahead of them this afternoon or this evening, and she can think of no one she'd rather do nothing with.

CHAPTER 45

This must be what flying feels like. Or floating more like, because Debbie doesn't feel like she's soaring so much as drifting, weightless, happy, suspended, with all her cares left behind on the ground. Up here she is completely present, in her body, and doing exactly what she is meant to be doing.

Even as she looks out and sees the show-goers looking back at her, she still feels like she's elsewhere. But at the same time she is here. Right here. In Bellbird River Showground, at the annual Bellbird River Show, with its rodeo riders and cattle-judging, its sideshow alley, dagwood dogs and fairy floss, with the choir behind her and the microphone in front of her, and Warwick on the keyboard that they brought on stage in lieu of the piano, and some high school lad on guitar and some other high school lad on a small set of drums.

This song is coming from somewhere deep inside her but also somewhere that is not her. She has always felt like her voice passes through her when she sings. That it doesn't belong to her. It's just never seemed as obvious – as undeniable – as it does today.

With her solo over, the choir joins her for the chorus, and she smiles as she sings. There's no disappointment that her moments are finished, only excitement at the idea that she has achieved something she worked so hard for: excellence, bliss, rapture.

Then – applause. A beaming smile from Warwick. Debbie takes her usual place amidst the other singers and the crowd waxes and wanes in size as their set continues.

Some singers wouldn't want to perform in a dusty showground with girls on ponies being led past and noisy children hurtling by, but Debbie doesn't care. This is more than she could ever have hoped for a year ago when she had no idea what she would do with her future. This is perfect.

With the performance over, Debbie finds herself mobbed.

'You were amazing!' says Alex, with a big hug and a kiss on her cheek. Kim slinks up from the crowd and smiles at her without saying anything.

'Nice,' Janine says, shrugging then nudging her lightly.

When Gabrielle appears before her Debbie feels her throat tighten in anticipation of professional criticism.

'My dear,' says Gabrielle, taking her hands, 'how wonderful.' She gives her a kiss on each cheek. 'You are our star.'

'I don't think so!' Debbie splutters. 'You're the opera singer!'

'Ah, but I could not sing that piece as beautifully as you just have. Congratulations.'

Then she's gone in a waft of heavy perfume and Debbie is dropping her sheet music into her handbag.

She feels a hand on her shoulder blade and looks up to see Warwick smiling down at her just before he pulls her into a firm hug. Her heart flutters and she hopes the blush she feels on her cheeks subsides before the hug ends.

'Thank you,' he says, muffled.

'For what?' She releases him and steps back. Then steps back again because her heart is still fluttering.

'For doing such an exceptional job,' he's saying. 'You must be thrilled.'

'Oh.' She blinks, still thinking about the hug. 'Yes, I am. It went better than I thought.'

'It went *exactly* as I thought.' His smile is so big that she feels slightly proud for being the cause of it.

'I'd better get going,' she says.

'Are you going to look around the show?' He pushes his long fringe off his face and tucks his hair behind his ear. He has such lovely long fingers, just as a pianist should.

She blinks again, trying to refocus. 'Maybe,' she says, smiling tightly, turning away.

'I'm going to the chicken display if you'd like to join me?'

That makes her stop and turn back. 'Chickens?'

'If you've never seen a chicken display at a country show, you haven't *lived*. They're beautiful. So many different types. Just wait – you'll see. Let me pack up the keyboard and I'll be right with you.'

'I, um . . .' She should tell him that she's due back at Wattle Tree in an hour or so, but she supposes it can't take long to look at chickens. They can't be that interesting. Bea has some laying hens but Debbie's never bothered to learn their names, even though Bea chats about them regularly.

Debbie waits for Warwick in front of the stage, watching as the high school lads amble off and give her a desultory fare-well wave.

'Ready!' Warwick says.

He's put a blue jumper over his blue shirt and it suits him. Not that she's going to say that. Because it would be a personal comment and she's not going to make those, even if he wouldn't take it the wrong way. Because he *might* take it the wrong way and think he has to explain to her that he's not interested in her like that and oh god, why does it feel like she's sixteen and he's the cutest boy in school?

'Where's the keyboard?' she says.

'In my car.'

'Will it be safe?'

He gives her a funny look. 'It's Bellbird River, Debbie. We have precisely zero crime that doesn't involve speeding down Drury Street.' His face clouds. 'And some man occasionally belting his wife.'

'Oh,' she says.

He offers her his arm. 'Shall we look at some chickens?'

She looks at his elbow. Is she meant to take it? That seems so . . . friendly. Are they friends? That seems like a lot to hope for.

'I'd be pleased to escort you,' he says in a light tone, and she knows he's trying to make the moment less awkward than she's already made it.

'Thanks,' she says, slipping her hand through the crook of his elbow, feeling like she's being taken to a dance.

As they pass a group of three women around her own age she sees them glower and turn away. Immediately she thinks it's about her. They know what she did. Where she's been. She stops involuntarily.

'Don't mind them,' Warwick says blithely, and tugs her on.

'Who?' she says, because if she pretends she doesn't know what he's talking about she won't have to say why she thinks those women behaved that way.

'Those women. High school mothers.'

'How – how do you know them?' She can hardly get the words out as she thinks about how she's going to tell him.

'I used to teach their children when they were in primary school.'

'Mm-hm,' she says, swallowing hard, as they pass a hot dog and fairy floss vendor.

'Don't you want to know why they turned away?' he says teasingly.

'Um.' She swallows again.

Now Warwick stops. 'Are you okay?' he says, looking concerned.

'It's fine,' she says. 'I'm fine.'

'You're *not* fine.' He puts his other hand on her shoulder. 'Were they mean to you too?'

Now she's confused. *Too?* What's he talking about?

'They drove me out of my job,' he says, raising his eyebrows.

Debbie knows what he's saying is terrible but she feels as though she could laugh. So this isn't about her. It was never about her. She's a self-involved idiot. Who needs to immediately make it right.

'That's awful,' she says. 'What happened?'

Warwick starts walking again and Debbie can see a large marquee up ahead with cages inside. The chicken display presumably.

'They're quite religious,' he says, 'and they decided that I'm gay and therefore I shouldn't be allowed near their children.'

'It's none of their business,' Debbie murmurs.

Then something filters into her brain. They *decided* that he's gay? So he's not? Oh, she needs to let go of his arm right now, otherwise she's going to send herself the wrong signals, let alone him. Except if she lets go he'll think it's because she's judging him too. Instead she hangs on for dear life and lets him steer her into the marquee with its squawking occupants.

'No, it's not,' he says. 'And thanks for saying that. Now – here we have a very handsome fellow.' He pats her hand then drops the arm she was holding, and she feels disappointed and relieved all at once. 'A Wyandotte. You don't see them much around here. And look, there's an Old English Game. My mother bred those.'

He strolls away from her, a look of delight on his face. She has never met a man who takes such joy in so many different things.

So much for her trying to dampen her crush on him. Here she is, indulging it. And feeling so hopeful about it that she's going to embarrass herself, and him. If she missteps she'll have to leave the choir, and she really doesn't want to do that. So she should probably leave the show instead, before she spends any more time with him.

'I, uh, Warwick, I have to go,' she says, pointing at her watch. 'It's later than I thought. I have to get back to work.'

His face falls. 'Really? I was hoping we could spend a bit of time together.'

'That's, um, that's really nice of you.' She laughs nervously. 'I have to make dinner for everyone. Roast.'

It's not true – she made pies this morning and they're sitting there, waiting to go into the oven – but it's plausible.

'Perhaps we could have dinner before choir practice next week?' He looks so hopeful.

'Yes. Maybe! I'll see you.'

She pivots and almost trots away from him. Barely noticing the din and bustle of the show she accelerates towards her car, and it isn't until she's put on her seatbelt that she feels the day's emotions cascade over her. She had a triumph on the stage, and a connection with a man she admires, and it's really all too much to handle.

Her solution is to put on a Wendy Matthews CD and sing all the way back to Wattle Tree.

CHAPTER 46

'**N**ow, we keep the slacks over here, folded neatly – see?' Gabrielle smiles and nods, smiles and nods, as Belinda points to a pile of nylon trousers in an array of pastel shades. What she really wants to do is grimace – who could *possibly* wear those things? They can't be flattering to a single woman on this earth, not even one of those supermodels. Gabrielle can only hope that wearing the merchandise is not a condition of working in the shop.

Belinda's Beauties, it's called, and while Gabrielle was absolutely and utterly convinced when she applied for the job that the name had to be ironic, the owner – Belinda – appears to want to prove her wrong.

'Look at those ruffles,' she says, gesturing to a blouse that would better belong on an engagement-era Lady Diana Spencer. 'Aren't they *gorgeous*?'

Restraining herself from pointing out that 'gorgeous' is meant to refer to colours rather than ruffles, Gabrielle smiles and nods again. If she doesn't verbally agree it's not real assent.

'You must have seen some beautiful ruffles on those costumes,' Belinda says, grabbing Gabrielle's arm with a little too much force, her heavily mascara'd eyelashes batting. She's quite an attractive woman underneath the eye make-up, the two-tone blush and the ill-advised separates, but most likely she'll stay hidden there.

'Yes, opera costumes tend to be laden with ruffles,' Gabrielle says merrily in reply.

At the interview she told Belinda that she had experience in costuming for opera – not strictly untrue – once it became clear that her name rang no bells with Belinda whatsoever. It seems that in Tamworth she can get away with not being 'Bellbird River's own' Gabrielle Reynold.

Now that she's in the shop, where the local country music radio station seems to be playing constantly, she understands why Belinda doesn't know her. This woman probably thinks 'aria' is a pasta dish.

'Opera?' she'd said when Gabrielle mentioned it on the phone during her initial enquiry about the job. 'Like *The Pirates of Penzance*?'

'Mm-hm,' Gabrielle had replied, not wanting to agree or to give offence. She needs this job if she is to save any money at all to give to Laurent. It cannot be Victoria's responsibility alone, as appealing as that sounds.

'So,' Belinda says as she stops in front of a spinning rack full of dresses. 'I'll leave you to get acquainted with everything. Mondays are slow so we shouldn't have many customers. When you're in on Thursday and Friday it will be busier.'

She smiles brightly, as if she's trying to sell Gabrielle on the job when it's Gabrielle who should be smiling at her, thankful to have three days work a week. Belinda told her that she hoped Gabrielle would eventually be able to run the place on her own on Mondays, 'so I can get back to the tuckshop'.

It had taken Victoria to decode that for Gabrielle: Belinda must be volunteering at her child's school tuckshop. Actually *children's* school, as Gabrielle has found out: Belinda has two girls, a year apart, both in primary school, and when her last shop assistant left Belinda had to give up her tuckshop shift. She's spent two months trying to find someone suitable to fill the position and is very pleased that Gabrielle is a 'mature lady' who can be responsible.

Gabrielle only phoned on Thursday. On Friday she was in here for a meeting. Now she is employed. Again. Not in anything she's qualified to do, but that's her reality now, she thinks.

Victoria has loaned Gabrielle her car so she can come and go to town. Luckily Peel Street isn't so busy that Gabrielle can't park it out the front and keep an eye on it all day. She wouldn't want anything to happen to it – Victoria has been through enough. Gabrielle has a strong desire to wring Arthur's neck for even *suggesting* that Victoria's house is partly his. It is married with a forceful urge to kick that Celeste in the shins if she ever sees her again.

She heard a rumour – from Warwick – that Celeste has been asking about the choir and if it's open to new members.

'Don't worry,' he said, 'I told the person who told me that I'm definitely *not* looking for new members. Although I could use a bass or two if you happen to know anyone. Don't think she qualifies!'

Bless Warwick, she has become quite fond of him. What a pity Ivan is taken or she'd think of setting them up together. It must be hard for Warwick to meet someone nice in Bellbird River. Or meet someone at all. Why on earth does he stay?

'See anything you like?' Belinda says, and giggles.

'Oh – so many things!' Gabrielle giggles back, although she has been absent-mindedly going through the dresses without paying attention to any of them.

'We'll have new stock soon.' Belinda pulls out the sleeve of a chartreuse number. 'I *love* it when there's new stock. It's so exciting. And I get first dibs!'

'Hooray,' says Gabrielle as Belinda turns and goes to the counter, where a woman in jeans, boots and an enormous jumper greets her with familiarity.

Drifting over to a rack holding an array of lightweight tops, Gabrielle tries to make herself focus. There has to be an order to how Belinda has hung these up. Are they colour coded? Maybe. Or by sleeve length? She'll have to ask. She doesn't want to get it wrong.

Her brain wafts off into music, as it likes to do. Last week Warwick introduced the Men at Work song 'Down Under', which was popular during the time Gabrielle was living overseas. She didn't know it was some kind of theme tune for *Australia II* in the America's Cup. She especially didn't know that it features a flute, which in her opinion has no place in a contemporary song. But some town burgher has decided the song would be just right for a party he's throwing for local councillors from the entire Liverpool Plains area. As if they don't already know they live 'down under'.

Softly singing the first verse, then the chorus, almost against her will – because she believes music moves through her, that she sings not of her volition but because she has no choice – she continues to ponder the tops. There really must be a system. She'll ask when Belinda has stopped talking to that lady.

Turning, she sees two sets of eyes staring at her and mouths dropped open.

'*Ohmygod*,' Belinda says. '*Ohmygod ohmygod.*'

'What's wrong?' Gabrielle looks at the rack. Did she damage something?

'You're . . .' Belinda glances at the boot-wearing woman, then back to Gabrielle.

'You're *famous*,' she says, her mouth dropping open again.

Gabrielle's face tenses and disappointment curls her toes. She shouldn't have sung. She was bound to be found out.

The other woman is approaching her, hand outstretched, as if seeking alms from a prophet.

'I saw you sing in Covent Garden,' she says, and for a second Gabrielle thinks she's going to curtsey. Not that she'd mind that. She's always been partial to a genuflection done for her benefit.

'You were . . .' The woman gasps. 'You were *sublime*.'

'Thank you.' Gabrielle blesses her with her most munificent smile.

'What are you doing here? In . . .' She looks around the shop. 'Tamworth?'

'I'm staying with my cousin in Bellbird River. Taking a break, you know.' Gabrielle pats her throat. 'My voice needs a holiday sometimes.'

It's the closest she's come to admitting the truth to anyone but Victoria, and that's only because she hasn't prepared a fiction. Which she really should have done, except who would have thought anyone would recognise her in this shop?

The woman looks perplexed and Gabrielle realises she needs to continue the story.

'And I'm getting underfoot,' she says, laughing, waving a hand, as if – *tra-la-la* – life is so hard for her living with her cousin. 'I just *love* clothes, and I saw this advertisement – perfect! I can work in this *divine* shop and give my cousin some space.'

'Who's your cousin?' It's Belinda, those eyelashes batting again.

'Victoria Crighton. *Reynold*. Victoria Reynold.'

Belinda's face drops. 'Oh,' she says.

'What's the matter?' Gabrielle tries batting her own, considerably less weighty, eyelashes.

'My, ah . . . my husband's sister is Celeste.' Belinda looks slightly afraid.

The woman in boots looks mildly titillated.

Now it's the turn of Gabrielle's face to drop. Seriously? *Seriously?* She knows Bellbird River is small but she hoped Tamworth would be less small, in all the ways that count. Socially, in particular. That was stupid of her, though, because the towns in this area have always been intertwined. Just because someone lives in Bellbird River doesn't mean their life is separate from someone in another town. As Gabrielle has just been reminded.

'I see.' She steps away from the rack of tops. 'Then I believe we have a problem.'

'I don't mind,' Belinda says quickly. 'Honestly. I'm so glad you took the job.'

Gabrielle purses her lips and nods slowly. 'I understand. But I *do* mind. My cousin has been very badly hurt. If I work with you it will not help.'

She walks to the counter and pulls her handbag from underneath it.

'Thank you for giving me the chance,' she says, nodding once at Belinda then smiling briefly at the other woman. 'I'm sure you'll find someone else.'

Years ago she perfected a sweep off the stage – head high, shoulders back, arms held by her sides, feet slowly and deliberately placed one in front of the other. She practised it in the mirror, instructing herself to look not just regal but imperious, like Queen Victoria when she was cranky. For a seasoned performer, such things can become an unconscious act. Not second nature so much as inner nature. Gabrielle hardly needs to give herself an instruction to do it; she just does it.

So she is barely aware that this is how she sweeps out of the shop, but once she's in the car, feeling upset because she doesn't have a job after all, because her cousin's awful husband and his grubby business keep haunting them, she remembers where she first got the idea for that sweep. It was from her very own Queen Victoria of Bellbird River, who handled disappointments and dramas by sweeping away from them down the street or out of the house or off the train platform.

Gabrielle smiles, knowing she's heading home to that same queen. She is sure that, between the two of them and their inherently regal natures, they will find a way to muddle through together.

CHAPTER 47

Alex doesn't believe she's ever been on a date before. On the rare occasions she has socialised with a man one on one it's never really seemed like a date – more like they tripped and fell on each other. She never formally dated Kimberly's father – he was just there, and she was just there, and they hung out because that's what you do at that age, then she was pregnant and he wasn't hanging out with her any more.

When George called her the day after she met him at the pub – she'd told him her name and he'd looked it up in the phone book – and asked her if she'd like to go to dinner with him, she wasn't sure she'd heard correctly. She's never been asked out to dinner before and isn't sure what will be expected of her.

At choir practice on Tuesday she told Janine about the impending dinner, which was to take place on the Thursday night.

Janine had glanced towards Debbie and said, 'Do you mean Debbie's friend?'

'Yes,' Alex squeaked as she had a sudden, clutching thought that she should have checked all this with Debbie first.

'Wow.' Janine raised her eyebrows and shrugged. 'I didn't think any of them knew how to ask a girl out any more.'

'Any of them?'

'Country boys. Boys like him who run around on horses and quad bikes. Sometimes they're not . . .' She shrugged again. 'Socialised.'

Alex felt relieved that Janine didn't have a Debbie-related objection. 'Oh. Right. He seemed well-behaved enough.'

Janine nodded. 'That's a good start.' She smiled hesitantly, like she was practising being happy. 'I'm really pleased for you.'

'Well, let's see how it goes! Maybe *I* won't be pleased for me.'

'It's nice,' Janine says with a weak smile. 'I'm sure you'll have a good time.'

Alex had asked Janine what she should wear.

Janine pointed to the pair of jeans she wears all the time and the worn-out shirt she had tucked under an old jumper and said, 'You're asking the wrong person.'

The thing is, Alex didn't have anyone else to ask. She was hardly going to confide in a colleague, or her mother. Or Debbie, because they don't know each other well enough for that. Nor was she going to call any Sydney friends, because they'd want to know all about George and there wasn't anything to tell – yet. So Janine was it. And she was clearly useless when it came to dates and clothes.

Given that she and George are dining at the Bellbird River pub, and Alex has observed how local women dress when they go to the pub, she's chosen to wear a dusky pink shirt tucked into jeans, flat shoes instead of the boots she's taken to wearing lately, a heavy leather jacket because it's cold, and an Albert chain around her neck. After seeing all the local women wearing one of those chains, she decided it must be some kind of social signifier and she needed to have one. A jeweller in Tamworth had sorted her out with an 'antique' – most likely just plain old second-hand – silver necklace that didn't cost her as much as she'd feared.

George said he'd pick her up at home, which seemed strange until she remembered that she'd read *The Rules* and this is how it's supposed to be done. She's being courted, or at the start of being courted, and he's showing respect by not expecting her to make her own way there.

As she waits for him to arrive she feels nervous. Or maybe she's just hungry. Kim is at her colleague's house. They could have stayed here but Alex didn't want to introduce George to Kim, or vice versa, and *not* introducing them would have been strange if they were all in the same space.

She told George about Kim the night they met. He said something about his niece and how she's more into bikes than Barbies, and without thinking Alex said, 'My Kim was always more into *books* than Barbies.'

The expression on his face may have changed briefly; or it may not have. It's possible she saw something that wasn't there, because she's always so ready to defend her position as a single parent, to explain to people that, yes, she's on her own and she's managing just fine, thank you.

Fleeting expression or no, he smiled and said, 'How old is she?'

'Eleven,' she said, smiling back. 'And before you ask, her father's not around.'

That, right there, was the moment she realised she was attracted to him. Why offer that information other than to let him know she's single?

George had nodded, then his mate had sloshed beer over them both and the conversation changed to how George might get his revenge.

Alex checks her watch. Six twenty-seven. He's picking her up in three minutes.

A knock at the door tells her that, actually, he's picking her up right now.

When she opens it she sees that he looks freshly showered, his hair still damp and combed to the side, and he's wearing a crisp-collared shirt and a heavy sports coat and jeans and boots.

He grins and holds out a small bunch of jonquils. 'Hi,' he says. 'You look lovely.'

It's not that Alex hasn't received compliments before – sometimes from fathers of students who are trying to crack on to her, or making an attempt to get their child's marks improved, or both – but never at the door of her home from a man bearing flowers. She's flustered and it probably shows.

'Thank – thank you,' she says, taking the flowers. What should she do now – invite him in while she puts them in water? No, he shouldn't come into her home. She doesn't know him.

'I'll just run and put these in the kitchen,' she says, then inhales the jonquils' scent. 'I love these, thank you. Won't be a sec.'

She almost skips down the hall to the kitchen, grabs a glass, fills it with water and shoves the stems in before returning to the door.

'Thanks for picking me up,' she says as he gestures for her to walk ahead of him down the path.

'Of course. It's my pleasure.'

He holds the gate open for her, then the car door, flustering her further. She's simply not used to having someone do things like this for her, and it feels almost indecently wonderful.

When they reach the pub he parks his ute across the road and goes to shut his door with the keys still in the ignition.

'Wait!' she says. 'Your keys.'

He grins – that bright, easy smile she liked so much the first time she saw it. 'Nah, we always leave 'em. It's in case someone needs to get home. They know they can just take the truck and bring it back later.'

Her mind dances around the possible outcomes of this practice. 'How will they know it's yours?'

He laughs and shrugs. 'Everyone knows everyone.'

'And how would you get home?' She knows she's asking a lot of questions but this is a fascinating local custom.

Another shrug. 'Someone'd drive me. No one minds.'

As he offers her his arm and they walk into the pub, she immediately sees what he means by 'everyone knows everyone' – Warwick is sitting at a table in the corner, lively and engaged in conversation with some man Alex doesn't know. He sees her then smiles and waves, and she waves in return.

As George guides her to the dining room she spots Janine's man friend, sitting with a woman and two children. His eyes meet hers then he looks away.

'Georgie,' she hears, then someone is slapping George's back and hands are being shaken.

It takes them ten minutes to walk ten metres.

'Half the town seems to be here,' she mutters as they reach their table, where George holds out her chair.

'I hope you don't mind,' he says as he sits. 'The pub is really the only place to have dinner.'

'No, it's fine,' she says, attempting a smile, although she knows she'll be interrogated at choir practice, because Warwick will probably tell someone else who will tell someone else who will tell ten other people that Alex was on a date with George, because everyone seems to know George.

Life in Bellbird River has suited her, but now she realises how valuable the anonymity of a city can be.

George reaches across the table and puts his hand on hers. 'I won't be telling stories about you to anyone,' he says seriously. 'If that's what you're worried about.'

'Oh!' She laughs nervously. 'I'm just not used to being out to dinner and seeing so many familiar faces. Still adjusting to living in a small town.'

He picks up the menu, which is battered and food-splattered but that's what you'd expect in a pub.

'It must be weird,' he says. 'I didn't think about that.' He puts the menu down again. 'Next time we'll go to Tamworth.'

Her eyes widen. Next time? They haven't even made it through *this* time. Still, if he's trying to get her to relax, it works. He wants to see her again. Now she just has to work out if *she* wants to see *him* again.

'What's your recommendation?' she says as she looks at all the different ways she could be served steak.

'Ah . . .' His brow crinkles. 'You're not a vegetarian, are you?'

'No,' she says, and he looks relieved.

'I panicked there for a second,' he says.

Then he grins, and she feels something in the pit of her belly let go. So it was nerves she was feeling at home. Nerves because she likes him, and she wants tonight to go well. This is what being on a date must be like. Even if this turns out to be the first and last time she goes out with him, she is grateful that he's making it easy for her.

And when, at the end of the evening, he drops her home, she lets him kiss her, briefly, and hopes that the Tamworth dinner will happen sooner rather than later.

CHAPTER 48

'See you, Simmo.' Janine smiles weakly as what she hopes is her last customer of the day leaves.

Simmo often comes in late to see if he can buy left-over bread, because he knows Janine will discount it. Not for everyone, just for him. If someone she doesn't know comes in late, probably on their way through to somewhere else, it's full price.

She checks her watch. Fifteen minutes to closing. Ross didn't turn up last week, so she doesn't know if he's going to turn up tonight. Who knows what he thought when he arrived to a darkened shop because Janine was already heading to Werris Creek.

That was a long night, fishing Bradley out of lockup and taking him to Tamworth. She thinks the cop took a shine to her and that's why he let them go. Bradley still has to appear before a magistrate and Janine doesn't like his chances of finding a Legal Aid lawyer in time. They're stretched; they're always stretched.

She has a little bit of money saved from paintings she entered in an exhibition in Scone two years ago. The gallery put what she considered to be far too high a price on them but they sold the first day. It gave her hope. And cash. With nothing to spend that cash on in Bellbird River, it's been sitting in the bank. Paying a lawyer to help her brother is, she thinks, the best possible use for it.

There are two rock cakes left. Her dad will want those. She turns and surveys the bread. More of it left than usual. Maybe it will fit in the freezer here.

The door opens and she looks around.

'Debbie – hi.' She smiles, although she's wondering why Debbie is here so late. She's a morning shopper.

'Hi!' Debbie's smile is broad. It usually is. Janine has noticed this and she supposes it's a nice thing. 'Sorry, you're probably about to close. I'm hoping you have some loaves or rolls left – we have some unexpected visitors and not enough food to feed them!' She laughs, as if feeding them would be a pleasure.

'Yeah, we do.' Janine nods. 'How much are you after?'

'How much do you have?'

Janine steps aside and gestures to the racks.

'Great, I'll, uh, I'll take it all. We can always freeze it if we don't eat it this weekend. Thanks, you're a lifesaver.'

Janine nods and picks up a thin plastic bag to wrap around the first loaf.

'What do you think of the new song?' Debbie asks.

'It's all right.' Janine shrugs. 'I'm not that keen on The Beatles.'

'Really?' Debbie is agog. 'I thought everyone liked them!'

'My brother loves them.' Janine remembers Bradley trying to slow dance to 'Michelle' with her high school best friend one night at a backyard party. Her friend was rapt; Janine had to explain that Bradley just loved that song and he'd take any opportunity to dance to it. He loved a lot of songs. She doesn't know if he listens to them now.

'I've just never been a fan,' she goes on. 'Elvis is more my speed – if we're talking old-school.'

'I don't think we'll be getting any Elvis at choir.'

'Probably not. Although Frank'll do "Blue Suede Shoes" if you ask him nicely.'

Janine turns to smile at Debbie, trying to be friendly, because she knows she could try being nicer. They've known each other for a while now.

That's when she sees Ross striding towards the shop and her heart feels like it stops. He's miles early. What's he doing? No one has ever seen them together and now there's a witness standing here waiting for her loaves of bread.

As the door opens Janine feels her chest tighten. Should she pretend she doesn't know him? No, that won't work. She's not one of those people who has a poker face. Debbie's going to be able to tell that something's going on.

'Hi,' she says, her voice higher than usual.

Debbie turns and looks curiously at the newcomer.

'Hi,' Ross says, glowering.

He doesn't appear to notice that Debbie is in the shop, but Janine sees her eyes flicker to his left hand, to his ring finger and the gold band on it.

Janine swallows. 'I'll, um . . . I won't be long,' she says and starts to put Debbie's loaves into a big plastic bag.

'Where were you?' Ross says, his voice low but calm. Too calm. Like he's holding something back to unleash it later.

Janine feels her breathing quicken. If she pretends she doesn't know what he's talking about, to keep up some façade in front of Debbie, there's no guarantee Ross will play along. If she responds to him she's admitting that they know each other well. He's snookered her. Which was probably his intention.

She feels that warning in her gut again. The one that told her to get out of his house. The one that's probably been there the whole time, but she's so used to distrusting her body – no, that's not it. She has actively tried to destroy her body, thinking it her enemy, something that can't be controlled no matter what she tries. It feels hunger. It feels pain. It needs touch. It needs comfort. This is how it betrayed her, by responding to Ross when he put his hands on her that first time. And, so used to the betrayal, she failed to heed the warnings that have been coming since. That tom-tom beat of her heart wasn't desire, it was fear. The butterflies weren't lust, they were nerves. This thud in her gut is the loudest siren of all because she didn't listen – or didn't want to listen – to the others. She's in danger from him, and all this while she's told herself he's a good person because that's what she wanted to believe.

But he's not. He's been with her when he should have been with his wife. He's been telling Janine he cares about her when anyone who genuinely cares about her would make sure he has no other involvements before becoming enmeshed with her. It's so very clear now: he doesn't care about anyone but himself.

Which means that whatever he does or says next will not be in Janine's favour. If he's sweet as pie it will be to get something for himself; if he's nasty the same motivation will be behind it. And she's allowed him to do this. To treat her as a means to his end.

Yes, she's stupid and she will never forgive herself for it. But she shouldn't complicate things further by being more of a liar than he's already made her.

'I had to go to Werris Creek,' she says.

Ross narrows his eyes. 'What's in Werris Creek?'

'My brother needed me.' Janine lifts her chin, trying to act defiant. Helping Bradley was an act of love but Ross probably wouldn't see it that way.

'You couldn't be bothered to let me know?' Ross crosses his arms and plants his feet apart.

'It was last minute.' Janine swallows again. 'I got a phone call.'

She glances at Debbie, expecting to see her watching avidly – which is what most people would do – but instead her head is bowed and she's leaning against the counter, almost like she's trying to get away from Ross.

'And you didn't call to apologise.' His irises are dark again. There's no light there at all. Maybe there never was.

Janine wants to laugh. Apologise – for standing up a married man? But laughing at him won't help calm down what she can see is his rising anger.

'I've been busy,' she says meekly.

Ross nods slowly and his chin juts forwards. 'I can see you don't think I'm a priority.'

Janine feels like laughing again – there's no way she is *his* priority. That's what *she* sees. But the time of tit for tat is past now. Her time with *him* is past. She knew it when she left here that night, because she did, indeed, choose her priority: Bradley.

'My brother needed me,' she repeats.

'And what about what *I* need?'

His face is pinched and she can see, now, not the cute teenage boy she used to go out with but the man he actually is: older, slacker, unattractive and unable to accept it. That's what he wants her for: to prove to himself that he's still appealing. That's her use.

'I think Janine has been clear,' Debbie says strongly.

When Janine looks over she can see that Debbie has planted her own feet apart, but her hands are by her sides, in fists.

'Oh yeah?' Ross says, but his left eye flickers.

Maybe no one has ever stood up to him before. Janine just can't believe it's Debbie who's doing it.

'I have to buy bread,' Debbie says, her face impassive, her knuckles white. 'You're holding me up. So you can get in the queue behind me or you can leave.'

Ross sniffs then he stares at Janine.

She's not going to make this moment all right for him. He does need to leave, for all their sakes. So she doesn't smile. She just stares back.

Without another word, he yanks open the door of the shop and goes.

'Thank you,' Janine whispers, trying to hold it together because the relief of his departure makes her want to cry.

'He's a bully,' Debbie says, stepping up to the counter, taking her wallet out of her bag. 'You can't let them get away with it.'

Janine has no idea where Debbie learnt to be so tough, and why she's been hiding it behind those plaits. She's not a religious person, so she doesn't believe in guardian angels. Or she hasn't so far. But she can't help feeling as if Debbie was sent here today specifically to help her.

'The bread's on me,' she says, because while it's a pathetically small token of her appreciation it's all she has to offer.

'No way!' Debbie shakes her head. 'You have a business to run. You can't give things away.'

'Please,' Janine says, pushing it towards Debbie and looking at her meaningfully.

They hold each other's gaze, then Debbie smiles, gently, sweetly. 'Thank you,' she says.

'I don't think I'm the one who needs thanks,' Janine murmurs.

Debbie shrugs. 'Swings and roundabouts.'

Janine doesn't really know what that means, but after she waves goodbye to Debbie and locks the shop door behind her, her legs wobble and she sits down, puts her head in her hands and wonders what the hell just happened.

CHAPTER 49

'Basses, we need to work on your part.' Warwick is smiling tolerantly but the rest of the choristers know that the basses *always* need work. 'Everyone else, have a break for about ten minutes. You're welcome to stay and listen, or go for a walk or something.'

Victoria turns to Gabrielle. 'I'm going to stay put,' she says.

'You don't feel like a stroll?'

Gabrielle sounds as if she really means to take a stroll, but Victoria can see that she's looking at the tea and biscuit table. It's the manifestation of a new tradition, suggested by Debbie – that everyone bring a treat of some kind, to go with their tea made using the council urn. Victoria is normally a fan of a treat but tonight she would rather just sit.

'I'm content to stay here,' she replies.

Gabrielle pretends to look disappointed. Victoria knows she's pretending because she has a mental catalogue of Gabrielle's many expressions and this one is straight out of the play-acting range.

'Go on,' Victoria says, waving her off. 'There are Monte Carlos.'

'What on earth do you mean?' This time Gabrielle's outrage appears to be genuine.

'You want a biscuit. Go on.' She shoos her again, having given up trying to curb Gabrielle's taste for sweet things.

Gabrielle attempts to flounce off but she's wearing so many layers of clothes to keep her warm inside this frigid hall that all Victoria can detect is a pursed lip and a lifted nose.

The basses really do need the practice. Victoria wonders if Warwick's tactic of making them do it in front of others is a form of public shaming, to motivate them to try harder and do better. Not that she really cares. She feels exhausted tonight. Has done all day. She was feeling light-headed in the early afternoon, possibly because she couldn't bring herself to eat lunch. An afternoon nap did nothing to ameliorate her condition and she wonders if she can get away with a day in bed tomorrow.

She's meant to see a couple of the bridge girls, and she needs to call her lawyer to talk to him about Arthur and the house. Perhaps she can cancel. It's not polite, and it's not something she's done since she went into labour with Leopold two weeks early and had to tell the CWA committee that she couldn't make the meeting. But needs must. She's sure it's a virus of some kind – this choir is probably a hotbed of bugs, with all the breathing and singing on each other that goes on. Rest will sort her out.

She feels a presence at her left side and turns to see Jimbo smiling down at her.

'Would you like a cup of tea?' he says.

'Oh, thank you. No. I'm fine.'

She smiles weakly because that's all she can manage, not because she's displeased to see him. He's a nice man, she's decided. Decent. Solid. And kind to her. He always asks after her health and her activities. If she didn't know better she'd say he's keen on her – as Gabrielle thinks – but at their age keenness is a relic of the past. The most they should aspire to is mutual respect.

'May I?' He gestures to the empty chair next to her.

'Of course.'

She's startled when he picks up her hand. Her instinct is to take it back, except his hand is warm and comforting, and for some reason it's exactly what she needs right now. How odd that he should know that.

She sighs, loudly, then winces. Her chest is feeling tight again. That happened this morning too. But she was so worked up about Arthur – telling Gabrielle her exact opinion of him as Gabrielle egged her on – that she thought it must be stress. She's not stressed now, though. Jimbo doesn't make her feel stressed.

'Are you feeling all right?' He's frowning.

'Am I . . . ?'

Now she feels like she's wafting away, although the pain in her chest is bringing her back to reality. Trying to breathe in, she finds her inhalation won't go very far.

'Victoria?'

Jimbo has taken her other hand too and he's squeezing them both.

'Victoria? Are you with me?'

Squeeze, squeeze. Now he's patting her cheek. That's a bit forward of him. But it feels nice.

She opens her eyes and sees him looking around. Warwick is conducting the basses. Victoria can see that schoolteacher – Alison or Alex or Alice. She *does* know her name. Why can't she remember it?

Now the teacher is frowning and moving quickly towards them, pushing chairs out of the way.

'What's happening?' she says to Jimbo.

Victoria closes her eyes and tries to focus on her breathing. Gabrielle showed her how to do some breathing exercises once. Where *is* Gabrielle? Victoria very much wants her back.

'I think she's in some distress,' Victoria hears Jimbo murmur.

Those basses are still singing. Sounding awful. Perhaps Warwick should cut them altogether.

'Debbie!' Victoria hears the schoolteacher call. She opens her eyes again and sees that small woman who works at Wattle Tree coming towards them.

'Can you call an ambulance?' the schoolteacher says quietly once Debbie arrives.

Debbie's eyes meet Victoria's and widen. Then her face settles and she smiles reassuringly.

'Sure,' she says, and she's gone again.

'Victoria, I'm just going to slide in behind your chair,' the teacher says and Victoria feels warmth behind her and hands holding her shoulders.

'What for?' says Jimbo.

'To keep her upright. I think I know what's happening to her, and if she collapses and slides onto her back, she may not be able to breathe properly.'

'You seem to know what you're doing.' Victoria can hear admiration in his voice.

'High school teacher. First-aid training, refreshing all the time.'

The basses have stopped singing. At last.

'Victoria,' she hears Warwick saying, and she half-opens her eyes. He's smiling at her, as if he's just come to say hello.

'We've called an ambulance for you,' he says.

'I don't . . .' she starts, but doesn't have enough breath to finish.

'What's going on?' That's definitely Gabrielle, and if Victoria couldn't tell by the voice she can by the wave of movement around her. Her cousin leaves a wake wherever she goes.

Jimbo squeezes her hands again and she feels reassured.

'Vicky?' There's a poke on her leg. '*Vicky?*'

'The ambulance might take a while,' she hears Warwick mutter. 'Debbie, Dr Hartford lives around the corner. Connaught Street.'

'Number twelve,' says Jimbo.

'There's a plate on his fence with his name on. Can you ask him to come right away?'

'Vicky, darling.' There's a kiss on the crown of her head and strangely Victoria feels like it's her mother giving it to her. 'You'll be all right, darling.'

Victoria half-opens her eyes and smiles weakly at her cousin, who is smiling back at her like she's just heard the most wonderful news. Probably to make her feel better.

'Love you, Gabby,' she says, then she closes her eyes and waits to find out what happens next.

CHAPTER 50

Gabrielle bustles along the hospital corridor ahead of Helena, who is almost trotting to keep up.

'She can't *stand* being in hospital, as you can imagine,' Gabrielle says over her shoulder.

'Gabrielle, can you slow down?'

'No.'

If that girl can't keep up with her mother's more-than-middle-aged cousin, she should take up an exercise routine.

'*Gabrielle!*'

Blowing air out of her mouth to make an emphatic point, Gabrielle turns and puts her hands on her hips. 'Can't you see I want to *get to her*? I haven't seen her since yesterday.'

'And I want to get to her too, but can you just stop for a second?'

Helena reaches out and touches her forearm. Gabrielle makes a face as if being touched is akin to being blowtorched.

Now Helena is holding her forearm and Gabrielle stares at her hand. She barely knows this young woman. The action is quite presumptuous – yet oddly comforting at the same time.

'I want to know how *you* are,' Helena says, shifting to let a nurse walk past her.

'Me?' Gabrielle blinks rapidly. 'Me?'

'Yes.' Helena's smile is sympathetic. 'It must have been a big shock. Mummy is always so strong. She's the last person you'd think would have a heart attack. If I'd been there I would have been so upset about it, to see her like that. It's . . . so wrong.' She looks stricken then rights herself.

Gabrielle inhales and holds it while she thinks, then exhales loudly.

'It *is* wrong,' she says. 'The universe is out of order.' She shakes her head quickly. 'That must sound silly.'

'It doesn't.'

They stand in silence for a few seconds.

'I really appreciated you calling me so soon afterwards,' Helena goes on. 'Sorry I couldn't get here earlier.'

'Oh, it's fine,' Gabrielle says, far more breezily than she feels. 'Your mother has been zonked out for a while so she wouldn't even know you haven't been here. I think they're sedating her just to keep her quiet. As you may imagine, when she's conscious she's trying to run the place.'

'I got on to Leopold.'

'And how is the king of Kangaroo Court?'

Gabrielle had seen Leopold once in London, where he was nesting in a community of expatriate Australians and proving to be quite popular with lads and ladies alike. The men all wanted to be his friend and the women all wanted to be his girlfriend. Gabrielle could see that he was on the same path to baldness as his father and silently hoped he enjoyed his popularity with women while it lasted. She has never, of course, told Victoria this.

'He sounded worried for about ten seconds then told me he's going to Portugal for the weekend,' Helena says.

'How nice for him.' Gabrielle didn't expect Leopold to come home immediately but she would have thought he'd *pretend* to want to return.

Not that Gabrielle is in any position to judge him: when her own parents fell ill, one by one, she didn't return. Nor did she when they died. Her rationale on the first count was that they were lousy parents and she owed them nothing; on the second it was that they were already dead so they wouldn't know that she wasn't there for their funerals. Victoria had taken care of all the arrangements.

And that's the thing: Victoria is an exceptional person. She's not just Leopold's mother, she's a towering figure in their lives and in Bellbird River. How can he not want to come home to see her?

Helena shrugs and makes the face only an understanding sister can make.

Gabrielle spins on her heel. 'Come along,' she says, determined not to lose any more time.

She leads Helena down the corridor and around to the right, stopping at the door of Victoria's room, which is ajar and allows a voice that is not Victoria's to float out.

As she enters Gabrielle sees that it is Janine sitting on the visitor's chair, and looking quite comfortable.

'Hello?' Gabrielle says accusatorily.

'Oh. Hi.' Janine jumps up.

'What are you doing here?'

Gabrielle told the nurse that it was to be strictly no visitors apart from herself and Helena. Admittedly, this was mainly designed to stop town busybodies and Arthur from barging in. Janine cannot be classified as a busybody but she's still not Gabrielle or Helena, so Gabrielle will be having a word to the nurse.

'Gabrielle, don't be so rude,' says Victoria from her propped-up position on the bed. Then her face relaxes. 'Darling!'

She holds out a hand to Helena, who grabs it, then buries her face in Victoria's neck.

'Well?' Gabrielle says to Janine, in no mood to have her enquiry go unanswered.

'I just wanted to see how she is,' Janine says, folding her arms tightly against her chest and leaning against the wall.

'But you don't even *know* my cousin!' Gabrielle can't recall Victoria and Janine talking at choir practice, or anywhere else.

'Of course I do,' Janine says. 'Everyone in Bellbird River does.' She dips her head briefly. 'My brother used to do her garden. When he was in high school.'

Victoria has never mentioned this; then again, how could Gabrielle expect her cousin to fill her in on the decades of town life that she missed? Victoria is the hub of the Bellbird River wheel, with all those spokes leading from and towards her. She probably has connections with everyone she passes in the street each day and she's too discreet to say anything. But there's something that remains puzzling.

'Then why don't you speak to her on Tuesday nights?' Gabrielle says.

Janine gives her a funny look. 'Why would I? She knows all about me. I don't need to tell her.'

There are aspects of living in Bellbird River that Gabrielle once accepted but which now confound her, such as the way its residents are in a constant flow around each other, acknowledging other people with a nod or a raised finger, and if an observer misses it they can think the individuals concerned don't know each other, when they might be siblings, or former lovers, or longtime colleagues.

Gabrielle has been an habitué of big cities for so long that she's forgotten the grace of the Bellbird River kind of living, in which everyone is important yet also knows they are part of the whole, existing in concert for the benefit of all. City life means, too often, a rigorous focus on the individual and what they can get out of that city. That requires the discipline of staying focused, not being distracted by passers-by, not making unnecessary connections because you don't have the time or the energy to foster them. In Bellbird River all connections are necessary, otherwise the town doesn't function. Casual contact is cursory and meaningful at the same time.

That is why Janine is here. She and Victoria don't know each other deeply yet they know each other intrinsically. It is, therefore, natural that Janine thinks she should visit to see how Victoria is.

'Very well,' Gabrielle says.

'I have to go anyway,' Janine says. 'Bye, Victoria. Bye, Helena.'

Helena too, Gabrielle presumes, is someone Janine implicitly knows.

Gabrielle nods her farewell and watches Janine leave the room. She's a slightly odd sort of person, really; Gabrielle can see that now.

Although everyone is slightly odd, when she thinks about it. Growing up to love opera isn't exactly un-odd. And that was in addition to Gabrielle deciding to collect Vogue patterns for a solid three years before she gave them all away yet kept her sewing machine. Which, as far as she knows, is tucked up in Victoria's house somewhere. Yes, that's odd. Yet human. She's a human being, after all, as much as she's always wanted to be so much more than merely human.

'You could be a little kinder sometimes, Gabby,' Victoria says, raising her eyebrows.

She looks wan, and sunken; not at all her warrior self. It makes Gabrielle feel frightened, as she used to when she was a child, in the time before Victoria's parents took her in.

It is the existence of Victoria, she realises, that has given her the fortitude to pursue her career, to travel the world, to meet people and be charming and effusive and brilliant. No, not just her existence – her love. Victoria always signed her letters with *All my love forever*. Gabrielle never really thought about it, nor did she reciprocate in kind. *Bisous* was her sign-off. How limp.

'More like you, do you mean?' she says, moving to Victoria's other side and taking her hand. Helena's head continues to rest on her mother's shoulder.

Victoria snorts. 'I'm hardly kind.'

'No,' says Gabrielle. 'You're very much more than that.'

She smiles mysteriously, then kisses the back of her cousin's hand before putting it on the bed again.

'I'll give you two some time alone,' she murmurs, and takes her leave.

CHAPTER 51

It took twice as long as usual to get Kim out the door this morning, and Alex is kicking herself for not anticipating this. Kim spent the school holidays with her grandmother in Sydney, and now she's back and even more miserable than before.

'I wish I never came home!' was last night's refrain.

'I hate you!' was this morning's.

'What did you do to her?' Alex asked Marta when she called her after Kim's first day home.

'I did nothing,' Marta said. 'She hates Bellbird River.'

Alex might have imagined the register of triumph in her mother's voice, but then again she might not have. In-between her expressions of anguish Kim has talked about the new bedsheets Marta bought for Kim's bed that is in the very special guest room of the house; about the goldfish Marta let her buy and which she promised to keep alive until Kim returns next holidays; and about the promise of a kitten or puppy 'in case you want to stay longer'.

'You are bribing my child to leave me,' Alex said, angry at her mother's games.

'No. She wants to live in Sydney. I am just making it nice for her if she does.'

'Mama! *I'm* your child, you're meant to be supporting *me*.'

But they both know the truth: that Marta and Alex have never really been friends, so they don't understand each other, yet Marta and Kim have some mystical connection that Alex can only hope to approximate with either one of them. It's a really uncomfortable feeling for a mother to realise that her child prefers someone else. Not that Alex's love is conditional on being Kim's favourite person – of course it's not, that's not the way parenting works. But it would be nice.

It's not going to happen today, though. That's what the look on Kim's face tells her as she parks the car near the schools and waits for Kim to get out of the back seat.

After a minute has passed Alex wrenches the door open.

'Kim, you have to go in. The bell will ring soon, and that means we'll both be running late.'

Kim's mouth is screwed up and she's pulling at her thick grey tights that have wrinkled around the knees.

'They're just going to be mean to me,' she says sulkily.

This is something Alex can't deny. The girls preying on Kim appear to have redoubled their efforts, and despite spending quite a bit of time trying to work out tactics for Kim to avoid or manage them, the small size of the school and its grounds means there are few options for hiding places. She probably shouldn't be thinking of how her child can hide but it's the only solution Alex has come up with.

'I know they are, sweetheart,' she says, crouching down next to the car. 'I'm really, really sorry. Can you go to the library at lunch, maybe?'

'They know I go there.' Kim rubs her eyes with the heels of her hands.

While Alex will never know what it's like to send someone to the gallows, she thinks this feeling must be close: dread, desperation, regret and inevitability mixed up together. It's so very tempting to let Kim sit in an office in the high school all day, but that only solves the problem of today, not tomorrow or the rest of the school year.

Homeschooling isn't an option because Alex can't earn a salary doing that. Maybe going back to Sydney *is* the answer. Except she likes it here, and she doesn't want to prove her mother right. Neither of those is a noble motive for staying put, and she certainly doesn't want to sacrifice Kim's wellbeing for them, but going back seems more drastic than moving here in the first place. It's an admission of failure. And it's a return to a place that Alex no longer wants to live in, even if her daughter does.

So the question she has to ask herself is: whose happiness is more important? And that's not something she can contemplate right now, with kids playing noisily in the primary school and teenage boys thumping each other in the high school playground.

'Kim, I'll have to drag you over there if you don't move,' she says, checking her watch. Ten minutes until the bell.

'All right,' Kim spits, picking up her bag from the floor of the car as if it's full of rocks and dragging it onto her shoulder.

Alex walks swiftly across the road, her hand on Kim's shoulder – because she half-believes her child will run away – and gives her a wave goodbye at the gate. No kiss or hug, because that will mark Kim further as a target for the vicious children who are probably watching them from somewhere close by.

Once she's inside the high school Alex half-runs towards the staffroom, and collides with Vince Sheridan in the doorway.

'Whoa!' he says, putting up his hands.

'Sorry. Sorry.' She makes a face. 'I didn't mean to run late.'

'It's all right. Classes haven't started yet.' He puts his head to one side and frowns. 'Something worrying you?'

'Why – does it show?' Her laugh is caustic.

His frown deepens.

'Still my daughter,' she continues. She'd told him once before that Kim was having problems at school and he'd been sympathetic. 'Those little bullies next door . . .'

Great, now she feels like she's about to burst into tears. She holds it together in front of Kim because she has to, but that means it's hard to find a way to let all this pressure out, because Kim is around her most of the time she's not at work.

'I've heard other children are having the same problem,' Vince says, stepping back into the staffroom as Alex follows him.

'The headmistress isn't doing anything!' Alex says, exasperated.

'And she won't,' Vince says seriously. 'I believe the chief instigator is the deputy mayor's daughter. Some of the others belong to well-established families.'

'Right.' Alex tries to calculate what this means. In Sydney it would have no import whatsoever. If a kid in a primary school was the child of the deputy mayor, well, so what? There are so many residents in a suburb that the deputy mayor would be just one of many so-called important people and his or her child would have no special treatment. In Bellbird River, though, clearly special treatment is expected.

'So,' she says, 'you're telling me it's never going to improve.'

He sighs and shakes his head. 'Not unless they find a new target.'

'Terrific. In order for my daughter's life to improve some other kid has to suffer.'

Vince makes a sympathetic face. 'You could move her,' he says.

'To where – Quirindi? How do I know it'll be better?'

'Not Quirindi. Tamworth. I could have a talk to a principal there.'

Tamworth? That's almost an hour's drive away. An hour each way. Each day. She may as well be back in Sydney. What cost, though, for a more peaceful life for her daughter?

'Um, thanks, I'll think about it,' she says, because the bell is ringing and she can't continue this conversation now.

'Just let me know,' Vince says, heading for the door.

'I will,' Alex says, although she may not. It's just one of those polite false promises we make to avoid saying the truth.

'Shit,' she mutters as she realises she's heading in the wrong direction for her first class and turns around at a canter.

CHAPTER 52

With a new warmth in the air winter is definitely on the way out, not that Debbie can tell from the trees in this park. All eucalypts, nothing deciduous, so there are no signs of new growth. The cockatoos are merrily tearing off strips of bark and chucking them to the ground, and from the squawks they're making it sounds as if they're bragging to each other about how much bark they're removing.

There's also a cluster of them on the roof of a house opposite the park, where they're ripping up little strips of something. More squawking, although this lot sound like they're cackling. They're so destructive yet so beautiful and so funny, and Debbie saw none of them during the years she was in jail so she's happy to watch them be themselves now.

It's the azaleas in the park that signify the change in season. Heavy with pink buds or white, depending on the bush, they're awaiting their signal to bloom. She'll have to remember to come back and see them in a couple of weeks time.

'Sorry we're late.' Julia is standing in front of her, smiling in a friendly yet cautious way.

'Oh, that's okay.' Debbie stands up. 'I didn't notice.' She glances towards the footpath, where Emily and Shaun are emerging from the car. 'Thanks for coming to Bellbird River.'

Julia glances around. 'It's sweet. Small.' She smiles again. 'Tamworth seems huge next to this.'

'Yes.'

The children are walking towards Debbie and she feels those nerves again. They got on fairly well last time – although Shaun still won't really engage with her – yet she can't help worrying that she'll have to start from scratch each time.

'Hi, kids,' she says.

'Hi,' they chorus.

'How's school?'

Shaun shrugs and glances at his sister, who smiles shyly.

'I got a merit prize,' she says.

'That's great!' Debbie hugs her without thinking, but Emily doesn't seem to mind. She even hugs back, for a couple of seconds.

'She's reading lots of books,' Shaun says softly, then he smiles too. 'More than I do.'

'I just like them.' Emily grins and shuffles her feet in the grass.

'Yeah, and I don't.' Shaun nudges her.

They're playful with each other. It makes Debbie happy.

'I know you like sport, Shaun,' she says. 'I thought you'd like this park because there's a fair bit of room to run around. I brought some tennis racquets and balls in case you want to have a hit.'

She gestures to the gear near her feet. Bea offered it, her boys having put tennis on hold for the winter.

'We've been meaning to start them at tennis,' Julia says, and Debbie flinches.

When she was away she didn't know what decisions were being made by Greg and his wife for the children. Now she does, and it hurts. They're not decisions she gets to make. They may be decisions she never gets to make again.

'Oh. Right,' she says quietly.

'There's a tennis club in East Tamworth. Greg plays twice a week. He keeps threatening to get the kids lessons.' Julia laughs, then sees Debbie's face and stops. 'Sorry,' she says.

'What for?' Debbie says, although she knows the answer.

Julia presses her lips together and shakes her head, then nods towards Shaun and Emily, who are watching them both.

Debbie smiles at her children. 'I guess you can get a head start on those lessons,' she says and points to the large grassy area a few metres away. 'Just be careful if you hit the ball a long way – the river is down there, past those trees. Call out if you need to go there.'

'Thanks, Mum,' Shaun mumbles as he picks up a racquet.

Emily is humming to herself as she does the same.

'What are you humming, Em?' Debbie asks.

'She's been doing it for days,' Julia says. 'It's Kylie Minogue, isn't it, Em?'

Emily shrugs and skips off behind her brother.

'I've been humming Kylie too.' Debbie looks wistfully after her children.

Julia puts her handbag on the picnic table. 'Really? Why?'

'I'm in a choir. We're doing a Kylie song.' Debbie turns and pulls open the plastic bag on the tabletop. 'I brought us some morning tea.'

'Thank you.' Julia smiles and swings her legs over the bench seat. 'I'm starving. Didn't get to have breakfast.'

Probably because she was busy running around after children who aren't even hers. It's the first time Debbie has contemplated the fact that Julia has been doing all the work of mothering and the children may never acknowledge what she's done for them. Somehow that doesn't seem like a good deal for Julia.

'Do you mind?' Debbie asks. Julia looks confused. 'Looking after the kids, I mean.'

Julia stares at her for a second, then a dreamy look crosses her face. 'No, I don't mind at all. I'm lucky, actually.'

'Not if Greg's as bad at housework as he used to be,' Debbie says. But she shouldn't have said that. It's mean, like she's trying to remind Julia that she was there first.

'He isn't,' Julia says before Debbie can add anything.

'He told me he wasn't much chop,' Julia goes on. 'Told me that you were working in that job . . .' She pauses, and Debbie knows why: it was in 'that job' that she committed her crime. 'And you still did all the childcare and the housework. And remembered all his family's birthdays and that sort of stuff. I said he didn't sound like much of a husband to you.'

Julia pulls apart one of the cupcakes that Debbie bought at Janine's bakery on the way here.

It was a quick visit; there were three other people in there all wanting different amounts of sauce with their pies, so Debbie didn't linger to chat. They didn't chat at choir either, which means neither has said anything about that Friday night when that man was there. Debbie wants to check on Janine, though. Wants to find out if she's okay. She just needs the right moment.

'I hope he's been a better husband to you,' Debbie says quietly, thinking of that man in the bakery and how he's someone's husband and not likely to be a good one. Not if he's there being mean to Janine, in front of someone else. That's a man who's not afraid to get caught doing something awful, and if he has no fear he has no limits.

'He has been.' Julia's mouth twists. 'But I feel mean saying that to you.'

Debbie takes a bite of cupcake. The cake part is fluffy and the icing is just the right thickness. She should remember to buy these cakes the next time Bea hosts a birthday party for one of the kids.

'It's not mean,' she says after she's swallowed her bite. 'It's just the way it is. I'm glad . . .' She stops and looks at the children, who are hitting, and mostly missing, a tennis ball to each other. 'I'm glad that he's better. With you. It's a good example for them.'

They both eat their cupcakes and watch the children.

'I love those two,' Julia says after a couple of minutes. 'Just so you know.'

Debbie wants to feel jealous of Julia. This pang in her heart surely means that she resents her for what she's just said. The wicked stepmother, claiming she loves Debbie's children. But there is no jealousy. Instead, a wave of something she can't name rises inside her, and to let it out she exhales through her mouth. Once, twice, again. There are pricks of tears in her eyes so she shuts them. If Julia sees her crying she might think she's angry. And she's not angry. She's . . . grateful. So she needs to let Julia know.

'Thank you,' she says, and she hopes Julia can tell how sincere she is. 'They needed a mother to love them and . . . I wasn't there. I guess I don't understand how you can love them, but . . . thank you.'

'You don't?' Julia looks at her curiously.

Debbie shakes her head. 'Maybe I'm not that nice a person.'

'I don't think it's that.' Julia breaks off a piece of icing and eats it. 'You just might not have had the chance I've had.'

They sit in silence for a minute, maybe longer, as the children become rowdier and make riskier shots. Debbie prepares herself to leap up and go after the ball if it's hit towards the river. She doesn't want them going near it. There's bracken everywhere and probably snakes on the riverbed.

'I can't have kids of my own,' Julia says softly.

Debbie doesn't know what to say. She and Julia aren't close friends and this is the sort of information only close friends share.

'So Emily and Shaun are . . .' Julia closes her eyes briefly and smiles. 'They're gifts. I honestly never thought I'd have the chance to be a mother of any kind.'

She swivels towards Debbie. 'I just want you to know that I know I only have that chance because of . . .' She shrugs. 'What happened. I know I get to be their mum because you had to go away. I feel so guilty about it sometimes because being around them is my favourite thing.' She laughs. 'More than being around Greg. Don't tell him!'

Debbie thinks about where her actions have led. The consequences she didn't reckon on. She could be angry about what Julia is saying, but the anger should only be directed to herself. There is one sole creator of this situation, and it's her. Now there is a triangle of care for these children: her, Greg and Julia. The best she can say about it is that there is love on all sides.

'I know what you mean,' she says. 'It was my favourite thing too.'

What she doesn't know – and can't expect Julia to know either – is what happens from here. Debbie can't ever have the children full time; she has accepted that. But she's spent a lot of hours wishing she can have them part of the time, even though the practicalities of that confound her. She'd need to live in Tamworth, which means finding work in Tamworth, which means leaving her understanding bosses and probably not finding the same degree of care elsewhere.

The one thing she should focus on, though, is what's best for the children. What she wants isn't necessarily the best thing for them, and as their mother that is powerfully hard to admit to herself. They should be in symbiosis, her and the children. Instead they are each their own organism.

'I really appreciate you letting me see them,' she says. 'I'm sorry if Greg has been tricky about it.'

'Oh, he's not now,' Julia says airily, like it's no big deal. She smiles at Debbie. 'I told him that Emily and Shaun need their mother.' She folds her hands in her lap. 'I've never done this before. Tried to share children, I mean. I don't know if I'm going to get it right. But I think . . .' She scratches the back of her head. 'I think if you and I just keep talking, that's the best thing.'

Her eyes are bright as they look into Debbie's. 'They're our joint project.' She smiles. 'Can we both be their mothers, do you reckon?'

This woman is a stranger to Debbie, yet not. In some ways she *is* Debbie. She is doing Debbie's job. Forming the lives of Debbie's children. Julia is a different person with her own background and life, but maybe the symbiosis now is the two of them.

'I think we already are,' Debbie says, just as Shaun hits a ball way over Emily's head and towards the river.

'I'll go,' she says, standing, brushing cupcake crumbs off her thighs.

'Thanks,' Julia says.

Debbie smiles and puts her hand on Julia's shoulder as she passes her, and is surprised when she feels a quick pat in return.

SPRING 1998

Eastern rosella

CHAPTER 53

The drama with Victoria messed up Janine's plan to talk to Debbie. They were all focused on what was happening to Victoria, on getting her into the ambulance and off to hospital in Tamworth, then Warwick said there was no point carrying on with practice. Janine had looked around for Debbie but she was gone. The following week Debbie left early so they had no chance to speak.

Tonight Janine's kept a close eye on her as practice winds up, and when she sees Debbie dart out the door she barely says goodbye to Alex before she's out after her.

'Debbie,' she pants, almost running to catch up.

Debbie turns, frowning, her car key in her hand.

'Oh. Hi,' she says, her face relaxing.

'You left quickly.'

'I have a bit of a drive to Wattle Tree.'

She smiles like Janine is a slightly irritating stranger whom she's tolerating. It makes Janine's resolve waver a little – but not completely. She has to say what she jogged out here to say.

'I don't want to hold you up. I just wanted to talk about the other night. At the bakery.'

Debbie hugs her arms around her. Winter is gone but the night air is still cool, and she's only wearing a T-shirt and light cardigan. 'Do you want to . . . ?' She inclines her head towards the car. 'It'll be warmer.'

Janine looks at the station wagon and wonders just who Debbie drives around in it. She knows nothing, she realises, about Debbie's work or life. She might have five kids and a shearer husband. Except Janine doesn't think so, otherwise why would Debbie be free to go to bands in Tamworth at night?

'Sure,' she says. 'Good idea.'

Debbie unlocks the passenger door, and Janine hops in and waits for Debbie to get in the driver's seat.

'You lock your car,' Janine states.

Debbie looks confused. 'Yes?'

Janine laughs. 'No need round here. Everyone knows everyone. If someone stole your car they'd be dobbed into the cop before you'd even noticed.'

'Oh. Right.' Debbie nods slowly. 'I'm from the city.'

'Right. Yeah.'

Janine examines her hands as if she wrote notes there earlier. Except the notes are in her head, because she was trying to come up with a story that made her sound blameless. She rehearsed it too. Then she hated herself for trying to avoid responsibility. So she's going with the truth.

'Sorry you had to be involved in that,' she says, glancing quickly at Debbie then back to her hands.

'It's okay, real—'

'It's not.' Janine swallows. 'It's not, because the whole thing wasn't okay. That man, Ross – he was my high-school boyfriend.'

Another glance tells her that Debbie is watching her closely.

'He moved back here,' she continues. 'With his wife and children.'

Now she bites her lip and looks out the window. Being the coward that she is.

No, time to face it. She looks Debbie in the eyes.

'We've been seeing each other.' Which is the truth, in a manner of speaking. 'We haven't . . . gone that far. But I shouldn't be doing it. I shouldn't have *done* it. It was wrong. Terrible.'

Janine shakes her head. Saying it out loud to someone else makes it clear just how wrong it was, because it's not something she wanted to admit. All this time, because she didn't have anyone to tell, she could convince herself it wasn't that bad.

It makes her think about the value of confession. If Catholics know they have to front up to a priest, does it make them less likely to do bad things? If she had her own version of confession – if she had a friend in whom she confided, if she still had Bradley to tell things to – would she ever have done this? We are not our own best gatekeepers, that much she is sure about. The rules of social interaction exist to help us keep a check on our more unpleasant instincts; when you exist outside those rules, by existing away from other people, that check is gone. She is living proof.

'You're not married,' Debbie states.

'No.'

Debbie shrugs and looks out her window, into the darkness of the main street. The council keeps saying they'll put up more lights but they've been saying it for a dozen years at least. When she turns back to look at Janine her eyes are bright.

'He's the one with the obligations,' she says. 'I mean – I know you're not blameless, but . . .' She shakes her head and laughs bitterly. 'Honestly, Janine, I'm not in any position to judge you.'

Her smile is wan. 'No one in there knows this.' She nods towards the town hall. 'But I was in prison.'

Janine is confused. And a little scared. 'For having an affair?' she says.

'No! No.' Debbie shakes her head vigorously. 'For a financial crime. *I* had obligations. A husband. Kids . . .' She looks out the window again and sighs.

Janine is astounded. Meek and mild Debbie – Debbie who seems happy when there are enough bread rolls for her to buy for 'the boys' at Wattle Tree – was in *prison*? And she has *a family*?

'I didn't fulfil my obligations,' Debbie murmurs. 'And now I don't have a husband and I don't see my children very often.'

She turns her head so she is looking at Janine once more.

'I let them down. I let myself down. *I'm* the Ross. So . . .' She makes a face. 'Like I said, I can't judge. Him or you.'

Janine fiddles with the band on her watch. It's something to do while she takes in this new information.

'You don't have to keep that a secret,' Debbie says. 'I'm tired of doing that myself.'

'It's not my news to tell,' Janine says. 'But . . . you didn't have to step in, the other night. Whatever else you did. You didn't have to do that.'

Debbie presses her lips together so hard that they almost disappear, then she smiles, tense. 'It's probably not my place to say this, but that man is cruel. The way he spoke to you . . . No man should speak to anyone like that. I let my ex-husband down very badly and he wasn't exactly perfect before then, but he's never used that tone of voice with me. He's not a cruel man.'

Janine thinks about the Ross she knew in high school and remembers a happy-go-lucky teenager. If she's honest with herself she has to admit she's been trying to see that boy inside the man he's become – but that boy would never talk to her the way Ross does. She just hasn't had experience of men like that before; she didn't know it was necessarily a bad thing. It's simply how men can be. Even so, she doesn't know if he's always like that or just like that with her.

'I probably did something to make him that way,' she mumbles.

'Janine,' Debbie says sharply, 'that's just not true. We don't *make* people do things. No one made me do what I did. I chose to do it. It was wrong. I've been punished.'

Her voice catches on the last word and Janine's heart goes with it.

They sit in silence for a few moments, and Janine can see others leaving the hall. In the darkness no one will be able to spot her in this car, which is good, because she doesn't want to have to explain it to anyone.

'Where are your children now?' she asks.

'They live in Tamworth. I'm, um . . . trying to see them more.'

Debbie's glance in her direction is full of pain. 'I stuffed things up,' she says, her voice ragged. 'You haven't. Yet. Please don't see him again.'

Janine is taken aback. Why should Debbie care so much about her? When she stepped in the other day it was because she happened to be there. It's not as if they're each other's guardians.

'I wasn't planning to,' she says quietly.

'Good.' Debbie nods once. 'You deserve better.'

'Do I?' Janine wonders what 'better' looks like at her age, in a town with no available men over the age of twenty-five.

'We all do,' Debbie says. 'And sometimes *better* is being on your own. You can make all the decisions for yourself.'

She clears her throat, and Janine recognises the signal.

'You have to go,' she says.

'I do.' Debbie puts the key in the ignition and Janine starts to pull on the door handle.

'But I wouldn't mind going to a band sometime,' Debbie says, and her face is full of hope. 'If you hear of anything coming up you could call me at Wattle Tree.'

Janine looks at her quizzically. 'Like, socialising? Just the two of us?'

Debbie laughs. 'Yep. I'm a bit rusty. But if there's a band playing I won't have to talk much, right?'

'Right.' Janine opens the door the whole way and steps out before leaning back in. 'I'll give you a ring.'

After she closes the door she pats the roof of the car, the way her dad always does before someone drives off. She waits to see Debbie go around the corner, then tucks her hands into her jeans pockets and turns towards home.

CHAPTER 54

'I've told you thrice now, *I'm fine.*' Victoria's nostrils flare as she bats away Gabrielle's busy hands, which are rearranging the cushions on the settee for the fourth, perhaps fifth or sixth time this morning. She knows that her cousin is worried about her but there's worry and there's annoyance, and Gabrielle is crossing that threshold far too often.

'But you're sick!' Gabrielle wags a finger and Victoria expects to hear a *tut-tut* but it doesn't come.

'I'm *recovering.*'

She's been home two days, with strict instructions, not to mention prescriptions, and neither involved a meddling family member. The whole heart episode business – she prefers the term *episode* to *attack* – has left her feeling vulnerable, and weak, and not a little frightened, but that's not to be Gabrielle's concern. Or Helena's. Or Leopold's, not that he's likely to rush home. The failure of her body is Victoria's to grapple with, and she'll do it in the quiet times – if Gabrielle will let her have any.

There's that finger again. 'You're convalescing. That's what the doctor said.'

'And there's a difference?'

'Of course.'

Gabrielle stands back and looks at her cushion handiwork in such a way that Victoria anticipates another rearrangement.

She sighs. 'I really wish you would take up a hobby or look for another job. And I will take this opportunity to state that my *convalescence* is neither hobby nor job.'

'I'm not leaving you,' Gabrielle says firmly.

'I really wish you would.'

A noise from downstairs gives Victoria a momentary reprieve as Gabrielle walks to the top of the stairs and peers down.

'Hello?' she calls.

'Door was open,' a baritone voice replies and Victoria is startled because it sounds like Jimbo.

She's hardly in a presentable state to see anyone other than the people who love her unconditionally. A person has their dignity, after all, and her particular personage has more than most. If Jimbo sees her looking so deflated – the word Helena charmingly used the other day – he may run off and tell every second person in town. And Victoria can't have that. Not when Arthur is still gadding about with that Celeste.

'Who is it?' she hisses at Gabrielle, whose twinkly smile in response tells her that it is, indeed, Jimbo.

Gabrielle likes Jimbo and his old-fashioned manners, and has decreed him a suitable beau for Victoria, who told her that the word 'beau' should only be used for men under the age of twenty-five.

'Oh, hello, Jimbo,' Gabrielle says sweetly, stepping back as he reaches the top of the stairs. 'How lovely of you to visit.'

'First chance I could,' he says. 'Heard she was home. Hope you didn't mind me coming in. The door was open.'

'We're leaving it open – so many visitors!'

Victoria spreads the blanket further over her lap, for some reason she doesn't know. Modesty? Her high-necked nightie and huge cardigan are taking care of that. Maybe it's just so she has something to do with her fidgeting hands.

'Oh, right.' Jimbo sounds disappointed. 'I only just heard she was home this morning.'

Victoria smiles to herself. He is indeed a very kind man, thinking to come and visit her as soon as he knows he can.

Gabrielle enters the room first like she's ushering in a debutante. 'Look who's here, Vicky!' She beams.

'Hello, Jimbo,' Victoria says, smiling as warmly as she can given she feels like the death she just cheated.

He looks extremely pleased to see her, and proffers a bunch of roses that appear to be handpicked. Perhaps he has a rose garden. Perhaps it was his wife's.

'For you,' he says.

Just before Victoria takes hold of them Gabrielle swoops in. 'I'll put them in a vase,' she says. 'And make you a pot of tea.'

She bustles out the door – not before turning to wrinkle her nose at Victoria and waggle her eyebrows.

'Please – sit down.' Victoria gestures to the chair next to the settee and Jimbo enfolds his long body into it, putting his hands on the arms.

'I saw your husband outside,' he announces, his voice mild, as if he's announcing the name of the winner of a meat tray.

Victoria wants to correct him – to say *ex*-husband – but Arthur isn't that yet.

'Oh,' she says. 'Was he about to come in too?'

She can't imagine why, unless it's to try to use her health problems as an excuse to move proceedings along. No point holding onto the house if she's not going to be alive to live in it, et cetera et cetera. It's horrible even thinking that the man she married nearly four decades ago could behave that way, but she's had an education this year in how people – and life – can surprise you. Also in how you can be fooled by someone for a long period of time.

It should make her wary and untrusting; therefore she has no idea why she's entertained Jimbo's company more than once. Perhaps because the aggregate of her experiences with humans tips in favour of the positive. She can't let one rotten husband poison her opinion of the rest of the human race.

'He was,' Jimbo says, settling back into the chair. 'I told him to get lost.'

Victoria gasps in surprise, then bursts out laughing. 'Why?'

'Because I don't want him bothering you. You've been unwell.' At this he reaches across and pats her wrist. 'All he'd do is upset you. Useless specimen.' He huffs and rolls his eyes. 'Imagine treating *you* like that. *You*.'

He turns up his palms in the universal gesture of helplessness and Victoria is touched.

'Thank you,' she says. 'You're right – he would have upset me.' She glances around the room. 'He wants half of the value of this house. And I'll either have to sell it to give it to him or sell him my half.'

'That's outrageous!' Jimbo is frowning. 'It's your family home.'

'I know. And I have a lawyer looking into it. It's just all so unpredictable.'

That, right there, is what makes her heart hurt: the uncertainty of her future. Her lawyer thinks Arthur doesn't have a case to make but he can't be sure. Nothing in the law is sure, apparently, which makes Victoria think that there's very little point in laws. They're written down as acts of parliament and in records of court cases and yet no one can predict how any judge or jury will interpret them. It's a capricious way to run a society – and not one that is conducive to her wellbeing.

'Sometimes I . . .' She takes a breath. One of her nurses told her whenever she feels upset she should try to practise breathing slowly. 'I think it might be easier to just let him have it. At least I'd know what's happening then. Certainty would be better for my health.'

She gives Jimbo a tight smile, the sort you make when you're trying to reassure someone without feeling terribly reassured yourself.

'Don't rush into anything,' Jimbo says seriously.

'Did you hear the part about my health?' Victoria's voice goes up, and she feels her blood pressure going up with it.

Jimbo's hand is on her wrist again, and this time he's holding on.

'I did,' he says. 'But think about how you'd feel if he ended up here and you had to go somewhere else. I'd wager that would be *worse* for your health.'

He's right, of course. When she was lying in that hospital bed her brain would go through all the possible outcomes, then the nurse would come and check her pulse and scold her for getting herself worked up, so Victoria would stop thinking about it for a little while. But it was just *there*: her inexorable future. Determined by Arthur no matter what she does.

When priests and pastors talk to engaged couples about marriage, she thinks, they really should ask the women whether they're sure they want to have the rest of their lives affected by the decisions of the man they're to wed, even if the marriage were to falter. Those supposedly wise men don't really cover the hard parts, do they? The parts where your husband does the wrong thing by you and can not only get away with it but determine how you live your remaining years without him.

'You may be right,' she says to Jimbo, hearing Gabrielle huffing up the stairs, china teacups and saucers rattling. 'I'll think about it.'

'And you can talk to me about it too,' he says earnestly, then removes his hand.

'Tea time!' Gabrielle announces, looking expectantly from Jimbo to Victoria. 'Have you had a nice chat?'

'Yes, and it's over now,' Victoria says, making a face at her cousin. 'You're here to entertain us instead.'

'Oh good,' says Gabrielle. 'Because I heard some gossip about the owner of the hotel that I really want to share with you.'

As Victoria watches her cousin pour the tea and listens to her gossip, she catches Jimbo's eye over Gabrielle's head and offers him a sincere smile. Somehow his presence in her house – if not her life – is more reassuring than she could have imagined.

CHAPTER 55

Pencil in hand, Debbie scans the shopping list written on the small, lined notepad on the kitchen bench. She always writes it in pencil even though she never erases anything; she just scratches things out if she makes a mistake. It's the opportunity for impermanence she likes, after years spent knowing exactly where she was going to be every day and what she was going to do at the same time every day. Music offers the same impermanence, each note ceding to the next, gone. It also offers transcendence: when she sings she's her but not her; in place yet also above and around and beyond. Maybe that's why she can't stop herself singing as she goes about the housework.

The other day Ryan asked her why she always sings and Steven said, 'Because she likes it, dummy.'

Ryan, of course, didn't like being called a dummy and Debbie, as usual, found herself stuck in the middle of a brotherly argument, wanting to intervene but lacking the authority to do so. She's not their governess; she's the housekeeper, and Bea hasn't told Debbie she's allowed to discipline them. Which means a jibe like 'dummy' goes unremarked and unpunished.

That day she cajoled the boys into singing along with her. She knows Bea makes them watch *The Sound of Music* every year when it's on television, so she tried them on 'Do-Re-Mi' and was unsurprised to discover the song is imprinted on their memories. After running it through twice they even seemed to be enjoying themselves.

Debbie never had the chance to find out if Emily or Shaun are musical. When they were toddlers she and Greg talked about what they'd like them to learn, and a musical instrument was on the list. Just not a piano, Greg said, because if they ever moved house he didn't want to be lumbered with that. They'd start them on whatever instrument it was at the age of seven.

It was an age each of her children celebrated without her. Julia hasn't mentioned if they're learning musical instruments and Debbie hasn't wanted to ask, but she feels like she's getting closer to being able to – perhaps even to gently suggest some things the children may like.

Not for the first time, though, she is aware that she has more influence over what Steven and Ryan do every day than she does over her own children's activities. It's an awful, hollow feeling. She may never be able to have that role in her children's lives again, but it won't stop her trying. Nor will it stop her doing the best she can for the two boys in her care.

Frowning at the list, Debbie can't remember what she wanted to write on it. Rice? Pasta? She moves to the pantry to check the supplies of both and almost collides with Bea as she flies around the corner into the kitchen.

'Oh good, you're here!' Bea says.

Debbie holds up the notepad. 'Doing the shopping list.'

'Great – I'll pop a couple of items on there when you're done.'

That's not their usual routine – Bea just tells Debbie what she wants – so Debbie looks at her quizzically.

'And I'll go in and do the shopping.' Bea nods as if she's trying to convince herself of the wisdom of the idea.

Debbie feels the blood drain from her face and her lips part in surprise. If Bea is going to do the shopping then . . . she doesn't want, or need, Debbie to do it. So she must be about to fire her. Debbie's done something bad, or the boys have complained about her. That's what it is. The boys don't like her any more.

Debbie feels her mouth going dry and swallows. 'Oh,' she says, swallowing again. 'Right.'

She turns away and puts the list and her pencil on the countertop. 'I'll leave it here,' she says meekly.

'But you were about to check the pantry?' Bea is looking at her like she's touched in the head.

'Yes. But, um, if you're doing the shopping now I guess I don't—'

'Debbie.' Bea is holding up her hand in the universal sign of *stop* and smiling. 'Don't get yourself in a tizz.'

'Um.' Another swallow. 'I'm not.'

'You *are*.' Bea laughs and shakes her head.

If Bea is laughing that's a good sign, Debbie supposes. But now she's confused about what's going on.

'I want to do the shopping,' Bea continues, 'because I'm hoping to take over the house duties again. If . . .' She crosses her fingers. 'You're prepared to do my job instead.'

Debbie thinks quickly. Bea's job is big: she basically manages the business and the workers while Phil makes the business decisions and goes off to meetings with people in Sydney and wherever. It's a lot more responsibility than running the kids to school and doing the shopping and the washing. She doesn't know what Bea is thinking.

'Why?' she says, hoping to find out.

'I miss the boys,' Bea says. 'Phil and I both think they need to see at least one of their parents more often. You've done a *great* job with them, but I don't want them going into therapy when they're fifty saying their mother never had time for them.' She grimaces. 'And, well . . . Phil and I both think you're more than up to managing Wattle Tree. You're organised, you're smart, you pay attention. You're good with details.' She grins. 'And the workers like you.'

'Do they?' Debbie's never really considered if they do or not. She's been spending the past few months just trying to figure out what happened to her life.

Bea winks. 'I think a couple of the older shearers think you're a good sort.' Then she looks mortified. 'Don't take that the wrong way! I know you're not old!'

Debbie shakes her head to signal it's all fine.

'And I know you get on with George and Jacko and those boys,' Bea rushes on. 'They respect you. And believe me, they don't respect that many people.' She laughs ruefully.

Debbie knows a little of what Bea does, and she also knows that the job takes more hours than what she's doing now. It also seems to be unpredictable, because farming doesn't happen only on weekdays. How will she see Emily and Shaun if she can't predict her days off?

'I, um . . .' She smiles vaguely. 'It's really kind of you.'

'I'm not being kind, I'm being practical.'

'It's a . . . It's a lot more hours.' Debbie wonders if she can just tell Bea what she's worried about.

'Oh, money! Money!' Bea claps her hands together. 'It's a pay rise, of course. We don't expect you to work longer for the same money. Sorry – I should have said upfront!'

'Thanks,' Debbie says, although the money hadn't crossed her mind. Funnily enough. Living out here she needs less and wants less than she did at that time when no amount of money was enough to fill the well she kept emptying. 'But I was more thinking . . .'

Bea looks at her and nods encouragingly.

'I've been hoping I'll get to see my kids more. Maybe once a week?'

That really is a dream at this stage but she wants to be prepared in case it becomes a reality.

'You'll have time off each week,' Bea says, saving Debbie further explanation. 'Of course! It won't be seven days a week like I do it. Phil's going to handle things on your days off and I'll be around to pitch in. Depending on the season we may not be able to give you two days off in a row.' She looks apologetic. 'But, look – just always tell me what you need, Debbie. This is a family business. You're part of our family now. We work things out, okay?'

Debbie is taken aback by what Bea's said. She's part of their family? She, who caused her own family to dissolve? It's more than she deserves. And exactly what she needed to hear. If only it wasn't turning her into a lip-wobbling mess, because that's what's happening now.

'Oh, Debbie,' Bea says as she hugs her and Debbie lets her. 'As I've said before, everyone makes mistakes. They shouldn't go punished forever. You're in a tough spot now but you'll come good.'

Bea pulls back and smiles. 'We're lucky to have you, I know that.'

'I think I'm the lucky one,' Debbie whispers.

'See if you still think that when you have to drag Jacko out of bed on a cold morning and yell at a supplier for being a week late.' Bea laughs, hugging her again. 'Come on – let's have a cuppa before I go into town.'

Debbie sniffles and nods. 'I'll make it,' she says.

'I'd love that.' Bea lets go of her and takes a seat at the kitchen table.

CHAPTER 56

Warwick is going to be so surprised when he sees her. Gabrielle is *never* early. Why should she be? It's better to make people wait because then they appreciate your arrival.

Victoria didn't notice she left the house early because she was already asleep. Not that Gabrielle thinks there's a benefit to having a heart attack but *if there were* it would be that a person needs rest to recover and that involves napping and sleeping. Victoria's slept more than she probably ever has.

When her cousin was a teenager, Gabrielle remembers, she would be up before dawn, pottering around the house. Gabrielle only knew this because their bedrooms were adjacent and she'd already be awake, afraid of what the day would bring. She was afraid quite often in those days: of her parents reclaiming her, of going to a school where she didn't really fit in.

The local school wasn't the most coddling environment for a slightly dramatic child who was prone to random fits of singing. One teacher told her there was 'no room for Sarah Bernhardts here'. But there was room in the Reynold household. Victoria and her parents never thought Gabrielle was strange – 'delightfully eccentric' was the phrase Victoria's mother used and Gabrielle wore it as a badge of pride. Victoria's father treated Gabrielle as his own. 'Two daughters are twice as good as one,' he'd say when there'd be presents for Gabrielle under the Christmas tree and a fuss made on her birthdays. If it hadn't been for Victoria's family, Gabrielle doesn't know who or where she'd be.

So she didn't mind when Victoria woke her up in the mornings. Sometimes she'd wander out and find her cousin baking or crocheting; there were always teas and fetes and birthdays and general occasions to which Victoria liked to make a contribution. She's been making a contribution her whole life, so she's overdue for a rest. And if Gabrielle can take advantage of her new sleep patterns to sneak out of the house, well, they both benefit.

The evening air is warmer now spring has really taken hold, so it's a pleasant walk to the hall. Gabrielle loves this time of year for the light, if not the warmth. European life suited her better; she's always been a cold-weather person, and the summers she lived through there didn't make her feel like her very bones were on a barbecue, unlike a January on the Liverpool Plains.

As she approaches the door she hears the piano being played. It's not one of the choir's pieces. It is, Gabrielle recognises, Chopin. Obviously Warwick likes to warm up with the classics.

The music stops as she pushes the door open.

'Gabrielle!' Warwick says, standing up. Then he looks around, as if he's expecting a trick.

'Hello, Warwick,' she trills.

'Do we have an appointment?'

Dear man, he's so well-mannered that he's trying to take responsibility for her barging in on him.

'No.' She strolls towards the piano. 'But I wanted to have a chat.'

Warwick looks like he's been scalded.

'Not about you! Or the choir. About me.' She pats his hand. 'About me *and* the choir.'

He looks relieved and steps out from the piano seat, walking slowly to one of the folding chairs that are set up for practice. He waits for Gabrielle to sit before sitting himself.

'Are you ready for a solo?' he says, looking eager. 'Because you know you can do any song you like.'

She smiles brightly. 'No! But it's lovely of you to offer. No, what I want to tell you is that I'm leaving the choir.'

She continues to smile, conceited enough to think she's softening a mortal blow to the man and polite enough to know that one should deliver a rejection as kindly as possible.

'But—' he splutters. 'What?'

'And before you ask: it's not you, it's me, darling.' Another pat on his hand. 'I've always wanted to say that.'

'I'm so sorry if we haven't been doing songs you like,' Warwick says in a rush. 'We can change the program. I'd be so happy to consult with you. Honestly, I—'

'*Warwick*,' she says, 'it's *really* not you. It's *really* me.'

This is the part she's rehearsed – the part where she confesses something to him that she still wishes she could lie about to herself. She knows she risks the information spreading; not even Ivan knows the truth, because as much as she loves him she also knows he's a gossip. Yet Warwick has always seemed like a self-contained person, not the sort to go running around town with news. Possibly because he's been on the other side of that sort of news. Victoria told her that people have been cruel to him. Because Gabrielle has worked for years in a world that has all sorts of characters in it, the idea of ostracising someone because of something they can't change is beyond her.

'Now I'm worried,' Warwick says. 'About you.'

I'm worried about me too, is what she wants to say. They are not, however, friends so she won't. She does worry, though. She hasn't stopped worrying since she realised, a few weeks ago, that months and months of trying have not given her top notes back to her.

'I have a . . . a problem,' she starts. 'It's why I couldn't do that solo. Before.' She bites her lip, uncharacteristically hesitant. 'Several months ago I had surgery on my vocal cords.'

He's watching her, his face a picture of concern.

'The surgeon warned me there might be some deficit afterwards but he assured me that I'd recover.' She presses her lips together in an attempt at a smile. 'The top of my range disappeared. Well, it's there – but not the way it was.'

Right, she's said it. If only she could feel relieved about it.

'But . . .' Warwick frowns and folds his hands in his lap. 'But you've been singing. I've heard you.'

'Most of my range is fine. Just fine!' A false laugh. 'And I've managed to avoid you hearing anything very high.'

He looks thoughtful. 'I hadn't noticed. But now you mention it, that's true.'

'I'm sure you appreciate, Warwick, that for someone like me it is distressing to not have those notes.' She pauses. 'Not "someone like me". For *me*. It is distressing *for me*. And as enjoyable as the choir has been, it's also a reminder that I can't sing the way I used to.'

He gives her a sceptical look. 'Enjoyable? Really?'

'What are you implying?' she gasps.

'Gabrielle, it has been an honour to have you here but I'm very much aware of how . . . rustic this must be for someone like you.' He grins. '*For you*.'

'Oh, darling, of course it's rustic but that's part of its *charm*. I honestly have enjoyed seeing people enjoying themselves.'

She meant it as flattery – to him – but she realises it's come to be true. This choir has grown on her.

'But?' Warwick prompts.

She sighs heavily. 'But . . .' She stops. Right now, here in this funny town hall, is when her disappointment feels like it's seeping into her marrow. Her shoulders slump and she wishes she could melt into the floor like the Wicked Witch of the West. Instead of a hat she could leave behind the tattered remnants of her career.

She attempts to sit up straight and lift her sternum. 'Singing and I have had a lovely relationship,' she says. 'The best of my life. But we're breaking up.'

Warwick laughs. 'How dramatic.'

'You're laughing at me?' She's not used to this – people always take her so seriously.

'I'm laughing at you thinking you're not going to be singing for the rest of your life.' He sits back in his chair like he's settling in for a long chat. 'Gabrielle, I don't think you know how to not *be music*. And your musical expression is singing.' His eyelids flutter. 'I've heard your recordings. I knew all about you before you came here. This may sound grandiose but I really think you owe it to the world to keep singing.' He raises his eyebrows. 'The issue of breaking up isn't really up to you. We *need you*.'

She stares at him. Victoria said something like this to her once – before she left Bellbird River. That her voice was a gift, that she brought joy to people, and having been given that gift she had a duty to use it. Victoria even went so far as to say that *God* gave her this gift. If Warwick thinks *he's* being grandiose he should have been present for that little guilt trip.

It made Gabrielle think, though. Her voice – her musical talent – doesn't belong to her. It's an innate part of her but she didn't create it. It was just *there*. She's fostered it, nurtured it.

Once, in Paris, she briefly met the American writer James Baldwin and she knows what he said about talent: that talent is insignificant, and there's a lot you have to do with it for it to endure. Or something like that.

Gabrielle's done the work. She knows that. Probably *because* Victoria told her that she had an obligation to do so, even if Gabrielle wasn't conscious of that. It really is annoying to discover that Victoria is continually right about so many things. However, when it comes to what she can do with her talent now, there is the little matter of a technical deficit.

'That's sweet of you,' she says to Warwick, 'but if I can't sing I can't sing.'

'You *can* sing,' he responds quickly. 'Just not everything you used to. But regarding those notes . . .' He gives her a curious look. 'If you'd permit me to hear what they're like, I may be able to suggest some exercises.'

Gabrielle is mortified at the idea of anyone actually hearing her. Yet the idea of assistance is equally strong.

'I've been trying exercises,' she says.

'But how do you know they're the right ones? I've worked with people before. In Melbourne. Years ago. Their voices came back.' He leans towards her. 'It's never *just* about the cords. As you know, the voice is a mystery. Fixing it is a bit of a mystery too, but I know it involves part belief, part work, and part magic.'

She thinks about how she's attempted to fix what's wrong by focusing just on the mechanics of it: that note feels a certain way in her body and has to keep feeling that way to be right. Magic is something she stopped accounting for when singing became her job, but she's prepared to believe him.

'You can still leave the choir,' he says, 'if you want. But I'd like to work with you if you'll let me.'

There is nothing to lose, she supposes, in trying. She doesn't have to tell anyone – not even Victoria – so if it fails no one else will notice. And it's not often that someone offers to help her; not often that anyone would dare. She should reward Warwick's chutzpah, and also let herself be the one who isn't the expert. It may even be a relief.

'Very well,' she says. 'Let's work together. I'll reserve my decision regarding the choir.'

She sees a fleeting expression of victory on his face.

'Wonderful,' he says. 'I'll think of a regular time we can do it and I'll give you a ring.'

She nods, then glances at the clock on the wall. The hordes will be arriving soon. She needs to leave so she can make an entrance in a few minutes time.

'Thank you,' she says, standing.

'No, really, Gabrielle, thank *you*.'

She knows he's probably just saying that but she's touched nonetheless. Turning, she walks to the door with her shoulders back and her chin lifted.

CHAPTER 57

Holding the phone firmly to her ear, Alex cranes her head around the doorway to see if Kim is still reading her book. She's relieved to see her daughter tucked up on the couch, nose deep in a novel, with only her eyebrows visible.

'Mm-hm,' she says into the receiver as George recounts a story about a sheep going rogue in the shearing shed.

Kim has no idea that her mother is talking to a man – a man Alex has now dined with three times – and Alex is relieved that the book is so engrossing that Kim's not going to ask her who's on the phone, as she normally does, always hoping it's her grandmother. George is a secret from Kim and he'll remain that way until Alex is sure she wants to keep seeing him.

One of her colleagues talked about how she had 'vetted' her husband for months before deciding he was worth continuing to see. 'And I keep vetting him,' she added. 'One slip and he's gone!'

Given that this husband picks up his wife after work each day and sometimes waits at the school gate with a bunch of flowers, the vetting thing appears to be a worthwhile practice. If Alex knew her colleague better she'd ask her about it, but she doesn't want to give anyone an opportunity to gossip. There aren't many eligible men around her age in Bellbird River or its surrounds, and given the way people in this town talk George's identity would be discovered. Which is why their last dinner was in Quirindi and the one before that in Tamworth.

'So there's a rodeo on this weekend,' George is saying as Alex refocuses on the call. 'Near Scone. Would you like to go with me?'

Alex calculates the distance to Scone and how long it will take to drive there and back, then adds a few hours for the rodeo. She doesn't know what she's going to do with Kim for all that time, and she certainly isn't going to take her along.

'I, ah—'

Loud knocking on her front door makes her stop.

'Hang on a sec, George,' she says, then pokes her head into the next room only to see Kim already on her feet.

'Kim,' she half-whispers, 'ask who it is *first*, don't just open the door.'

Kim gives her an I-know-that-already look and walks heavily to the door as Alex keeps one eye on it.

'I know it'll be a long day,' George is saying as Alex watches Kim's body language change. She's bouncing on her feet, now she's opening the door – and Alex can see Marta standing on the other side of it.

'Oh god,' Alex says.

'What's wrong?' George says. 'Too much?'

'Oh, um – sorry, George, I have a really unexpected visitor on my doorstep. Can I talk to you later?'

'Sure. I'll ring you tonight.'

'Thanks. Bye.'

She didn't want to be rude to him, and she doesn't want to be rude to her mother either, but she has a feeling she's about to be.

'Mama,' she says, as Kim pulls a big suitcase into the hallway, 'what are you doing here?'

'Hello, Alexandra.'

Her mother is smiling at her like she's an annoying stranger. That's the smile Alex saw a lot in her teenage years – the one her mother used to keep her at a distance for reasons Alex never knew.

'Mama?' Alex stands back as Kim drags the suitcase towards the spare bedroom. 'Kim, you shouldn't be lifting that!' she calls.

'It's too heavy for Grandma.'

There's a thud as Kim hits the door with the case.

'My Kimmy needs me,' Marta says as she steps inside.

'Kim needs a lot of things, including stability.' Alex glares at her. 'When did you decide to visit? Why didn't you call first?'

Marta smiles mysteriously. 'Not visit,' she says. 'Move.'

Alex feels instantly nauseated. Did her mother really say *move*? No, she can't have. Who just decides to move to a country town with no notice? Possibly a woman who once decided to move countries, granted, but ever since Marta arrived in Australia she's stayed put in Sydney.

'Come on, Mama,' Alex says nervously. 'How long are you really staying for?'

Kim has reappeared in the hall. 'Are you really moving here?' She's bouncing on her feet again.

Marta holds out her arms and Kim runs into them, leaving Alex feeling betrayed twice over. These two appear to have come up with a scheme and mutually agreed to not tell the person it most affects. Or else Kim has been given very strong hints during her regular phone calls with Grandma, and Alex – who used to listen in but started giving Kim privacy because that seemed like the appropriate thing to do – missed them. Either way, this development is not to her liking.

'Mama, you can't be serious about this.'

Marta lifts her gaze from the top of Kim's head and she has never looked more serious.

'My Kimmy isn't happy,' she says. 'We have to sort out this school. These bullies.' She gestures with her right hand. 'You are not coping.'

'That's not fair, I *am*—'

'*All year* she has been bullied,' Marta interjects fiercely. 'It must stop.'

'And how are you going to stop it? Don't you think I've tried?'

Marta walks down the hall towards the sitting room, still holding onto Kim, brushing past Alex as she goes.

'Go and sit, Kim,' she says gently, then she turns to face Alex. 'You forget, Alexandra, that when you were in Sydney I was helping you. Around the house. With Kim. Now you are doing everything and your job. You don't have *time* for her like you did before.'

'I have *so much time*, Mum! I see her so much more than I ever did!'

Marta shakes her head. 'You are here in this house, yes. But that doesn't mean you are *here*.'

Alex can't believe what her mother is insinuating – that she's neglecting her child. That somehow this is creating a situation where Kim can't break a terrible cycle at school. It would make her the worst mother in the world and she is very, very sure she is not that.

'Kim isn't being bullied because of the amount of housework I have,' she says quietly, her voice shaking.

She's surprised when her mother takes her arms. 'Maybe not. But she is not feeling strong enough to fight back because it is just you and her on your own.'

She squeezes Alex's flesh, and it feels reassuring; Alex was expecting punishment.

'She does not have new friends,' Marta says softly, 'to protect her. So I need to be her friend.'

She tucks a strand of hair behind Alex's ear and it makes Alex jump. Marta hasn't done that since she was a child.

'You are a good mother, Alexandra,' Marta continues. 'But you cannot do everything. You do not *have* to do everything.'

No matter how kindly her mother's tone, Alex feels like she's being scolded. No gold star for her. Corrections all over her homework. She's ashamed, the way she's always been when she's failed to meet a standard she set for herself.

'But I want to,' she says.

'You cannot.' Marta drops her hands. 'And that is why I am here.'

She turns to Kim. 'Kimmy, my darling, I have more suitcases. Will you help me?'

The pair leaves the room before Alex can ask questions, like what's happened to Marta's house in Sydney, and where does she think she's living in Bellbird River? Probably here, but Alex hasn't lived with her mother since she was in school.

She looks wildly about the room, immediately seeing all the things Marta will criticise: the magazines not stacked neatly, a cushion on the floor, the rug looking threadbare in one spot. This will be her life again now. In her own home this time. There's no way this can work. They'll be yelling at each other before the day is out, and that won't be good for Kim either.

Alex sticks a fingernail in her mouth and starts to chew.

Great. There's something else she hasn't done since she left school.

But she keeps chewing as she watches Kim struggle in with another suitcase, and switches to a different nail as she heads out the front door to Marta's car to bring in the rest.

CHAPTER 58

It would be quite easy to become accustomed to this lifestyle, Victoria thinks. Spending her days with a blanket over her knees, like the Queen in a horse-drawn carriage. Being waited on by others so she doesn't have to fetch even a glass of water for herself. Gabrielle checking on her welfare; friends ringing or dropping by. There is very little incentive to tell anyone she's feeling better, especially when the biggest benefit of this new phase of her life is having her daughter visit so regularly.

Helena used to go months without returning to Bellbird River. Victoria understood – life in a city is always busy because there are so many options for how one spends one's time. There are art galleries and concerts and botanic gardens; in Sydney there are harbour beaches and ocean beaches and beachside walks and beachside cafés. Bellbird River has one carefully maintained civic park, some riverbanks, the annual show, an occasional attempt at amateur theatre, and a straight road to Tamworth. It also has a paucity of the sort of young men Helena would find interesting. Or perhaps she finds young women interesting. Victoria would never ask, just like her father never asked two of his brothers why they didn't marry.

Understanding why Helena doesn't want to spend much time in Bellbird River does not, however, mean that Victoria has ever stopped missing her. Leopold is another matter: he was so quick to abandon not just Bellbird River but Australia that she learnt how to put him out of her mind. Every now and again she'll feel the pang of his absence but there's no point indulging it because he has no plans to return. But with Helena still in New South Wales, missing her is a more present concern. Every time Victoria sees her it's another opportunity to be reminded how much she's not here. Also another opportunity to say goodbye. Which makes each visit bittersweet.

Victoria is trying to focus more on the sweet, but this weekend she has a subject to broach with Helena and with Gabrielle. So she's let them fuss around with morning tea, laying everything out, tucking her in on the couch, checking if she needs warmer clothing or cooler clothing, the window open or closed, classical music on the stereo or not.

Now they're settled with their own hot beverages and small plates of sweet treats, looking at her expectantly because Gabrielle has just told her that the mayor – Celeste's husband – has decided to run again and she'd like to know what Victoria thinks.

'I don't care,' Victoria announces.

'Reallllly?' Gabrielle widens her eyes.

'Why should I care? I barely know the man. Just because he and my husband have shared . . . Well, let's not go into it.' She shakes her head. 'There's something else I'd like to discuss. Helena, I'm glad you're here for it.'

Gabrielle and Helena glance at each other.

'That sounds serious,' says Gabrielle. 'Is it serious?'

'In some ways. But in others I believe it's a positive step.'

Victoria takes a long sip of tea. Her cousin isn't the only one who enjoys a dramatic pause and she quite likes making Gabrielle squirm from time to time. Right now she's almost jumping off the couch wanting to find out what Victoria has to say.

'Helena, Gabrielle may mind me saying this, but I think honesty is required. She has some debts to her manager.'

She risks looking at Gabrielle, whose eyes are on the ceiling as if something fascinating is growing there.

'Large debts. And he's not letting her out of them even though she . . .' Now Gabrielle looks stricken and Victoria knows that means she shouldn't reveal too much. 'She has no wish to return to Europe at this present time.'

'He sounds awful, Gabby,' says Helena. 'Want me to beat him up for you?'

'Ha-ha!' Gabrielle's smile is as fake as her laugh. 'No, thank you!'

Then she quickly glares at Victoria, who decides to ignore it. She has a mission, and she's staying with it.

'This house is the only asset I have,' Victoria says. 'And it's an asset that would have passed to you and Leopold, of course. Except your father thinks he's entitled to half of its value.'

'That, um . . .' Helena's discomfort is obvious – and of course it would be. While she's made her disapproval of her father clear, he's still her father and as much as Victoria would like Helena to pick a side – hers – it's not reasonable to ask her to do so.

'That doesn't seem fair,' Helena finishes.

'No. It's not. But he won't be dissuaded. I think his . . . *little piece* wants to live here.'

'Mummy, don't be mean.'

'About Celeste? I think I can be.'

'Daddy's as much to blame.'

'I absolutely realise that, Helena, but I do not think she slipped and fell on his penis by accident, so I can assign as much blame to her as I wish.'

'*Mummy!*'

Helena's cheeks are red, but Gabrielle's eyes are streaming with tears of laughter.

Victoria is quite enjoying her daughter's outrage. Sometimes these younger people can be quite prudish while at the same time thinking their parents are just *so* old-fashioned and close-minded.

'At any rate,' Victoria continues, 'I think *she* wants to live here and that's why Arthur is so insistent about wanting half the value of the house. He knows I'll be forced to sell it to pay him. Then they can buy it, because who else is going to want it? No one else in Bellbird River would dare buy my house.'

It's the explanation that makes the most sense to Victoria. Arthur knows she doesn't have a lot of cash to pay a lawyer, therefore she won't want to go to court to fight him over the house. The cheapest course of action is to sell it to pay him.

'I don't want them living here!' Helena cries.

'I don't either. But I also know that the money from the sale will help Gabrielle. And that's why I've decided to stop caring about who buys the house. All I care about is that I've decided to sell.'

She turns more towards her cousin. 'Gabrielle, this house isn't worth as much as a house in Sydney but if Arthur really wants it I believe we can drive up the price. What I want is enough for you to discharge your debt and for me to invest.'

Gabrielle looks rattled. 'You can't do that, Vicky! This is your family's home.'

'That doesn't mean anything any more.' Victoria smiles sadly. 'They're all dead, darling, apart from you. Why would I hold on to history just to prove a point? If my father had needed the money he would have sold without hesitation. This house is here to be used to our benefit.' She reaches over and pats her cousin's cheek. 'And it's not just my family's home. It's *our* family's home. The title may be in my name but you should benefit from the place too. So I've decided, and that's that. It's going on the market.'

'But . . . where will you live?' Helena asks.

She appears to be crying, and Victoria realises she should have considered what it would mean for her to have her childhood home sold. Except none of them can afford sentiment now. It's far too expensive a hobby.

'I don't know. I'll rent somewhere. I'm eligible for the aged pension. We'll work something out.' She smiles quickly at Gabrielle. 'You may wish to go to Sydney, Gabby. I don't expect you to poke around Bellbird River with me.'

Gabrielle's mouth opens but she doesn't say anything. Instead, she sniffs and looks down at her hands.

'Thank you,' she whispers. 'I never expected anyone to do something so grand for me.'

'Well, we're related, aren't we?' Victoria says. '*Grand* is in our blood.'

Gabrielle sniffs again and nods. 'I've ruined you,' she says, her voice catching. 'I didn't mean to.'

Victoria huffs. 'Oh, for god's sake, stop being so melodramatic. You didn't ruin me, yourself or anyone. Things happen. Things we don't expect. All the time. Life is constant change wrapped up in an illusion of unbending routine. You and I have been through a lot together – your terrible parents, for one thing – and we'll make it through this. It's just more change.'

Now she looks at Helena, who is definitely crying. 'I'm sorry, darling. I didn't know the house meant that much to you.'

'It's not that, Mummy.' Helena tries on a smile. 'It's because I love you so much. You're . . . amazing.' She blinks back more tears.

'She is,' Gabrielle murmurs, and her own tears roll down her cheeks. 'And we almost lost her.'

'You two are *hopeless*. You didn't almost lose me, I just had a heart episode. And I'll have another one if you keep bringing me cakes like this.' Victoria gestures to the array on the coffee table. 'But let's have one or two while we can still afford them.'

She smiles to show she's joking. Except she's not, really. It's entirely possible that she won't be able to afford anything once she sells this place and settles everything else to do with the divorce. Arthur may be getting his way on this score but Victoria has the satisfaction of knowing she's doing it for her own reasons. Staying in this house would be worth nothing if Gabrielle were in trouble for years to come. Possessions are meaningless if we cannot take care of those we love. It's a philosophy that has guided her for much of her life and one she intends to carry to the grave.

CHAPTER 59

At the front of Bradley's house Janine is surprised to see neat garden beds filled with sweet peas, irises and woody shrubs. One of the residents must be doing the work because she's sure the state government isn't paying for a gardener.

Bradley's waiting for her at the front door, looking freshly showered, the collar of his shirt stiff, the hem of the shirt tucked into his trousers. He's wearing a belt and his shoes have laces. This is progress. Progress she could learn from herself.

The other day she gently lectured him about how taking care of himself isn't just about medication and eating healthily – he needs to wash, and brush his teeth, and dress nicely. Making an effort, she said, makes a difference to state of mind. It's something Debbie told her when Janine asked why her hair is always in plaits.

'I started doing it inside,' she said. 'It takes some time and fiddle to do properly. To make them look neat. It was my way of showing that I was prepared to make an effort to keep myself neat and tidy.' She'd smiled as if it was a good memory, which surprised Janine. 'Now it's a habit. But I still think it sends the same message. And it's easier than blow-drying every day!'

It was Debbie who encouraged Janine to talk to Bradley about what was on her mind. She said that he would want to know what's troubling her; and if she never confides in him he'll think it's because she doesn't trust him.

Janine had never thought about it like that but she believes it's true. She and Bradley were so close. Once he was diagnosed she stopped telling him much about her life because she thought he had enough to worry about. But, really, that kept them apart. She's been showing up for him in body but not in spirit; no doubt he's noticed.

So she called and said she'd like to go out to lunch with him. Not take him to lunch, as she knows he has his pride and he saves money where he can. He would want to pay for lunch; probably for her lunch too. They can have that tussle at the pub.

'You look handsome,' she says as she walks down the path, and she's rewarded with a smile.

'Thanks,' he says, rolling onto the balls of his feet and back to his heels, the way he always used to.

She feels almost shy when she reaches him, like they haven't seen each other for years. In some ways they haven't. The version of Bradley before her is the one who is taking all of his medication, so he's slower, flatter, than the brother she grew up with, but his smile is as she remembers it. She's missed it.

'We're going to the Tamworth Hotel,' she says, 'up on Marius Street. They have a nice dining room.'

'Yeah, I remember,' he says, stepping off the verandah. 'Near the station.'

'That's the one.'

She takes his arm and fancies that he stands up a little straighter as they walk towards the car.

'You look healthier,' she says.

He grins. 'I'm making an effort.'

'It suits you.'

He opens the gate for her and stands back as she walks through, then he opens the driver's-side door and closes it after her.

As they set off she decides that she's just going to say what she wants to say, before lunch. She'd like them to sit and enjoy each other's company without having to hash over problems. Being in the car makes it easier, too, because she doesn't have to see his face and any reactions he may have.

'I want to tell you something,' she says as she drives through the streets of West Tamworth, heading for Bridge Street.

'Oh yeah.' He rolls down the window a little and the breeze ruffles Janine's fringe.

'I've been doing something stupid.' Her throat tightens but she's not going to back out now.

'Oh yeah?'

When they were younger she used to take Bradley's short responses to anything she had to say as an indication that he perhaps didn't care. Now she thinks that he might simply have been creating space for her to speak. There's no judgement in that space, just an invitation. It makes her brave.

'You remember Ross,' she says, flicking on the indicator.

'Yeah. I do.'

The way he says it makes Janine think that the memory isn't a pleasant one, except they always seemed to get along. Or maybe she just wanted to believe they did.

'He's back in Bellbird River. With his wife and children.'

She thinks of those photos in Ross's house. Of the letter she wrote him this week, saying that she had behaved badly and they shouldn't see each other any more. Taking all the blame, acting as if she was the temptress, knowing that if she didn't he'd tar her with that brush anyway and come to see her to do it.

If he feels blameless he'll just skate on with his life, and they'll pass each other in the street sometimes, and no doubt someone she knows will be his friend or his wife's friend and she'll hear stories, but he'll become just someone she used to know and a mistake she once made. And there will be no in-person confrontation. He won't have the chance to get angry with her, to make her feel afraid. Because she's realised that's what he made her feel that night in his house, and seeing him afterwards. Once she knew that he didn't care about her, only about what he could get from her.

'I was seeing him, Brad,' she says. 'Romantically.'

She laughs involuntarily, for what they were doing was hardly romance. Yet she doesn't want to tell her brother that they were half-naked in the back room of the bakery. That sounds as tawdry as it was, and only she needs to know that.

'Right,' he says and he rolls the window up again.

'I shouldn't have done it,' she says, and she's not laughing any more. 'We didn't, you know, *do that*. But it was bad enough that I was seeing him.'

Out of the corner of her eye she sees him shift in his seat. This car is too small for him. It was too small the night she drove him home from Werris Creek, when he curled up on the back seat and fell asleep. But it's what she has.

'Doesn't sound like it was the best idea,' he says. 'But, ah . . .' He scratches the side of his head. 'It's not that easy being human, is it?'

'What do you mean?'

'We try the best we can,' he says slowly, deliberately. 'But sometimes it's not the best idea. Y'know?'

They cross the Peel River and head up Brisbane Street. As they near the *Northern Daily Leader* building she puts on her left blinker.

'I do,' she says. 'But I shouldn't have done it.'

He sighs, and it startles her.

'You're too hard on yourself,' he says. 'Always have been.'

Her laugh is without mirth. 'I think I need to be *harder* on myself, if anything.'

'Nah.' He shakes his head. 'You try, Neenie. You try so hard. You were always helping Mum around the house when she didn't ask. You came to footy with me all those times when I knew you didn't want to.' He pauses. 'You stayed friends with that girl who was mean to you because she didn't have any other friends.'

She pulls up near the hotel and puts the car into reverse, angling into a parking spot, trying to see it through her tears. All those years she didn't know if Bradley cared about her as a person or just as his little sister. Now she knows he was paying attention after all.

'So you made one mistake,' he says as she turns the engine off.

She looks at him, and he's smiling at her like he used to: in that indulgent big-brother way.

'I'll forgive you,' he says, 'and maybe you should try to forgive yourself too.'

She doesn't know if she's ready to forgive herself, but she doesn't want to argue the point with him. It's enough that he doesn't think she's a horrible person. That makes one of them.

They spend lunchtime talking about all the people they know in Tamworth and speculating about what they're doing now. Then she drives him home, and drives herself home to Bellbird River. When she arrives she goes into the shed and locks the door, and she paints.

She lets her brush move on the canvas without thinking, and what emerges is a wedge-tailed eagle like the ones she sees sometimes when she's on Jumbuck Way, and the one that used to fly near the outcrop where she and Bradley hung out when they were kids.

On her canvas the eagle is in flight, her brushstrokes creating its feathers in motion. She can feel the wind beneath it, lifting it up, carrying it along. She paints the countryside below it, the same she has always known. And as she moves and creates she feels that this eagle is free, without limits on its life. That makes her think of all the limits she has put on herself, and how that has stopped her being free.

The biggest one has been this: that she gets scraps of love from other people because that's all she gives. She may well have tried her best, as Bradley said, but she hasn't done it with her whole heart.

She can change though. She can set herself free. Free of who she's been, of what she's done; free of expectations and disappointments. She doesn't know what she will be like if she flies free, but she's prepared to find out.

CHAPTER 60

'That was a change,' Debbie says, turning to smile briefly at Warwick as she collects the sheet music.

'"Ave Maria" isn't in our usual repertoire, no.' He smiles back at her, then turns to stack some chairs against the wall.

When Warwick announced their new piece at the start of practice there were groans from some of the older choir members, followed by complaints that the piece would be too difficult. Debbie expected Warwick to say that Gabrielle would take the solo, except Gabrielle wasn't there. She never imagined he'd ask *her* to do it. She's had her time in the sun.

Except no one else protested, and when they had their tea-break Janine leaned over and said, 'You're perfect for this.' Alex had looked slightly disgruntled but she'd also been out of sorts most of the night, sighing and moving around in her seat.

They'd worked on the choir parts all practice, with Warwick saying he'd rehearse with Debbie separately for the lead vocal.

'They'll start to think you're giving me preferential treatment,' she says as he picks up two chairs at once.

He grunts as he puts them down, then flashes her another smile. 'I don't care.'

Debbie isn't used to not caring what other people think, although she imagines it would be quite liberating.

'You have the voice for it,' he says, 'and I've been waiting for someone to come along who can sing it. Pop songs are great but . . .' He shrugs. 'There's more we can do. I think the good people of Bellbird River would appreciate it.'

'Is there an occasion coming up?' She pushes the sheet music into a tidy pile.

'Yes – the Christmas concert. And this time we'll be the sole performers. No school choirs. No church choir.'

That makes her stop. A whole concert, just for this choir? Everything else they've done has been a song or three at most. A whole concert is a lot of pressure. On them, on her. It's different to standing up at the local show when everyone is walking past or thinking about having a hot dog for lunch. At a concert they'll be sitting down, paying attention. There'll be no hiding her mistakes. Or herself.

'Wow,' she says. It's the only way she can express her reservations.

Warwick glances at her over the top of some chairs. 'You sound *thrilled*.'

'Oh no, it's just . . . scary. That's all.'

'Debbie, if I didn't think you could do it I wouldn't ask you to.' He pushes the last of the chairs against the wall. 'All right, we're done. How about a drink at the pub?'

'Wow,' she says again, and this time it's because she's genuinely surprised. She has no idea why he's suggested this but presumes it has something to do with 'Ave Maria'.

He gives her a curious look. 'The pub's not *that* special.'

'Um . . . no. It's not. I just . . .'

'We haven't caught up outside of the choir before,' he says, nodding slowly. His fringe falls in his eyes and he scrapes it back. 'If you don't want to, that's fine.'

'No, I do!' she says quickly. She doesn't want him thinking she's going to ostracise him like some other people in town. Or that she's too nervous around him to be alone with him, even though that's how she feels. 'I'll just get my bag.'

That done, she waits for him to turn off the lights in the hall and lock up.

'Do you mind if we walk there?' Warwick asks as they reach the street. 'I'll walk you back to your car later.'

Debbie shakes her head. The pub is only around the corner. It would be ridiculous to drive there. They take a few steps in silence.

'Will the pub even be open?' she asks.

She's never stayed in town after practice, and only feels she can do it now because she doesn't have to get up to see the boys off to school. Bea is handling that, and Debbie's own hours, while longer than before, are more flexible accordingly.

Warwick laughs. 'I'm not sure the pub ever shuts. Sometimes the doors are locked but there are still people in there. Friends of the publican.' He waggles his eyebrows. 'If you know what I mean.'

'Are you a friend of the publican?'

Debbie notices that Warwick is keeping pace with her, his much longer legs matching her slower stride. It's polite of him.

'I teach his kids piano,' he says.

'Oh. I didn't realise you were doing that.'

'I'm not at the school any more, obviously.' He makes a face. 'But some of the parents asked me to teach their children privately. I have quite a few students in Tamworth too, for voice and piano. I'm actually turning people away.'

'That's wonderful.'

She hasn't stopped to think, before now, about how Warwick makes his living. The choir is a group of volunteers and that includes him.

'We're lucky to have so much of your time for the choir,' she says as they reach the pub.

'I love it. Highlight of my week.'

He yanks on the pub's main door and they enter. There's a handful of men in the public bar, a couple of them surrounded by a cloud of cigarette smoke that makes Debbie cough.

'Let's go to the saloon bar,' Warwick says, gesturing for her to go ahead of him.

There's no one else in there so they have the pick of the seats.

'Great,' he says, 'nice and quiet. What would you like to drink?'

Once she's given her order he disappears to the bar and she chooses a table with banquette seating. He returns with their drinks and a packet of chips.

'I'm *starving*,' he says. 'Hope you won't judge me for eating junk food.'

He rips open the packet and offers it to her.

'Thanks, I'm fine,' she says, picking up her beer and taking a sip.

He sips his own, then noisily crunches on a chip. 'Is this weird?' he says after he's finished it. 'That I asked you here, I mean.'

'Um . . . a little.' No point pretending she thinks it's normal. They have a professional association – as professional as two volunteers can get – and they both love music. That's it.

'I probably should have been more clear about it.' His eyes are half-lidded as he looks at her, almost like he's trying to gauge what she's thinking. 'I don't want you to think I've railroaded you.'

'Into "Ave Maria"?'

'No.' He smiles bashfully. 'Into spending time with me.'

'Oh,' she says, trying to work out what he means. 'Do you . . . want to be friends?'

She wants to tell him that she's out of practice making friends, but that would mean telling him why. Janine didn't seem to think less of her for telling the truth but Warwick may not be the same.

'I think we've started down that path already, don't you?' Warwick says, sipping his beer. 'I, ah . . .' He fiddles with his coaster. 'I'd like to see if we're more than friends.' He still looks bashful but also hopeful.

Then he shakes his head and waves a hand around. 'It's been so long since I asked anyone out. I'm sorry. I should have asked you out properly instead of surprising you with a drink at the pub. This is hardly appropriate.'

'It's fine,' Debbie says, a holding phrase while her brain whirs through this new information. She feels flustered and amazed and unsure all at once.

She frowns. 'Warwick, I'm confused.'

He bites his bottom lip. 'What about?'

'Aren't you . . . gay?'

His face is impossible to read. Has she offended him? She hopes not. She simply wanted to explain why all of this is a surprise, because even after what he told her at the Bellbird River Show – about what the parents at the school had thought of him – she had kept him in a particular category in her mind. The not-interested-in-her category.

'Is that what people told you?' he says, and his smile is sad.

'I, ah . . . I might have decided that myself. Kylie Minogue songs?' She shrugs.

'Oh, that's the secret entry code. Right, right.' He raises an eyebrow. 'I'll have to make a mental note.'

'And you knew all about Gabrielle's career,' she adds.

'Because she's world famous.' He sips his beer.

'And you don't seem to have girlfriends or an ex-wife or anything.'

She's sounding desperate now – desperately trying to justify the conclusion she leapt to that she now knows was erroneous.

'No.' His face clouds briefly. 'I realise that a single man in his forties is unusual, particularly around here.' He swallows. 'I had a wife. She died, about . . .' His eyes close. When they open, they're shining. 'Fourteen years ago. I really shouldn't have to stop to think about how long ago it was, should I?'

Debbie goes to say *I'm sorry* but stops. It's a bit of a cliché and she thinks he deserves something else. There's just not a good alternative, though.

'That's awful,' is what she comes up with.

'It was.' Wistfulness comes across his face. 'It was a freak thing. A stroke. At her age.' The coaster is in his hands again. 'I moved here to start over. I haven't looked for anyone else since. And I wasn't looking when you walked in the door, either.'

Their eyes meet. Debbie is still trying to work out if this is real. Her crush on him has waxed and waned, as crushes do, but it's never really gone away. Although she has wondered if the main reason she likes him is because she thought her interest wouldn't be returned. He was a safe re-entry into the world of romantic attachment. And now he's not.

'Guess I've been good at hiding it,' he says, and his smile is kind. 'You had no idea, did you?'

She shakes her head.

'Would you like to pretend I never said it?'

She shakes her head again, then sits up straighter and smiles at him. 'No. I think it's lovely.'

It's the truth, and she made a policy a while ago that telling the truth is always easier than telling a lie.

'Then . . .' He drops the coaster. 'I'd love to take you out to dinner on Saturday night.' He looks around. 'It will probably be here. But the food's pretty good.'

'I'd love to have dinner with you,' she says.

Then they pick up their beers and drink, smiling at each other over the rims of their glasses.

CHAPTER 61

'Is that Jimbo?' Victoria wants to stomp her foot for emphasis but she's not strong enough so she settles for bashing her fist on the arm of the settee, which only makes her hand hurt and reminds her that dramatic gestures are better left for divas like her cousin. Or her younger self. This old version of her, with its weaker heart and slowly seeping loss of dignity, isn't up to them.

'Yes,' Gabrielle says meekly as she treads down the stairs.

Victoria hears voices – polite tones. How *dare she* be polite to him! *How dare she!* The man walked into the real estate agent's after Gabrielle told him at choir practice – just mentioned, as casual as you like, without checking with Victoria first – that Victoria was planning to sell the house, probably to Arthur, and told the agent that he wanted to buy it. There's only one real estate agent in town so it was a solid bet that's who would be looking after the sale, but still – presumptuous! Unbelievably presumptuous!

The first thing Victoria knew about it was the agent calling her, as giddy as a newborn foal, telling her that he had a buyer and wasn't it wonderful, Mrs Crighton – *Ms Bloody Reynold, thank you!* Before he'd even put a sign in the window a local man had made an offer. Fastest sale ever.

'But I haven't signed a contract with you yet, so you have no business selling the house,' Victoria said acerbically and was pleased to hear noises indicating fluster on the other end of the line. Still, she needed information from him.

'Who was it?' she demanded.

More fluster.

'*Who. Was. It?*'

'I can't possibly say, it's confidential.'

'I'm not your client so it's not!' She had yelled a few more things she's not proud of, but in the end she'd extracted the name.

As soon as she hung up she rang Jimbo and yelled a few things at him. Now, unsurprisingly, he's here. And Gabrielle is probably going to make herself scarce, as she should, because Victoria can't believe she's been so indiscreet. This town has known enough of her business this year. Why should they have a sneak peek at the sale of her house?

Gabrielle practically bows and scrapes as she shows Jimbo into the sitting room.

He looks remarkably calm considering what Victoria said to him on the phone – something along the lines of wishing he would rot in hell, or Adelaide, whichever came first. She's never been fond of Adelaide but it's been a long time since she's pulled out that particular insult.

Victoria's nostrils flare as he sits down in the chair nearest her.

'Victoria,' he says, smiling with his mouth closed.

'What did you think you were doing?'

'Hold your horses,' he says mildly. 'I haven't bought it yet.'

'Nor will you ever. I mean to sell it to my husband. Ex-husband. Husband.'

Victoria always wants to say he's her ex but he's not, technically. It seems cruel not to be able to use that prefix straightaway in circumstances such as hers.

'Now, why would you want to do that?' He looks quizzical.

Victoria glances towards the landing, unsure if Gabrielle is loitering outside the room or not. Oh well – Gabrielle went spreading her business around so it probably doesn't matter if Victoria is similarly indiscreet.

'My cousin has debts,' she says. 'I mean to clear them. The only way to do that is to sell the house and use the money. Arthur keeps saying he wants half the house – well, now he can have it, by buying the whole thing. For the maximum price I can get.'

'He doesn't deserve any part of this house,' Jimbo says gruffly and for a second Victoria likes him again.

'I agree, but we so often get things we don't deserve.' Her smile is saccharine and sour all at once.

'If he buys it, he benefits from what he's done to you.' Jimbo sits further forwards. 'I can't let that happen.'

'Oh, can't you?'

He appears to have appointed himself her white knight. Well, such a personage is a myth and Victoria gave up believing in that myth when she had her first baby and realised Arthur was more interested in his 'projects' than parenthood. The supposedly romantic man who had wooed her never brought her so much as a chrysanthemum again.

Jimbo stares at her, then sits back in the chair, crossing one long leg over the other. He's settling in for a while, apparently, and his presumption irks her. She wants an explanation, then she wants him gone.

'I've known you a long time, Victoria.'

She sniffs.

'Not known you well, but we both grew up here. We know each other.' He smiles wryly, his wrinkles deepening along his smile lines. He must be a man given to merriment – not that that makes her like him more.

'I had a crush on you for years,' he says. Then laughs. 'Knew it was no good. Your father wouldn't have let me near you. Not enough money.'

Victoria can't ever remember Jimbo acting as though he was interested in her, possibly because she barely noticed him. She wasn't so much the queen bee of Bellbird River – that was her mother and grandmother before her – as the princess pretender, bustling around with her friends, going to parties and houses and properties, accepting the attention of boys or discarding it when she felt like it. Her family's status brought her a lot of benefits, even if fundamentally she didn't feel she'd earned them. She was a semi-talented pianist and an average student, not the prettiest girl in Bellbird River but not the ugliest. She had nicely turned ankles but her mother said her legs were too muscular from horse riding, and Victoria should try to slim if she were to find a husband. Life when she was young felt like a sometimes wretched game of trying to meet the expectations of others while never satisfying her own. Perhaps that's why she had been so willing to listen to Arthur's flattery.

She closes her eyes, trying to imagine a life in which a man who actually cared for her had married her. Too late, too bad. And she can't say she regrets the children.

When she opens her eyes again Jimbo has a strange look on his face, almost like he's studying her.

'Maybe I shouldn't have said that,' he murmurs.

'No, you should have,' she replies quietly. 'The truth is always welcome. To me, at least.'

'Then I met my Sal,' he goes on. 'And we were very happy. I didn't think about you again, not like that. Not until just recently.' His eyes are bright. 'You're a magnificent woman, Victoria. But I always knew you would be. You're strong. Brave.'

She snorts. 'Strong? That usually puts a man off.' That's what she was always told.

'Only a man who isn't strong himself.' He smiles kindly. 'Not that I figured Arthur to be that kind of man.'

'He got me at a moment of weakness,' she says.

That weakness was, simply, her youth, but she isn't about to explain that if only she'd waited until she was older to marry she might have chosen a better husband.

'And he shouldn't make you weak again,' Jimbo says, sitting up straighter. 'Which brings me to the house.'

'Oh. Yes.' She's let her mind wander from this very important matter – he almost got away with it.

'I want to buy it so you can stay in it,' he says eagerly, like it's Christmas morning and he's bearing her presents.

'I don't understand.'

'I have my home,' he explains. 'I don't want to move in here. And I don't want Arthur to either. That's not right. He has no place here. Neither do I. It's the Reynold home.'

Victoria's breath catches. To think that someone else can see this as plainly as she does – the nature of this house, and why it has meant so much to her.

'You wouldn't know it to look at me – or my house – but I made some money on shares,' Jimbo says. 'In fact, I keep making money. It started off for my nest egg but now . . .' He raises his arms. 'Let's just say I can pay cash for this place and I'll make sure it's a good price.'

'So you would . . . be my landlord?' As kind a gesture as this is, Victoria doesn't know if she'd like paying rent on her old home.

'No,' he says firmly. 'You won't pay me anything.'

Her brain almost turns inside out at this announcement. And keeps turning. She is flattered by the gesture – incredibly so – but it is too much. And as much as she would like to trust Jimbo and his good intentions, she's not sure she can trust anyone any more except Gabrielle and her children. Not that she's completely sure about Leopold. He's only called twice since she left hospital. Rude.

'Jimbo, I . . .' She sighs and shifts her gaze away. There are moments – not often – when she feels as if life is so tiring, its problems so overwhelming, that she would simply like to close her eyes and not open them again. It's not that she wants to die; she simply wants to not feel like this any more.

But then she'll hear Gabrielle playing the piano, or an eastern rosella with its multicoloured feathers will pluck away at one of the bushes in the garden, or sunlight will catch the branch of a tree just so, and she will be reminded that beauty is everywhere in this world and joy is present in flashes, and those flashes, aggregated, can make each day very pleasant indeed. That gives her the strength to move past those other, harder, moments.

When she looks at Jimbo again and sees the kindness in his eyes, and the warm familiarity in his smile, there is another flash. That is his true gift to her today. And that must be the extent of it.

'I can't let you do that,' she says. 'It is the most generous thing anyone has ever offered me, but if I don't own this house I don't want to live in it. It won't be mine any more. And that's all right.'

She gives him her bravest smile and he nods slowly.

'If you don't mind me asking,' he says, folding his hands together in his lap, 'what is your greatest priority – Gabrielle's debt or getting rid of Arthur?'

It's a very good question and one that Victoria hasn't contemplated before. But the answer comes very quickly and clearly.

'Gabrielle is my priority. If everything isn't right with her, there is no point scoring points over Arthur.'

Jimbo nods again. 'Then if you're really sure about the house—'

'I am.'

He smiles. 'I thought you might be. So I have another solution. I'll lend Gabrielle the money to pay back her debt. She can repay me as and when she can. And I'll *give* you the money to fight Arthur over the matter of the house.'

Victoria opens her mouth to protest, but Jimbo quickly uncrosses his legs and leans across to take her hand.

'Please don't refuse this too,' he says firmly. 'I want to help you.'

She stares at him. 'But why?'

'Well, I gave up on that crush, Victoria, but that doesn't mean I haven't been aware of you all these years. You don't know how much you've done for this town. You're in this association and running that group. You visit people when they're sick and bake them cakes and whatnot. People feel like this town is a community mainly because of *you*, Victoria. You listen to people. You take chances on them. You're kind.'

'I am not!'

He laughs. 'Too bad. Secret's out.' He puts her hand back in her lap. 'Like I said, I've done all right financially. I have money just sitting there. Paying for a red-hot lawyer for you is the least I can do to show my appreciation for everything you've done for this town.'

Victoria swallows and looks away again. This is really all too much to digest. She had herself worked up to yell at him and now he's gone and done this lovely thing, for her and her cousin. Oh god, Gabrielle will be *unbearable* when she finds out. Smugly pointing out that she's always known Jimbo is *such* a gentleman.

'Thank you,' she whispers, then sits up straight herself. 'Thank you,' she repeats, more loudly.

Jimbo smiles and those wrinkles return. 'How about a cup of tea?'

'Of course. *Gabrielle!*'

Victoria hears a thud and realises that her cousin has been just down the hall, listening in to the whole thing, but she'll pretend that she's far away and accordingly will take her time to appear.

'She'll be here shortly,' Victoria says, smiling back at Jimbo.

'I don't mind waiting. I'm happy to sit.'

So they sit, smiling at each other, until Gabrielle appears, acts shocked when Victoria tells her the news, then leaves to make them tea.

CHAPTER 62

'This can't be right!' Frank is looking indignant as Janine ambles past him into the hall. Last rehearsal he wasn't happy about his four bars of solo and tonight he's clearly upset about something else. And there's Jimbo, trying to calm him down as usual.

Jimbo raises a hand to greet Janine and she nods and raises one back. She heard a rumour from Mr Fordham that Jimbo is paying for Victoria's divorce lawyer, and while Janine doesn't discuss rumours she's secretly hopeful that Victoria will leave Arthur with nothing – not even the remaining hairs on his head – and if Jimbo wants to help her do that, good. Victoria's loaned money to half the town over the course of her life – although they were never really loans. Everyone just pretended they were to save face. The people she gave the money to weren't in a position to repay her. So it's no wonder Victoria needs someone else to help her pay for a lawyer.

'We cannot sing "Last Christmas"!' Now Frank is really worked up. 'We don't have enough time to rehearse! And that is a *teeny-bopper song*!'

Janine smirks; she didn't know anyone used the word 'teeny-bopper' any more. And she can't resist weighing in on this issue.

'Wham! had great songs, Frank,' she says. 'They're not just for kids.'

She remembers how 'Wake Me Up Before You Go-Go' used to motivate her to actually get out of bed some mornings, when all she wanted to do was curl into a ball and never face the world again. Music as medicine. Maybe that's the real reason she's stuck with this choir.

'Janine is right, Frank,' says Warwick as he looms over them. 'And George Michael is an excellent singer so we really need to do the song justice. I know it's a late addition to the concert schedule but I think the audience will love it.'

'But . . . we're performing in a *church*,' Frank cries, although as far as Janine knows he hasn't had a relationship with any kind of religion for many years.

'Not all music performed in a church needs to be holy. As long as our intentions are pure I'm sure God will understand.'

Warwick smiles beatifically, and Janine stifles a snort. She can never decide if he likes to wind up Frank on purpose or it just happens naturally.

'We have the Kyrie Eleison to start,' Warwick goes on, '"Ave Maria", four traditional carols as well as "The Three Drovers". I think "Last Christmas" will fit in nicely.'

He nods, as if the matter is settled, although Frank makes a face like someone just trod on his foot.

'C'mon, Frank,' Jimbo says, patting his shoulder. 'Let's go and look over the music.'

Janine sees Warwick and Jimbo exchange a glance before Warwick turns to her.

'Now,' he says grandly and smiles. 'I really came over to talk to you.'

'Oh?'

'Your cakes.' He looks at her expectantly.

'Yes?'

'I wondered if you'd consider making some Christmas-themed cupcakes for the party after the concert? I've been assured,' he glances over to where Debbie is chatting to some other choir members and for an instant his face softens, 'that no one decorates cakes more beautifully than you.'

Warwick only ever comes into the bakery for bread and as far as she knows he's never looked at her cakes, so he must have received the intelligence from Debbie. Not that it's any of Janine's business.

'I think it's more that no one else in Bellbird River decorates cakes at all,' she says.

Warwick raises an eyebrow. 'Don't undersell yourself.' He leans a little closer. 'I bought one of your paintings a couple of years ago, so I know exactly what you're capable of.'

Not even bothering to conceal her surprise at this news, Janine takes a step back and collides with Alex, who laughs and grabs her.

'Anyway, we have a budget so I'm not asking you to do it for free,' Warwick says quickly. 'A donation has come in and I'd like to use it to buy the cakes.'

'Oh, sure,' Janine says, because it's not as if she doesn't have the time and she's already been thinking about what to do for Christmas decorative icing.

'I'll come by the bakery tomorrow,' Warwick says, then looks around the room. 'Now I'd better get this mob under control.'

As he departs Alex steps in front of Janine. 'How's it going?' she says. 'Have you been practising?'

'Probably not as much as Warwick wants us to. You? Or has George been keeping you busy?'

Janine grins. Alex grimaces and Janine immediately feels bad. 'Oh. Sorry.'

'Not your fault,' says Alex. 'He, uh . . .' She sighs. 'He says having my mother here is more than he bargained on. He was fine about Kim but . . .' She runs a hand through her hair, as if an answer to it all might be in her follicles.

'Did he meet your mother?'

'No. I think it's her presence alone that's a problem.'

Janine had wondered, after Alex told her that Marta's moved in, how long it would take George to break it off. He's younger than Alex and none of the blokes he runs with are interested in settling down. Of course, they'll probably all hit forty and complain that no women will go near them – Janine has seen it before – but for now they all think their twenties are for fun. She'd been surprised that Kim hadn't put George off before he and Alex even got to this point – in fact, she'd thought maybe it meant he was different to his mates. But she's not sure she can blame him. He and Alex have only been out a handful of times and learning there's a mum as well as a kid on the scene would spook most people.

'So . . . what? That's it?' Janine says.

'I guess so. Or maybe that's it until Mum goes back to Sydney. Which may never happen.'

Some other members of the choir walk past them into the hall and Alex nods her hellos.

'Are you okay?' Janine says quietly.

'Sure.' Alex smiles weakly. 'It's not like I fell in love with him or anything.'

Janine nudges her. 'Never mind. Country boys aren't all that great anyway.'

Alex laughs. 'I don't think that's true, but thanks for saying it.'

'I'd offer to set you up with my brother but . . .' Janine shrugs. 'He's not right in the head.'

She watches Alex's face to see her reaction. Bradley has never been a subject of discussion – in fact, she's not even sure she told Alex she has a brother.

Alex frowns but says nothing.

'He's schizophrenic,' Janine goes on, and she feels that twinge her parents must have felt all those years ago: shame, rising. Even though there's no conscious part of her that doesn't accept and love her brother the way he is, she can't help what she's feeling. It makes her wonder – perhaps her parents can't help it either, and she's never given them the chance to explain it.

'That's really tough,' Alex says, and Janine is glad she didn't use a 'poor-you' tone of voice. She's had enough of that over the years from various people, mainly about her own health or her unmarried, childless state.

'Yeah,' she says, and there's a frog in her throat that's holding on. She coughs to dislodge it. 'I love him to bits, but it's hard going for him. For me . . .' She stops. 'For all of us. I'm trying to figure out how to help him more.'

'I think if you love him, you start with that and let that guide you,' Alex says. 'We don't love that many people unconditionally in this world. I love Kim. My mother.' She smiles ruefully. 'I should probably take my own advice there.'

Janine isn't sure whether that's an invitation to talk further or Alex's only statement on the matter, so she says nothing. It's the safest option.

'I tend to think my mother and Kim gang up on me,' Alex continues. 'I should really just stop and remember that they love me as much as I love them.'

'Nah, Kim wouldn't,' Janine says. 'Kids can be selfish.' She grins to show she's joking. 'Although I think it's safe to say that your mum loves you as much as you love Kim.'

Alex's eyes widen and Janine wonders if it's the first time that idea has ever occurred to her.

Suddenly several notes of the piano are being pressed simultaneously and Janine jumps.

'Guess Warwick wants us to shut up,' she mutters.

'Probably. Quick – we need to sit down.'

Alex leads the way to their seats, and the two of them pull out their sheet music just in time to hear Warwick announce that they're adding 'Last Christmas' to the concert, without a peep from anyone in the choir.

CHAPTER 63

'So let's hear those three notes again, running the G into the G sharp then the A.' Warwick has a serious look on his face – more serious than Gabrielle is used to seeing. It's the look he tends to reserve for the basses when they're off-key. It's also a look no one has dared to give her for decades, laced as it is with frustration and disappointment.

'There's really no point,' she says fiercely, putting one hand on her hip and glaring at him.

'Of course there's a point, Gabrielle.' Warwick's face relaxes and he almost smiles. 'You've come to my house two weeks in a row to practise this because there's a point. And you know what it is.'

She doesn't just know what it is – she *lives* what it is. She needs these notes back otherwise she'll never be Gabrielle Reynold again. Not *the* Gabrielle Reynold. She'll be the version who is Victoria's cousin and a town curiosity because she returned after years away. That's not a bad version but it's not the version she wants.

'Fine,' she huffs. 'But I'd like to do F into F sharp first.'

'Your F sharp is fine,' Warwick says, a little dismissively.

'I don't want it to be *fine*. I want it to be *exceptional*.'

How can he not understand that? The standards of other people – not that she'd say this out loud, but the standards that *he* might be willing to accept – are not hers. Her career only came about because she set ever-higher standards for herself then kept rising to meet them. Some may say that makes her conceited, or hubristic, but she doesn't care what *those* people think. She only cares what *she* thinks. And sometimes what Victoria thinks. In short: those standards still exist and she wants to meet them.

'All right.' Warwick smiles tightly and presses the key on the piano.

It's his piano – a decidedly better-maintained affair than the one in the hall, which Gabrielle believes is steadily going out of tune a little more each week, with clearly no one available to fix it. She's also more comfortable doing this practice in his home, where there are no witnesses, as there may be in the hall and definitely would be in Victoria's house.

Gabrielle closes her eyes and hums the note to herself. Almost imperceptibly she runs up B, C, C sharp, D – then she opens her mouth wide for the D sharp, holds it for a few seconds and tries to slide up to E. But she can feel the catch in her vocal cords and stops.

'The note's there,' Warwick murmurs reassuringly. 'You just have to be brave enough to approach it.'

'Oh, for god's sake, don't lecture me about bravery,' she snaps, and is impressed to see he doesn't wilt from the heat of her anger. Most people do and she loses respect for them immediately, which is, obviously, perverse but she feels no need to explain herself to herself.

'I've been brave,' she says. 'I left here knowing no one in Sydney, then no one overseas, and I made a life. A *great* life. A *successful* life. That's where bravery took me.'

Warwick nods slowly, his face serious once more. 'And where,' he says quietly, 'has it taken you now?'

She stares at him and feels her eyes blink rapidly. God damn him, he's provoked tears. Crying is for people whose vocal cords aren't their tools of trade. Crying always affects her voice and that's why she will not do it when she is even thinking about singing. Has trained herself out of it. So what is this? *Tears* because of something said by someone she hardly knows? Outrageous and inconvenient. Just like his question.

'It's brought me home,' she responds, equally quietly but with far more steel.

'Home to Bellbird River, yes. But you're not at home in your voice.'

'What's that supposed to mean?' Gabrielle asks, although she knows. She just doesn't want to let him think he's right. Because he is.

'Your voice, Madama Reynold,' he arches an eyebrow, 'is your identity. Or so you think. I actually think that *music* is your identity, and your voice is how you express your musicality.'

'You're not making sense.'

'I'll put it another way: you feel that because your voice isn't working the way it used to, you're not who you used to be. My perspective is that because your voice is just one way you express your true self – which is music – you are still very much who you used to be, but you need to adjust your idea of how you express it.'

'You mean you can't really help me get those notes back.'

She knew it. She *knew* he wouldn't be capable of it. A music teacher in a small town could never have the expertise she needs.

'I believe I can,' he says. 'And we haven't been trying for long enough to say one way or the other. What I want to know, though, is why you're clinging on to those notes when, as far as I can see, you could express yourself in other ways. You play piano, don't you?'

'Yes.'

'Any other instruments?'

'Violin. Harpsichord.'

Warwick looks triumphant.

'Tell me,' he says, 'what do you feel when you sing?'

Gabrielle recalls the best moments of her career. She's about to tell him how she felt standing on stage at La Scala as she delivered a flawless Turandot, or at an outdoor concert in Vienna one summer performing 'O Mio Babbino Caro'. But that's not what he means. He's asking her what she feels when she *sings*, not how she feels when her ego is satisfied by the volume of the audience's clapping.

She sees that he's watching her, his face impassive.

'I feel,' she starts, not quite sure what she's about to say, 'as if I'm drawing my notes from a dark well. The deepest, darkest well on earth. Maybe they even come from the past. From history.' She stops and briefly closes her eyes, recalling the sensation of a note as it rises within her. 'Then they move up through my body. And I want to bring them to the light, so they emerge. I open my mouth and they keep rising. They leave me and they don't belong to me after that. They belong to everyone. To the world.' She blinks a couple of times, and concludes, 'That's what I feel.'

'I understand,' Warwick says softly. 'So why are you fixated on a couple of notes, when *all* notes give you that feeling?'

'I'm not *fixated*.'

'You are. That's why you're here.'

'I'm *determined*. Because I want to restore what used to be mine.'

'But you just said the notes don't belong to you. They belong to the world.'

She presses her back teeth together to stop herself yelling at him for being right.

Her nose lifts just a little. 'I would really prefer,' she says, 'that you do not use *reason* and *common sense* when you argue with me.'

Warwick looks surprised, then he laughs. 'Fair enough. So I should just accept whatever it is you say and let you be miserable about three notes that you're allowing to stop you enjoying that very experience you just described to me?'

'*Reason* and *common sense*.'

He laughs again. 'You're an original, Gabrielle, I'll give you that.'

'Thank you. I've spent my life trying to be so.'

Warwick presses the D sharp again and Gabrielle hums it automatically. As a little girl she would sing along to whatever was playing in the house and never be conscious of it until one of her parents told her to shut up.

'There's a lot you have to offer, musically speaking,' Warwick says, taking his hand away from the keys. 'And I wonder if realising what you have to offer others may help you reconnect with what you really need for yourself.'

Gabrielle has no idea what he's talking about and she's about to say so when he starts to speak again.

'I teach singing and piano to children,' he says. 'Varying ages. And I have more requests than I can handle. So I say no to some of the children who live furthest afield, like Tamworth. I would really love to be able to pass those requests to someone else.'

She still has no idea what he's talking about, only that it's not about her and her voice.

'To you, Gabrielle,' he continues. 'I would love it if you could take on those Tamworth students.'

'Me?' She begins to laugh. '*Me?* I'm hardly the teacher type.'

'You've been a student for years, haven't you? From what I can tell professional singers continue to have lessons throughout their careers.'

'Yes. So?'

'There is no better preparation for being a teacher than being a student for a long time.'

'That makes it sound as if you're denigrating our education system. The inmates should be running the asylum – something like that?'

He laughs. 'No. I'm just trying to convince you to give it a go.'

Gabrielle thinks about what it might be like to transmit her knowledge to others. Young people. That may be hard. She is quite convinced she was never a child, just a world-weary adult stuck in a small body. But it would also be a challenge, and lately she has been without challenges of her own making. In her career she liked to take on difficult roles to challenge herself. The challenge with her voice was forced on her.

'May I think about it?' she says. 'Perhaps talk to Victoria.'

'Absolutely.' Warwick smiles and presses the D sharp again. 'Shall we make another attempt?'

Unbidden, his remark about bravery pops into her head. Perhaps she isn't being as brave as she knows she can be. Her voice has always come from a place that isn't physical. It's a place of connection, of faith. She has been focused on the technical aspects of these notes and has forgotten that she can conjure them from a place other than her vocal cords. If only she could be brave enough to try, to see what emerges.

'Of course,' she says with a smile, and hums as he plays the note once more.

CHAPTER 64

The lengthening days have revealed to Alex a whole new aspect to living in Bellbird River. When she first arrived, in January, the solstice was weeks past and while daylight saving meant there was still plenty of sunshine at the end of the day, she hadn't seen the gentle easing into summer that happens now it's November, as the daytime extends and the clocks have gone forwards. Lately she's been spending early evenings in the back garden, enjoying the just-right air temperature and the golden light.

The turning season has enticed Kim into the garden as well, lolling on the grass as she reads or chats to her grandmother. That's where Alex left them this evening as she headed for choir practice.

After she's parked the car she half-wants to stay near it to watch the light fade, instead of going inside only to emerge when night has fully committed itself to bringing out the stars.

She's also been going outside at night to look up. There's a whole universe out there, twinkling back at her, reminding her that she's one small human on one small planet. It's enough to help her put things into perspective on the occasions when she needs to. Such as when Marta irritates her. Alex is learning to stop and ask herself whether her mother is really doing anything to annoy her or if Alex is just presuming she is. She tries to remember to put her mother into context: Marta has a brace of experiences that influence her reactions to things, just as Alex does. As everyone does.

'Hey,' Janine calls softly as she walks up to the hall entrance.

'Hi!' Alex's smile is so broad she can feel her cheeks moving.

Janine looks at her questioningly. 'You're chirpy.'

'Yeah, I . . .'

Alex stops, because she was about to give a pat answer: that the end of the school year is almost upon them and she's looking forwards to holidays, or of being free of the teenagers for a while, or being able to sleep in. Answers of the variety she tends to give whenever someone asks, 'How are you?' Because we all tend to give those rote answers just to keep the social wheels spinning. One of the things she's learned living in this town, though, is that because so many people know your business, those social wheels don't spin the same way. If you give a fake cheerful answer to 'How are you?' someone is liable to say, 'But I hear your dog died.' There's no hiding – from other people or, Alex has realised, from herself.

'I'm actually getting on really well with Mama. Maybe I'm . . .' She makes a face. 'Even enjoying having her here.'

Janine's mouth drops open and Alex holds up her hands.

'I know, I know, I'm as shocked as you are.' She sighs happily. 'But I'm a bit freer now. Like tonight – I can come here and not worry about Kim getting bored or grizzling about something. And I completely understood why she'd be bored but . . .' Another sigh. 'I kind of just want to not feel like I'm letting her down by doing things like this. And now I'm not! Because she's with Mama and they both love that.'

'Cool,' Janine says, nodding slowly.

They enter the hall and see Debbie in animated conversation with Gabrielle as Warwick watches on, looking fairly delighted.

'It also means I can think about being away from Kim for longer than a couple of hours on a Tuesday night,' Alex says, manoeuvring herself so she's in front of Janine. 'So I was wondering . . .'

Janine cocks her head to one side. 'Yeah?'

'How about a day in Tamworth? I need to buy Kim some clothes, but I figured we could have lunch, see a movie . . .'

'I can't remember the last time I went to the movies,' Janine murmurs, her face scrunching.

'I think *The Truman Show* is still on,' Alex says, to a blank look from Janine. 'It's meant to be good.'

'Sure. I could, um . . . I could go this Saturday, if that works?'

'Can you get away from the bakery?'

'Dad doesn't mind filling in if I ask nicely.'

Janine's smile is unsure but Alex doesn't want to press any further. 'Great! I'll pick you up at ten.'

As the din in the hall grows, Alex sees Gabrielle split off from Warwick and Debbie and make her way towards the soprano section.

'I'm just going to ask how Victoria is.' Janine nods in Gabrielle's direction.

'Okay.' Alex wonders if she should go with her but she doesn't feel as though she knows either Victoria or Gabrielle well enough. Instead she moves towards her usual seat and sits down.

'Hello, Miss Markovich.'

Alex looks up and sees Vince Sheridan beaming down at her.

'Vince!' she says, standing. 'Is something wrong?'

Her immediate thought is that the school must have burnt down or something else serious to bring the principal here.

'What? Oh!' He laughs. 'I see – you think I'm here on school business. Because I, ah, called you Miss Markovich.' He looks sheepish. 'I was trying to be funny.'

'Oh, right.' Alex's shoulders drop a few centimetres.

'I'm joining the choir,' Vince says with a hint of triumph.

'Really? Now?'

They've already started rehearsing for the Christmas concert – it seems an odd time to join.

'I bumped into Warwick at the shops. He said he needs a bass.' Vince turns his palms up. 'I happen to be one.'

'You sing?'

'Only in the shower.' He blushes. 'You know what I mean.'

'I do. And yeah, me too. But the choir is my . . .' She looks around at the people in the hall, all busy chatting or looking at sheet music. She feels the energy here. The anticipation of enjoyment. That's what it is. Choir practice is *fun*. She just hasn't given it that label before. It's also meaningful – they make something beautiful together. Well, ultimately it's beautiful but even the faltering rehearsals have their lovely moments.

'It's really special, actually,' she concludes. 'I don't go to church but it feels a bit like that sometimes.'

Vince looks at her quizzically. 'Really?'

'And we're doing "Ave Maria", so . . . I guess that makes it holy.' She smiles but she's not joking.

'Here I was hoping for some "Nessun Dorma".'

'Put in a request. Warwick might give up one of his Kylie songs for you.'

Vince's eyes widen and Alex laughs.

Janine returns and Alex can see the enquiry in her eyes, but just then Warwick walks to the piano and they all know what that means.

'We're about to start, Vince,' Alex says, and in reply he waves once and moves towards the bass section.

She wonders if Warwick is going to make him audition in front of everyone – or maybe being the high school principal gets you past 'go' automatically.

'I'll tell you later,' she says to Janine before the question has even been asked.

She's rewarded with a rare smile, then they settle into the evening's practice. It's all carols tonight.

There's something comforting about singing such well-known songs, especially in the company of people she has come to know and respect, and soon Alex feels like she is in the groove of this music, this choir and this town for the first time. And maybe in the groove of her life, too. She cannot deny that Marta's presence has changed Kim for the better. The girls at school are still giving her trouble but Kim isn't as upset any more, and Alex has noticed that the incidents are fewer than they were.

Marta has been taking Kim to swim at the council pool; she's teaching her to sew. Things Alex wanted to do but with all the housework and the shopping and the cooking she rarely had the energy to contemplate. That doesn't make her a bad mother, though – as her mother keeps reminding her. It just makes her a busy one, and that's why – and her mother *loves* reminding her of this – Marta needs to stay with them for the foreseeable future.

'Are we not all happier, Alexandra?' she said the other day.

And as much as Alex doesn't like to admit her mother is right, that time she knew she was.

CHAPTER 65

'So what do you think of it?' Janine steps back to allow Bradley to walk past her into the living room of the small house on Lancaster Street. A house so quick to welcome people that it has no patience for a hallway, or much of anything. Living room, two bedrooms, bathroom, kitchen, laundry. Oh, wait – the laundry is outside. It was probably the dunny once upon a time. There's also a shed in the back garden, which is what convinced her the place is right for her. That, and the fact that there aren't a lot of rental properties in Bellbird River, let alone any she can afford.

'Let me get a look at it first,' Bradley says.

He's walking slowly at the moment. Lumbering, you might say. His doctor introduced a slight increase to the dosage of his medication and his brain and body are still adjusting.

The low ceiling of the house is almost in contact with his head and Janine giggles.

'I don't know who built this house,' she says, 'but they were obviously shorter than you.'

His smile is lazy but she knows it's real.

'Come on, show me the rest of it,' he says.

She chooses one of the two doorways, the one that goes to the larger bedroom. The other goes to the kitchen, and the smaller bedroom is accessible from that. It looks like it was added on after the original build. This was probably a worker's cottage. A modest house for people of modest means. Well, that's her. The bakery has never brought her riches, although her parents have never charged her rent so she's ahead there.

'It's nice,' Bradley says when she points out the relatively modern features of the kitchen.

'And there are some citrus trees in the garden.' She points to the large window that looks from the kitchen out to a lawn and garden that takes up almost the same amount of space as the house itself.

'Orange juice for you, then.' He smiles, and sighs.

'Are you feeling tired?'

'A little bit.'

'Um . . .' There aren't any chairs here. Nothing of anything yet. Her parents said they'd give her some furniture they no longer need, but she has to go to Tamworth to buy the rest.

'It's all right.' He leans against the wall and gives her a thumbs-up.

'So . . .' Her smile is tight, as is her chest. She feels nervous about what she's going to ask him, mainly because she wants him to say yes and she's not sure he will.

He looks at her enquiringly.

'It's a two-bedroom house,' she goes on. 'And I thought the big bedroom could be yours. If you'd like to move in with me.'

The information takes a few seconds for him to process – she can almost see it happening.

Then he squints and cocks his head. 'What?'

'I'd like you to move here. With me. I don't want you living in that group home any more.'

His squint deepens until his eyes close. He scrunches them, then opens them again. 'But I think I have to stay in the home.'

'No, you don't. I spoke to your doctor. I hope you don't mind, but I wanted to make sure it's possible before I mentioned it to you.'

'It's fine,' he says.

'The home is there so you have someone who can watch out for you. But they're not there all the time, are they?'

He shakes his head.

'I won't be here all the time either, but . . .'

She gasps, because the emotion of what she's been thinking about, dealing with, planning and talking about, has been sitting just below her skin. Standing here, telling him about it, has put pinpricks in her outer layer and it feels like everything is leaking out. It's hard, when you're not a demonstrative person, when you're not someone who knows how to express herself any other way than through a brush on a canvas or a decoration on a cake, to communicate what you feel and make sure the other person knows it's real. When they've never heard it before, how can they trust it, even if they trust *you*?

Janine hasn't even been sure she trusts herself lately, but she has always known one thing: she is Bradley's sister. At times when she hated herself for her behaviour about a range of things, when she felt at her most worthless, she would bring herself out of it by coming back to that surety. She is Bradley's sister and if she needs a compass to find her way home, he is it.

He'd probably laugh at that if she told him, because he's so wobbly on his feet these days. Which is why she's not going to say it like that. She's had to come up with another way.

'I don't want you living with strangers, Brad. I want you to live with me. I'll be taking care of you, but I think you know you'll be taking care of me too.'

He shifts his position against the wall. They stand in silence, looking at each other.

'That's always been the way,' he says softly. 'But . . .' His focus drifts.

'But what if something goes wrong? If you wander off? If you become upset with me?' She needs to say it plainly, so they both know what they're up against.

Now his gaze is locked on to her once more. 'Yes.'

She gives him a funny little smile, then turns and walks back to the living room, beckoning him to follow her.

'See?' She points to a building across the street. The police station, with the police officer's residence next to it. 'All I have to do is run over there.'

It's a fluke that the house is so close to the station, but if she were a religious person she'd take it as a sign from God that they're meant to live here together.

Bradley's doctor told her the risks of his illness: that he might not recognise her one day, or he might develop a delusion about her that could make his behaviour unpredictable. That's not enough, she told him, to stop her giving her brother what she knows he needs: love, care and attention.

Bradley smiles, then his face drops and he puts a hand over his eyes.

'I'm so sorry,' he says, his voice ragged, 'for everything I've put you through.'

She takes hold of his hand and pulls it down. 'I'm not. I don't ever mind anything you put me through.'

She is surprised when he hugs her, his long arms squeezing her against his chest. It can still reassure her, this hug; it reminds her that she's not as alone as she sometimes wants to think.

'What if you want to have a boyfriend here?' he says slowly, teasingly, after he lets her go.

'There aren't going to be any of those,' she says firmly.

'Come on, Neenie. There might be.'

That's something else she had to think about when she was contemplating all of this, until she realised that she has no interest in a romantic relationship. Not because Ross put her off, but because she's come to believe that the intensive search for a romantic partner can sometimes be the result of a vacuum of love in a person's life. They feel empty, so they go looking for someone to fill them up. It's the wrong motivation, but she knows it happens. She's seen it in people she went to school with, people she knew when she was younger, paired off for that reason.

It's taken her all these years to discover that she hasn't felt the same imperative because she's never been unloved, not by Bradley and, in their own way, not by their parents. Her failure to love herself wasn't their fault. In many ways it was hers.

At first she just started hating the way she looked – or that was the line she took. Because in reality she hated what was happening in her life. The loss of control over it. Her wonderful brother, disintegrating in front of her. From there it built, one spiteful thought at a time, and all of it directed at herself. When all you want is to rail at the world and there's no one specific to blame, sometimes you find the target within yourself. But she's tired of it.

Moving in with Bradley is a way to begin to change. Because she's also worked out that the best way to stop thinking about your own problems is to help someone else with theirs. She is not the centre of the universe. Things that have gone wrong, that never worked out, are so very minor set against the love she feels for her brother and just how much she wants to look after him. If she's been looking for a purpose in life, she was looking too hard: it was in front of her the whole time.

'Brad, I assure you, if there's a bloke in my life at some point we'll worry about it then.' She walks back towards the kitchen. 'I just want to make sure you're all right first.'

'Do Mum and Dad know about all this?' he says from behind her, and she pivots to face him.

'Yes.'

They took it better than she thought they would; perhaps they've been feeling guilty about how they've treated Bradley. Or haven't treated him. Haven't seen him. Haven't spoken to him.

'And?'

'Their reaction wouldn't have influenced me either way,' she says, because she wants him to know. 'But they were fine.'

'Really?'

'Yes.'

She walks into the kitchen and gazes out at the garden. A magpie is hopping around the lawn. It stops and lifts its head, looking at her. She smiles; she knows magpies recognise people and no doubt they'll see each other again.

'They may even come to visit,' she tells Bradley, and feels pressure lifting from her. This was the last piece of information she needed to deliver to him.

He's standing next to her now and she glances up at his face, which is hard to read.

'That's good,' he says at last. 'I'd like to see them.'

Nodding, Janine turns her attention back to the magpie. It hops around a couple more times then flies onto the fence, right near a banksia tree that Janine didn't notice the first time she visited.

They'll be happy here, she thinks. Her, Bradley and the magpie.

Maybe the magpie will bring some friends. Maybe she will too. Over time, Bradley might have some of his own. Might reconnect with people he cared about before. He's still him, just with some different layers on his personality.

And who doesn't have those? Who, after years on this earth, hasn't covered themselves with what they imagine is protection only to find themselves trapped inside it?

The way to slough it off is to remember who you are at your core.

She is Bradley's sister. He is her brother. They can start again from that. It's enough; it's everything.

CHAPTER 66

When Debbie went into labour with Shaun she was nervous. Panicky. The pain wasn't like anything she'd experienced before. She broke her arm once, falling off a bicycle; it was painful and she was scared. But labour wasn't the same kind of pain, or the same kind of fear. After she fell off the bike and knew she'd broken the bone it all seemed contained; finite. A cast would go on, stay on for a few weeks, then be removed and her arm would be fine. Labour and the birth that would inevitably follow seemed so vast and unknowable, and the length of time she'd have to endure them together so indeterminate, that the pain that came with them was terrifying. So she panicked.

Her sister was there to hold her hand and tell her that it was a shock, yes, all this pain, but they'd give her an epidural and it would be over soon. It was reassuring, even if it allayed none of Debbie's fears.

Her sister isn't here today, and Debbie probably won't ever see her again. That's the price she's paid for the decisions she made long after Shaun was born. But she wishes someone could hold her hand, because today she feels that panic rising once more, even if there's no pain to trigger it. Panic because Shaun and Emily – whose birth was over so quickly Debbie barely noticed the pain – are coming to Bellbird River. To be dropped off by Julia to spend a few hours with Debbie on their own.

'Greg's concerned,' Julia told her a couple of days ago on the phone, 'but I think it's necessary. They're your children, Debbie. It's important they have a relationship with you. Without us interfering.'

Debbie had wondered how Julia could be this generous, and so helpful, then she remembered that Julia actually gets to be the kids' mum for real and Debbie is still a visitor in their lives. Granted, Julia gets the drudgery of school lunches and home-work and fights over TV shows. But she also gets the funny little highlights that come with each day. A sentence here, a gesture there; the ways your children fill up your life with memories.

Debbie's been living off the same memories for years and she's desperate for a cache of new ones. She'll have to settle for this piecemeal arrangement they have now, but at least Julia seems to trust her enough to leave her alone with the children.

She sees Julia's car turn the corner and pull up, Emily's and Shaun's faces turned in Debbie's direction. The edge comes off her panic slightly; maybe part of it was her worrying that they wouldn't show up.

The biggest element is definitely her concern that they'll hate spending the day with her and never want to see her again. Which is why she's starting off with a bribe. Not ideal parenting, but it's the only idea she came up with. She asked Julia to meet her outside Janine's bakery, where they're going to buy cupcakes. Then they're going to Wattle Tree, where Bea has arranged with Phil and the boys for a tour of the shearing sheds and a ride on some farm equipment.

'Hi,' Debbie says meekly as Julia steps out of the car.

'Hi!' Julia beams as she walks over and gives Debbie a hug, then turns to make sure the children are on their way.

'Hi, Emily. Hi, Shaun.'

The children give Debbie little smiles in return and she feels like her heart might explode.

'Hi,' they chorus.

'I'll have them back here by four,' Debbie says to Julia.

'All good – if you're running late I'll wait for you.' She kisses Debbie on the cheek. 'Have fun. Bye, kids.'

'Bye.' Another chorus.

'It's so good to see you both,' says Debbie. It's cheesy, but it's true.

The children squirm as if they're embarrassed, except those little smiles have come back.

'I thought we'd start with some cupcakes.'

Their eyes light up and Debbie yanks open the bakery door to let them walk in.

As they enter Janine gives her a quizzical look. 'I saw you standing out there,' she says. 'Wondered why you didn't come in.'

'I was waiting for the children.' Debbie glances at Shaun and Emily in turn. 'My children.'

Something shifts in Janine's face and it ends in a warm smile.

'This is Shaun and this is Emily. Kids, this is my . . .' Debbie hesitates. She hasn't had to introduce Janine to anyone before and hopes she gets it right. 'My friend, Janine. And this is her bakery.'

'Hi, Shaun, hi, Emily.' Janine rests her forearms on the countertop. 'It's great to meet you.'

'Janine decorated those cakes.' Debbie gestures towards the special cakes in the side display. 'Isn't she talented?'

Emily's head nods slowly as she wanders over to have a look.

'Can we have one?' she says.

'No, Em, we'll burst if we eat that much cake!' Debbie stops. She wishes so very dearly that she could call her children 'darling' and 'sweetheart' and 'baby' again, all the time. Those have to be earned, though, and she's still working on it.

'Janine has some lovely cupcakes,' she continues. 'Have a look. You can have a couple each. And I'd love you to pick one each for me.'

She smiles as she watches their heads bow together in front of the cabinet.

'That's great,' Janine says.

'Hm?'

'Having them here.' She nods towards the children. 'Isn't it great?'

'Yes.' Debbie nods slowly. 'I don't know if I ever believed it would happen.'

'I did.' Janine smiles more broadly than Debbie has ever seen.

They haven't spoken much about the children. Janine knows what the situation is and how Debbie wishes she could see the children more, and on her own. But as far as Debbie could tell, Janine had no thoughts about it at all.

'Really?' she says.

'Yeah. You're a good person. There was no reason not to let you see them more.'

Debbie's mouth opens. It's not voluntary. It's because she's surprised that anyone would call her a good person. Goodness is a quality she believed she possessed before it became abundantly clear that it was incompatible with her being sentenced to prison. There were so many ideas she had about herself that needed to be tossed out or rearranged once that happened. For quite a while – and with plenty of time to contemplate – she wondered if the version of Debbie who existed before prison wasn't real and the version who was in prison was. And if so, what sort of person did that make her? By the time she was released she'd come to the conclusion that both versions were real, and had to coexist; and in the process of figuring that out, she hasn't solved the question of whether or not she's good. But she appreciates Janine giving it a nudge.

'How's Bradley?' she asks.

Janine told her this week at choir practice that she's rented a house and her brother was about to move in. She also told Debbie why he'll be living with her, and what sort of care she'll have to give. If anyone's going to be labelled a good person, Debbie thinks it should be Janine. Yet she knows Janine would eschew that label. She has her own reasons for not believing in her own goodness and Debbie can't judge them. All she can do, as Janine's friend, is try to help her see all the positive qualities that Debbie can see.

'He's adjusting,' Janine says and pulls a face. 'They had a cleaner in his group home and he's not impressed that he'll have to do some cleaning at home.'

'I'm sure he'll get used to it. We all do.'

'Yeah. Made a choice, kids?'

'Yep!' says Shaun, grinning as he lifts his head.

As he and Emily indicate their selection and Janine puts them in paper bags to keep each child's cakes separate, chatting all the while to them about school, Debbie revels in the ordinariness of it all. To some parents this would be drudgery; to her, it's the closest thing to heaven she's had in a long while. Being with her children, being present at the small, seemingly insignificant moments in their days, is a privilege she didn't even realise she had before it was gone. She will never take it for granted again. Not one of their smiles will go untreasured by her. No tear will be ignored. Whatever story they want to tell her will have her full attention, and she will commit herself to this quotidian work of being a parent, even if it's at a distance most of the time, because she can't imagine any work more important.

She's been given a second chance, by the grace of a woman she didn't know a year ago. By her ex-husband, if she's honest, because none of this is happening without his tacit approval. He could go to court to have it stopped, and he hasn't.

These past few years Debbie was convinced she would never be worth much again, especially to her children. But she is. She has to be. Worth something to herself too. Because she's still here, trying to be good. It's the project of a lifetime, and of her life.

'We're going to Wattle Tree,' she tells Janine as the children head outside with their bags.

'That'll be fun,' says Janine just as the bakery door opens. 'Hi, Mr Fordham.'

'See you,' Debbie says and turns to go, before turning back. 'Maybe you'd like to come to Wattle Tree one day, for dinner?'

'I'd love it.' Janine flashes a smile and waves goodbye before she gives her full attention to Mr Fordham.

'My car's down here,' Debbie says to Emily and Shaun, who are peering inside their cupcake bags, looking pleased. 'We have a bit of a drive then we'll be on the farm.'

'Cool,' says Shaun, then he skips ahead a little and Emily copies him.

It's the most beautiful thing Debbie has ever seen.

CHAPTER 67

While she has never been what one could call the athletic type, it wasn't until her little heart episode that Victoria realised how active she was. Trotting around town going to the shops, to friends' homes, to the library, to the council chambers kept her quite fit. Which, the doctor told her, might not have prevented the heart episode but will help her recovery.

'But all I do is walk everywhere,' she told him. 'I am not a *jogger*.' She'd made a face. She thinks jogging is uncivilised. Either run flat out or walk. Jogging is for the indecisive or those who want to be seen to be exercising without putting in much effort at all.

'That's enough,' he'd said. 'Regular incidental exercise is just as good as, if not better than, something like jogging three times a week.'

So it had taken her until this age to find out that she's actually quite a robust physical specimen. How pleasing. And how frustrating, because now she has to get *back* to that level of fitness. Which is why she is taking what Gabrielle refers to as her *passeggiata*, walking slowly along the paths she has trodden for so many years.

'It's a stroll, Gabby,' she'd retorted the first time her cousin used the word. 'I don't need a fancy name for it.'

'But don't you think it sounds so much more *enticing* when you call it that?'

Victoria had raised her eyebrows. 'Who is meant to be enticed – you or me?'

They'd discussed the fact that Gabrielle really needs to exercise herself, because for all they know heart episodes run in the family. So a deal was struck: the pair will walk around town late in the afternoon each day at an easy pace.

That's why Gabrielle's arm is hooked through hers and they are passing the supermarket.

'Hello, Diane,' Victoria calls to a woman her age who is entering the shop.

'Victoria,' Diane says with a nod and a wave. 'Gabrielle.'

'Who's she?' Gabrielle hisses in Victoria's ear. 'How does she know who I am?'

Victoria looks at her in surprise. 'For someone who was so impressed with her own reputation not that long ago, I can't believe you have to ask.'

Gabrielle's nostrils flare. 'That's unkind.'

'Yet true.'

'Hm.'

'And she's someone I went to primary school with. She married a grazier and they had a property near Gunnedah. One of her children is here, so she visits a lot.'

'Right.'

'Her husband is one of Arthur's friends.'

'Have you heard from Arthur since you asked that barrister to represent you?'

'Strangely, no.'

At least once a day Victoria recalls the feeling of glee she had when her lovely new barrister – working in concert with her Sydney solicitor – called and said that his suggestion that she and Arthur go to court over the house was met with a retraction of his demand regarding that very house. As she knew it would be. Arthur is cheap and a court case would cost him a lot of money in legal fees. Presumably Celeste wasn't willing to fund it either. Although Victoria wasn't sure about the barrister when Jimbo had insisted, he had turned out to be right that the mere fact of hiring the man would save her time, money and angst.

'Poor Celeste won't get to be the queen of the castle.' Gabrielle pouts.

'Poor Celeste won't get much of anything now. Not from me. And I don't know what Arthur thinks he's going to live on for the rest of his life.'

'What an idiot.'

'I couldn't have put that better myself. Now I just have to wait for the year to be up and we can start the divorce proceedings.'

They walk past the town hall, which in daylight hours is fulfilling its usual role of being the centre of municipal business.

'You haven't spoken about the choir for a while,' Victoria observes.

'Oh – did I need to?'

'Not necessarily. I suppose I mean that you haven't criticised Warwick's musical choices for a while.'

'I don't appear to notice as much now.'

'Now that he's been so kind to you?' Victoria smirks.

Gabrielle opens her mouth and her eyes widen, then her face softens. 'You're right. Yes. He's been *very* kind.'

'Well, I'm glad you're teaching. I think it suits you.'

The past few weeks Gabrielle has been taking Victoria's car and heading to Tamworth for the lessons. She pretends to find it all very boring yet she's come back each day with bright eyes and colour in her cheeks. Even the driving doesn't seem to bother her. Who knows what they'll do, though, once Victoria is up to her usual speed and needing the car to drive to all her usual spots. She has no intention of becoming Gabrielle's chauffeur.

'It's made me reconsider things,' Gabrielle says.

'Oh?'

'Perhaps I can return to opera, working with a company. Helping the singers.' She turns to Victoria, her face full of hope. 'Maybe my career isn't over after all.'

Victoria knows her first reaction should be to feel pleased that Gabrielle is making plans for her life. Yet if her cousin joins an opera company it will, at the very least, be in Sydney and more likely further afield. In Europe. There are, as far as Victoria can tell, no opera companies in the Liverpool Plains area.

'Oh,' is all she can say in reply.

'Would you miss me?'

'Of course I would,' Victoria snaps. 'I'm used to having you around. More importantly, I enjoy your company.' She smiles, hoping to mitigate her display of temper.

'I enjoy yours too.' Gabrielle squeezes her arm. 'And I'm not going yet. But I do need to think about earning more money if I'm to pay off that debt before I'm ninety.'

They turn into Bendon Street. Three houses from the corner, in the front garden, stands Jimbo, leaning on his front fence.

'Right on time,' he says, his face crinkling into its smile.

'Hello.' Victoria gives him her biggest smile. Not because he's earned it – although he has – but because she is happy to see him.

When he offered to help her it didn't create an obligation between them so much as an opportunity for them to spend more time together. He's an interesting character, and he has

416

plenty of stories to keep her entertained. Sometimes she feels like she isn't offering enough in return, but he seems to like being around her.

'Hello, Jimbo!' Gabrielle says.

She lets go of Victoria's arm as Jimbo steps onto the foot-path and closes his gate behind him. Then Victoria takes his arm and the three of them start their own *passeggiata*, slowly taking in Bendon Street on the way to the river.

'What are your Christmas plans?' he asks.

'Are we there already?' Victoria frowns. She feels like she's lost some of the year by being unwell, but she didn't think she'd lost *that* much.

Jimbo chortles. 'Oh no. A month to go yet. But it always seems to take a lot of planning.'

'I'll have to talk to Helena,' says Victoria. 'See what she wants to do.'

This will be the first Christmas without Arthur, and Victoria hasn't yet thought about how it should work. Helena will likely have to split her time between them. Or maybe Arthur will fall on his head, die and save them the hassle.

'May I propose something?' Jimbo says, angling his body slightly towards hers as they continue to walk.

Victoria catches sight of Gabrielle, whose face is a picture of anticipation.

'Of course,' she says.

'I'd like to have Christmas lunch with you and Gabrielle. Either at your house or mine.'

'I *love* that idea,' Gabrielle exclaims.

'What about your children?' asks Victoria.

'It's their turn with their in-laws,' Jimbo says. 'Next year they'll be with me. And they come to visit on Boxing Day anyway.'

Victoria thinks about how this Christmas might look: her, Gabrielle, Jimbo. Helena if they're lucky. It's so different to the Christmases of her childhood, when there were relatives everywhere and the women in the family ended the day exhausted and never wanting to see a roasted bird again. But her own family has been contracting. Once Leopold went overseas their festive gatherings changed, because he and Helena often used to have at least one stray friend joining them.

There is, of course, nothing to say that a large gathering is better than a small. She and Gabrielle can have fun even if it's just the two of them; they do that every day. But she has come to cherish Jimbo's company and she would be delighted to have him there.

'I'm with Gabrielle,' she says. 'I love that idea. And I would love it more if you could come to our house.'

Jimbo nods slowly, a look of satisfaction on his face. 'Wonderful,' he says. 'We'll work out the particulars closer to the time.'

Victoria presses his arm gently to communicate her approval. With her other hand she takes hold of Gabrielle's arm and they walk three abreast down the footpath, looking into the setting sun, surrounded by long shadows.

Ahead is the riverbank and its tufts of hardy trees. Above there are long, thin streaks of clouds tinged with pink.

'Red sky at night,' murmurs Jimbo and Victoria nods: she knows what it means.

A car goes past and Victoria sees a hand wave. She checks the numberplate: it's Brian from the council.

She doesn't wave back though; her hands are occupied holding on to her oldest friend and her newest.

SUMMER 1998

Magpie

CHAPTER 68

While Gabrielle would not voluntarily go to church for a service or a prayer or even a plea to God – she likes to issue those on an ad hoc basis – she has willingly gone to various churches and cathedrals to perform, often on the occasion of a Christmas concert. So that isn't the reason she feels uncomfortable entering St Thomas' Anglican Church on Connaught Street, with Victoria not far behind her. It's because this is where Victoria and Arthur were married, and Gabrielle is quite sure that Arthur – so fond of his so-called status in Bellbird River – will come to this evening's concert to parade himself and his consort.

Victoria had dismissed Gabrielle's concerns when she'd raised them. 'I don't care,' she'd said, nose in the air, a hand waving her off. 'He's tried his worst on me and I'm still here. He can parade his filly around the ring if he wants.'

That doesn't mean Gabrielle wants to see it, however. Victoria may be feeling sanguine about the whole thing, but Gabrielle is prepared to hold a grudge against Arthur for the rest of her life. It's her job as Victoria's cousin and, if she's honest with herself, one she relishes. So she insisted that Victoria come with her at the time the choir is to assemble, so she can take a seat down the front and not have to see anyone who may eventually sit behind her.

'Gabrielle,' Warwick says as he steps forwards to greet her, taking her hand and kissing the back of it.

'So formal!' Gabrielle says, slightly breathless. She does enjoy a courtly gesture.

'It's a formal occasion,' he says, then he appears to bow his head to Victoria. 'Victoria, lovely to see you. I hope you'll come back to us soon.'

'If you're lucky,' Victoria says. 'But I shall be singing along to the carols tonight, of course.'

Jimbo appears from behind the altar and Gabrielle notices little buds of pink forming in Victoria's cheeks.

'Hello, Victoria,' he says, eyes only for her.

'I'm here too!' Gabrielle waves a hand in his direction.

Jimbo nods. 'Hello, Gabrielle.'

Gabrielle makes sure Victoria is in the best seat before she moves towards her own seat in the sopranos. She watches the others start to arrive. Janine and Alex have their heads bent towards each other, chatting.

When Debbie appears, Gabrielle notices her glance towards Warwick. Their eyes meet and Gabrielle recognises that look. It's been a while since anyone has looked at *her* like that, but a person doesn't forget that combination of respect and desire that mark a truly romantic attachment. She's surprised, she'll admit that. Warwick seemed to be completely uninterested in women in that way. But good on them.

And good on her, too, because she is quite sure that by insisting on Debbie taking that solo months ago she created an opportunity for the pair to spend more time together. Yes, she is definitely going to take credit for any romance that may be developing between them.

Debbie appears to be positively gliding over the floor as she approaches.

'How are you feeling?' Gabrielle asks her.

No matter how well she knew a role and how many times she performed it, she always felt nervous before a performance. Good nerves, not sick-making nerves. Yet nerves they were and she is sure Debbie is feeling them.

'Um . . .' Debbie makes a face. 'A bit like a fraud.'

'What?'

'It should be you singing this.'

Gabrielle is quite sure Debbie is saying this just to flatter her but it's completely welcome all the same.

'Don't be ridiculous!' she cries. 'It is *absolutely* right that you are singing it. You have a lovely voice and . . .' She pauses, wondering how to phrase it. Singer to singer, that's how. 'You understand the piece. Where it's coming from. You feel it, right here.' She puts her hand over her own solar plexus. 'Don't you? I know you do.'

Debbie nods quickly, then sniffs and turns her head away. 'Sorry,' she says.

'For what?'

When she turns back her eyes are shining. 'It's so nice of you to say that.'

'*Nice?*' Gabrielle snorts. 'I think you know that I'm nothing of the sort. And if you're thinking about crying, please don't – it's no good for your voice so close to a performance.'

Debbie looks startled but there are no tears on her cheeks. Instead her face transforms as she smiles broadly, looking towards the back of the church.

Turning, Gabrielle can see two children in the company of a man and a woman.

'Friends of yours?' she says.

'My son and my daughter,' Debbie replies, and the sniffing starts again.

'*No crying!*' Gabrielle taps her on the arm. 'Honestly – do you want to make a great singer or don't you? Pull yourself together.'

She'll find out the gossip about the children later.

Debbie gasps then starts laughing.

'That's better,' Gabrielle says. 'Now off you go – say hello, make it quick, and don't get emotional.'

She watches as Debbie trots up the aisle and bends down to hug the children. As she goes to sit down again Victoria catches her eye.

'It looks like a family reunion,' Gabrielle calls, nodding towards Debbie.

'They're the best kind,' Victoria calls back. Then she blows her a kiss.

Gabrielle feels something catch in her throat and starts to blink rapidly. No. *No*. She can't have tears. Not after lecturing Debbie. Bloody Victoria, upsetting her like this.

Doing her best to bring her feelings under control, and failing, Gabrielle organises her sheet music the way she likes it, lets herself have a quiet sob into the crook of her elbow, then sits back and waits for the other choristers to take their seats.

As Warwick strikes the first chord on the piano, and the choir launches into the first verse of 'O Come, All Ye Faithful', Gabrielle half closes her eyes and feels her voice melding with the others, each of them performing their parts.

She is not the soloist here today; she may never be a soloist again. This time last year that was the thought that panicked her most: life as she knew it would be over and she had no idea how to go on.

As it has turned out, life as she knew it did end. But she did not. She found her way home, not necessarily to Bellbird River but to Victoria.

Opening her eyes she sees her cousin smiling at her beatifically, the way she used to when Gabrielle was a teenager performing at local concerts. Victoria was proud of her then and she is proud of her now.

Oh *really*, she cannot cry now, right in the middle of a carol. How unprofessional.

She looks down a few places to where Debbie is singing her little heart out, with a smile bright enough to light up the entire church. Next to her Janine and Alex are doing their best.

That's all anyone can really ask of another person, isn't it? If we all do the best we can, every day of our lives, we are that much further ahead in making life better for everyone.

That's how Gabrielle will go on. And if she ever needs an example of what to do, she need look no further than the people around her.

The carol comes to an end almost without Gabrielle realising it. There's no applause – they're in a church, after all – but she can see from the smiles on faces in the audience that they've done a good job. How lovely; how satisfying. Gabrielle is sure she's had something to do with it, because no doubt she has set a standard, but that is a notion she'll keep to herself.

Pages are turned to the next piece of music. Victoria gives her a wink.

On they go, to the first note, and the next, into the melody, into the harmony, into the magic that they have gathered together to make.

ACKNOWLEDGEMENTS

Thank you to the many people at Hachette Australia who make it possible for this book to reach readers, including but not limited to Fiona Hazard, Rebecca Saunders, Louise Stark, Lillian Kovats, Kate Taperell and Melissa Wilson.

Thank you to Karen Ward, editorial choirmistress; editors Celine Kelly and Nicola O'Shea, and proofreader Julia Cain.

Thanks to my agent, Melanie Ostell, for calm advice and astute editorial feedback.

Christa Moffitt makes each of my book covers more beautiful than the last – thank you, Christa, for creating magic.

All the love in the world and thanks to my parents, Robbie and David, and my brother, Nicholas, for your support.

There are never enough words to thank Jen Bradley for being the shining star she is and Isabelle Benton for being divine.

Neralyn Porter put me in her band almost two decades ago, we played the Tamworth Country Music Festival and that set me on a path that has pretty much led to this novel. Thank you, sweetie, for all the musical riches you've brought to my life.

For their support and interest in my writing, huge thanks to Ashleigh Barton, Marg Cruikshank, Anna Egelstaff, Kate Farquharson, Richard and Robbie Hille, Chris Kunz, Amelia Levido, Col Porter, Tammie Russell, Kate Sampson, Veronica Sywak and Jill Wunderlich.

This book was written and rewritten on Borogegal land. I acknowledge the Traditional Owners of this land and pay my respects to Elders past, present and future.